IN SHINING ARMOR

Visit us at www.boldstrokesbooks.com

By the Author

In Shining Armor

Written as Rachel E. Bailey

Dyre: By Moon's Light

IN SHINING ARMOR

by

E. L. Phillips

2016

IN SHINING ARMOR

ISBN 13: 978-1-62639-827-6

This Trade Paperback Original Is Published By
Bold Strokes Books, Inc.
P.O. Box 249
Valley Falls, NY 12185

First Edition: June 2016

CREDITS
EDITOR: JERRY L. WHEELER
PRODUCTION DESIGN: SUSAN RAMUNDO
COVER DESIGN BY JEANINE HENNING

Acknowledgments

To Joanne, the person who got me started on this particular journey of a novel, by prompting me with this: "I was walking in the woods for about twenty minutes. I followed the green trail markings, but soon they'd disappeared altogether…" (Joanne, I meant for this to be a short story, but it got *real* big when my back was turned.)

To my first beta readers, especially Thom Oldford, himself a talented writer; and Marcela, burgeoning writer/book editor, without whom, the final draft wouldn't even have existed. Similar thanks goes to my editor at Bold Strokes Books, Jerry Wheeler, without whom this book wouldn't exist in any publishable form—and it'd be rife with *sliding, slipping*, and *cupping*.

To all the friends and followers on Facebook and Twitter who cheered me on whenever I posted or tweeted about *In Shining Armor*: Thank you for your timely cheerleading, and for always believing I could do it, even when *I* didn't believe it, myself.

To the country—yes, the *entire country*—of Wales. Thank you for inspiring this novel and for continuing to be awesome. When I make my first big, fat pile of cash, I'm coming your way.

Dedication

For my mother: I know this probably has a lot more sex in it than you'd like, but it *doesn't* have unicorns, dragons, robots, *or* zombies, and that's certainly something…thank you.

For my friend, Thom Oldford: What can I say? You were my sounding board, my inspiration, my cheerleader, my devil's advocate, my beta reader—you wore a lot of hats in the making of this novel. All of them invaluable. Without you, this novel wouldn't exist, let alone be worthy of publishing. Thank you, my friend. Thank you.

And last but not least, for my friend and the second beta reader of *In Shining Armor*, Marcela: adverb extinguisher extraordinaire, and the person who kept the grammatical side of the final draft sparkling. Without you, there'd have been no second half of the novel, let alone a final draft. Thank you, Marcela. You rock!

PART I

CHAPTER ONE

L et's go camping, Krish!' they said. 'We'll spend the night in the freezing-ass woods, and then spend the next day at the local tourist trap festival!' they said. 'It'll be a fun way to end our backpacking tour of Wales!'" I muttered to myself as I stopped my headlong rush through the trees and leaned against one that didn't look too mossy or damp. "'It's impossible to get lost, Krish! There are markers *everywhere, Krish*!' Yeah, right. Hansel and Gretl had the right idea."

I had been walking in the woods for twenty minutes and had dutifully followed the green trail-markers, but soon they'd disappeared altogether. So, I'd stumbled along through the foggy forest, worried for another half-hour, before finally admitting I was completely lost.

I looked up at the overcast sky. It was already getting dark, the leaden light fading quickly. I hoped it wouldn't rain, but the way my luck had been going since we'd left Cardiff for the countryside, I had no doubt it'd be flood conditions before I found my way back to the campground and my waiting friends.

I sighed, burying my face in my grubby hands. John and Dierdre had probably already gotten the campsite set up and were roasting S'mores while I was still trying to find the rental car to grab the forgotten boom box so we could listen to some music. But I was utterly adrift beyond the range of the ubiquitous, but not very helpful green markers.

I'd been so sure that I was walking in the right direction. Even without the green markers, I'd recognized landmarks: a boulder, broken and splattered with bird shit; a fallen tree blocking the path

John and Dierdre clambered over on the way to the campsite, while I'd simply gone around; and a small pond that we'd *all* walked around.

Having gone way past those landmarks and way past the point where the car and the road leading out of this outdoors hell-hole should have been, I was starting to doubt the way I'd come. After all, I was no wilderness expert. This, in the boonies of Wales, was my very first camping trip, though not John and Dierdre's.

Sighing again, I came to one conclusion. I had to swallow my pride and retrace my steps back to the campsite. Let John or Dierdre go after the boom box if they were so keen to have music. I straightened up and looked around, noticing the fog was now so thick I could barely see around me for more than a few yards. And it was nothing but trees and damp, loamy earth that hadn't held my footprints.

"Fuck," I breathed. "This isn't good."

Starting to panic, I began walking back the way I *thought* I'd come, trying not to think things like *death by bear* or *death by exposure*. Of course, the way I was going seemed to take me deeper into the heavy fog, until I couldn't even see five feet in front of me.

Panic mounted, causing me to pick up my pace until I was running. And I knew it was dangerous bolting pell-mell through a thick forest in such an impenetrable fog, but the sensible part of me was drowned out by the frantic need to get back to a place and the people I knew.

I ran and ran until I tripped over the root of a tree and went sprawling on my front, face in the dirt. The fall knocked the wind out of me and I groaned, spitting out soil, while my right ankle screamed like a wounded mountain cat. I was near tears when, out of nowhere, I heard it…faint, but there.

Hoof-falls. Unhurried and relatively nearby, if they could be heard in the fog and damp, squishy earth.

"Help!" I yelled, scrambling to my knees, and then to my feet. My right ankle was useless agony that couldn't bear my weight, but I hobbled toward the hoof-falls nonetheless. I even began waving my arms, though the rider probably wouldn't see me till he or she was almost on top of me because of the fog. "Help! Please! I'm lost!"

The hoof-falls stopped. Then they began to canter toward me through the fog, which moved and thinned with the advent of a stiff breeze.

"I'm over here! Help!"

In another few seconds of heart-pounding panic and hope, a shape emerged from the grey murk. It was a large brown horse, almost as big as a Clydesdale, wearing fancy blue tack, like something out of a Ren-Faire. And on its back, in keeping with its theme of medieval splendor, was…

A *knight.*

I blinked. Then blinked again as the knight, in full mail armor and surcoat, stared down at me from his lofty height. Dark, wary, grim eyes took me in, and the knight unsheathed a huge sword that may have been a Claymore.

He pointed the maybe-Claymore at me and spoke commandingly in Welsh, his words clipped, incomprehensible, and angry.

"I…I don't understand you," I said, shrugging and shaking my head. The knight frowned even more ferociously and gestured tersely with his sword. He repeated whatever it was he'd said the first time, and when I continued to stare at him blankly, he made a sound of distaste.

"English?" he said gruffly, looking me over once more. I didn't know if he was asking if that was what language I spoke or if I was from England.

"Uh, I *speak* English. But I'm *from* America." I held up my hands slowly to show I meant no harm, just in case the sword was real and this guy took Ren-Faire a bit too seriously. "I was camping with my friends, and I got lost. I was hoping you could…"

And there I fell silent. I couldn't give him directions to the campsite since I was already lost, but he probably knew where the road was. And if I could get to the road, I could find my way to the rental and wait there till morning, or whenever John and Dierdre took it into their heads to come looking for me.

"Could you just tell me where the road is?" I finished with a squeak as the knight quickly dismounted with a jingle of metal. He took a few steps toward me, sword still held up, and I began to limp back, wincing and hissing. For every step back I took, he took one forward until I hit a tree.

The knight, still looking grim but less wary, came close enough that I could smell sweat, metal, and horse. He was an inch or two shorter than me, and what little of his face was visible in his mail helmet was pale and slightly dirty. His nose was long and crooked, as if it'd been broken and badly set. Perhaps more than once. His dark eyes were round and wide-set. His beard and mustache were neatly trimmed and barely hid a thin, down-turned mouth.

"You are strangely dressed, lad," he said in the musically lilting accent I'd come to associate with Welsh English. He reached out and rubbed the material of my dark blue parka and looked me over once more before meeting my eyes, looking a bit puzzled. "From whence do you hail?"

Oh, boy, was this guy really into his role as brave Sir Knight. I was just glad he knew English, after all. "Like I said, I'm from America. San Francisco, to be specific." I fought not to roll my eyes as he stared at me blankly. Obviously those place names meant nothing to him. How deep into the Welsh countryside *had* I wandered, anyway?

"I'm from really far away," I settled for saying as the knight stepped even closer and *sniffed* me. "Uh, personal space is not just a concept, pal."

"Your speech is even stranger than your attire," the knight noted, and I huffed.

"Well, that's the pot calling the kettle—hey, could you please stop sniffing me? It's weirding me out."

The knight took a step back and shook his head. "Methinks you are from farther afield than I have e'er been," he said. Then he said something else, this time in what was clearly Spanish, and I could only shrug again. The knight sighed. "I had taken you for Spanish because of your dark looks, yet you do not understand me when I speak that tongue. Odd."

"Not really, when you consider that I'm *not Hispanic*." I rolled my eyes. In my life, I'd been mistaken for Hispanic more times than I cared to count. Not a bad thing in itself, but I was *Indian*, not Puerto Rican, not Mexican, not Cuban, and *not* from Spain. I just didn't expect to get it in Wales. In the middle of a forest. From a guy pretending to be from Ye Olde Wales in his spare time. "Look, can you just tell me how to get to the road? I need to get back to my car before it gets too dark to see."

The knight bit his bottom lip for a moment. "I can stand you better than mere directions, lad. I can offer you a ride to the Great

Road." He sheathed his sword and looked me over yet again, his gaze lingering at my right foot. "You are injured, are you not?"

"Uh, I guess. I think I sprained it." Blushing, I tried to put weight on the ankle and hissed again when agony shot up my leg, hot and sharp. I began to rethink *sprained* in favor of *broken*. Just my luck. "Damnit!"

"Hmm." The knight looked around us, then up at the sky. Within the hour, it'd be full dark, and there was no moon to light the way. "It grows late. Night approaches."

"Yeah, I—*hey!*" I squawked as the knight darted forward and scooped me up in his arms like I was some damned damsel in distress. Like I weighed next to nothing, which okay, maybe I did. A buck fifty-nine soaking wet is pretty skinny for my height. I flailed and swore while the knight carried me in his arms toward his patient horse. "Put me *down!*"

And he did. On his horse. With no help from me. I barely thought to swing my right leg out of the way of the horse's barrel body as the knight placed me on the animal. Then I was sitting astride, gazing down at him with a mixture of awe and fear.

"Boy, you really take this Ren-Faire shit *seriously*, don't you?" I asked, and he frowned.

"I know not of what you speak, lad," he replied, shaking his head just as I had a few minutes ago. Then he was swinging up behind me, pressing his body to mine as he slid his arms past me to grasp the reins. I, for my part, grasped two handfuls of the horse's mane and tried not to clench too hard. "But tell me how you are called, that I may address you properly."

"Krish. Uh, Krishnan Nayar." I leaned forward a little as the horse began to walk, trying to put a little space between my body and that of good Sir Knight. "What's *your* name?"

A few moments passed before he answered. "I am Bleddyn ap Rhys, of *Sir Gaernarfon*," he said quietly, his breath warm on my neck. I shivered and blushed, glancing around to distract myself. I spotted a semi-familiar boulder that looked like the one John, Dierdre, and I had passed to get to the campsite, only it wasn't broken, nor was it covered in bird shit. It looked brand-spanking-new, if a boulder can be said to look that way.

There's a simple explanation, dumbass. It's a different boulder, I told myself, but I couldn't quite believe that. Except for looking newer and cleaner, it was exactly the same size and shape as the boulder I remembered.

"Where the hell *am* I?" I muttered to myself.

Bleddyn ap Rhys heard me, anyway, and said, "You are in Gwydir Forest, on the baronet's lands, between Trefriw and Llanrwst."

Which sort of made sense. I remembered Dierdre pointing out those weird-ass names on her ever-present map. But I said nothing, merely looked around while we still had light so that, if necessary, I could find my way back to—well, the spot where I'd turned up lost in the first place.

A sudden howl went up from the woods far behind us and I tensed. Bleddyn ap Rhys leaned closer to me.

"Worry not, Krishnan of Nayar," he murmured softly. "For the wolves herein are neither bold nor famished. Merely curious and watchful."

"Famous last words." I shuddered and grasped the horse's mane a bit tighter, not wanting to fall off when freaking *wolves* were about, though that was unlikely with Bleddyn ap Rhys's arm bracketing me.

With a click of his teeth, Bleddyn urged the horse on a bit faster. And sooner rather than later, the trees began to thin, until I could see the road ahead. Only it wasn't paved anymore. The asphalt was gone, and in its place was a well worn, wide, but nonetheless *dirt* path.

I couldn't even find the words to express my dismay till we were actually on the so-called road, and a glance down it in either direction showed nothing but more unpaved glory, filled with ruts and holes.

"Where'd the road go?" I demanded.

"We are on it," Bleddyn said stolidly, reining his horse in.

"No, I mean where'd the asphalt go? Where's the road itself?"

"I know not what az-*vault* is, but you sit in the Great Road of Baronet John Wynn's lands. The only road that runs from Trefriw to Llanrwst."

"But where'd the paving go?" I asked again, almost close to panic once more. I craned my neck to see farther down the dirt road, but what I could see was all dirt, too.

"*Pave* the *Great Road*?" Bleddyn sounded amused. "With *stones*? Know you how far this Road runs, Krishnan of Nayar?"

"No, but I *know* it was paved the last time I was on it. And our car was here, too!"

"Car?"

"Excuse me, our *auto*. It was *right here*. I *know* it was," I said, my voice gone shrill and anxious.

Bleddyn put his gloved right hand on my arm comfortingly. "Calm yourself, lad. You're confused and perhaps bestartled on top of being lost, but there's naught to be gained by panic."

I glanced over my shoulder at him. "Easy for *you* to say. *You* haven't lost your friends, your car, and an entire road!"

"No, I have not." Bleddyn sighed. "Perhaps, in light of the pass you find yourself in, you should accompany me to my lord's castle, and there we may be able to help you."

"Castle? There's a *castle* around here?" I demanded, for a moment wondering why, when we could've gone on a tour of a castle and probably slept in a cozy B&B, John and Dierdre had dragged us all camping.

"There is. Gwydir Castle is but a brief ride from here and where I was bound, till I heard your cries for aid."

All right, I thought with relief. *Gwydir Castle must be where this whole Ren-Faire thing is based. Maybe I can crash there until I can get a forest ranger or whoever to help me find John and Dierdre.*

"Okay, sure. Take me to your castle," I said, too tired to keep freaking out about the road. Maybe I'd wandered farther in the forest than I'd thought, and made my way parallel to the road to some part of it that was under construction.

Yeah. That *had* to be it.

Chapter Two

G wydir "Castle" wasn't really much of one.
      It was more like a fortified manor house, two stories of
stone and sprawling. As we rode into a muddy courtyard that smelled,
I gazed around wide-eyed at this ultra-realistic rendition of a medieval
castle and environs.

There were actors around, "working," though who-all they were
working for was beyond me, since I didn't spot a single person who
looked like a tourist. No one dressed like me. Everyone was dressed
in their period outfits and occupied with period duties. But that didn't
stop them from double-taking when they saw me, reflecting my own
gape.

"Your friends are all staring at me," I whispered to Bleddyn,
whose hand had migrated from my arm to my waist and stayed there
during our ride.

"You are strangely dressed and obviously a foreigner to these
lands," he said, and I laughed a tad nervously.

"Sir, your sweet words of flattery will completely turn my head
if you're not careful."

For a moment, Bleddyn stiffened behind me. Then he was
stopping his horse near what could only be the stables and was
swinging down with the ease of long practice, when someone called
his name from behind us. We both looked around to see a tall-ish
man approaching us on foot. He was even more solidly built than
Bleddyn and dressed much the same, with thatchy blond hair and a
conventionally handsome face.

"Bleddyn, *lle wert ti? Mae'n hwyr,*" he said easily, his open smile revealing long, slightly discolored teeth. He looked from Bleddyn to me, dismissing me before looking back to Bleddyn. Then he looked at me astride Bleddyn's horse, and his friendly, open expression closed as he pursed his lips. "*Pwy yw hwn? Mae rhai bachgen sipsiwn potsio ar diroedd yr Arglwydd John?*"

Oddly enough, I could sort of understand a little of what he'd said. Something about how late it was and was I a gypsy? But his voice was frosty and disapproving underneath its seeming good humor. I looked down at Bleddyn and he looked up at me, his brow furrowed in concern.

"Fear not for your safety, Krishnan of Nayar, for you will find naught but friends here," Bleddyn finally murmured, holding out his hand. I searched his serious eyes and nodded, taking the offered hand and Bleddyn helped me down, all under the hostile, watchful gaze of the blond.

"This," Bleddyn announced in English, no doubt for my benefit, "is Krishnan of Nayar. He became injured and lost in the forest. I heard his cries for help and have brought him here to be seen by Lord John."

"Oh, aye?" the blond said in the same frosty, but superficially jovial tone, his eyes ticking between us, and then back down at our hands, which were still clasped. We both quickly let go. The blond's smile didn't change, but his eyes grew colder and hooded. "Welladay."

We three stood for almost a minute in the most uncomfortable silence I'd ever been privy to. The blond finally snorted and turned away, striding off toward a long outbuilding near the castle. "*Mae eich tad yn edrych ar eich cyfer gynharach. Roedd yn dymuno siarad â chi,*" he tossed over his shoulder as he went, his bearing stiff and angry. I could pick out the word for *father, earlier,* and *speak,* from what he'd said.

Bleddyn sighed, shaking his head and watching the blond go with confusion and no small amount of frustration. "*Diolch, Dafydd,*" he called, an obvious *thank you.*

Huh, I thought, looking back and forth between my rescuer and his *friend.* When Bleddyn caught me staring at him, he cleared his throat and turned back to the stable, calling out a word I couldn't quite make out. A few moments later, a boy of about twelve came to take his horse, and we made our way in the squelching mud to the "castle."

❖

It all looks and smells so real, I thought as I limped, with Bleddyn's assistance, into Castle Gwydir, garnering more stares as I went. It was really starting to grate on me.

"Look, Bleddyn, you've been great, helping me and all, but can you just take me straight to a phone? I'm really starting to worry about my friends," I said as we made slow progress down the front hall of Gwydir Castle. It was all damp, but clean stone, tapestries, and ancient, yet new-looking furniture I couldn't put a name to. Whoever had set all this up had really outdone themselves.

Bleddyn hitched my arm more firmly across his shoulders and tightened his arm around my waist. "I know not what a *phone* is, Krish-lad, but if your companions are a-lost in the Forest, my lord may be willing to send out a party of men to search for them."

I rolled my eyes. "Okay, you get an A for effort and acting ability, but isn't it time to stop this Ren-Faire baloney and just talk like a normal person?"

Bleddyn frowned and opened his mouth to answer, but at that moment, a voice hailed Bleddyn from down the long hall. It belonged to a man of my height, wearing mail armor similar to Bleddyn's but for the lack of helm. His dark hair, beard, and mustache were shot through with grey. He approached swiftly, the jingle of his mail loud in the cavernous hall. As he drew closer, his eyes darted to me, then *back* to me, widening as he took me in.

He demanded something of Bleddyn in Welsh and Bleddyn tightened his arm around me again.

"This is Krishnan of Nayar. He was lost in the Forest and injured himself," Bleddyn said in English, for my benefit, I imagined. The man who'd greeted him so harshly sneered at me as Bleddyn went on. "He was separated from his traveling companions while in search of the Great Road."

"And what, pray tell, were ye doing on Lord Wynn's land?" the man asked me suspiciously. His version of English was thicker and even more antiquated than Bleddyn's. "Poaching?"

"What? *No*, I wasn't. Look, I appreciate your dedication to realism and everything, but this is getting out of hand!" I said, standing straighter and leaning less on Bleddyn. "Can you guys all just cut the crap and let me use a phone, for God's sake? I need to get back to my friends so we can get the Hell out of here and back to Cardiff before anything else crazy happens to us!"

Now the man was frowning. "Caerdyf, mean ye? And what be ye're business there?"

I found myself getting defensive. I didn't like his tone, the way he'd spoken to Bleddyn, or the way he kept glancing at Bleddyn's arm around my waist with that look of suspicion increasing, as well as burgeoning disgust.

"My business there," I began with poisoned patience, "is leaving this awful country as soon as humanly possible. It's been one thing after another since the day we got here. I just want to get back to Heathrow, catch my flight back to the U.S., and pretend I never came here if that's all right with you!"

"Ye're impertinent, lad," the man noted grimly, ignoring almost everything I'd just said. "Has nane thought to teach ye proper respect for yer betters?"

"Father," Bleddyn started before I could show this jerk what *real* disrespect was. Then I was glancing between the two men in shock. *Father*? "He is exhausted and injured, and among strangers after being lost in the forest. Surely he may be excused his impertinence and extended the hospitality of the castle?" Bleddyn cleared his throat. "I have promised him at least that."

"That was not yer promise t'make, Bleddyn." The man glared down his long nose at me and sighed with great irritation. *Of course* they were father and son. They had the same ski-slope schnozz, though this man's nose was crooked in the other direction. But they also had that same grim look in their dark eyes, not to mention the way their brows furrowed.

Bleddyn's father turned on his heel and walked away. "I'll let the baronet know we're to have a guest."

"My thanks, father!" Bleddyn called after the man's rapidly disappearing back. Then he was helping me walk again, taking the same route down the hall his father had taken.

"He seems like a swell guy," I muttered.

"Please excuse his bluntness. Such is the manner of soldiers," Bleddyn said, sounding rather nonplussed. I shrugged, and didn't say that I thought his father was simply a boor of the first water. We limped along in silence for a minute before I could think of anything to say.

"Um. Where're you taking me, now?" I asked wearily, my hopes of finding a phone and help dwindling with each labored, aching step I took.

"To a bathing room, where you may make yourself more presentable for his lordship." Bleddyn replied as we turned off into a stairwell. A *long* and winding one, which made me sigh. We began to climb. "You look to be approaching my cousin in stature, and I am certain his clothing will fit you."

"But if I'm wearing *his* clothes, then what will your cousin wear?" I said with pointed snark, and Bleddyn was silent a moment before speaking.

"William is dead," was all he said, without inflection, and I gaped. Either Bleddyn ap Rhys was the best actor in the world, or I'd just stuck my foot in it without even trying.

The latter being a common enough occurrence, I hung my head. "I'm...so sorry, Bleddyn. I didn't mean—"

"It...was a long time ago. He rests, now, in the arms of the Savior. The time of grieving for William is done," Bleddyn said, also without inflection. I wisely refrained from asking why, if that was the case, Bleddyn still kept William's clothes.

This was, I'd decided, not a Ren-Faire or tourist trap, after all, but some sort of cult or sect, like the Amish, that lived like it was the 1600s. These people weren't actors, they were really *living* this squalid, no electricity, no running water, let's-ride-horseys kind of life. The only explanation that fit was that this was a bunch of people hearkening back to their medieval roots. I may not have *seen* them, but I was sure weirder sects had to be out there.

Bleddyn lead me to a bathing room that contained several wooden tubs and asked me to wait there, while he went to retrieve William's old clothes.

So, I leaned against a wall near the door and waited. Eventually, the door opened and in came several women, each bearing two buckets of steaming water that *I* wouldn't have been able to lift. I blushed when the last one came in and put her buckets down, looking me over.

Like everyone else I'd seen in this place, she was dressed in period clothes, her homespun calico dress topped by a pristine white apron. She had a matronly air, and blonde hair escaped from her bonnet in wisps and strands.

"Ye must be the Spanish lad Bleddyn found wandering the Forest," she asserted, arms akimbo on ample hips.

"I must be," I sighed, not bothering to correct her. She smiled, showing three missing teeth.

"Ye're a *handsome* one! But don't you go stealin' the hearts of my girls!" she admonished, only half-joking.

My eyebrows shot up, and I snorted. "Yeah, you don't actually have to worry about that," I said dryly.

"Hmph!" The woman turned and began directing the others to empty their buckets into one of the wooden tubs, shooing me away when I offered to help.

So, I found myself leaning against the wall again when Bleddyn came back sans his armor. He seemed less bulky and more wiry, and he was carrying folded clothes not so different from what he was wearing: a pullover grey tunic, breeches, and hose, all somewhat faded, probably from washing.

He actually smiled when he saw me, and it transformed the harsh planes of his features. Surrounded by a corona of dark, slightly flattened curls, his face looked younger than I'd initially thought. Almost boyish, especially with those smudges of dirt on it.

"Uh," I said with my customary quick intelligence, taking the clothes he was offering and blushing. "Thank you."

"You are most welcome, Krishnan."

I grinned my most charming grin. "Please, call me *Krish*."

"Krish." Bleddyn's smile widened, showing off teeth that were a little crooked, but clean and all there. "I'll, erm...I suppose I shall leave you to your ablutions."

Or you could join me, I thought, but again refrained from saying it. I didn't know how it'd go over, and I couldn't pull off a line like that to save my life. Not even as a joke. "O-okay, Bleddyn. But, um, when I'm done, do I just wait here for you?"

Sketching a shallow bow, Bleddyn nodded once. "I will return at the chiming of the great clock in the hall, for that is when supper will be served."

"So that gives me almost an hour?" The clock had chimed once already, as we were climbing the stairs. Prima donna that I am, I figured even I could repair the damage wandering around the ass-end of the U.K. had done in an hour.

"Supper with his lordship is at half-six. It is now ten past."

"You mean I have *twenty minutes*?!" I groaned and ran my hands through my hair. Just then, the women who'd brought in the hot water hustled out of the room, including the matronly woman, who winked at me as she was going. As she passed, she grabbed Bleddyn's arm and tugged him after her, saying something about someone named Gareth being inconsolable without him all afternoon.

"It's because he missed you," she said gently as they left. Bleddyn sighed.

"He'll understand in time why I'm so often gone. Just as I did when—"

Then the door shut behind them, and I was alone in the bathing room, wondering who in the Hell this *Gareth* person was, why he was so inconsolable over Bleddyn's absence, why Bleddyn sounded so genuinely guilty and aggrieved—heartsore—and why *I* was suddenly feeling what most certainly could *not* be jealousy.

Hey, even Welsh guys who live like it's medieval times can have boyfriends, I told myself sternly. *And why do I even care? It's not like I'm even going to be here at this time tomorrow. No sense crushing on a guy I'll never see again. And for all I know he's straight. Happily married to a woman, with six kids...*

But something in me rebelled at that. My gaydar was as accurate as it came, and Bleddyn may have been many things, but happily married to a woman was not one of them. Which left only one thing I could figure, and, yep, that was definitely jealousy I was feeling in response to it.

I can't believe he has a boyfriend! Why are the good ones always taken?

Then the clock chimed, a muffled bell-tone that rang throughout the castle. While I'd been woolgathering about this Gareth person and what his relationship might be to Bleddyn, five minutes had passed.

"Fuck my life," I said to absolutely no one. Then I was hurrying out of my dirty clothes.

❖

Once I was as clean as I could get myself in fifteen minutes with hot water, the washrag, and a huge chunk of brown soap, I opened the door to the bathing room and limped into the cool air of the hall. Bleddyn was waiting for me, leaning against the wall opposite the door. He looked up when I came out, and he smiled again. Cue my heart beating faster in a way I was not exactly thrilled about, considering.

"You look well," Bleddyn said, still giving me the eye. I blushed and tugged on the waist of the buckle-up breeches. The clothes were the right length, though a bit loose on me. The woolen hose itched.

"Thank you. I mean, for the bath and the clothes," I fumbled out, running a hand over my damp hair and grinning anxiously. "I feel much better. Even my ankle. It's like my mother always says, there're few bad things in life that a good, hot bath can't cure."

"She sounds like a wise woman," Bleddyn said approvingly, and I laughed.

"*She* thinks so, at any rate."

We stared at each other for a few moments, me blushing, him doing the same. At least until I cleared my throat. Then I remembered all this blushing and banter was pointless, since Bleddyn already had a...*Gareth*.

"Is, uh, Gareth doing better since your, um, return?" I asked tentatively, putting on what I hoped was a concerned and altruistic tone. Bleddyn's smile widened and relaxed at the same time.

"He is as ever he is—a little hellion. Much as I was, at his age." Bleddyn chuckled, confusing me. Was he dating some barely legal twink? "But a cup of warm milk and the beginning of a bedtime story, and he was asleep in mere minutes."

This last was said fondly, tenderly, and I was starting to doubt my gaydar all over again. But then, I had a sudden realization. "How old is he, if you don't mind me asking? How old is your son?"

"He is three years old," Bleddyn said proudly, but he also sounded baffled, as if wondering where and how the time had gone. Then he sighed and met my eyes again. "In another few years, he'll be too old for stories from his *Tad* and cups of warm milk."

"But you'll never be too old to want to give them to him. To soothe him, and send him off to dreamland sweetly," I said, nodding, even as Bleddyn nodded. "Your son is lucky to have such a dedicated father."

Bleddyn's smile faded a little. "I am often too busy and too far away to be called that. Gareth is lucky, yes, but that's because since his mother's death, the women of the castle have had the raising of him, and they have lavished him with love that his dead mother and absent father could not," he finished softly, with muted regret, and I was keenly aware of having stuck my foot in it, yet again. Only this time, it was worse than a dead cousin. It was a dead *wife*.

"I'm sorry, Bleddyn. So sorry for your loss."

Bleddyn's waved his hand. "There is nothing to be sorry for. Rhiannon, like William, rests in the arms of the Savior. In a place where sickness and pain cannot touch her. And she smiles down on her son and, I hope, me. And one day, if I live a virtuous and good life, I will join them both in our Eternal Home."

Tears sprang to my eyes at the wistful note in his voice. It made me sad that the only thing this man felt he had to look forward to, aside from telling his son bedtime stories, was dying to join his family in the afterlife.

But I could totally understand the feeling. For I missed my father, now eight years dead. And I missed my mother. I missed Dierdre and John. I missed *home*, and that pang of homesickness was so great it nearly swallowed me whole.

Bleddyn frowned. "You are upset?"

"No, no, I just—I'm worried, I guess. About my friends."

"I have already spoken briefly with his lordship about your companions, and he is willing to begin a search of the Gwydir Forest for them on the morrow, after sunrise."

Ecstatic, I whooped and threw my arms around Bleddyn, hugging him tight. "Oh, thank you, *thank you!*" I said into his hard shoulder, so relieved I didn't even care I was embracing a near-stranger. Bleddyn, for his part, hugged me back after a moment, *for* a moment, then cleared his throat and let me go almost reluctantly. When he stepped back, he was blushing so deeply, he looked like a beet. My gaydar began pinging again, bringing with it an unnamed hope and joy I immediately dismissed as silly.

"It is not *my* generosity, but his lordship, the baronet's," Bleddyn said quietly, not meeting my eyes.

"Maybe. But you're the one who talked him into it, admit it," I said, chuckling and linking my arm through his. Together, we began to hobble down the hall, but it was definitely a faster hobble than I'd been capable of half an hour ago. I cautiously upgraded the status of my ankle from *possibly broken* to *badly-sprained*.

Things were, at last, finally starting to look up.

The baronet's personal dining room was windowless but relatively cozy, with dark, baroque furniture and a fully set table with food already awaiting us.

At the edges of the room stood serving women, and when we entered, his lordship was already seated at the head of the table and awaiting *us*. Also seated at the midsized table, was the man I recognized as Bleddyn's father and several other men of varying ages.

Everyone stood when Bleddyn and I entered, and I let go of his arm. He glanced at me and bowed to the baronet and I copied him, despite my ankle's unhappiness with the motion.

"Good evening, Bleddyn and young Master Krishnan," his lordship said, smiling. He had a keen, clever face, white hair, and bright blue eyes. He reminded me of my PoliSci professor back in college, who'd always purposely fostered more questions than he'd answered.

"Good evening, my lord," Bleddyn said. Again I copied him and bowed once more for good measure. The baronet smiled again, as did a younger man to his right, with the same bright blue eyes, and dark blond hair.

Another father and son, I thought, *along with a brother to their right*. He bore the same blue eyes, but his hair was dark brown and he was frowning quizzically.

"Sup with us, will you, lads?" the baronet asked, waving at the two unclaimed seats to his left.

With a hand placed lightly on the small of my back, Bleddyn guided me to the chair immediately next to his lordship. After bowing again, just in case, I sat.

❖

"So, Master Krishnan, Rhys tells me you are from Spain," Baronet Wynn said to me when the table had resumed its talking and the women had begun to serve food. Dinner appeared to be mutton, vegetables in gravy, and fresh-baked bread along with giant steins of some sort of alcohol I could smell before my server poured it.

"Uh," I said, looking at my stein with trepidation. Would I be expected to finish it? Or would a few sips for politeness's sake do? "I'm actually from the United States of America." I hoped against hope his lordship, at least, would recognize the name. But from the curious look he gave me, he didn't. "Um. From very far away. I'm not, Spanish, though. I'm actually Indian—"

"Ah, from the East Indies! Of course!" The baronet leaned in, his interest genuinely piqued, as far as I could tell.

"Well, my parents were. They left when they were my age." I blushed, feeling Bleddyn's gaze on me, just as curious as Baronet Wynn's. "But they used to tell me stories about growing up in Kannur, and the places they used to travel to in Kerala State. It's a beautiful place, filled with history and monuments and, uh, stuff."

I fell silent, thinking of my father, dead of a heart attack at forty-three, and my mother, still alive, but so far from me now. For the first time, I began to wonder if I'd ever see her again.

Of course I will! This is just a bump in the road! It certainly won't last forever! I thought, glancing at Bleddyn, who smiled reassuringly, as if he knew what I was thinking. On the table, his hand brushed mine briefly before he picked up his stein and drank a few long swallows.

"And are your missing companions from the East Indies, as well?" his lordship asked, and I turned my attention away from the intriguing sight of Bleddyn swallowing.

"Um, no. John and Dierdre are both from the United States, like me. But John's family is originally from Italy, and Dierdre—I think her family's mostly Irish," I said uncertainly, wondering what they were doing right now. They were probably worried about me. I'd been gone for at least two hours.

Or perhaps they hadn't even noticed how long I was gone and were using this unexpected alone time to get reacquainted. It'd been weeks since they'd been together without me along as a third wheel. They were probably fogging up their tent, having forgotten all about their tag-along. The thought should have irritated me, but instead I fought not to smile.

The baronet was watching me, one still-dark eyebrow quirked halfway to his white hairline. "Something amuses you, Master Krishnan?"

"Just thinking about my friends, my lord," I murmured, looking down at my mutton. I tried to muster up an appetite but couldn't quite, even though everything smelled delicious. "I miss them. And I'm worried for them."

The baronet patted my hand. "Do not worry overmuch, Master Krish. If indeed your companions are out there, we will find them and reunite you all."

And for some reason, with the baronet to my right and Bleddyn to my left, I felt…reassured.

After supper, everyone except Bleddyn and I retired to the baronet's office.

We limped down the drafty hall in an expectant silence. His arm was around my waist again, and it felt nice enough that I didn't mention my ankle felt better and his assistance wasn't needed.

"Where am I to stay for the night?" I asked, sliding a hesitant, nervous arm around his shoulders.

Bleddyn smiled a little. "His lordship has given you a guest bedroom on this floor. That is where I am I taking you now."

"I see. And, uh, where do you and Gareth sleep?"

Bleddyn blinked over at me, seeming surprised. I looked away just as he started to turn that deep, beet-red again.

"Gareth sleeps with the other motherless or orphaned children of the household in the east wing of the castle. I take my rest with the unmarried men and widowers in the barracks," Bleddyn said slowly, thoughtfully. "I had thought Lord Wynn would quarter you with us, but he has been most gracious to you." Bleddyn and I turned right at an intersection and he helped me to the first door on the left of this shorter arm of the corridor. "This is the guest room he has allotted you."

And Bleddyn opened the door.

The room was small by non-Welsh cult standards and didn't have a window, but it had a high, narrow four-poster bed complete with drapes, a giant piece of furniture that might have been a garderobe, a small table with a basin of fresh water and an ewer on it, and a small chest at the foot of the bed. A multi-colored tapestry adorned the wall across from the door, though I couldn't quite make out what it was depicting.

On the small night table on the right side of the bed a lamp burned low, and the bed itself was turned down rather invitingly. I opened my mouth to speak, and a yawn came out. Bleddyn laughed.

"I see that the chamber meets with your approval," he noted wryly, and I laughed, too.

"It's been a very long day," I agreed as we walked into the room, Bleddyn leading the way through the narrow doorway. "It's not every day I get lost in the back woods of Wales, and stumble across, uh… what do you guys call yourselves?"

Bleddyn helped me to the bed, and I sat gratefully. The look on his face was puzzled, however. "What do we call ourselves? Welshmen."

I smiled. "No, I mean the name of your sect."

"Sect?"

"Yeah, I mean the people who live the way you do, like you're in the 1600s, instead of 2000s? Surely you must have a name for yourselves." I tugged on Bleddyn's arm, and he obligingly sat next to me on the bed.

"We are Lord Wynn's men, and that is the only other name we go by. As to the year, it is *not* sixteen hundred," Bleddyn said, chuckling. I scooted a bit closer to him and chuckled, too.

"Of course, it's not."

"It is the year of our Lord, sixteen hundred and *twenty-six*," Bleddyn said calmly, and in the act of nodding along with him, I froze.

And gaped.

"Um," I finally said, laughing. But Bleddyn wasn't laughing with me, merely watching me as if I was something both interesting and mystifying.

"Sixteen twenty-six?" I asked, and he nodded.

"Spring is upon us early," he added with great satisfaction and with such a straight face, I began to chuckle again. And again, Bleddyn didn't join me, only watched me quizzically.

And I realized, in that moment, it was entirely possible he hadn't been joking.

Chapter Three

U h," I began, my chuckles turning a tad anxious. "Springtime of sixteen hundred and twenty-six? Haha, very funny."

Frowning, Bleddyn searched my eyes. "I made no jest, Krishnan of Nayar."

That's what I was afraid of. "Yeah, right. You're telling me it's sixteen twenty-six?" I snorted. "Maybe on you *guys's* calendar."

Bleddyn blinked. "I swear that the year is as I have said. Do you use a different calendar in this United States of America from whence you hail?"

"We must," I muttered, thinking I was pretty sure America and most of the world went by the Gregorian calendar. Or was it the Julian? Either way, however, I was certain if a different calendar was used in Wales or even by just Bleddyn's sect, it wouldn't be off by four hundred years.

Would it?

And if it was, what date were they counting from? I'd assumed Bleddyn's sect were religious in nature, at least partly. And the presence of Christian art and icons gracing the castle bore that assumption out. If not counting from the birth of Christ, what date would a *Christian* sect be counting *from*?

Because it was most definitely *not* 1626.

But suddenly I was thinking of the boulder in the forest, strangely unbroken and not white with centuries' worth of bird shit. I was thinking of the unpaved road I was suddenly certain was the road where we'd left the rental before making our way into the forest.

I was thinking of that creepy, thick fog I'd walked through, and how eerily fast it'd come on, then disappeared. I was thinking—

No. That's impossible, I told myself, unwilling to even entertain what my brain was trying to posit.

"You seem troubled, Krishnan," Bleddyn said, his concern cutting into my thoughts. I tried to smile, but I don't think I fooled him.

"Bleddyn, I know you guys don't use any technology here, but tell me, you *do* know what it is, right? That beyond this place there are telephones and airplanes and cities and indoor plumbing, all manner of things the rest of the world enjoys? You know what these things are, right?"

Bleddyn shook his head *no*, and I was about to ask him how he *didn't* know, for surely he'd looked up and seen an airplane or had other lost people turn up on the baronet's doorstep, bearing their cell phones and iPods and other tech.

How could they *not* have? At least once in a while?

Because most people don't get lost and wind up in 1626, my brain whispered, and I shook my head to free it of such a crazy thought. It was *not* 1626. I had *not* traveled back in time. That only happened in books, television shows, and movies.

But in real life, people didn't get lost in one year, straggle through some fog, and wind up nearly four hundred years before they were born.

"Bleddyn, I—" I started to say shakily, suddenly *very* cold, to the point of shivering. "Do you...do you think—I mean, do you *believe* that time travel is possible?"

"I do not know what you mean by 'time travel,'" he said simply, and then he put his arm around me, pulling me close against him. He felt warm and solid. "But I *do* know that you have gone quite pale and are shivering despite the warmth of the room. Speak, and tell me what troubles you, Krish."

This near to Bleddyn, I felt both safe and surprisingly comfortable. Safe enough and comfortable enough to say whatever came to my mind. "Do you think it's possible to start out your day in one year, and by day's end, be back nearly four hundred years before you were born?"

Bleddyn's dark eyes widened. "You mean as if by spell or curse, to have been thrust back into a time that is not one's own?"

"I guess. Because where I come from, by our calendar, it's almost four hundred years later than sixteen twenty-six. That is, I was born in nineteen ninety-three." I watched Bleddyn's face change as I said this, from concerned and puzzled to concerned and awed.

"Speak you truly?" he asked almost breathlessly, and I nodded once. He searched my eyes again then smiled. "'Tis a most wondrous thing, this time travel of which you speak, to bring you so far from your own time, and to mine!"

I could only gape. "You don't think I'm crazy?"

Bleddyn's raised his dark brows. "Of course not. You are no madman."

I laughed, burying my face in my hands. "You don't know me. For all *you* know, I could've escaped from a psych ward."

"Psych ward?"

"A mad house, Bleddyn." Then I laughed once more at the thought of a man who'd surely lost his mind explaining the concept of a psych ward to another man who was probably even crazier. "I must've gone mad or hit my head or *something*. All I know is, this can't be real. It just can't be. I'm lying in a ditch in the woods, bleeding from a gash in my head and imagining all this. Or maybe I had a psychotic break in Heathrow. Who knows? But *this* can't be happening."

Bleddyn closed his calloused hands on my wrists, and he gently pried my hands away from my face. It wasn't until air hit my skin that I realized tears were on my face. Bleddyn wiped them away with his thumb and smiled solemnly.

"If, by the Grace of God, you have been brought to this time from your own, then it is by that same Grace that you will find your way back. And as long as I have breath in me, I pledge myself to aiding you in that pursuit," he said softly. "Ever will I protect and guide you as best I may."

More tears ran down my face, and I looked away. "You don't have to say that, Bleddyn. Don't have to act like you believe me. How could you possibly believe what I say?"

Bleddyn turned my face back toward his. "I have seen with my own eyes, Krishnan of Nayar, how differently you speak and act. The strangeness of your attire. You are as familiar with the ways of my time as I expect I would be with yours, which is to say not at all. You are a true stranger, having little in common with the ways of this age. *Ignorance* is not the same as madness. And if you are merely ignorant of this time and not mad, then what you say must be true."

"Oh, jeez, Bleddyn." I laughed through my tears, which he again wiped away. "How can you believe me when *I* don't believe me? Time travel is impossible!"

"*Anything* is possible, through our Lord, Krishnan."

I snorted. "And what if it wasn't your *God* who sent me back in time?"

Bleddyn's eyes widened once more. "You speak of the Adversary?"

"I dunno *who* I speak of, only that I'm scared and confused, and I just can't believe that I'm in sixteen twenty-six!"

"Believe it," Bleddyn said grimly. "For you are. And every minute spent here must convince you of that."

He was right about that. Yet even as I was convinced, my doubts intensified. Which was more likely, after all? That I was crazy, or that I was a time traveler? But then, what would be *better*? Continuing to live like I was trapped in a nightmare or delusion and continuing on in what could be dangerous denial, or behaving as if I genuinely *was* in a different time, and maybe find a way of getting back? Hadn't I lived most of my life since my father died as if I was waiting to wake up? And look where it'd gotten me.

I sighed and hung my head. "I don't know what to think Bleddyn. Or what to *do*."

His arm around me tightened. "As I've said, Krish, I will look after you while you are here. You are my charge. As such, will you follow my guidance until you are prepared to navigate this time more adroitly?"

I nodded. "Yes, Bleddyn."

"Will you trust me?"

I took a deep breath and let it out slowly. "I will."

"Then," Bleddyn said quietly. "Do not speak of this time travel with anyone else, for I fear that you may be taken for a witch or a madman if you speak of such things to anyone."

My own eyes were the ones to widen, this time. "A *witch*? But didn't witches used to get burned at the stake back in the sixteen hundreds?"

Bleddyn nodded. "It is not so bad as once it was. And certainly not here. His lordship does not hold with superstition, nor with burning the unpopular and accused as if they were heathen sacrifices," he said proudly. Then he sighed. "However I fear *he might* think you mad, and if he were to think that, I do not know that he would not send you to a mad house."

I shuddered. The idea of being placed in a seventeenth century madhouse was horrifying. "Don't let them do that to me, Bleddyn," I begged, and Bleddyn shook his head.

"Never, Krish. But you must follow my instruction and tell no one else of your time of origin."

"Believe me, I can barely tell *myself* any of this stuff, so telling other people? Not even on my radar." In response to Bleddyn's blank look, I found myself smiling just a little. "You have my word I'll keep my mouth shut about when I come from."

Bleddyn returned the smile, clearly relieved. "That is well, then." He let go of me and stood up hesitantly, turning beet red again. "I shall leave you to your rest, for on the morrow, we begin the search for your companions. Though in truth, we shall be searching for a way back to your time."

I sighed again, daunted by even the prospect of what lay ahead. "Yes."

"Do not look so downcast, Krish, for I believe that we *will* find the way home for you," Bleddyn said, reaching out and tilting my face up. He was smiling again, and I couldn't help but smile back, for in that moment I believed him, even though I didn't believe I had traveled back in time. But I would.

I would.

I didn't think I'd be capable of falling asleep after *everything*. But I was wrong, as was proven when I was startled out of sleep by a gentle knock on the door.

For a few moments, I thought I was back in the hostel in Cardiff, and that John or Dierdre was knocking. "Come in!" I called, rolling over on a firm but unexpectedly pokey mattress. I squinted open my eyes to total darkness suddenly pierced by lamplight as the door opened, then shut.

And that's when everything came rushing back to me.

"Oh, oh, my God," I groaned, sitting up and burying my face in my hands as the light grew closer and someone sat on the edge of my narrow bed. They placed the lamp placed on the night table, and wound their strong arms around me and held me as I wept, all the fear and feelings of being trapped returning even though I'd had a full night's sleep that'd featured no dreams.

"Hush, Krish," Bleddyn said. "I will look after you."

He cradled the back of my head with one of his hands and swept the other soothingly up and down my bare back. At first I was comforted, and then...not so much. My fear and anxiety gave way to other feelings entirely with each pass of Belddyn's rough hand, and I began to shiver.

Then a moan slipped out, one that Bleddyn could not possibly take for anything other than what it was. And indeed, he didn't. He paused his hand at the small of my back, and he sat back, looking into my eyes.

"Krishnan," he said lowly, and the way he said my name sent such a thrill through me that I moaned again. Bleddyn looked away, blushing. "You gaze at me as if..."

"As if I want you to kiss me?" I asked without thinking, and then I blushed too. Feeling daring, I reached up and turned his face back toward mine. He still wouldn't meet my eyes. "There's something between us, Bleddyn. Maybe I'm the only one who feels it, but every time you touch me, I—"

"This is wrong," Bleddyn said firmly, or perhaps it would have sounded firm if not for the quaver in his deep voice. "You are but a lad. You know not what you court by your actions and speech."

"Actually, I do," I said, smiling and brushing my thumb across his sharp cheekbone. His eyes fluttered shut for a few moments before he turned his face away once more.

"Krish, lad—"

"I'm *not* a lad. I'm a grown man. I know what I want, and I know what I need."

Bleddyn's eyes darted to mine for a moment before darting away just as quickly. "It is an abomination for a man to lie with another man as he lay with a woman."

"Not where I come from."

Another glance, this one startled. "Truly, you say?"

"Truly. Two men or two women can even marry where I'm from."

Now, Bleddyn looked doubtful and disbelieving. "Even if that is so, you are *not* where you come from. You are *here*."

"So you keep reminding me." I let my hand fall away from his face, but before I could turn away, Bleddyn caught my hand and pulled it up to his lips, kissing it lingeringly.

"I swore to protect and guide you, Krish of Nayar," he murmured on my palm. "I would not break such a promise at all, let alone mere hours after swearing it. I would not ravish you as if you were some catamite whore when your innocence shines forth from you like a beacon of loveliness and light. I would not sully what I find most beautiful about you with base carnalities."

Turning so red I had no doubt it showed up even on my complexion, I cupped Bleddyn's face in both hands, this time. "Bleddyn, what if I *want* you to be basely carnal with me?" I asked him and he sighed. "No, I'm being serious. It's not as if I've never had a lover before."

Bleddyn frowned, and if I didn't know better, I'd swear he looked *jealous*.

"You have lain with another?"

"Of *course* I have! I'm twenty-two!" I exclaimed, laughing, letting go of his face to push back the heavy coverlet and sheet. I was naked and not especially ashamed of that fact. And it did my heart a world of good to see Bleddyn's eyes widen as they traveled up and down my body, lingering at my groin every time.

Then he closed his eyes tight and stood up, pacing to the door where he paused, his hand on the knob. "You tempt me," he said, his voice soft but tight. "I came only to waken you, and you tempt me most unmercifully, Krish."

I swung my legs off of the pokey, straw mattress bed and stood up, crossing the small room to place my hands on Bleddyn's grey-shirted back. He was the one to shiver, this time. Feeling greatly daring once more, I leaned in and lightly kissed the nape of his neck, brushing his dark curls aside to do so.

Bleddyn shivered again, but didn't pull away. Not even when I slid my hands around to his chest, then down it, till I was grasping the hem of his shirt and pulling it up to get to the waist of his breeches.

"We should not be doing this," Bleddyn breathed shakily as I unbuttoned his fly. He wasn't wearing the seventeenth century's equivalent of underwear, so the first thing I felt after a solid six-pack, was a hot, damp, *hard* handful of cock. Bleddyn let out a low moan as I began to stroke him, nibbling my way to his ear. "Krishnan, we *should not*."

"Who says?"

"*God* says!" Bleddyn hissed, then hissed again when I ran my thumb across the head of his cock. "He did not send you here for *this*."

"How do *you* know he didn't?"

Bleddyn had no answer for that. At least not for most of the next minute, during which his breeches and hose became a puddle at his feet, and I'd stopped stroking him off in favor of trying to remove his shirt.

"My father—"

"Is not here."

"If he were to catch us like this—" Bleddyn shuddered and it wasn't from pleasure. "He has already caught me so once, and I have found that once was quite enough for my lifetime."

"Your dad caught you *fucking another guy*?" I asked, horrified. My father had died when I was fourteen, and I was still a virgin as far as my mother knew. A gay virgin. And until I got married, that was the way it was going to stay. "Holy shit, that's—that's awful!"

Bleddyn turned to face me, and I stopped tugging on his shirt to wrap my arms around his neck and lean our foreheads together.

"We were barely old enough to grow hair where it counted, William and I," Bleddyn whispered with a sad smile I could just make out. "My father beat us both most soundly and sent William to be fostered in another county. And that was the last I saw or heard of him until shortly before his death."

"Oh, Bleddyn, I'm so sorry," I whispered back, hugging him tight, then leaning back to kiss him. He gasped in surprise, and then he kissed me back hungrily, intently, settling his hands on my waist. Then he them slid around to my ass and pulled me flush against him till his cock was nestled against mine and we both moaned.

I don't know which of us began backing toward the bed, only that suddenly we were laying on it, Bleddyn on top of me, driving his hips down into mine hard and fast. I spread my legs till I could wrap them around his thighs, like my arms were around his neck. He kept groaning my name between panting kisses, squeezing my ass. He brushed his fingers between my cheeks, at first tentatively fingering me, then less tentatively, till I arched up against him and came, biting down on his sinewy shoulder to keep from waking the whole castle with my shouts.

Then I was a limp, sated pile of time traveler, letting my body be used for another's pleasure. Bleddyn grunted and groaned his way to a climax that seemed almost to pain him, from the look on his face before he buried it in the hollow place between my neck and shoulder.

He slipped and slid against me in come and sweat, till with a low groan he finally came, too, hot and a lot, all over my stomach. Then he, too, was collapsing into a heavy pile on top of me. But his weight felt good and right anchoring me, so I didn't mind. When we'd caught our breath, Bleddyn made to lever his body off my own, but I held on to him and waited for him to meet my eyes. When he did, I smiled.

Bleddyn smiled back and leaned down to kiss me good morning.

Chapter Four

O f course, the kiss turned into necking, then into Bleddyn grinding down against me, half-hard and pinning my wrists to the mattress.

"This is wrong," he murmured against my collarbone before kissing it so tenderly, I shivered and tried to wrap my arms around him. But he was stronger than me, and my wrists stayed pressed into the mattress. So I settled for wrapping my legs around his and arching up to meet his thrusts against my abdomen. "We should not—"

"We most definitely *should*," I breathed, angling my head to give him more access to my neck, access he immediately took advantage of, nipping my throat with gentle teeth then laving the spots he'd nipped with his tongue. "Oh, *Bleddyn...*"

"I have wanted you thus from almost the moment I first laid eyes upon you, Krish," Bleddyn whispered feverishly, his lips roaming up to my mouth again. He kissed me sweetly, and freed my wrists. Then he sighed as I wrapped my arms around his neck and pulled him down firmly on top of me. He would not meet my eyes. "And having had you, I thought such illicit desires would be slaked. That I would commit such a delightful sin, repent, and crave you no more, yet..."

"Yet?"

Now Bleddyn met my eyes, his dark ones as somber as a Sunday morning. Which it might very well have been in 1626, for all I knew. "Yet having you has only made my yearning for you keener, sharper. My desires have grown teeth." He shook his head. "My desire for William I had excused as nothing more than childish exploration, for I had not yet a man's appetites. But even as a man grown, even as I lay with my sweet wife, never have I felt anything like this. Anything like *you*. You overwhelm me so, Krishnan of Nayar." Bleddyn kissed me again, hard, hungrily, briefly. "I know this is sin, pure and inexcusable, and yet I would gladly buy my passage to Hell with even just one morning spent between your thighs."

I shivered again. Even medieval dirty talk was enough to turn my crank. *Bleddyn* turned my crank. Everything he did, everything he said, everything he *was*.

I caressed Bleddyn's face before cupping it in my hand. "I wish I could convince you what we're doing isn't wrong, Bleddyn. But I guess I can't compete with a lifetime spent living in this time, with everyone, including your father, telling you that desiring another man is wrong. Hell, even in *my* time, some people still insist what we're doing is wrong. That somewhere, up in the sky, there's a God sitting on a cloud, judging who we love despite having given us the will to love freely. But *I* don't believe that. If there *is* a God out there, somewhere, it loves us and wants us to love each other and be happy. It doesn't want to see us suffer and be miserable and make everyone else that way because of narrow-mindedness and fear." I wrapped my arm back around Bleddyn's neck again and leaned our foreheads together. "I don't want to hurt you, or scare you, or make you regret what we've done."

"But that is where my sin is compounded, Krishnan. For I regret *nothing*." Then Bleddyn was kissing me once more, pulling me up with him as he sat, so I was straddling his thighs and half-sitting in his lap. I could feel his cock nudging past my balls, and he grasped my ass with both hands, squeezing and kneading before he teased his fingers between my cheeks again.

"Don't stop," I moaned, clutching at him tighter as he pressed the tip of his finger against me, then into me with a fierce and addictive burn I hadn't felt in over a year. Only it'd never felt this *good* or this *right*. "Oh, God, don't stop!"

"I could not. Even if I wished," Bleddyn said, nuzzling my throat as I kissed his curly hair. His finger made its way inside me and was quickly followed by another. Then he began scissoring them gently, till I was writhing on him like an agitated cobra. "Krish, the heat of you sears me like the heart of a sacred flame. I can maintain only one thought, one desire—to feel you around me, to lose myself in your fire until I am ash."

"Fuck, Bleddyn, please tell me you have something? Like lube or lotion."

He looked up at me, puzzled. "I know not—"

"Something slippery? I can take you. All day, if it were up to me, baby. But I can't take you *dry*." I clenched around his fingers and sudden understanding dawned in his eyes. Understanding and regret.

"I have not oil to ease my way," he said, frowning. "I did not expect—"

"Neither did I," I said, cupping his face in my hands again. I did my best to hide my frustration, seriously considering taking him with nothing but spit. It'd be like the night I lost my virginity all over again.

Yeah, let's not *revisit that pleasant little interlude just now. Or ever again, if possible.* I sighed and kissed Bleddyn. "It's okay. I suppose we could just—"

"Salve!" Bleddyn burst out, and I blinked at him.

"What?" But Bleddyn was laying me back down and practically springing out of bed. He padded over to the garderobe and yanked it open, scanning the contents of the mostly empty piece of furniture. Then he bent low and picked up something I couldn't make out, mostly because I was staring at his ass again.

"Gwynedd mentioned last night that she had left a soothing salve for your ankle in yon garderobe, and I was to relay that information to you before you took your rest," Bleddyn said in a rush, standing up with a small pot of what I assumed was the aforementioned salve. He grinned, and it made him look barely old enough for his mustache and beard. Then his grin turned rather sheepish. "Of course, I forgot her admonishment entirely, but t'will now serve us in a similar capacity."

"Uh, do you know what's *in* the salve?" I asked as he approached the bed and climbed on. "I mean, it's nothing gross, is it? Or burn-y?"

Bleddyn's grin gentled into a reassuring smile. "This salve is gentle and mild enough to be used on teething babes. Gwynedd used it on Gareth when he was teething and mayhap even on *me* when *I* was teething. It relieves pain and eases aches, nothing more."

I thought it over for a few moments, then shrugged, tossing over my misgivings. If it was good enough for Gareth's and Bleddyn's gums, I supposed it was good enough for my asshole. "All right, bring on the salve. And I don't mean sparingly," I added, looking at his cock. It was my first *good* look at it, what with all the frantic rubbing off on each other. I remembered just how hard and fast he'd seemed to like thrusting it. And it was *not* little.

"Be gentle," I told him as he removed the lid of the small pot and tossed it over his shoulder. "It's been a while."

Bleddyn nodded, that hint of jealousy flaring in his eyes again, but only for a moment. Then he was running a hand up my thigh to grasp my cock and stroke it.

"My desire for you almost incapacitates me with its fierceness. I wish to have all of you at once," he murmured, running a finger over the tip of my cock before leaning down to kiss it. I made a garbled sound low in my throat like a squabbling crow.

"Bleddyn—" *for God's sake, fuck me!* I was about to say, but Bleddyn slid his hand between my hip and the bed, urging me to roll over onto my stomach.

He didn't have to tell me twice. Though there's a lot to be said for missionary, there's just such a dirty thrill to be had from getting it doggy-style.

I grabbed the bed's lone pillow and crammed it under my hips, wriggling around a little to get into a comfortable position. For a few seconds, Bleddyn did nothing, merely stared down at me. I could feel his gaze, as weighty and hot as July sunlight. I gave a low, breathy, porn-star moan and spread my legs, looking over my shoulder at Bleddyn. Never let it be said that Krish Nayar can't put on a decent show. He was staring at me, mouth agape, with a dollop of translucent salve on his fingers. It looked like petroleum jelly.

"I'm waiting, Bleddyn. *Take me.*"

Bleddyn let out a breath and began stroking himself with the salve, never once taking his eyes off me. I hiked my right leg up higher to give him a better view.

After another few seconds of gazing, Bleddyn moved closer, till I could feel the heat of him all along my back, ass, and legs. Two slippery, salve-y fingers trailed down from the small of my back to my asshole before pushing back into me with that same burn, though lessened. I didn't know if it was the salve, if I was just getting used to being fingered after going so long without, or if it was a combination of both.

Whatever it was, it definitely felt more good than bad. Bleddyn began scissoring his fingers again and while doing so, brushed my prostate. I lit up like a JACKPOT sign in Vegas, moaning his name.

Bleddyn leaned down to kiss my ear and whisper, "Are you ready for me, Krishnan?"

"*Yes.*"

Bleddyn kissed my ear again and sat up, removing his fingers. I instantly missed the feeling of fullness and pressure, but not for long. Something a lot larger than Bleddyn's fingers brushed me, then pressed against me, then pushed *into* me without hesitation or delay.

"Blehhhhhttthhhyyyyyyn!" I yowled his name as he filled me, slowly, surely, and implacably. For his part, Bleddyn was whispering my name like a prayer, pushing my thighs wider with his big hands before settling them on my ass again.

I was torn between pleasure and pain—between that really amazing feeling of being filled and that feeling one is about to be split like a cord of wood.

But even as I was wondering just how big his cock was, the closet size-queen who lived in my head was cheering and gleefully taking it. Would have taken it *all* till the end of the world, if necessary.

Bleddyn was leaning over me, drops of sweat dripping onto my back. When he at last could go no farther, when I could swear I felt cock nudging my epiglottis, he stilled, panting and groaning.

"Oh, Krish." His breath was hot and moist on my shoulder. "Never have I…"

He trailed off and fell silent for so long, I began to worry. "Never have you *what*, Bleddyn?"

"I have never taken a man thus," Bleddyn said, and I glanced over my shoulder, surprised.

"Not even William?"

"I let *William* take *me*. Once. And there were a few others. After him and before Rhiannon." Bleddyn nuzzled my cheek. "But never have *I* taken another man."

"Wow," I exhaled softly, then grinned. "Feels good, doesn't it?"

"Never have I felt its like. Nor yours." He placed a damp, gentle kiss on my temple.

"I promise it only gets better," I purred. "But first, you have to pull out, then—ah! God!"

It may have been his first time pitching, but Bleddyn had great instincts, because before I could even finish the sentence, he'd pulled out and driven his way back in, hard and fast, leaving me speechless and breathless, and scrambling in the sheets for purchase.

"Have I harmed you, Krishnan?" Bleddyn was as still as a statue, on me and in me. My insides, however, were all aflutter trying to accommodate him. Soon, I began to clench and release around him like a fist. I arched up against him, bearing myself up on shaky arms.

"Harm me some more, baby," I gasped out, then clarified just in case Bleddyn took it the wrong way. "Take me, Bleddyn. Until neither of us can walk right."

Bleddyn leaned down and kissed my shoulder. Then he was pulling out fast and thrusting back in the same way. I yowled again, loud enough that if the castle wasn't already awake, they surely were after *that*.

Bleddyn grasped my hips and began pulling them back for every thrust and pushing them away every time he pulled out, grunting and swearing in, I assume, fluid Welsh, interspersed with my name. I risked bearing up on one arm and began stroking myself off—even I wouldn't expect a reach-around from a virgin—not that I had to stroke hard or long. By luck or innate skill, Bleddyn struck prostate more often than he didn't and soon, I was coming *hard*, Bleddyn's name ripped raggedly from my throat.

Through the haze of completion I floated in for an eternity afterwards, eventually I felt Bleddyn's body still on and in mine before he pumped out his release with a loud groan that sounded like it was trying to be my name.

Then for a little while, I knew nothing but gentle darkness, and Bleddyn's body anchoring me to Earth, his heartbeat thudding in time with my own.

Chapter Five

"S o, what's the plan of attack for today?"

I was lying in bed, still wrapped up in the most satisfying afterglow, wishing I could spend the rest of the day that way. But Bleddyn had already levered himself off me and was sitting up. I took the opportunity to ogle the way his muscles moved with ease under his pale skin. He stretched and stood, giving me a drool-worthy view of his ass which was still, in a word, *perfect*.

I watched as he first went to the small table near the garderobe and splashed his face with the water in the basin. Then he picked up a wide piece of flannel lying next to it, one of three, and gave himself a quick spot-clean, quickly wiping away come and salve. Last of all, he retrieved his breeches, hose, boots, and shirt and pulled them on efficiently. Not once did he look at me, nor did he speak, till my afterglow had begun to recede and turn to something less pleasant.

"The plan," he said, his head finally inclined toward me, his expression rather grim. "Is we search the Forest for your companions, in case they, too, were sent back and know not that they were. If we find traces of them, we shall track them and reunite you with them. If we do not, then we shall continue the search for them to cover our true quest, the way to send you back to your own time. God willing."

"Yes. God willing," I said, remembering where I was and what was happening. That the last thing I wanted to be doing was tying myself to a time that wasn't my own. Something Bleddyn had clearly figured out before I did.

Though, perhaps unfortunately, not before we'd created one hell of a complication.

But it doesn't have to be complicated, does it? I asked myself, but I didn't receive an answer. No answer that I liked. *We're just two guys who got together and got off. It doesn't have to mean more than that. Maybe chivalrous Sir Knight, here, doesn't understand that, but I do. And I can make Bleddyn understand, too. I have to, or else the rest of my time here is going to be really awkward.*

I sighed and sat up, watching the stiff, tense line of Bleddyn's broad shoulders and found myself at a loss for words. I tried, nonetheless. "Bleddyn, I—"

"I'll leave you to prepare for the day," he said before I could find out what I would have said. "I must see to my son before we leave, and you'll have to break your fast as we ride."

"If you say so," I mumbled just as my stomach let loose with a ferocious growl. I'd only picked at my dinner the night before, too nervous and keyed up to have much of an appetite. But after this morning, I suppose I could've eaten a horse.

Bleddyn turned to face me and I blushed, not meeting his eyes, even though I could feel his gaze on me, considering and intent.

I wanted to hear him tell me he still regretted nothing. That he'd enjoyed being with me, that being with me was a game-changer. I wanted to hear him say he would stop trying to bury who he was under his father's expectations or his people's and go after what he truly wanted, wherever that lead him.

I wanted to tell him to be proud and unashamed.

I risked looking up at him, meaning to say these things and more, but the words died on my lips at the grim, closed off look on his face. He looked, in that moment, just like his father.

So in the end, I said nothing, and Bleddyn simply turned and left.

"Master Krishnan? I—I have a boon I would beg of you."

Wincing and twinging at the discomfort of riding just an hour after getting the fucking of my life from Bleddyn, I looked up from the back of my pony's head and over at Owen Wynn.

"I'm at your disposal, my lord," I said listlessly. My ass *hurt*, and my stomach was churning as it tried to process the two hard, dried apples and chunk of bread I'd recently fed it while horsed on the slowest, most wobbly-gaited pony known to man.

When I'd first seen the damn thing—sway-backed and not on the young side—I'd eyed it with some trepidation, glancing at Bleddyn as if to ask *are you serious?* Bleddyn, who'd been at best lukewarm to me since our assignation, had frowned.

"I suppose this was father's doing," he'd muttered to himself with a sigh, and I'd raised one eyebrow.

"Oh, you mean the man whose favorite person I am? Well. That's just awesome." I rolled my eyes but didn't protest when Bleddyn helped me onto the pony, which was named, of all things, Queen.

Around us in the courtyard, armed men mounted up on sturdy horses, including Owen, the baronet's second oldest son, and Bleddyn's father, Rhys, who hadn't looked at me or acknowledged my presence once since he'd greeted me with such touching warmth yesterday. The handsome blond who'd been the first to greet me and Bleddyn upon our arrival at the castle yesterday was also along. He kept staring at me and sneering as if I was a sideshow freak. His manner was at once disdainful and condescending, and I flushed, knowing he'd been laughing at me as Bleddyn had helped me mount up.

Whatever. Who cares what he thinks? I asked myself. *Who cares what* any *of them think?*

When Bleddyn mounted and joined his father at the head of our small company of eleven men, Rhys gave the signal to ride out. And out we rode, through the muddy, stinky courtyard and down the road.

I'd once read somewhere that when horses are walking or cantering with other horses, they'll all keep pace with each other, whether they're being ridden or not, no matter how lazy or ornery an individual horse may be. Queen was, of course, the exception, for from my vantage point of last rider, I got a lovely opportunity to eat everyone else's dust along with my cold, tough breakfast.

Everyone had gotten just far enough ahead of me that all I could see were horses' asses and the glint of metal. Having resigned myself to getting lost in the Forest twice in two days, I half-heartedly clucked at the pony to get her to move faster, but she wouldn't. And I wasn't about to call for the macho dicks on their mustangs to slow down. I wouldn't have given Rhys, Bleddyn, or the disdainful blond the satisfaction.

So I'd rode along, my ass and stomach complaining, gazing at the bay pony's mane and trusting the animal to be able to follow her nose to wherever the others fetched up. But I'd been so enmeshed in my own world of misery and confusion, I hadn't noticed one of the riders slowing his horse and waiting for my slow-ass pony to catch up.

Now, I waited for Owen to make his request, whatever it was. I looked him over when his brow furrowed as he sought to phrase whatever it was he would say. He was a handsome man, like his older brother and father, only with darker hair and a paler complexion. Yet he had the same Wynn-canniness about his square, fine-featured face.

"I would hear a tale of where you come from," Owen finally said in his husky, cautiously excited tenor, his blue eyes round and almost childlike in their anticipation. "A tale directly from the shores of, erm, from where, again, do you hail?"

"America," I said, mentally shrugging. They'd never guess from the name that I was a time traveler.

"Yes, America!" Owen said, as if he said the name every day. "It must be a truly grand kingdom, indeed, to nurture so many kinds of people from so many places."

"Oh, yeah. The good ol' United States of America is one big melting pot." I laughed at the irony of that statement and glanced over at the baronet's son again. "But I'm no story-teller. I get details mixed up and leave things out. I have to backtrack just so people know what I'm talking about. I mangle the stories I tell."

Owen's frown bordered on a pout. "Any tale you could tell me that I haven't heard before would be most appreciated, Master Krishnan. I would be your captive audience," he added, blinking those big blue eyes at me. I blushed, glancing ahead of us at the asses of all the other horses. I couldn't spot Bleddyn or Rhys leading the party, such as it was.

"Well," I hesitated. "There's *one* story I'm especially fond of. It's a, er, tale of a ring of great power. *Magic* power," I muttered with some anxiety, wondering if Owen would freak out at the word 'magic.'

But he looked even more excited than he had before, leaning slightly closer to me like a kid anticipating a really *good* bedtime story.

"It began with the forging of the great rings of power: Three were given to the Elves, immortal, wisest, and fairest of all beings..."

❖

Half an hour or so later, Rhys called a halt.

"*'I ain't been droppin' no eaves, sir, honest!'* Samwise Gamgee exclaimed, frightened as the wizard held him down on the table and aimed a fierce glare at him," I told Owen, who was still listening with unhidden fascination, when the call went up to stop. Owen and I both blinked at each other, looked up and ahead, then back at each other and laughed.

"It appears," he began, grinning, "that we have reached the place where Bleddyn found you," he said, looking around. This spot looked like every other bit of Gwydir Forest we'd passed through. Perhaps if there'd been fog, it might have looked more familiar.

Owen and I nudged our horses to catch up to the others, and, for a wonder, Queen obeyed, picking up her unhurried pace to a slightly hurried one, but still not managing to keep pace with Owen's horse.

When I drew even with the others, they were already dismounting. I groaned under my breath and told myself it'd be a cinch. I'd just swing my way off Queen and hop to the ground. Neither ass nor ankle would be jarred badly. It'd be simple and painless.

Yeah, right, I thought, and took a steadying breath before standing slightly in the saddle and lifting my leg to swing it over Queen's back. I'd just managed to make my aching leg cooperate despite my aching *ass*, when a pair of firm hands settled on my waist and lifted me down, placing me gently on the ground.

Blushing and swallowing my pride, I turned to thank Bleddyn and found myself facing Owen, instead.

"You, seemed to be having a spot of trouble dismounting," he murmured, his blue eyes steady on my own. I found myself smiling and still blushing.

"I was," I admitted. "But lucky for me, the rumors of chivalry's demise have been greatly exaggerated."

Owen smiled at me, his own cheeks turning red, and we stared and grinned at each other, not saying anything, when I heard someone clear his throat to our left. Bleddyn stood there, looking grim and unhappy.

"Lord Owen. Master Krishnan, this is where I found you, last evening," he said in a formal tone, his gaze shifting between Owen and me before settling on me. "If you'll join me at the front of the party, we may be able to retrace your steps and locate your companions."

"Right. My companions," I replied with a final small smile for Owen. "Excuse me, my lord."

"Of course," Owen said warmly. Bleddyn took me by the elbow, and we made our way to the head of the group of men and horses. But I could feel Owen's warm gaze lingering on me.

Well, when it rains, it pours, I thought bemusedly, glancing at Bleddyn's grim profile. I willed him to look at me, but I realized that wasn't going to happen after a few seconds. So I sighed, looking dead ahead at the tangle of forest that looked like every other tangle of forest I'd ever seen.

"Is it that you hate me, now?" I clapped a hand over my mouth, mortified. I had no idea where that question had come from. I certainly hadn't meant to even think it, let alone say it.

Bleddyn's hand tightened on my elbow for a moment before relaxing and dropping away.

"Never could I hate you, Krishnan of Nayar," Bleddyn murmured, still not looking at me, though I was watching him from the corner of my eye. When we drew even with Rhys, he was frowning, as if finding me utterly distasteful. The feeling was mutual, and I let it show on my own face, which seemed to take him aback before he merely looked affronted.

Then Bleddyn was leading me past his father and the disdainful blond—who seemed thick as thieves—with a light touch to the small of my back. That touch steadied me, and we began to look, in earnest, for any signs that my friends had traveled back to 1626, too.

"This is it," I said about two chilly hours later, looking around the empty clearing where my friends and I had made camp yesterday. Or four hundred years from now. I didn't see any sign anyone had ever been there. Not even a single gum wrapper or wadded-up tissue.

But I was certain this was the spot. We'd passed the like-new boulder and the stupid pond, which was nearly a small lake in 1626. We didn't pass the fallen tree, but it was probably still standing now.

"Are you quite certain?" Bleddyn asked me, scrutinizing the empty site with narrowed eyes. I nodded.

"I remember Dierdre chose this clearing because it looked the cleanest. Huh. If only she could see it now," I muttered.

Behind us, the rest of the men led their horses forward and began fanning out in the clearing. Rhys barked orders, sending his men off in pairs in three of the four cardinal directions, instructing them to search, "*a few miles hence for any signs of the wayward travelers*," and took himself and the last of the men off in the fourth direction, leaving Bleddyn and I alone in the clearing.

Bleddyn immediately knelt and studied the grass for goodness knows what, leaving me to stand there twiddling my thumbs. For lack of anything better to do, I limped over to Queen and patted her side. Bleddyn wasn't going to talk to me, and I certainly wasn't going to be the one to go crawling for companionship.

Queen stood still and impassive, neither stamping her feet nor champing the grass. She stared ahead of her, ignoring my sudden bout of affection. Apparently I was *persona non grata* to everyone that day. Sighing, I leaned against her and turned to watch Bleddyn investigate the empty clearing. Because of his armor, I couldn't even ogle his ass or his muscles.

This promised to be a long day, and it wasn't even noon yet.

"Your friends did not travel back with you."

I'd finally given in and sat cross-legged in the grass, my back against a tall, solid old tree. Wary of spiders or bugs at first, I'd tried not lean against it, but I eventually closed my eyes only to have them fly open when Bleddyn spoke. He was standing over and staring down at me, an unreadable look on his face. I yawned and sat up. "Well, *I* coulda told ya *that*. This clearing is way cleaner than it is in my time. It's pristine, in fact."

Bleddyn grunted and held his hand out to me. After a few seconds of reluctance, I took it and let him pull me to my feet. Bleddyn not only hauled me up, but hauled me close, still holding my hand as he settled the other on my waist.

He locked his eyes on my mouth as if he wanted to kiss me but didn't dare. So, I took the matter out of his hands and gave him a quick, teasing kiss that he didn't respond to at first. As I was pulling away, my face gone up in embarrassed flames, Bleddyn made a low, growling sound in his throat and kissed me back passionately, possessively, sliding his arms around me and holding me close. His mail armor was chilly and hard through the thin material of my shirt, but I could feel that wasn't all that was hard on Bleddyn.

He pushed me back until I was pressed between him and the tree. He freed my hand, seeking out the hem of my shirt. I lifted my arms, and I was bared to the chilly spring air in seconds. Bleddyn traced the skin of my chest with his large, hot hands, their calluses leaving gooseflesh in their wake. He did the same on my back before sliding under the waist of my breeches. He gripped and kneaded my ass slow and hard.

"Bleddyn," I exhaled when his hot kisses wended their way to my ear. "Please, *please*."

"How is it you've ensnared me so?" Bleddyn mumbled like a man drunk. "What spell am I under that I desire you with such intensity? That even *having* you is not enough to sate me for more than mere minutes?" And so saying, Bleddyn thrust himself against me *hard*, pinning me to the tree, and I groaned, sliding my arms around his neck.

"If it's a spell, it's a *good* one," I purred in his ear, and Bleddyn tensed in my arms, leaning back to look at me, that grim, Rhys-look back on his face. "Is it the same spell you would cast over my lord's son?"

Confused, I blinked. "What?"

Bleddyn's frown turned into a scowl. "Think you that I noticed not how closely you rode with him? That I noticed not how you enchanted him with your talk and your eyes? That I noticed not how *his eyes* linger on you in a way most covetous?"

It took a few seconds to parse all that, but when I did, I was nonplussed. "You think I'm trying to *seduce Owen*?"

"*Lord Owen* is falling under your spell as surely as I—" and here Bleddyn fell silent and simply scowled harder. "Is that your aim? To steal the hearts and minds of every one of Lord John's men? *Are* you a witch, sent to sow havoc and licentiousness among us?"

I laughed and shook my head, both irate and stung. "This morning, you didn't have any problem sowing havoc and licentiousness yourself. You didn't seem to have any qualms about being *ensnared* when you were fucking me raw! Tell me, is this how you treated William after you had *him*?"

Bleddyn looked shocked, and all the color drained from his face. I immediately wanted to take back the last part of what I said. It felt like a low-blow. Way lower than anything Bleddyn had said so far.

"Bleddyn, I'm sorry," I said, trying to hold his gaze to show him how sincere I was. "That was below the belt and I shouldn't have said it. I was just angry and hurt. I didn't mean to—wait, Bleddyn—"

But Bleddyn had already let me go and was walking away. I felt instantly colder for his absence. "We should ride for Llanrwst or Trefriw. Mayhap, if your companions *were* swept back in time as you were, there would be some sign of them there."

I swallowed and kicked myself, wiping at my dry eyes to quell the stinging behind them. "But I thought you said my friends hadn't come back with me."

"They likely have not, Master Krishnan. But if they did, and they arrived at some other point besides the Forest, then Llanrwst and Trefriw will be the places to start." Bleddyn paused at his horse's side but did not mount.

I slowly approached him, making noise so as not to startle him. And when I was within touching distance, I put my hand on his shoulder. He tensed under my touch.

"I'm not—I'm not trying to ensnare Owen Wynn, Bleddyn," I whispered. "He is someone who could be a good friend, I suppose, if I'm here for long enough. But I'm not trying to seduce him. I wouldn't. Flirt with him? Perhaps. It's my nature to be flirty. But seduce? Not if it causes you such pain and consternation."

Bleddyn hung his head. "Always has it been my great besetting sin to desire that which I cannot or should not have, Krish. And I desire *you* greatly."

I found myself smiling and blushing. "I desire you greatly, too, in case that wasn't made clear this morning, when you fucked the common sense out of me."

Bleddyn relaxed his shoulders a bit. "When I saw the way his lordship was gazing upon you, I could not see *past* that, nor past my own jealousy and covetousness. The merest thought that he should desire you the way I do, might want to *lay* with you, as I have lain, undid me and overthrew my reason with the ease and capriciousness with which a child topples a house made of playing cards."

Turning to look at me, Bleddyn took my hands and held them up to his face, kissing them. His eyes were solemn and sorrowful. "If you wish me to stand aside so that you may follow whither your affections lead, you have only to say so, Krishnan of Nayar. For never have I seen Lord Owen look at either person or thing the way he looked at you today."

Bleddyn bowed, and let go of my hands.

I was left speechless in the wake of his assumptions. Bleddyn's obvious *feelings* for me ran deeper than was wise for either of us, and maybe he wasn't alone in that. But I could only dig in the voluminous pockets of my borrowed clothes. I came out with a small, hard apple, which I tossed in Queen's general direction, and the pot of salve that I'd yet to use on my poor ankle.

I held it out to Bleddyn, who took it with a shaking hand and looked at me with questions in his eyes. "You brought the salve with you? Why?"

In response, I smiled, and hooked my thumbs in the waist of my breeches and pushed them down. I stepped out of them and my unlaced hiking boots.

"What can I say? I thought it'd come in handy one way or another."

Glancing around the clearing, Bleddyn took a step toward me, then another. Then we were in each other's arms, kissing and pressed tight against each other. Bleddyn cupped my face tenderly while groping my ass, the pot of salve still in it.

Meanwhile I was scrabbling under his mail shirt for the waistband of his woolen breeches, then pushing them down, dropping to my knees with them.

Eye-level with his cock, I finally looked away from his wide-eyed gaze, held up his mail shirt, and took another good look at him. He was above average in length and *girthy*, just the way I liked 'em. He was also brick-red, rock-hard, uncut, and leaking at the tip. I stuck my tongue out like a kid trying to catch snowflakes and licked the head of his cock slowly, like it was a lollipop, and he made a noise I've never heard another man make: choked, high-pitched, and half-squawk.

I was flattered.

I continued to lick and nibble at his cock before finally sucking him in and doing my best to deep-throat him. Bleddyn, for his part, held dead-still and said nothing, though he did utter a few more of those weird squawks. I could feel his heated, awed gaze on the top of my head, and I angled myself so I could meet his eyes while sucking the rosy flush off his cock.

"Krishnan, I—" he started to say, his voice tight and strained. I took him as deep as I could for a few seconds, and he began groaning like he was about to come, so I backed off with care, clamping down on the base of his cock.

"Not till you're in me," I said, my voice firm as I held his gaze. Bleddyn nodded, closing his eyes and breathing deep, measured breaths.

I let go of Bleddyn and picked up the pot of salve, which Bleddyn had dropped early on in the proceedings, opened it, and scooped out some of the slippery stuff. I let it warm a little before slathering the lion's share of it on Bleddyn's cock, without touching him *too* much, or for too *long*, because he was obviously near the edge.

The rest of the salve left on my fingers, I stretched and prepared myself under Bleddyn's wide-eyed, almost salivating gaze. I bit my lip in the midst of moans that made Bleddyn's dark eyes glaze over and his cock hug his abdomen. With a bare modicum of time and preparation I was mostly ready. I turned away from Bleddyn, going on all fours, and spread my legs as wide as I could.

I felt Bleddyn devouring me with his gaze, then he held me open with his fingers and skewered me with his cock in one hard, fast thrust. I keened, high and long, and scrambled for purchase in the grass and soil. Behind me, Bleddyn moaned softly, sliding his hands down to my hips as he pulled out, then drove forward again. I saw stars and gasped out Bleddyn's name, shuddering all over like an old jalopy.

And so it went, Bleddyn filling me again and again, setting off fireworks in my body and behind my eyes. Every once in a while, he'd lean down to whisper in my ear that I was beautiful and lovely and *his*, and he'd kiss my shoulder or my nape, then carry on fucking me cross-eyed.

After one of those whispered endearments, he took it into his head to give me a reach-around. Not that he had to do much reaching or arounding. I was ready to explode, and just a few passes of his rough, calloused hand on my hot, uber-sensitive dick was enough to send me to the stratosphere.

Bleddyn came a second after me, each tangible throb of his cock adding to my own climax, as did the wet, hot pulse of his release. It was pleasure greater than I'd ever had with anyone else, familiar and new, and as right as anything I'd ever done. Righter, even. Something about Bleddyn made *everything* better, and my last thought before the world whited out was that maybe being stuck in 1626 wouldn't be so bad, after all. For a little while, anyway.

Chapter Six

When I returned to myself, Bleddyn and I were laying spooned together on our sides, and he was still inside me. One arm pillowed my head, though not too well what with all the armor, and the other was around my waist. He was kissing my ear and nibbling the lobe, still languidly thrusting his half-hard cock within me. I was quite sore after just now and earlier this morning. It felt beyond *good*, but I was trying with all my might not to imagine the ride to Trefriw and Llanrwst, then back to Gwydir Castle.

"You are so lovely," Bleddyn kept murmuring with quiet urgency and nuzzling my hair. "And I desire you so. The more of you I have, the more of you I *want*."

I chuckled, leaning back into his embrace and turning my head in time to get a teasing kiss. I moaned and lifted my leg, putting it back over Bleddyn's so he could sink more fully into me. He slid his hand up my stomach to my chest, making slow circles around my left nipple with his index finger. "You can have me whenever you wish, as often as you wish, Bleddyn."

Bleddyn's finger stilled, and he laid his hand flat over my heart. "T'would be unwise to have any more of you than I have already tasted, for even now, I know the time comes when I shall have *none* of you. Nothing but a memory of your warm arms and sweet lips."

Swallowing an unexpected lump in my throat, I looked into Bleddyn's dark eyes and tried to smile. I didn't want to think about going back to my own time. At least not at that moment. "Then let's make as many fantastic memories as possible. Whaddaya say?" I clenched every aching, sore muscle I could around him, and he shut his eyes and rocked his hips forward as he held me tight.

Half-hard became three-quarters hard, and sooner rather than later, Bleddyn was fucking me again. Not hard and fast as he had the other two times, but slow and tender, his kisses mixed with words of praise and affection, and his caresses as light and tender as butterfly kisses.

Our legs tangled as we rocked together, working toward a second climax, this one almost painful in its searing, languorous intensity. When we came, it was like something out of a cheesy romance novel: at the same time, holding hands, our fingers linked together. I had tears in my eyes, and Bleddyn called on his God for salvation even as he filled me with the hot, copious evidence of his eventual damnation.

❖

"So, now that we know my friends haven't come back in time, too—at least not to the same spot I did—we go to the nearest town and do some investigating, just in case?"

Bleddyn nodded as he pulled up his breeches and his hose. "*Discreet* investigating," he said, adjusting his clothes and armor and looking at me. I stood in the center of the clearing, naked but for my boots, unwilling to get dressed yet. Being dressed meant leaving this clearing, and leaving this clearing meant facing not only the fact that I had traveled in time, but receiving irrefutable proof of it. Also, it meant facing the fact that I might not be able to find my way back to the time I was from.

I looked up when Bleddyn approached me, his arms held out. A second later, I was in them, fighting tears as he held me tight and close, stroking my hair and my back.

"What if I never get home?" I mumbled to Bleddyn, clutching him panic-tight and burying my face in the taut, hollow junction where his shoulder and neck met. "What if I'm trapped here for the rest of my life? What will I *do*?"

"Hush, Krish, hush. Have I not promised that I would look after you for as long as you're here?"

"But you have a life of your own and duties that won't be helped by caring for some guy you barely know, who can't even fend for himself!"

"That matters not," Bleddyn said, so gently that I *did* start crying in earnest, sniffling and everything.

"B-but, I can't e-even start a *fire*! No matter how many times I rub sticks together, it never works! I can't hunt, I can't fish, I can't fight, I get lost *all* the time, if that hasn't become super obvious! I—"

Bleddyn chuckled, leaning back to kiss my forehead, then my eyelids, so, *so* tenderly, it caused more tears to leak out, and I sniffled some more.

"All those skills are skills that can be taught with patience and practice," Bleddyn said softly. His smile was fond and kind. "I will instruct you in whatever you need to learn to sustain yourself in *this* time. It would be my honor."

"Really? You'd—you'd help me?" I asked, wiping my eyes and blushing. Even at my best I'm not the *most* manly man, but weeping in front of a butch guy like Bleddyn? Absolutely mortifying. I felt foolish and silly and overwrought in the wake of my little crying jag. "You'd show me how to do that stuff?"

"For certain I would, Krish of Nayar." Bleddyn turned my face up to his own and kissed me. The kiss was sweet, even though it tasted like my tears. But no more tears were forthcoming, something which filled me with relief. I was sure I'd find other occasions to cry at some point down the line if I didn't get back to my time soon, but I'd try my best not to cry in front of Bleddyn or anyone else.

After the kiss ended, Bleddyn gathered up my discarded clothes and helped me into them. When I was once more dressed, we made our way over to Queen, and I groaned at the thought of having to sit my thrice-sore ass through another few miles of riding her. But Bleddyn only took her reins and led her to his horse, Arwel. He secured Queen's reins to Arwel's saddle, then held out his hand to me. I hobbled over to him, confused, until Bleddyn helped me up onto Arwel. I went with a wince and a gasp, but was soon seated and looking down at Bleddyn, who smiled, and climbed up behind me.

With one hand holding Arwel's reins and one arm wrapped around my waist, Bleddyn clicked his teeth, and we were off.

❖

"Awaken, Krish, for we are near Trefriw," a familiar voice whispered into my hair before placing a lingering kiss in it.

I started a little, opening my slightly stinging eyes. The forest was gone, receding to fields on either side of us as we cantered down the Great Road. The sky above was overcast, but clear enough that I could tell the sun was almost directly overhead. It was almost noon.

I stretched and straightened up, wincing at the literal pain in my ass and legs. And neck. I'd dozed off with my head angled back to lean on Bleddyn's mailed shoulder. Not the most comfortable of sleeping positions, but I did feel a bit refreshed for my micro-nap.

"I didn't mean to fall asleep on you, Bleddyn," I yawned, rubbing my eyes as I craned my neck to see this village of Trefriw coming up. A rather large part of me was certain it'd look like the town John, Dierdre, and I had traveled through to get to Gwydir Forest, and that this whole thing would be just a weird dream, even Bleddyn. It was a thought which caused a pang I chose not to examine. "Did I miss anything?"

Bleddyn nuzzled my hair and my neck, then heaved a heavy sigh. "Nothing of import. I would have let you sleep for as long as was needed, for clearly you are weary, but Trefriw nears and I think there is aught we must speak of before there we arrive."

Sensing a sudden change in mood, I glanced back at Bleddyn. "What's the matter?"

"The matter is," Bleddyn's mouth pursed a bit under his mustache. "The matter is our behavior toward one another."

I frowned. "I don't understand."

Sighing again, Bleddyn stopped Arwel, and took my hand, bringing it to his lips to kiss it reverently. "In your time, two men sharing affection may not be unusual. But in *my* time, it is unusual to the point of being criminal. It is illegal for men to lay together as we have, and such a crime is punishable in Britain by death."

I was speechless. I had, of course, assumed that homosexuality was frowned upon in this century, and punishable by jail-time or flogging, or something medieval and unnecessarily punitive. But death? I could only look back at Bleddyn in horror, certain he *must* be joking but seeing soon enough that he wasn't. His long face was deadly serious and sad, to boot.

"I say this only to warn you that our actions while in the view of others, no matter how we may behave in private, must be circumspect. There are those whose only aim in this life is to cause trouble, and bring it down on the heads of those who do not deserve it. I fear, not for myself, but for you, Krishnan, who have no one to speak for your character but myself."

I felt cold. All the blood had drained from my face and I felt cold. "No, don't worry about me. I know how to behave myself in public, Bleddyn. Especially when the stakes are so very high." I sighed, too, and reached up to caress Bleddyn's cheek. "I'll do better than my best to not give anyone any suspicions or ammunition to use against either of us."

Bleddyn turned his face just enough to kiss the pad of my thumb. "Fear not, Krish, for none in this county have yet been convicted of such a crime, though rumors have abounded about more than a handful of my lord's tenants. The tenants in particular behaved beyond reproach in public, and though many cast a doubtful eye their way for a while, never were charges brought. None had a wish to bring death on the head of a neighbor," Bleddyn said. I sensed he was trying to reassure me, but I was less than reassured.

"But that's the big difference between them and me. I'm *not* a neighbor or tenant. I'm a *foreigner*, and if anyone took it into his head to get me into trouble, things could go south for me very quickly," I murmured, trying to smile for Bleddyn's sake. He looked about as convinced as I felt. "Don't worry," I said. "It won't even come to that. I'll be as circumspect as anyone could want."

I started to face forward again, but Bleddyn caught my face by the chin and turned slightly, kissing my cheek and down to my jaw, all passion and possessiveness, intensity and wantonness as he nipped and sucked and licked my neck. By the time he pulled away, both of us were panting for breath, and I could feel him stirring against my ass. He wasn't the only one taking serious interest in the proceedings, as he discovered when he dropped his hand into my lap to grip and stroke me.

"Oh, Bleddyn."

"Already I look forward to the next time I lay with you," he exhaled, leaning his forehead against mine and adding a few squeezes to his strokes. "If, that is, I am not being too presumptuous of your favor, Krish."

"*Bleddyn*," I moaned, bucking up into his touch. "Believe me, you're not being presumptuous. The next time we have some privacy, I expect you to bend me over the nearest flat surface and *fuck me raw*."

Bleddyn made a sound somewhere between a groan and a sigh and with a final stroke, he let go of me and nudged Arwel into a walk. Each step of the horse's sure gait brought Bleddyn's semi-hard cock into contact with my ass and the rest of the ride to Trefriw was sweet torture.

The village of Trefriw was not much smaller than its futuristic self, still smelled like livestock, poop, and fresh soil, and was populated by, like, four people, mostly women.

On approaching, all I could see was a handful of huts and larger buildings that were probably businesses. We crossed a stone bridge over the Afon Crafnant at one point, the river rushing to join with the Conwy once it passed the Fairy Falls. We spoke to everyone we saw in town, but most of the men and women were out working in the fields and not available to answer our questions.

Except for greetings and actual descriptions of John and Dierdre, Bleddyn did the talking, which I felt was for the best. None seemed to think that was strange and all were deferential but not fawning or servile with Bleddyn. A few of the women even mentioned that he could come in and sample some of their eldest daughter's cooking if he liked. A request to which Bleddyn demurred, citing the lord's business and others to speak to on Wynn's behalf.

"You're very popular in Trefriw," I noted, half-amused and half-jealous. Bleddyn, walking Arwel and Queen, glanced at me, smiling lopsidedly.

"Very popular amongst the mothers of unmarried daughters, that is," he replied with a clandestine whisper, glancing around us as if expecting to see hordes of unmarried farmer's daughters overrunning us. "I am rather old for an unmarried and unspoken-for man and yet I am still considered eligible. I suspect that is because I am seen as a challenge."

I snorted. Little did they know. "And how old *are* you?"

"I turned nine and twenty on the first of April."

Surprised, I found myself looking at Bleddyn again. I tried to imagine him without the neatly-trimmed beard and mustache and decided that yes, he could indeed be twenty-nine without the face fuzz. His eyes, of course, were older than the rest of his face. They spoke of experiences beyond those of any twenty-nine year olds I'd ever known.

"So, you're an April Fool of a baby?" I asked, grinning. I refrained from taking Bleddyn's arm and leaning on it as I'd have done in back in my time with any lover as we walked along.

Bleddyn's wry smile faded a little. "Aye. William used to call me his 'April Fool.' 'Twas more endearment than jest at my expense, though in truth, I was ever his fool."

Looking away from the raw heartbreak still to be seen in Bleddyn's eyes, I sighed. I didn't know if I was more sympathetic or jealous. "I'm sorry you lost him."

Bleddyn shook his head once, either in negation or simply to shake free his thoughts of William. "It has been fourteen years since his passing, and yet some days it feels as if mere hours have passed since word was delivered," he whispered, studying the ground at his feet. In that moment I wanted to embrace him, death penalty be damned, but I somehow fought the urgent need to do so. It took everything I had to resist comforting Bleddyn with my arms and kisses.

We walked along in silence, then we paused to gaze at the Fairy Falls once more. I took Bleddyn's hand, and he squeezed it tight. I glanced over at his grim profile and dark, melancholy eyes, and I could almost feel something in the region of my heart turn over, restless, as I sought to name what *I* was feeling in response to Bleddyn's obvious distress.

Finally I squeezed his hand back, and he faced me even as I faced him. In that moment, he looked *very* young, barely older than me. I reached up and brushed his cheek with my fingers.

Bleddyn wrapped his arm around me and pulled me close, leaning in to kiss my eyelids, and then my lips. "Fourteen years, and still I grieve for my sweet William, as a widow grieves for her lost husband," Bleddyn murmured against my mouth before kissing me again. "And yet, some of that grief and loneliness lifts now. My heart's desolation is o'ertaken by a queer relief that I cannot countenance, and a joy that I fear I cannot long hide."

Looking into his dark eyes, I could see that relief and that joy, both solemn things composed more of hope than anything else. I could only imagine the power of such a look when it was unleavened by grief and regret. How Bleddyn's whole being must've *shone* in William's presence.

Their love must have been obvious to everyone with eyes, which meant Lord John's people must have been much more tolerant than Bleddyn realized. I had no doubt William had loved Bleddyn, because even as shuttered by life's sorrows as he was, I found it impossible not to fall myself.

William was a lucky man, to be on the receiving end of a look like this. He was a lucky man to be Bleddyn's hope and his heart, I thought as I closed the distance between our lips, uncaring and unheedful of any eyes that might be on us. In that moment, *I* wanted to be Bleddyn's hope. To be his *heart*. I wanted, at long last to find a home in someone I could trust. Someone who, once I gave my own heart, I could trust to take care of it.

I knew, just *knew*, right then and there beyond all doubt, that Bleddyn was *that guy*. And when our lips met, I could've sworn I heard choirs of angels, saw fireworks on the backs of my eyelids. I couldn't even begin to describe that kiss. It was like coming home. Like my birthday and Fourth of July and Halloween all rolled up into one, with Valentine's Day thrown in for good measure. It was every special moment of every special day, and it wasn't just happening on my lips and in my mouth, but in my *heart*, which was beating faster and faster, like it had the first time I'd kissed my first major crush. Only instead of the disappointment that that kiss hadn't been more, this kiss was *everything* every kiss should be.

In those perfect moments, held in Bleddyn's arms, I knew one thing, and one thing only:

This is it. This is who I'm meant to be with and why I was sent back here. I'm falling in love with him, and not just because he rescued me. Not just because he took me in and pledged himself to take care of me. Not even because he's so fantastic in bed. But because we were meant to be together like this. I've been waiting all of my life to find Bleddyn. Looking high and low, not knowing what I was looking for and never realizing I was looking in not only the wrong place, but the wrong time. Oh, God, I don't even believe in soul-mates, but I think Bleddyn is mine.

I moaned my way out of the kiss before I was even more overwhelmed, tears running down my face that I didn't want Bleddyn to see. But when I tried to look away, Bleddyn turned my face back to his own, his eyes questioning and solicitous.

"Speak, Krishnan of Nayar, and tell me what troubles you so," he murmured, kissing my forehead. A tear slipped down his own face. I sniffed and tried to smile.

"I think I understand now why I came back here to 1626. Why I was *sent* back," I whispered.

Bleddyn's eyes widened. "Say you truly?" I nodded, and he smiled, too. "Will you not tell me, then, that we may divine a way to s-send you home?"

"Perhaps—perhaps one day I *will* tell you," I said, smiling again. "At best, it's only a guess. A wish, maybe. But one thing I know for sure, now." I took another deep breath. "There *is* no going back for me. This is where I belong. Where I'm m-meant to be."

Bleddyn searched my eyes, frowning. "But, Krishnan, your companions and kin—"

"Are beyond me, now. And I can only hope they don't grieve too long for my loss. That they can move on with their lives, even not knowing what happened to me." I looked down for a moment, then back up at Bleddyn as I tried on a grin. "Looks like I'll be holding you to that promise to teach me how to be a man of the seventeenth century."

Still searching my eyes, Bleddyn shook his head. "Are you certain? For there may yet be a way to send you home."

"And what good would that do me when I'd be leaving a part of me behind?" I asked, then I blushed, kicking myself for letting whatever sappy, idiot thoughts my heart stirred up come tumbling out of my mouth.

"And what part would that be, Krishnan of Nayar?" Bleddyn asked, swallowing.

The part of me that's you, I wanted to say, but I didn't. Just because Bleddyn had fucked me didn't mean he wanted to have me gushing about how I felt for him. Especially so soon after we'd just met. "Perhaps I'll tell you that, too, someday. For now, suffice it to say that *here*, in this time, is where I want to be. I think it's where I'm needed. And hopefully wanted."

Bleddyn leaned his forehead against mine. "I will not deny that if I could be granted one boon, it would be for you to find a home and happiness here, for as long as you choose to stay."

"I'm happy right now," I told Bleddyn. "Happy to be here, with you."

"My heart swells with that news, Krishnan, for I am happy to be here with you as well. Happier than I ever thought it my lot to be."

And then we kissed again, in front of the Falls, I wrapped my arms around Bleddyn's neck and felt his arms wrap around my waist. I don't know how long we stood there like that, where anyone in the small and empty town could have seen us, when we heard someone clear her throat to our left.

"Never did two hearts love so true," a familiar voice said as Bleddyn met my eyes. Blood draining from both our faces, but for entirely different reasons, we turned to face the speaker.

She was wearing a tan and black calico dress similar to the one Gwynedd, the head housekeeper who'd drawn my bath yesterday, had worn. But instead of being pinned and tied up under a bonnet, her dark, curling hair fell freely around her oval face and past her shoulders, as wild as the green eyes that watched Bleddyn and I with more than a little amusement. "And never did two hearts fight so valiantly to be reunited."

I blinked, rubbed my eyes, then rubbed them again when she didn't disappear, but just stood there grinning.

"*Dierdre*?!" I finally exclaimed, just before I sagged in Bleddyn's strong arms and everything went black.

Chapter Seven

*R*unning. I was running.

Heart pounding in my ears, my own laughter trailing out behind me like a skein of cloth, I darted behind a tree and silenced myself, grubby hands covering my mouth. Then, after peering around the tree to see my pursuer nowhere near, I stealthily made my way through the outskirts of Gwydir Forest, creeping along until I found a recent deadfall.

A smug giggle escaping me, I crawled under a gap in the downed tree behind the shroud of a bush and settled in to wait. I knew he'd never find me.

And I hadn't settled long before I was, in fact, found. I was playing with a beetle crawling on my right trouser leg when a pale, triumphant face appeared just beyond the shroud of the bush hiding me.

"Found you!" Startled, I sat up and bonked my head on the deadfall.

"Ow!" I saw stars and fireworks, and I rubbed my curly head while the other boy laughed and laughed. By the time I finished investigating my head for lumps and abrasions, my pursuer had climbed into the limited space under the deadfall and behind the bush, and was wedged in with me, brushing my hands away from my head. With gentle efficiency, he searched my scalp for injury and upon finding none, pulled my head down and kissed the crown anyway.

"There," the other boy said with no-nonsense satisfaction, his dark, dark, solemn eyes shining. "That's better, isn't it, Gwil?"

"I s-suppose," I stammered, blushing and batting his hand away. "How is it that you always find me so quickly?"

A lopsided, seldom-seen grin was my only reply till I pouted, and he sighed with fond patience. "When you run, you leave behind a trail anyone can follow of trampled grass, broken branches, and disturbed earth. Were we playing hide and seek in the castle, I might not have found you so quickly. But Tad's been teaching me to track. And he can find anything," he said in a worshipful and reverent tone.

I spared a thought for my own Tad, dead before I was even born and Mam had shortly followed. I sighed, wishing my uncle liked me better. Perhaps he might have taught me to track, at the same time as he taught his own son. I learned fast. Everyone said so. I was better at reading and sums than any other boy my age and many who were older. Perhaps—

"You're it!"

*With a stinging smack on the cheek that shook me out of my reverie, he was wriggling out of the small crawl-space and running away, laughing himself. And I—*I blinked and was staring up into two pairs of concerned eyes: one dark brown, the other bright green.

"Cefnder, aros! Peidiwch â gadael i mi...!" I called out: "Cousin, wait! Don't leave me!" I bolted upright and startled both people who'd been leaning over me backwards. I was breathing hard and fast and looking around me as if I'd misplaced my best friend.

Then I was scrutinizing the two people again. One of them was Bleddyn, who smiled a worried smile at me, reaching out to caress my face.

"Wyt ti gyd â hawliau, mae fy nghalon?" he murmured, and I shook my head. I knew he was asking if I was okay—well, I was pretty certain he was.

"Huh?"

"Nid wyt ti yn deall yr hyn yr wyf yn ei ddweud?" Bleddyn asked, his brow furrowing, and I gave a weak laugh, putting a hand to my suddenly aching head.

"Of course not. You know I don't understand Welsh, baby."

Now Bleddyn was the one to blink. "But you most certainly did, just now, as you awoke. As you answered the question I just asked. You understood me perfectly well."

"Did I?" I asked, unable to focus on anything but that heart-pounding sensation of being about to lose, or maybe already having lost my best friend. It'd hurt like a knife in the heart, and my mind shied away from remembering it or anything related to it. "Oh-kay. If you say so."

And I glanced at the woman sitting next to him. Though she looked a lot like Dierdre, from the oval face and green eyes, to the cleft of her chin and the wave and curl of her dark hair, she was *not* my best friend. I had to remind myself that Dierdre was both younger and paler still than this woman, and instead of the Dierdre's pertly-upturned, freckled nose, this woman had a longish, straight nose with nary a freckle on it.

Still, I supposed a swoon and a faint was, if not the most manly thing I'd ever done, at least somewhat understandable under the circumstances.

I supposed everyone had a doppelganger somewhere. It made sense that even in this time, when there were billions fewer people, that people strongly resembled other people for no other reason than the fact that they just *resembled* each other.

I couldn't take my eyes off the woman, however, and she, in turn, kept staring at me as if she knew me. *Maybe she knows my 1626 doppelganger,* I thought, then I shuddered. That was too much coincidence, even for a man who believed in such a thing.

"Who *are* you?" I asked her, leaning closer to Bleddyn, who obligingly put his arm around my shoulders and turned his solemn gaze on the woman, too.

Her canny gaze traveled between us and she smiled serenely. Then she got to her feet, dusting off her dress. "I am Gwenllian Robert, of *Llyn Tynymynydd.* And you are Krishnan of Nayar, a guest of Lord John's who has been separated from his companions."

I glanced at Bleddyn, who was still frowning up at Gwenllian. "Word travels fast, I guess."

Gwenllian chuckled, low and throaty, nothing like Dierdre's ridiculous, dainty *tee-hee-hee,* and offered me her hand up. "Indeed, it does. Especially in the countryside."

Before I could decide whether to take her hand, Bleddyn had leapt up and was helping me to my feet. The world wobbled for a few moments, during which Bleddyn held me upright more than my own legs. The disorientation quickly passed, as did the inexplicable headache, but even when I was steady, Bleddyn held onto me with one possessive arm around my waist.

"*Gweddw* Robert," he said with sudden gravity, inclining his head. "I thank you for your concern, but as you can see, Lord John's guest is just a bit shaken from his swoon, a circumstance which will be remedied by a swift return to Castle Gwydyr."

I would've whole-heartedly agreed with that, had I not been fascinated by this woman who bore such a striking resemblance to my best friend. Could she be some distant ancestor? After all, Dierdre's family had roots in the U.K. I couldn't remember where, exactly. I was certain her father's side was all Irish, but I didn't remember for sure what her mother's side was, other than some kind of Briton.

"Lord's blessing upon thee," Bleddyn said with formal finality, steering me away from Gwenllian and the Falls, toward the horses.

"But Bleddyn, she looks almost *exactly* like one of my friends! Dierdre! You can't think that's a coincidence?" I hissed as he dragged me along. I kept looking behind us, and Gwenllian was watching us go with a contemplative look that made me shiver. "What if she knows something about how I got here? Bleddyn, *slow down*! Let me *go*!"

But Bleddyn shook his head and dragged me on toward the horses by my arm. His grip was like iron. "Krish, this is one of the instances where you must rely on me to lead you a-right. And away from *her*," he said under his breath, as if afraid that Gwenllian could still hear us even from that distance.

"What do you mean? Is she not trustworthy?" I asked as we got to Arwel and Queen. Bleddyn helped me up onto Arwel then mounted behind me. When I looked back at the place we'd left Gwenllian, she was gone. I couldn't spot her anywhere nearby.

"I do not know how trustworthy or not *Gweddw—Widow—* Robert is. What I *do* know is that she is looked upon with disfavor by many in the county, since the death of her husband. No, since before he married her, there was disquiet about her," Bleddyn said, sighing and clicking his teeth. Arwel started to walk, Queen no doubt right behind him.

"But why was there, um, disquiet about her? What is she? Like, a golddigger? A trophy wife?"

"Trophy wife?"

"Never mind." I snorted as Bleddyn settled his arm around my waist, and I leaned back against him slightly. "Tell me why she's viewed with disfavor."

Bleddyn sighed again, his warm breath stirring my hair as he nuzzled it briefly. "Ten years ago it had been said none could snare the heart of Eirian ap Robert, Lord John's head gamekeeper. For years, many a maid and widow tried and none succeeded in capturing his fancy until *she* arrived, fresh off a merchant ship from Caerdyf, seeking a position at the castle.

"She got it immediately, as Gwynedd can always use extra hands around the castle. And Gwenllian Jones captured Eirian's eye before that first week was closed. Within that first month, she was Gwenllian Robert. The unmarried women of the county and their mothers were most displeased."

I snorted again. "I can imagine."

Bleddyn made a noncommittal sound. "The whispers began shortly after their marriage. Rumors that Gwenllian Robert was no ordinary woman. That she was a faerie maiden come to work mischief among men—"

"Oh, Lord," I muttered, rolling my eyes. This was what happened when people didn't have cable television and the internet.

"—and it certainly did not help matters that she was, by Gwynedd's own mouth, an uncanny hand at healing the sick. Always did her tonics and tinctures work to cure the ill. After a few winters in which Gwenllian Robert saved many from fevers and maladies that might have cost lives, all those unhappy maidens and their mothers found it within themselves to accept her in their society."

"How big of them."

"Two winters ago, however, when sickness fell upon the county faster than healers could work to combat it, Gwenllian Robert was nowhere to be seen near the middle of winter. For days, no one saw her or Eirian. I found them when I was dispatched to find out why the lord's gamekeeper had not reported to his job in so many days Eirian ap Robert was in his bed, several days dead of fever, and Gwenllian Robert barely clinging to life at her hearth-side. Her fever had broken not long before I arrived and she was stirring, but weakly."

I frowned. "So, because she couldn't save her husband, she fell back into disfavor with the county at large?"

"In part."

"Then what's the *other* part?"

Bleddyn was silent for a bit before answering. "There are some who say she *could not* save her husband. That her skills simply failed her when she needed them most, and that the Lord called him home. And there are others, still, who say that she *would not* save her husband."

It took a moment for that to sink in. When it did, I glanced back at Bleddyn's serious face. "And what do *you* think?"

Sighing again, Bleddyn met my eyes and smiled a little. "I *believe* that Eirian ap Robert's wife tried her best to keep him by her side when the Lord called him home. And, falling ill, herself, would have followed Eirian hence had I not been sent to collect him."

I shook my head. "Why do people believe she let her husband die? Were they having problems? Fighting? What would make them *think* such a horrible thing about someone?" I demanded, angry on Gwenllian's behalf. "After all she's done for the people of this county!"

"People will often believe the worst with little or no provocation," Bleddyn said, shrugging and holding me tighter as we left Trefriw proper behind. "Which is why I urge you to mind being seen with her. For she does not enjoy the reputation she once did, and though she is, I sense, a well-meaning woman, many do not see her that way, and would see anyone who associates with her as tainted. They may cast a suspicious eye on that person and scrutinize them both closely and harshly."

"And the last thing I need, is close, hard scrutiny," I murmured, thinking of the way Bleddyn and I couldn't keep our hands off each other and how lucky we'd been that no one had yet caught us.

No one except Gwenllian, of course. And I sensed she wouldn't be in a rush to spread the news all over the county.

No, she'd seemed neither surprised nor disgusted to come upon Bleddyn and me kissing, which was odd for a woman of her times.

There's more to her than meets the eye, I thought, leaning back into Bleddyn's arms, sighing when he tightened them around me. *I have to see her again—have to talk with her. I know she knows more than she's said about where I'm from, not to mention something about why I'm here, now. I could see it in her eyes.*

But then Bleddyn kissed my neck and I filed my thoughts on Gwenllian away for later consideration. "Are we going back to the castle?" I wondered aloud, thoughts of my tiny room, and of Bleddyn and I on my narrow, pokey mattress dancing in my head.

"I wish nothing more than a private space and time with you," Bleddyn said fervently. "But as we are already on the road which leads there, we may as well make the trip to Llanwrst. Though I suspect nothing will come of that."

"Least of all *me*," I half-groused, then laughed a little, marveling at how even just a smidgen of nookie turned me into an insatiable, come-hungry slut. "Llanwrst, it is. Then, after *that*, the castle?"

"Indeed, *fy un annwyl*."

I smiled. I knew an endearment when I heard one. Even when it was in Welsh. "Welsh isn't a romantic language at all, is it?"

"In truth, it is not, Krish. It is not a derivative of Latin, though some common words are. What brings you such amusement, Krish?"

"Nothing, Bleddyn," I said, still chuckling. I angled myself and turned my head, kissing him till he stopped frowning. "Nothing at all."

❖

Llanrwst was, of course, a bust, and in exactly the same way as Trefriw.

It wasn't quite as quaint and pretty, but more people were around to talk to. More mothers trying to secure Bleddyn as their son-in-law. I knew I'd be teasing him about it, later. *Perhaps as we lay in bed together,* I thought, feeling smug as one mother's face fell when Bleddyn declined her invitation.

By the time we returned to Gwydir Castle, the sun was westering. The courtyard was busy as people finished up their day's work in a hurry before they lost the light.

We rode up to the stables and Bleddyn dismounted and helped me down, holding onto my waist longer than necessary. He reluctantly let me go when the stable boy came to take Arwel and Queen.

"Think we have time to get up to shenanigans before supper?" I whispered.

Bleddyn smiled outright, though it was tinged with apology. "I'll be expected to report my findings to father. He, Lord Owen, and the other men will have returned some time ago."

"But since we didn't find anything, reporting shouldn't take long, should it?" I murmured, stepping close to him. After a quick glance around, I put my hands on his mailed chest for a few moments. "If I wait in my room for you, will you come see me, if you're able?"

Bleddyn's dark eyes smoldered. "I will. For I mean to make small work of my report and spend as little time with father as I may."

Swell guy like that, I can't imagine why, I thought. I took Bleddyn's hand briefly and squeezed it. "I'll look forward to seeing you, then."

Bleddyn glanced around, took me in his arms and kissed me, hard and quick, lingering to explore my mouth forcefully, before pulling back and whispering: "I wish to lay thee down and worship thy body as my one true God. And I will move Heaven and Earth to see you between now and supper, *fy un annwyl.*"

Bleddyn marched off toward the castle, leaving me to stare after his receding form, while my knees relearned how not to deposit me ass-first in the mud.

I was still in a daze when I reached my room, pleasantly absent-minded. Nonetheless I was surprised to see Lord Owen waiting at my door, like a man who'd been there hours and was prepared to stay.

I wondered, with a twinge of dismay, if he wanted to hear the rest of, ahem, *my* story, *now*, and what Bleddyn would think if he came to see me and found me entertaining his lord's son, however innocently.

"Lord Owen," I said, my voice shaking a little. I barely remembered to bow, and Owen smiled a little.

"Please, simply *Owen* will do, at least in private. And you needn't bow every time you see me."

I straightened and smiled back. "I'm a stranger in a strange land. I don't wish to seem disrespectful."

Lord Owen shook his head. "You are anything but, Master Krishnan. Your ways are strange, but far from disrespectful. You are quite a pleasant guest. Certainly the most pleasant we've had in some time. And I must say, you tell an excellent story."

I grinned, hoping Tolkien and Jackson weren't spinning in their previous lives. "Aw, thanks, Owen."

He blushed and looked down at his booted feet. "I speak only the truth. I take it you and Bleddyn were unsuccessful at Trefriw and Llanrwst?"

My grin faltered, and I cleared my throat and tried to look innocent. "No traces of my friends were found, and no one has seen them. At least around here."

"That is, indeed, most odd. None of the men found anything either, though we scoured the Forest in all directions." Owen sighed, his big blue eyes meeting mine. "I am sorry we could not find your companions, Master Krishnan."

"Please, it's just Krishnan. Or *Krish*." I said and smiled to show him I wasn't upset. "And you've all been so kind to me, extended me genuine hospitality and gone out of your way to help me find my friends. There's nothing to be sorry for."

Owen wrung his hands and frowned. "It's just that I wonder what will you do, now? Will you attempt to travel back to your America alone, and hopefully be reunited with them there?"

Not likely, I thought, imagining what the odds were of me surviving a trip to America on a ship in 1626, and then my odds of surviving small pox, or lynching, or enslavement, or being accused of witchcraft. I didn't like those odds one bit. "I, that is, *they*, my companions, have our traveling papers and money. Even if I wanted to go back, I wouldn't be able to without them."

"I see," Owen murmured, frowning harder still, his lips pursed. Then he looked up at me, his eyes narrowed in thought. "Are you a learned man? That is, have you any skill at figuring and sums and perhaps some at reading and writing?"

"Um, yes. I mean, I'm pretty good at everything up to and including calculus." I shrugged. "And I can read in English. And I suppose Welsh, too, since it's the same alphabet. I just have no idea what I'm reading or saying."

"Hmm." Owen was frowning at his feet again. Then, a second later he was beaming up at me. These mood changes were quite impressive, if a little dizzying. "I must speak with father about a certain matter, Mast—*Krish*. But I will see you at supper. Oh! You're cordially invited to supper in father's private dining room, tonight. You and Bleddyn, of course, for he wishes to hear all about the search."

"Okay," I said to Owen, who was already halfway down the narrow corridor that led back to the main hall. As he turned the corner, he saluted me and kept going, clearly a man on a mission. "I will see you shortly!" he called back at me.

After puzzling over this—the second hot guy to take off on me in twenty minutes—I shrugged and let myself into the room, my mind already on other, Bleddyn-related matters.

I must've fallen asleep again because, when I woke, it was to a tender kiss on the corner of my mouth, followed by several more of which I sleepily, but heartily, partook.

"You made it," I breathed on Bleddyn's lips, then yawned as he sat on the bed and smiled down at me.

"That I did," he whispered, reaching out to brush my hair off my forehead. "But you are weary. Perhaps the time before supper would be best spent in rest."

"Nuh-uh, no way, Mister Sweet-talking Welshman. You promised me shenanigans, and it's shenanigans I demand," I said, sitting up and stretching. Bleddyn looked at my torso with obvious yearning, despite my shirted state. In fact, the only thing I'd taken off before laying down had been my boots.

When I was done stretching, I put my arms around Bleddyn's neck and pulled him close. He came obligingly, kissing me again, putting his arms around my waist.

"How'd the reporting to dear, ol' dad go?" I panted when he let me up for air.

"As well as can be expected. It was brief, at least," he said, but he didn't continue. Not that I was exactly badgering him for deets when what I really wanted was for him to be riding my ass like I was wearing a saddle.

"Mmm, well, how much time do we have until supper?" I asked. Bleddyn smiled and bore me down to the bed, pinning my hands to the mattress on either side of us.

"Time enough," he promised, and he kissed me gently before freeing my hands to pull off his shirt. He tossed it at the garderobe, and I ran my hands up his strong arms and over his broad shoulders, then down his ridiculously defined chest, to the waist of his breeches. Everywhere my palms passed, muscles jumped and twitched.

I pushed his breeches down his narrow hips, careful not to snag the fabric on the slight curving of his cock, and I looked up into his eyes. They seemed to burn into mine, and I knew no one had ever wanted me quite like this or as much.

"Time is *never* enough," I said, suddenly bereft for no reason I could put my finger on. But I shivered and tried to smile when Bleddyn brushed his thumb across my lips. I doubt the attempt passed muster, but Bleddyn smiled back, and then we were scrambling to get *my* clothes off. When we were both naked, our bodies crashed together like opposing waves, our hands everywhere at once as we traded kisses and endearments back and forth between us like a glass of wine. One that, for all our sipping, could never go empty.

Never say never, a quiet and watchful part of me whispered from the back of my mind, even as Bleddyn pushed his way inside me, and I cried out before literally biting my pillow. After that, the voice was silent, leaving me to enjoy Bleddyn's body on and in my own.

And I, for my part, submerged myself wholly in the pleasure and rightness of having Bleddyn in me and anchoring me, letting concepts such as *tomorrow* and *what next?* drift as far from me as each powerful thrust could drive them.

CHAPTER EIGHT

B leddyn?"
     "Yes, *fy un annwyl?*"
I turned my head on Bleddyn's chest to see his face. He was staring at the ceiling with a blissed-out smile on his face and I grinned, leaning up to plant a kiss on the underside of his jaw. Then, because I could, I trailed them up to his ear and nibbled on the lobe till he started to chuckle and try to catch my lips with his own. Eventually I let him, and his chuckles turned to moans, as he pulled me even closer, tight against him.

We kissed and kissed and touched and touched, until Bleddyn, having rolled on top of me, caught my hand. He brought it to his lips and kissed it, too, lingering till I giggled. "What is it, *ngoleuni fy nghalon?*" His eyes were fond and content. I wanted to see them stay that way, but considering what I had to ask, I doubted they would. I doubted this afterglow would last, and that made me both sad and frustrated, but I had to ask about Gwenllian. I *had* to see her, and Bleddyn was the only one I could trust to take me.

"One of these days I'm gonna be able to speak Welsh, and *then* what will you call me?" I asked playfully, putting off the moment of my asking. Bleddyn smiled and pressed my hand to his cheek.

"Then I will still call you *ngoleuni fy nghalon,*" he said, his voice soft and tender, as he searched my eyes. I blushed and reached up to run my thumb along his high cheekbone.

"Will you tell me what that means, then?"

Bleddyn kissed me briefly, but so sweetly, I almost forgot what we were talking about. "*Ngoleuni* means *light*. *Fy* means *of my*. And *Nghalon* means *heart*." Bleddyn ducked his head a little, his face going up in flames of embarrassment.

That simply would not do.

I turned his face back to mine and smiled. "*Ngoleuni fy nghalon*," I said, trying not to stumble over the words. Bleddyn nodded.

"Yes. That was handsomely said, Krish." He smiled. "You'll be a dab-hand at learning *Cymraeg*, which is the language of the Welsh. I doubt it not."

I rolled my eyes. Bleddyn was being slow on the uptake. I blamed all the cripplingly good sex. "No, Bleddyn. *Ngoleuni fy nghalon* …as in, *you are the*." And I hugged him close, just in case my meaning was still unclear. After a few startled seconds, Bleddyn embraced me back, almost panick-y tight, and moaned.

"You do not have to say such things because I say them," he whispered quickly. "My intention was not to force affection from you."

"Oh, you're not forcing *anything*, Butch, trust me." I laughed and leaned back on my elbows to look at him. He had been wiping at his eyes but stopped as soon as we were facing each other again. "I've only known you a day, and I'm already gone on you. Absolutely gone." When Bleddyn furrowed his brow, I clarified. "I'm falling in love with you, Bleddyn. I'm addicted to the way your eyes light up when you see me, the way you talk. the things you say, and the way you touch me. You're my hero. My knight in shining armor. You saved me and have done so much for me, all without expecting repayment or even thanks. Though I'll say now, *thank you* for all that you've done for me."

Bleddyn turned red again and looked down. "What you feel is gratitude, which I appreciate and am humbled by. But it is easy to confuse hero worship with adoration, when—"

"Bleddyn." When he stopped talking and looked up at me, I sighed. "Don't tell me how I feel. Or *what* I feel. I've already dated that guy, and I left him for a reason."

"I do not understand."

Wincing, I tried to smile. "Nothing, just trust me when I say I know my heart now more than I ever have. I've never felt for anyone the way I feel for you. Not one tenth the passion, the power, the need, the desire, the frustration, the impatience, the yearning, the worry, and the hope that maybe someday, you could feel the same way I do." I shook my head and flopped back down to the pillow with another gusty sigh. "I know the difference between gratitude and the beginnings of love, Bleddyn. And I dunno about you, but my heart beats faster just at the sound of your name. I've *traveled back in time four hundred years* and yet the most amazing thing that's ever happened to me was stumbling across *you*."

"Krishnan, I—" Bleddyn swallowed, his Adam's-apple bobbing. "I am not worthy of such sweet words or such deep affections." Bleddyn held up a hand just as I was about to gainsay him. "But that does not mean that I will not try, with every breath and every day given me, to *be worthy* of them. And of you."

"Ditto," I said. "That means I'll do the same."

Bleddyn caressed my face, brushing my lips, chin, and throat, and he came to a stop at my collarbone. At the necklace my mother had given me when I was eighteen.

"What does this figurine depict?" he asked, running his finger carefully across the gold pendant. I smiled and held it up for him to examine in the flickering lamplight.

"Where my parents come from in India, we have different gods, many more of them than you do here in Britain. Our religion is Hindu." I shook the pendant a little. "This is the *devi*, or goddess, Parvati. Goddess of beneficence and love, among other things. She is the wife of Shiva, the Transformer; sister of Vishnu, the Preserver; and mother of Ganesh, the deva of intellect and art, and a lot of other good things." I scanned Bleddyn's face to see how he was taking me talking about my heathen gods. His face was a study in concentration, but otherwise unreadable. So I went on.

"Anyway, this pendant depicts Parvati. She's a symbol of many kinds of love. This pendant was originally a gift from my father to my mother on the day of their wedding. And it was given to me by my mother on my eighteenth birthday, four years after my father passed away." Now I was the one to swallow. It'd been eight years, but the pain of my father's death still affected me deeply. "It was her way of telling me she'd love me forever, just as my father had told her, once upon a time. If my family can be said to have an heirloom, it's this. It is precious to me beyond words."

Bleddyn placed the pendant back against my skin, then leaned down and kissed it and me.

"It is as lovely as its bearer," he whispered, and I smiled, wiping my eyes.

"Oh, go on, charmer."

Bleddyn chuckled and laid next to me, pulling me into his arms so that we were spooning, his breath warm and moist in my hair. "Tell me, *ngoleuni fy nghalon*, do all the gods of India have so many arms?"

I burst out laughing. "Some have even more! Parvati only has four! You should see Krishna or Ganesh!" Snorting and giggling, I leaned back and settled further into Bleddyn's arms. "See, all the arms are so that they, the *devas*, can have different *mudras*, which are symbolic gestures that involve the hands and fingers, mostly. This *mudra*—" I held up my hand and made the *Kataka mudra*,"—means 'fascination' and 'enchantment.' Parvati always uses one of the front two hands to make that *mudra*. And this one is *Hirana*, and it symbolizes the power of nature and the supernatural. And for the two back hands, there's *Tarjani* and *Chandrakal*, which represent contempt, and the moon and intelligence, respectively."

I let go of *Chandrakal* with a flourish, and Bleddyn caught my hand, pulling it to his lips again. "Is there nothing about you that is not graceful and lovely?" he murmured on my palm, and I snorted.

"Oh, honey, there's *plenty* about me that isn't graceful and lovely. You've seen me try to mount a horse, right? So much for *graceful*. And you've seen me first thing in the morning, too. So much for *lovely*." I laughed, and Bleddyn squeezed my hand and kissed my shoulder blade.

"I have seen you handle hours of riding with grace and patience. And I have seen you fresh out of sleep thrice, now. Each time, you were more beautiful than the last," he breathed, hot and fervid on my shoulder, draping his arm and my own over my waist.

Boy, have you got it bad, *buddy,* I almost said, but that would've been the pot calling the kettle black. So I shut my mouth. Yet I couldn't stop the huge smile that threatened to crack my face in two.

"Well, maybe I'll take your word on that," I finally replied, and Bleddyn swept his hand up and down my chest.

"That is well, then," he said with a sigh. "Now, tell me more about this Devi-Parvati, of yours."

I groaned. "What *is* it with you Welshman and your love of stories?" I asked, half-teasing and half-serious. Bleddyn's smile was warm and wide on my shoulder.

"'Twill keep my mind on other things, rather than on my unslaked desire to have you again and again and again." And with that, he pushed his cock against my ass. He was getting hard once more.

I looked over my shoulder at him again, eyes wide. "You really *are* insatiable."

Blushing, Bleddyn looked away from me in shame, and I kicked myself for not thinking before I spoke. "I didn't mean that in a *bad* way, Bleddyn. I meant only to thank the goddess Parvati that she's at last blessed me with a man who can keep up with *me*!"

Risking a glance at me, Bleddyn's brow smoothed out little by little, and he ventured a quiet, "I do not mean to continue to push my unseemly desire upon you."

I turned in Bleddyn's arms till I was facing him, and I pushed him onto his back. He gazed up at me with wide eyes as I straddled his thighs and stroked him nice and slow. It didn't take long to get him flagpole-stiff. I got to my knees and inched up the bed, till his cock dragged past mine and behind my balls. Bleddyn hissed and placed his big hands on my thighs, gripping them hard enough that there'd probably be bruises later.

Since he already had such a steadying grip on my thighs, I felt free to reach behind me and hold myself open. I spread my knees farther apart and sank down slowly, until the head of Bleddyn's cock nudged at my asshole.

"Or would you rather hear the tale of Parvati?" I asked, lowering myself onto his cock despite my sore, aching muscles. Bleddyn, his wide eyes still on mine, shook his head with intent vehemence and bit his lip as he was engulfed by my body. Then his eyes fluttered shut, tight for the rest of the time it took for me to slowly impale myself on his cock. But when they opened, bright and mesmerized, I smiled and, balancing myself with my hands on Bleddyn's spread legs, I levered myself up off him as much as I could. When my arms began to shake with strain, I sat back down hard, and we both hissed.

Then Bleddyn surprised me by bucking his hips up hard and fast, and I threw my head back and yelled in pleasure and pain that were so intertwined, I couldn't tell where one left off and the other began.

That was how I was starting to feel about Bleddyn.

❖

Afterward, we cleaned up quickly, but with more than a few caresses and stolen kisses.

The last such kiss turned into a clinch that made me think about skipping dinner with his lordship and undressing Bleddyn again. But Bleddyn broke the kiss, panting and leaning his forehead against mine.

"I must go to the east wing before supper," he breathed. "For I promised Gareth I would see him before he went to sleep."

I blinked, then whapped Bleddyn on the arm. "Why didn't you *say so*, doofus?" I took Bleddyn's hand and dragged him toward the door, even though I didn't know which wing was the east wing.

I paused at the main corridor and let Bleddyn take the lead. I quite lost my way, but Bleddyn seemed to know where he was going. Indeed, after a few minutes of twists and turns, I could hear peals of childish laughter. My eyes wide, I stopped at the turn-off for another dead end hall, with only two doors, one to each side. Bleddyn stopped, too, looking back at me. "Krishnan?"

"I can wait here while you see your son, if you like."

Bleddyn smiled a little. "Would you like to meet Gareth?" he asked, seeming amused at my obvious nervousness.

"I—" *never dated a guy with a kid before…don't know if I'm ready to meet your son…wonder what you'll do if he doesn't like me… wonder what* I'll *do if he doesn't like me.* "—would love to."

Bleddyn's smile widened. "Excellent. Even the babes have heard of Lord John's visitor from a strange and foreign land. Gareth, especially, has been asking what you look like, what you sound like, and if you have any gifts for him."

I burst out laughing. "Oh, wow. He sounds like me, when I was a kid."

"He is quite an intelligent and curious child. He gets that from his mother," Bleddyn said, but he sounded proud nonetheless.

Then he was leading me down to the door on the right, and knocking on it.

A tall, slim, matronly woman in a soft-looking blue dress opened the door, smiling. She wore a clean apron and matching bonnet on her head, from which grey wisps escaped.

"Eirwen," Bleddyn said, grinning.

"Ah, Bleddyn," she replied, seeming pleased to see him. Then her eyes met mine she nodded, curtseying like a young girl. "And you must be Krishnan of Nayar," she said in slow, lilting English. "Welcome to Castle Gwydir, in case no one has told you already!"

I laughed. "Thank you," I said as she stepped aside and waved us into the room. Bleddyn preceded me, walking quietly despite the laughter of the children—all boys, all seven of them—who were bouncing on their beds and running around, rather than preparing for bed. They looked like little ghosts, pale in their oversized sleep-clothes. The room was chaotic with over-excited children who would probably not be going to sleep any time soon. One boy got a look at me and stopped. And pointed.

Then Bleddyn and I were being surrounded by small boys, in age from three to seven. All the boys seemed fascinated with the color of my skin, which was about thirty shades darker than theirs. They were asking me questions in Welsh at light-speed, and though I could pick out a word here and there, it was still spoken too fast for me to really understand. I glanced at Eirwen and Bleddyn for help.

Laughing, Bleddyn reached into the gaggle of boys and scooped up the smallest boy, a tiny ash-blond, still in toddlerhood. The boy giggled almost uncontrollably as Bleddyn hugged him tight and kissed his cheek.

"*Tad! Tad!*" he screamed in his high, delighted voice. Then he garbled out something in Welsh, leaning back to look at me with Bleddyn's dark, shining eyes, in a perfect elfin face.

Bleddyn spoke to him briefly in Welsh, and the boy nodded—dutifully, it seemed—and Bleddyn nodded back, looking satisfied. Then he turned more fully toward me. "Krishnan of Nayar, this hellion is my son, Gareth. *Gareth, mae hyn yn ffrind tad, Krishnan o Nayar.*" Which I somehow understood to mean: *Gareth, this is a friend of dad's, Krishnan Nayar.*

And like that, all the questions stopped and every eye, including Gareth's, was trained on me.

"*Beth ydym ni'n ei ddweud i ffrindiau newydd?*" Bleddyn asked his son, kissing the boy on his cheek again. *What do we say to new friends?*

Gareth giggled and wiped his face. "*Croeso i Gastell Gwydir, syr!*" *Welcome to Castle Gwydir, sir!*

Bleddyn turned his proud smile on me. "He says welcome to Castle Gwydir."

"I know." I found myself grinning at Gareth. "How do I say thank you?"

"*Diolch yn fawr,*" Bleddyn leaned in to whisper to me.

"*Diolch yn fawr,* Gareth!" I said, taking his right hand in my left and giving it a faux-solemn shake. He giggled again, hiding his face against his father's neck.

Then the room was erupting again into questions from the other six bright-eyed waifs, some of them bouncing like soccer balls to get my attention. I laughed and looked at Bleddyn helplessly. He laughed with me and began speaking in Welsh again, his voice not loud, but commanding. The six boys perked up for a few seconds, then ran for their beds, giggling and laughing, while Bleddyn carried Gareth to one of the room's two remaining unoccupied beds. I followed him while Eirwen went around to tuck the other boys in.

When Bleddyn had Gareth situated and tucked in, he kissed the boy on the forehead and whispered something that was probably *I love you*. Gareth chirped it right back, his adoring eyes on Bleddyn before they drifted to me, where I stood near the foot of his small bed. He grinned at me again. "*Nos da, syr!*" *Good night, sir!*

"And a, um, *nos da* to you, too, Gareth," I replied, and the boy yawned, grinning as his eyes closed. Bleddyn began to sing to him in a soft tenor, one hand holding Gareth's, the other stroking the fine blond hair back from his face.

My heart did that appalling turning over-moving-thing again as I watched Bleddyn sing his son to sleep. I accepted the feeling with as much grace as I could, for I had given up on trying to corral my heart before it gave itself away.

No, at this point, it beat for Bleddyn. And maybe a little for Gareth, too.

We were late to supper.

Lord John, however, welcomed us as if we were not, as did his sons. Owen grinned at me so winsomely that if I wasn't so stuck on Bleddyn, I might've been tempted to see just how much he *really* liked me.

Meanwhile, Rhys was glaring at Bleddyn and me for no reason I could tell. Then Bleddyn hastily let go of my hand, which neither of us had realized he was still holding from when we'd sneaked out of the guest room together.

Rhys looked away from us, scowling.

❖

After dinner, when Lord John's men went off to discuss the business of running the castle and smoke their pipes, Bleddyn and I excused ourselves and took a slow walk back to the guest room. The halls were empty, which wasn't surprising. By seventeenth century standards, it was pretty late. Bleddyn took my hand in both of his, clasping it with one and covering it with the other. When we took the turn-off for the guest room, he raised my hand to his lips and kissed it with tender affection.

I smiled and stepped closer to him. And closer still, till we were in each other's arms and gazing into each other's eyes.

"Spend the night with me," I said, and Bleddyn frowned yet again. "I...should not..."

"And we're back to *this* again," I said only half-jokingly, rolling my eyes. "I promise your god won't smite you for cuddling with me and keeping me company tonight, Bleddyn."

"On my word, Krishnan of Nayar, if I were to spend the night in your bed, I would get up to more than merely keeping you company," he whispered, leaning our heads together and swaying us both, his hands fanning out on my ass. I smirked and kissed him.

"That's entirely the point, Master Bleddyn."

"I see," Bleddyn breathed, and he kissed me deeply, intently. Before I knew it, we were leaning against the door to the guest room and Bleddyn's hand was down the front of my borrowed breeches, stroking me till I got hard, which I did embarrassingly fast, despite having last made the beast with two backs just two hours ago.

Bleddyn broke the kiss to look into my eyes while still stroking me, then sank to his knees, taking my breeches and hose with him. I felt my eyes get saucer-wide as Bleddyn pushed my shirt up and gazed at me for the better part of a minute.

"Meditating?" I inquired with pointed sweetness, and he smiled a little, running the tip of his finger along my dick to my balls and cupping them in his hand. He squeezed gently, and I moaned.

"Merely appreciating," he said, meeting my eyes. I almost came just from the look he was giving me. Then I nearly came again when he kissed the tip of my cock, his tongue flicking out to taste me. My head fell back against the door with a loud *thunk* and a short, strangled laugh sounded. It must've been mine, since Bleddyn's mouth was already preoccupied with the top third of my cock.

"You ever done this before?" I asked, breathless with anticipation. Bleddyn hummed around my cock, scraping his teeth down the shaft and across the tip before pulling off altogether.

"A time or two," he said with wry self-deprecation, and I laughed again. I wondered if the *time or two* had been with William or with other men. Or both. And in wondering, I felt a surge of jealousy. Not that other men had had *my* Bleddyn this way, but that William had had him *first*.

But luckily for me, Bleddyn put his mouth back to work and proceeded to erase every thought and feeling that didn't have direct bearing on the hummer he was giving me. I ran one hand through his dark curls, gently thrusting my hips forward, moaning as I slid deeper into the warmth of his mouth, and he swirled his agile tongue around me, always returning to the tip as if he couldn't get enough of tasting me.

Getting a good grip on his hair, I tested the limits of his endurance by pushing my cock toward the back of his throat. When I felt minute twitches on the tip of my cock, like Bleddyn was going to gag, I pulled back some, murmuring, "It's okay, baby, it's okay…don't stop."

Bleddyn groaned. I looked down at the top of his head, and my hand clenched in his curls. "Look at me, baby."

It took a few moments, but Bleddyn did, without pulling off me. His eyes were watering and he was drooling, which should've looked ridiculous, but was sexy as hell on him. I licked my lips. "Touch yourself, Bleddyn," I commanded, letting go of his hair to wipe at a tear-track with my thumb. "Touch yourself while you suck my cock."

Bleddyn groaned again, blinking as another tear fell, and he took his hands from my calves and scrabbled at his waistband. I couldn't see much of what he was doing from that angle, but I knew when he had himself in hand. His eyes closed again and his tongue and lips went still for a few moments, then he was stroking himself and sucking again with renewed fervor.

"You like having my cock in your mouth?

Bleddyn nodded and made a moan I took to mean *yes*

"You like the way it feels on your tongue and pushing at the back of your throat?"

Another nod and moan.

"I can tell you like it. You're so fucking *good* at it." I smiled and leaned my head back against the door. "If you like taking my cock so much, one day soon, I'm gonna have to switch things up. I'll lay you down on my bed, on your stomach, spread those strong legs of yours and…"

Bleddyn whimpered and moaned around me and the wonderfully obscene sounds of skin on skin and flesh in flesh grew louder and more urgent. I smiled, closing my eyes as my orgasm uncoiled from my balls and the base of my spine.

"First thing I'm gonna do when I have you on your stomach, Bleddyn, is taste you all over. And I *do* mean all over. I'm gonna taste your tight little hole and tongue-fuck you until you're screaming for me to give it to you hard and fast. Then I'm gonna hold you open and fill you with my cock—" another startled whimper-moan from Bleddyn "—and fuck your gorgeous ass until you can't come anymore. And then I'm gonna *keep* fucking it until *I* can't come anymore."

With a muffled shout, Bleddyn went still around me, every muscle, even his tongue, tensing, only to release as he started gasping for breath around me. I pinched the base of my cock between two fingers and let him catch his breath for a few minutes, thinking neutral thoughts while gazing up at the ceiling.

He's so much fun, I decided as he began sucking my cock again with real vigor, his hands locked around my calves once more.

"I'm gonna come soon," I told him with hard-won calm, letting go of my cock and letting my oncoming orgasm pick up right where it left off. Balls tingling? Check. Base of the spine thrumming? Check. Cock painfully hard and burning from the inside out like it was about to combust? Double check. "Gonna *come.*"

Bleddyn grunted and speed up the tongue-swirling, letting go of one of my calves to take my balls in hand. He squeezed and tugged in time with his sucking, and I looked away from the ceiling, at him. Just the sight of him on his knees like a supplicant or a submissive was all it took. I could count the time left to my endurance in nano-seconds. "Fuck—Bleddyn...coming."

And for a while, that was all she wrote.

When I came back to myself, Bleddyn was standing up with another grunt, pulling my breeches and hose up with him. He looked disheveled and drop-dead *sexy.* His hair was a mess from my hand, and he had come in his mustache and on his lips.

A lazy smile crept across my face, and I put my nerveless, thousand-pound arms around his neck, pulling him close for some rather intensive grooming.

"*Fy nghalon, fy nghariad, fy dechrau a diwedd?*" he mumbled as I lapped at the come on his face. My Welsh was still really spotty, but he spoke slowly enough that I could make out what he said: *My heart, my love, my beginning and end.* "What spell am I under that I care for nothing any longer, nothing but you?"

He scooped me up in his arms and, kicking the door open, carried me into the guest room. He kicked the door shut behind us and with me still licking his face, made for the turned-down bed and laid me on it, capturing my mouth in a kiss as desperate and yearning as if we hadn't kissed in a year.

"Stay with me?" I practically begged when he broke the kiss to lean our foreheads together. Bleddyn sat back just enough to look into my eyes, his own full of so many different emotions, I couldn't even begin to read them.

But he nodded, and for the moment, as sleepy as I was, that was all I needed to know.

Somehow, between kisses, we maneuvered each other's clothes off. Once we were naked and pressed together, Bleddyn pulled the sheet and coverlet up over us and settled in my arms, his face on my chest, over my heart.

"I will stay with you, my lovely enchanter," he murmured, kissing my chest. *Am byth ac yn oes oesoedd."*

"No fair, if it's in Welsh," I yawned, even though I was pretty sure that last part had meant *forever and ever.* My eyes closed in satiation and contentment. Bleddyn kissed my right nipple, which sent sleepy arousal zinging through me. But even that wasn't enough to wake me fully.

Soon, I was out for the count, murmured Welsh endearments winging me off to dreamland.

❖

I woke up to Bleddyn's strong arms around me and his soft, even breaths on the back of my neck. Before I even opened my eyes, I inhaled deeply and smiled, enjoying the intermingled scents of the lamp oil and Bleddyn, who was a mixture of metal, horse, and clean sweat. Whether or not I had dreamed the night before, I didn't remember. But I knew they were sweet ones, if I had. How could they be otherwise, when sleeping in my love's arms?

I snuggled back against Bleddyn's ambitious morning wood and he sighed in his sleep, squeezing me tighter and burying his face against the back of my neck. Smiling, I opened my eyes, meaning to turn over and wake Bleddyn up in a way I was pretty sure he'd approve of—and let out a startled scream.

Rhys ap Thomas stood glaring and sneering over Bleddyn and me.

I lay there, wide-eyed and frightened, unable to move even to cover myself. Bleddyn had hogged the covers, leaving me to give his father the full Monty, however unintentionally—for what felt like an eternity as he looked at me and Bleddyn.

Bleddyn...

I started to reach behind me to shake him, but I needn't have. Bleddyn caught my hand and sat up behind me.

"Father," he said, without inflection. And Rhys looked at me and his son, his eyes hardening.

"Ye and yer catamite get dressed, Bleddyn. Lord Owen wishes ye t' break yer fast with him," Rhys spat. With another death-glare for me, he turned on his heel and marched out of the room.

"Father. wait!" Bleddyn called without hope, and it was indeed already too late. The door was slamming shut behind Rhys, leaving Bleddyn and I alone in the deafening silence, a silence I was unwilling—no, *afraid* to break, even by breathing. Even by *moving*. Finally, Bleddyn let go of my hand and rolled away from me to stand up.

As if released from a spell, I could finally move. The first thing I did was bury my face in my hands and listen to the sounds of cloth rustling as he got dressed and strode to the door. It opened and, after a long moment of hesitation, shut quietly.

When it did, the first sob took me by surprise, but the ones that came after it were rather expected.

CHAPTER NINE

I got up and got dressed in a slow daze, not even bothering to wipe my eyes after the first few minutes of crying. I felt like I could barely breathe. Like I couldn't get enough oxygen and my heart wouldn't stop pounding, like it wanted to burst out of my chest in search of air. I was colder than even springtime in Wales could account for, and it felt as if I'd never be warm again.

Bleddyn had chosen to go after his father and explain? Apologize? Lie, somehow? Whatever he chose to do, the weight of his upbringing and his own shame and fear would always be a barrier between us. He could never be as comfortable in his own skin and with his own needs and desires as I wanted him to be. At this very moment, he was trying to walk back what his father had witnessed. Right now, his father was no doubt convincing him that he was hell-bound for being with me. And right now, Bleddyn was believing him. Listening and believing and regretting and maybe even blaming me for "ensnaring" him.

It would be the easiest explanation his father would accept. Maybe the easiest explanation *Bleddyn* would accept, too. In the cold light of day, the word and deeds we'd shared likely meant less than nothing to him. I wasn't his *ngoleuni fy nghalon*. I wasn't the light of his heart. I was the shameful secret he hadn't been able to keep. It was time I recognized that and accepted it. Ours was no great romance. I wasn't the balm for his bruised and battered heart, and he wasn't the person I could at last trust mine with. It'd just felt that way because our desires for each other were so intense.

Who knew, better than me, how intense desire could overwhelm one, dragooning common sense and practicality to leave one clamoring for the society of the least suitable person? I'd said I'd never let it happen to me twice, and here I was, washed up on the shores of disillusionment and heartbreak much sooner than expected.

I was a fool. Worse, because even in those awful minutes, all I wanted was Bleddyn's arms around me again, and his low voice telling me I was the light of his heart, and that everything would be all right. That he'd meant all the things he said and didn't regret having been with me. That he would *still* be with me, no matter what.

Like I said, worse than a fool.

Once dressed, I stepped out of the guest room and looked back, hoping to catch a memory of Bleddyn and I rolling around like puppies or simply talking while we held and touched each other. But all I could see was the look of disgust and regret I'd imagined on his face as he'd left minutes earlier.

More tears spilled out of my already sore eyes, and I closed the door to the guest room behind me.

Lord Owen was waiting.

❖

It wasn't till I'd been wandering about the castle for nearly ten minutes that I realized I didn't know where Lord Owen took his breakfasts. Finally, I stopped a serving woman and asked. She was in a rush, but directed me to Lord Owen's rooms with patience and deference for my still aching ankle and slow, painstaking hobble. I knocked on Lord Owen's door.

"Enter!" came from inside, and I thanked the serving woman and let myself in.

The main chamber of Lord Owen's rooms was neat and well-lit, neither large nor small. A large desk took up most of the windowless room, covered in maps and papers and *books*. Lord Owen sat behind this desk, studying a book. It took nearly a minute before he looked up at me and smiled. I tried to smile back and must not have done too kosher a job, for his smile faltered and he stood, skirting his desk to approach me.

"Is there some trouble, Krish? You look as if you've been weeping," he said, all interest and genuine concern. That concern made my smile a little less of a grimace, and I waved away his worry.

"No, just missing my friends," I lied, looking away from his eyes. I've never been much of a liar. "It all hit me suddenly this morning that I may never see them or my family again."

Lord Owen's face fell, and he reached out to me, taking my hand the way Bleddyn had last night, holding it with one hand and covering it with the other. "I sympathize with your plight," he said, squeezing my hand. "In part, that's why I've brought you here this morning, not merely to share a breakfast with you."

I frowned. "I don't understand."

Lord Owen opened his mouth to explain, then laughed a little. "But what sort of host would I be to keep you standing here famished, while I prattle on?" He drew me toward a narrow entryway at the other end of the main chamber.

It was his bedchamber.

For a moment I was stunned. And a bit panicked, thinking I'd have to put up or shut up, regarding to my flirting with the lord's son. But then Owen was leading me to a corner of the bedchamber with a small table set up, three chairs, and what appeared to be breakfast. I breathed a sigh of relief, not that it would've been a chore to fuck Lord Owen. But I'd courted enough disaster by sleeping with one man in this time. No use courting more by sleeping with *two*. And a *lord's* son, nonetheless.

I watched as Lord Owen pulled out a chair and gestured for me to sit. Which I did, after bowing. When Lord Owen was seated, he immediately began buttering a piece of bread. I did the same. We ate in comfortable silence for a few minutes, before he inquired as to how I had passed the night. I told the truth, this time, that my night had been wonderful. I kept mum about the morning, however. At any rate, he didn't make small talk for long, choosing, instead, to come to his reason for inviting me to breakfast.

"Since you are at loose ends," he began, smiling a little, "and in want of money, lodging, and employment, I have spoken with my father and he has agreed we have more than enough to occupy your time here at Gwydir Castle, were you of a mind to stay on."

I gaped and stammered. "That's very generous of you, your lordship, but—"

"In private, to you, I am simply *Owen*, remember?"

"Owen," I corrected myself, blushing under his frank regard. Then I shook my head. "But I'm foreign to your ways, more foreign than you know. I can't do the things most of the men of this time—I mean this *place* can do. I can't chop wood or ride a horse properly or fight or farm. I can't even find my way about the castle, let alone anywhere else, here. I can't cook, I'd probably mess up at any real cleaning, I can't—"

Owen laughed. "You'll forgive me for saying so, Krish, but *that much* is obvious about you to anyone with eyes." When I blushed again, Owen's smile turned apologetic. "You are or were a scholar where you came from, unused to harsh and manual labors. I'm right, am I not?"

"Well, yes," I said, still red and getting redder. I looked down at my plate. "I guess it *would* be pretty obvious I've never seen a day of hard, physical labor in my life."

Owen sighed and reached across the table to take my left hand in both of his again. He examined it, first the top then the palm, folded it in his, and smiled at me. "These hands have not seen labors that would mar or roughen them. They are gentle, genteel hands. I would not see that change."

He let go of my hand almost as if he hesitated to do so, his fingers brushing it as they withdrew. I shivered and felt all the excess blood that gravity had been kind enough to drain from my face, return there in a rush.

"You would not?" I asked, breathless and unable to look away from his eyes.

"No," he whispered. "I would not. I would not change anything about you, least of all your hands."

Then he was clearing his throat and standing up to pace to his fireplace. "My father's accountant, Islwyn, has handled father's money for many years, but he is growing older and somewhat infirm. He has asked of late that we seek out a suitable lad to be his 'prentice. Now, you are, of course, a man grown, not a lad. However, you *are* already learned, and no doubt know much about figuring and sums that he would not have to teach you. In essence, however, he would be training you to fill the role of castle accountant when he is no longer up to that task."

Owen paced toward me, resplendent in his dark-blue wool tunic, black breeches, and hose. Not as built as Bleddyn, but not a chore to look at, either. "This is a duty with heavy responsibilities attached. It would require of you specificity, exactitude, a certain tirelessness, integrity, honesty, and a keen mind. All of which I would wager my life you have in spades."

I blinked. I didn't know what to say. Owen was smiling at me, waiting for me to say something, and I was speechless. This was a marvelous chance to get a place to stay and something to do to support myself in one fell swoop. And I could be close to Bleddyn, but I remembered that was probably not something Bleddyn wanted anymore. No doubt, if he had his way, I'd be as far from him in time and space as humanly possible.

Looking away from Owen's happy face, I closed my eyes as they began to blur with tears. I tried to blink them away, but they fell nonetheless.

"Krish?" Owen came up to me and knelt, trying to see my face, but I turned it away. "Krishnan—speak, and tell me what troubles you."

And hearing such unintentional mimicry of Bleddyn at his most solicitous undid me. I buried my face in my hands and wept silently, unable to stop the flow of tears or the way I shook. I was unable to hide my mortification at Owen seeing me like this.

After what felt like an eternity but may have only been a minute or two, Owen pulled me up to my feet and into his arms. He was taller than me by just enough that he could rest his chin on the top of my bowed head. He swept his hand up and down my back.

"You will see your home again, Krishnan of Nayar, this I promise," he murmured. "Your home, your kin, and your companions."

I laughed without mirth, removing my hands from my face so I could hide it against his shoulder. He smelled of wool and old books. "It's not that!"

"Then what causes such tears from you? What other loss prompts you to shake and shiver so? Tell me."

"I can't," I exhaled, looking up at him, pleading. He was looking down at me, frowning in concern once more. "You wouldn't understand, and it's not my tale to tell."

"I see," Owen said, biting his lip and searching my face. He sighed and reached up to brush my hair out of my eyes. "Then tell me what I may do to bring back the smile you wore just this past evening? For a day without such a smile to start it, is a day when the sun does not rise in the sky."

And of course, I smiled. Just a little. Probably not the smile he was hoping for, but more than anyone except Bleddyn could've wrung out of me at that point.

"There it is," Owen murmured, returning my smile. And I don't know what I was thinking, what made me do it, but I bobbed up on my toes and kissed him. On the mouth. Even as I was doing it, I was screaming at myself that I just *got* myself hanged or put in front of a firing squad, or however guys like me were put to death in 1626.

But after a few seconds, when I started to pull away, *Owen didn't*. In fact, he held me close and leaned into the kiss with a soft sigh, tasting my lips with his tongue and parting them.

Well, I guess that answers that *question*, I thought, placing my hands on his chest and kissing him in earnest. It was nice. Better than *nice*, actually, but it was nothing like kissing Bleddyn. For that reason, it felt subtly wrong—then less subtly as the seconds wore on. Finally, I pulled away again, breaking the kiss with several smaller, tender kisses, before leaning back to look at Owen and gauge his reaction.

His eyes were wide-open, and his lips were still parted. Still kiss-swollen and inviting, and despite the urge to taste them again, I felt that pang of *wrong* and stepped back out of his arms. He let me go reluctantly.

"I—I apologize for my behavior, your lordship," I stammered, bowing, trying to think of a way to explain what had just happened. Perhaps I could pass it off as a custom between men in America to swallow each other's faces as a sign of friendship. "Please, forgive me."

"Krish, there's nothing to forgive," Owen said, laughing a little, then covering his mouth with one hand as if to stifle that laughter. I met his eyes warily. They were almost all pupil, yet narrowed, as if he was receiving confirmation for something he'd long suspected. Then he shook his head and smiled. "You've done nothing wrong."

"But—but the *law*—"

"Bugger the law, and I do mean that quite literally," Owen said, his tone sharp and disgusted. "That law is ridiculous. A waste of ink and paper, not to mention the untimely deaths of innocent men and women in counties that aren't as willing to turn a blind eye as father's."

I was gaping again. "So, you're not going to hang me?"

"Oh, for Heaven's sake, *no!*" Owen snorted. "What sort of hypocrite would that make me?"

I shook my head. Surely this was all a dream, right? Right now, I was laying in Gwydir Forest, having tripped and hit my head, as well as sprained my ankle? There'd been no time travel, no castle, and no Bleddyn or Owen. "Does that mean that *you* are...um..."

"I have lain with men before, yes. As I don't doubt you have." Owen challenged me with a look, and I blushed again.

"I might have lain with a few men in my time," I said, and then I covered my mouth when I realized that could be taken more than one way. "I mean—"

"I know what you mean, Krish." Owen stepped closer to me and reached out to brush my hair out of my face again. He sighed, a melancholy thing, but kind of wry, too. "And know that if your affections weren't so clearly spoken for by another, I would dally with you here all morning."

And from the emphasis he put on *dally*, I knew he didn't mean we'd be playing chess and reading scripture if we stayed here. I turned all kinds of red, and then I blanched as I processed the rest of what he'd said. "Spoken for? My affections aren't spoken for. How could they be? I've only been here two days." I laughed nervously, and Owen's eyebrows stayed quirked up in that challenging way.

"I see more passion and affection in one glance between you and Bleddyn than I've seen in entire marriages, Krish. The two of you are deceiving no one, at least not anyone who isn't blind."

At his words, my eyes filled with tears and I looked away, not even bothering to deny what he'd said. "Well, maybe yesterday. But today? That's all over and done. There *is no* 'the two of us,' anymore."

Owen frowned. "I do not understand. Are you claiming that Bleddyn no longer returns your affections?" he asked doubtfully. I nodded, feeling dull and listless.

"This morning—well, last night, we slept together in the guest room, and this morning, his father found us there together."

Owen's frown turned into a scowl. "Rhys ap Thomas is a bitter and ugly man who has never had a kind word for either Bleddyn, or poor, dearest William," he said, his eyes flickering with something I couldn't read. "And when he caught William and Bleddyn together, he had to be restrained from beating them both to within an inch of their lives. I was one of the men who held him back. I was horrified, and heavily did my conscience weigh, for it was my fault that William even took it into his head to—" Owen felt silent, closing his eyes and covering his mouth.

I put my hand on Owen's arm. I had a bad feeling about this. I didn't want to ask or know, but I felt like I *had* to. "Why was it your fault, Owen?"

Owen opened his eyes and looked down at my hand on his arm, then into my eyes.

"Bleddyn does not, as far as I am aware, know this," he said, his gaze gone flat and hard.

I shook my head. "Nor will he ever know it from me."

Owen searched my face again and sighed, taking my hand. He led me to his bed and sat on the foot, leaving room for me to join him, so I did. He did not let go of my hand, and I didn't move to free it.

"Back in aught-eight, I was sent to be apprenticed with a merchant of the Staple for several years. When I returned to Wales, it was to see there had been many changes, but the one that struck me most was how William ap Warren had grown into a fine young man whilst I'd been away." Owen paused and hung his head, shaking it. I thought I knew where this was going, but I let Owen tell it in his own way, and in his own time. After a minute, he went on.

"He was easy to charm with tales of the world and its ways. He had stars in his eyes, that one, and had he been born to a different family, might have gone to Cambridge just as I had, for he was quick and intelligent and personable.

"Before the month had gone 'ere I was home, I'd tumbled the lad repeatedly. I deflowered him and, when my fickle interest turned to a pretty young maid, I abandoned him. I left him with his newly-discovered desires and to his own ends. Only to find out months later, from Rhys's own mouth that the boy had been buggering Bleddyn!"

I nodded. It was pretty much what I'd thought. Except for one thing. "Rhys told *you* what happened?"

Owen snorted again. "He told the entire castle. He was shouting at the top of his lungs about what the two boys had been getting up to. And he beat them in front of everyone. None dared lift a hand against him until Richard and I came running outside to find out what all the yelling was. Rhys barely stopped beating them to explain. It took both Richard and me to hold him back."

I sighed, myself, putting an arm around Owen's shoulders, hugging him close. "How old were you? How old were William and Bleddyn?"

"I was nineteen," Owen said quietly. "William was sixteen, I believe, and Bleddyn would have been fifteen."

"You were all so *young*," I breathed, and Owen turned a morose gaze on me.

"My youth does not excuse my culpability in this matter. William was an innocent. 'Twas *I* that introduced him to buggery and the pleasures of the flesh. 'Twas *my* careless, thoughtless neglect of him that drove him to seek out Bleddyn."

I shook my head. "I don't think it was. I think William and Bleddyn always loved each other. That William turned to you because he was attracted to you, and because he liked the things you taught him. But that his affections were always oriented toward Bleddyn."

Owen frowned as if he wanted to believe but didn't quite dare. "Think you so, Krish of Nayar?"

"Yes, I do. Speaking as someone who's falling in love with Bleddyn, once that happens, there's really no turning back no matter how much better it'd be if one *could* turn back." I smiled sadly, and Owen squeezed my hand.

"Rest assured of one thing, Krish. Bleddyn ap Rhys does not give his heart away easily, or at all. Not since William passed on. That he has given it to you so plainly and without reservation speaks volumes to the esteem in which he holds you. Whatever setback you face now, 'twill be overcome in a matter of time," Owen said with warmth and gentle kindness. "In the meantime, will you think about my offer to be 'prenticed to Islwyn?"

I found myself smiling just a bit. "I studied Liberal Arts in college. That's nothing like accounting, you know?"

"Whatever you need to know that you don't already know, Islwyn will teach you."

I rolled my eyes but kept on smiling. "I'll think about it," I promised, thinking with a mental sigh, that whether or not I stayed on depended entirely on how Bleddyn felt about me. But I knew that he probably despised me now, thanks to Rhys.

Tears sprang to my eyes again, but this time I blinked them away with stubborn determination. I decided right then and there that seeing as I had no other prospects in 1626, I *would* take Owen up on his offer, and grin and bear it if I had to see Bleddyn every day and deal with his contempt and hatred. So be it. Avoidance was all well and good, but one couldn't fill a stomach or keep the rain off with it.

Owen stood up, offering me his arm. I stood and took it and let him lead me back to the breakfast table. He saw me seated, then sat himself.

"So," he said, a bit awkwardly after everything we'd shared. But he met my eyes squarely. "What is on your agenda for today?"

I shrugged. "Not a single thing, I—wait, actually there was somewhere I wanted to go today. Someone I wanted to speak with."

Owen drew his brows together slightly. "You have but to tell me, and I shall have you brought whither you will."

I let my own eyebrows rise in challenge. "Is that so?"

"That *is* so, Krish of Nayar." Owen gave me a quick but flirty once-over.

"I need to see Gwenllian Robert of Llyn, uh...I wanna say *Llyn Ten-a-minute?*"

Owen's smiled. "It's *Llyn Tynymynydd*. And might I inquire as to why you wish to see her?"

"To have her look over my ankle. It, uh, still hurts really bad," I lied again. My ankle wasn't great, but it definitely felt better than it had two days ago.

Owen hummed and buttered another piece of bread. "Then, as you say, it shall be done. I'll have one of the men take you there by mid-morning."

Relief. The tension flowed out of me so fast it left me almost limp. I reached for Owen's hand and took it, squeezing it gratefully. "Thank you, Owen. Thank you so much!"

"Think nothing of it. In fact, Bleddyn can take you," Owen said, looking up and over my shoulder. My heart rose at the same time that it sank. I didn't even have to look around to know who was there. "Ah, Bleddyn, old man, we've almost finished breaking our fast without you! Come, sit, and break your fast!"

"I apologize for my lateness, Lord Owen," Bleddyn murmured, stepping past me to bow to Owen before sitting in the third chair. He did not look at me, and that hurt more than I could've said. "But my father had something important to discuss with me, and we lost track of time, I fear."

I blushed so brightly, I could've guided Santa's sleigh on a foggy Christmas Eve.

"Perfectly understandable, my good man," Owen dismissed. Bleddyn inclined his head, then paled when his eyes landed on my hand, where it covered Owen's. Frozen, I didn't know whether I wanted Bleddyn to think the worst or not. I was torn between holding on to Owen's hand and letting go. All the while I could see Bleddyn's jaw working, and a vein at his temple throbbing. When his face started to turn an angry red, I decided it might be best if I let go, after all.

As I did, Bleddyn finally looked me in the eyes. I don't know what he saw there, but I couldn't read *his* eyes to save my life. So I looked down at my breakfast and started eating again, even though it was tasteless now.

"You've actually arrived at a providential moment," Owen went on to say, taking a bite of his bread. "I was just telling Master Krish that you could take him to *Llyn Tynymynydd* to see Gwenllian Robert."

Bleddyn froze in the act of selecting a slice of bread and looked at me, surprised and unhappy. Grim-faced, like his father. I glanced away, sighing.

"I *need* to do this, Bleddyn," I whispered. After a moment, from the corner of my eye I could see him take the piece of bread and start buttering it with angry, choppy strokes.

"Of course. It shall be as Master Krish commands," he said without any inflection, and I winced.

"Yes, his ankle still pains him quite a bit, poor fellow. But that should fall well under the Widow Robert's purview," Owen said, as if utterly oblivious to the tension between Bleddyn and me. Knowing how intelligent he was, I knew it was pretense. "She'll have you feeling better in no time, 't'all."

"Yes, she will," Bleddyn said stiffly, and I seriously thought of asking for a different guide, even with Bleddyn sitting right there. But in the end, I held my peace and finished my breakfast while Bleddyn ignored me and Owen chattered on with what I could only imagine was false enthusiasm about anything and everything.

It was going to be a long day, and it hadn't even really begun, yet.

CHAPTER TEN

So," I said when Bleddyn and I had been riding along for what seemed like eternity in uncomfortable silence. We'd just reached the outskirts of Gwydir Forest after traveling along the road for a bit, he on Arwel, me on a horse whose name Bleddyn hadn't told me. But her gait was much better than Queen's. "What is *Llyn Tynymynydd*, anyway?"

Bleddyn, riding just far enough ahead of me that I couldn't see his face, didn't answer for a few minutes. When he spoke, his voice was matter-of-fact. "It is a lake. *Llyn* is the Cymraeg word for *lake*. *Ty n-y-mynydd* means *the mountain house*."

"Oh," I said, blushing for no reason and wishing I hadn't asked. Then we rode along in silence thereafter for another eternity. Till the silence got so loud and obnoxious, I *had* to break it. "How was Gareth, this morning?"

"I do not know. I had not the time to check in on him."

Ouch. Another thing that could be laid at my doorstep. I sighed. "So, are we gonna ride all the way to Mountain House Lake in this lovely, companionable silence, or are we gonna talk about what happened?" I asked him with more than a little reluctance, my voice shaking just a little. To be honest, I didn't know which would have scared me more, a yes or a no.

Bleddyn, meanwhile, tensed up so much I could hear the slight jingle of his armor when his muscles shifted and tightened.

"There is nothing to speak about, Master Krishnan."

So, we're back to that, I thought, closing my eyes on the tears that filled them. Even though he wasn't looking at me, I didn't want to give Bleddyn the satisfaction of having made me cry. Though I seemed to be doing it a lot lately. And all thanks to him.

No, all thanks to *me*. It was hardly Bleddyn's fault I'd let myself grow so attached to him so fast. Of the two of us, I surely knew better than to fall for a guy just because he was hot and an epic lay.

But Bleddyn had been more than that, or so I'd thought. He'd been my knight in shining armor. My Prince Charming, so to speak. He'd treated me, in the uber-brief time we'd been sort of together, better than all my previous boyfriends combined. He'd been tender and sweet and protective. Possessive in a way that made me feel special, but not controlled. And the way he'd looked at me, he'd made me feel about ten thousand feet tall.

And now, here I was, let down *again*, playing the *Smiths' Greatest Hits* in my head because I'd just gotten kicked to the curb *again*.

I wiped my eyes and wished I knew how to slow my horse down so Bleddyn could pull ahead of me far enough that I could cry and do my Morrissey impersonation in private. But as we rode on, my tears began to abate some. Though not the heartache; that felt everlasting. But I guess there's a ceiling on tears no matter how bad the hurt, because I started singing just to keep myself company. It wasn't as if Bleddyn cared. He was probably off in his own world of Jesus and Hell and which virginal maid he was going to woo and marry to please his father.

Braiding bits of my horse's mane, I began to sing *How Soon is Now?*, not caring if Bleddyn heard or didn't. And if I put a little extra emphasis on the chorus, especially the last two lines, so what? When I fell silent, I smiled to myself a little, and finished off another braid on the nameless horse. I put my brain on shuffle, hoping to come up with another Smiths' song that'd fit my current mood of raw heartbreak and weary cynicism. There were many, and like a jukebox, I cycled through bits of them all, each bit only serving to make what I was feeling even more intense, till tears threatened again.

This is ridiculous, I thought, swiping at my leaking eyes with impatience and self-contempt. *What difference does it make which song I pick or how bad it makes me feel? It won't change the reality of my situation. I'm stranded in 1626 with no marketable skills, and I've alienated my only defender because I just* had *to sleep with him. I'm essentially alone in a foreign place, in an even more foreign time, and living under the threat of a death sentence for being who I am. A reshuffling of priorities is in order, Krish! I should just be glad this little* thing *I had with Bleddyn didn't end with one or the both of us losing our heads to an ax, and be more careful in the future. Which, as far as I know, is going to be spent in the past*!

I'd just opened my mouth to start *What Difference Does it Make?* when I was startled out of my reverie by Bleddyn's soft, thoughtful words. "'Twas a lovely madrigal, Krishnan of Nayar. You have a fine voice."

Startled to hear him speak at all, let alone in praise of something I'd done, I looked up to find Bleddyn had slowed his horse and was riding almost abreast with me.

"Uh, thanks." I shrugged and looked back down at my fingers, still playing with the horse's mane.

"Is that a song from America?"

I snorted. "No. The name of the song is 'How Soon is Now?' by an English band called the Smiths. They were really popular in the 1980s and early 90s. A little before my time, but a really good band. They were the background music of high school, for me." I laughed a little. Steven Morrissey always reminded me of my fraught teenage years, and how sincere I was. How absolutely *naked*.

By the time I grew my adult armor, high school was over, and the adventure that was college had begun. I was a bit too jaded, and the sincerity and earnestness of my teens was replaced by the sarcastic, snarky bitch I am today.

"These Smiths—did they work metal as well as they sang?"

I glanced at Bleddyn. He seemed serious. As usual. I sighed. "They weren't *actual* smiths, that was just their name."

"'Tis a strange name to take if one is not a smith or the descendant of one," he noted, frowning at the woods ahead.

"Yeah, well, it gets even stranger. Strawberry Alarm Clock, Jefferson Starship, Toad the Wet Sprocket, Imagine Dragons—bands have to come up with some pretty weird names in the future to stand out."

"Say you truly?"

"Truly. All the normal names are taken."

Bleddyn *hmmed* and smiled just a little. It wasn't exactly a happy smile, but it was better than the grim look that made him resemble Rhys so much. I found myself smiling a little bit, too, and I looked away before Bleddyn caught me staring.

This time, the silence we rode in was much less uncomfortable, though still a little tense. And Bleddyn was the one to break it.

"I would hear more of these Smiths, if you're of a mind to sing further," he said, low and humble. Again, I was startled. When I looked over at him, he was red about the face, but met my gaze steadily, almost—Well, I knew how I *wished* he was looking at me. But surely that yearning on his face was my projection of my own feelings, and the desires of my own restless, broken heart.

"Why not?" I replied, looking away, at the forest ahead. At least I'd be distracting myself from wanting what I couldn't have anymore. "Okay, this one is called *What Difference Does it Make?*"

When I finished—I really shredded that high note, too, and usually that's the one place my voice would give out—Bleddyn was watching me with grave consideration.

"The words are strange, but filled, I sense, with heartbreak and loneliness, loss and despair," he decided finally, and I laughed a little.

"That's the Smiths. Sometimes listening to their songs is like an education in misery. Other times, it's a balm. Understanding in a world that feels as if it's going mad and taking me with it," I said, then blushed, realizing I might have revealed more than I was comfortable with.

Bleddyn tilted his head with almost unwilling curiosity. "And you say their songs remind you of your youth?"

I nodded. "In some ways. I found it easy to relate to their lyrics—um, words—and the feelings their songs evoked were feelings I knew. When I was just shy of fourteen, my dad died, and I experienced loss. When I was almost fifteen, my first boyfriend broke up with me, and I was heartbroken. At nearly sixteen, I fell in with a bad crowd and got cozy with the baddest of the bunch. It wasn't long before I learned how to despair. And ever since then, I guess I've been lonely." I shrugged again, uncomfortable with the territory we were treading on. "The Smiths and Morrissey make great music for masochists."

"For *whom*?"

"Nothing, nothing." I sighed, looking down at my horse's bunches of half-done braids and thinking I was a walking Morrissey song.

❖

By the time we reached the lake, the overcast sky had begun to rain steadily, if not heavily. Yet. We skirted the lake to the Northeastern shore, and then Bleddyn took us back into the woods for a bit. Minutes, really, before we came upon the cottage.

It was like something out of a fairy-tale: thatched roof, ivy-covered trellis, smoke coming out of the squat chimney top. Next to it on the right was a barn that was on the narrow side, but still respectable.

We clopped into Gwenllian's front yard, wary of the neat, sprawling herb and vegetable garden to either side of the front door. Bleddyn and I looked at each other uncertainly, then he shrugged and pulled ahead a little. He was the first to stop and get off his horse, but he waited for me to reach him before helping me off. I thanked him without looking at him, not wanting him to see whatever expression was on my face.

Then we were walking slowly, in deference to my damned ankle, up the stone-paved walk to her front door. Bleddyn raised his hand to knock, but then glanced at me as if to ask was I sure. I smiled limply and nodded. The only thing I'd ever been surer of was him. Though I kept that information to myself.

So Bleddyn knocked and we waited. And waited. And waited. He knocked again, more heavily, so that the knocking echoed in the clearing around the cottage. The only response we got was the sky opening up to rain even harder, soaking us both in under a minute.

"She is not at home," Bleddyn said, and I rolled my eyes, blinking out rainwater.

"You think, Captain Obvious?" I shivered, cold and damp and feeling miserable again. I'd been so dead-set on getting my answers, and now I was being put off. And I'd be riding back to the castle soaking wet. "So, what do we do now?"

Bleddyn shook his head and nodded to the small barn. "Methinks we can wait out the rain in there. Then, if *Gweddw* Robert has not returned by dusk, we will make for the castle."

"Oh-kay," I said as Bleddyn put an arm around my waist and began leading me toward the barn. "But she left a fire burning, so that means she'll be back soon, right?"

"'Tis merely banked, not burning. If the widow is tending the sick, she may be gone for days."

I groaned, and just then it began to rain even harder. Bleddyn and I hurried toward the barn as fast as my ankle would allow.

When Bleddyn saw me settled in an empty stall near the back of the barn, he went to get the horses, leaving me to look around.

The barn only housed three cows and two horses, not counting the ones Bleddyn and I had ridden to get there, despite having eight stalls. The hay was fresh, and the barn itself didn't stink of manure as badly as I'd expected. Above me I could make out the hay loft and hear the occasional drip of water in the hay. Gwenllian's roof needed tarring or whatever they did to prevent leaks.

I spread some of the hay out in the empty stall Bleddyn had left me in and sat on it. It was like sitting on the mattress in the guest room at the castle, pokey and a bit uncomfortable. But it was dry, and that was something to be said for it.

By the time Bleddyn had led the horses into the barn and gotten them settled in stalls, I'd removed and wrung out my soaked shirt and was wringing out my dripping hair. I'd heard him puttering around making the horses comfortable, but I'd drifted off into my own world, and so didn't notice when he came up to the stall I was in. I just looked up after I was done with my hair and he was standing there, still as a statue, staring at me with wide-eyed surprise. His face was flushed and his lips parted. If I didn't know better, I'd have sworn he was turned on.

But of course, after the tongue-lashing his father had no doubt given him, Bleddyn was probably put off me for life.

Trying not to sigh, I asked, "What's up?"

"I—" Bleddyn began, then flushed more, looking away and wringing his hands. "I've settled the horses. All that remains is for us to await the widow."

"All right," I said, frowning as Bleddyn started to turn away. "Wait. Where're you going?"

Bleddyn paused and took a deep breath and spoke without looking at me. "I think it best if I keep an eye out for the widow's return and leave you to rest in privacy."

"Oh."

Now Bleddyn glanced at me, his gaze unreadable as he took me in. I probably looked like a drowned rat.

"I'll leave you to your rest and privacy," he said once more, but he made no move to go. We just stared at each other for what felt like forever. I tried to smile, to not let it show that the only thing I wanted in that moment was for him to be kissing me and holding me, pinning me to the hay and pressing his hard body against mine.

But maybe some of that yearning *did* show. And maybe it disgusted him, because he abruptly turned away and marched toward the front of the barn.

❖

Weak...I was so weak.

I couldn't stir from my bed, to which I'd been confined for days now. I lay fevered and raving, sometimes almost lucid. But the pain in my gut was constant as I lay there, simply trying to breathe past the agony that assailed me.

Sometimes people spoke above me in hushed whispers. Sometimes they spoke to *me, but only ever to ask me how I felt. And I could only ever answer them with grunts and groans for them to please, please* make the pain stop. *Sometimes things were poured down my throat, bitter tonics that lessened pain and put me to sleep for many nightmarish hours. And when I slept, I dreamt of being beaten and chased, only to be awakened by my own thrashing. By the fresh agony of my disturbed wound and, sometimes, my renewed fever.*

They would have two or three strong lads hold me down when they cleaned the wound and stuff my mouth with a rag soaked in spirits to calm me and muffle my screams.

All I wanted was for the pain to stop. I didn't want the mother and father I'd never known. I didn't even want the boy I had loved to the detriment of my life. I just wanted the pain to stop.

And my waking nightmare of being on death's door would become confused with my nightmares of being beaten and chased. Sometimes I could swear I felt my love's hand in my own as we ran across the grounds of Gwydir Castle, no plan as to where we were going, only knowing we were going together.

Until he *caught up with us and beat us. Worse than ever he had. And as always, I didn't get the worst of it. As always, the worst of it went to he whom I loved and had always loved.* Would *always love. As I lay, half-insensate on the filthy stones of the courtyard, I could barely move to reach out a trembling hand. Could barely speak to beg* him *to* stop *hitting and* kicking *and* hurting.

"Ewythr, na, os gwelwch yn dda...peidiwch â brifo ef...! Yr oedd pob un fy ei wneud!!" Uncle, no, please. . .do not hurt him. . .! It was all my doing!

I kept repeating some variation of that over and over, not until he *stopped, but until he* was stopped *and dragged away from the limp, bloody, bruised body of my love.*

Surely he is dead, *I thought, and in so thinking, wanted to die, too. I tried to crawl toward him, to touch him, to kiss him once more before the fires of Hell came for us, but the world began to go dark and hands pulled me onto my back. Canny dark blue eyes stared down into my own, horrified and sad.*

"Gwil—" a low voice said, and then said no more. I rolled my aching head toward him, toward my love, who was being lifted up as if he weighed nothing. My vision was too compromised to make out who was doing the lifting, but it mattered not, for he was dead *and no amount of lifting would change that.*

And all I wanted was to die, too.

To die and be laid to rest next to him, but they were taking his body away from mine. Far away.

"Arhoswch i mi, Cefnder, canys mi a'th ganlynaf i ba le yr wyt ti yn myned—" I wept. *Wait for me, cousin, for I will follow thee whither thou goest—*

❖

"Arhoswch i mi, Cefnder. Arhoswch," I plead. *Wait for me, cousin. Stay.*

"Ni wnei di deffro, fy nghariad? Dim ond breuddwyd...dim ond breuddwyd."

I startled awake to a soft, concerned voice telling me it was only a dream and to wake up. To a gentle hand caressing my cheek. Bleddyn's worried face hovered over me, and I blinked in confusion, tears blurring my vision before rolling down my cold cheeks. "Bleddyn?"

"Ie, ngoleuni fy nghalon. Mae'n Rwy'n," he confirmed, still brushing my cheek with his thumb, spreading the wetness of my tears, as he began to cry himself. *"Rydych yn crio, ac yn galw allan am help wrth i chi gysgu."* *You cry, and call out for aid when you sleep.*

I flung my arms around Bleddyn and buried my face in his neck, sobbing for a reason I couldn't define. All I could do was shudder and mumble. "Don't leave me. Please don't let me go."

"Do not cry, gentle my love, for I will never leave thee."

Bleddyn's reply comforted me. His voice, soothing in my hair, and his arms around me, the feel of him against me was everything I needed, and it banished that awful dream to the deepest pit of my subconscious where it would hopefully stay, never to come bubbling to the surface again.

When my sobbing had subsided into occasional hitches, Bleddyn leaned back a little to look down into my eyes. His eyes were a little red from weeping.

"What did you dream, my love?" he asked, and I shook my head in complete negation. I didn't want to remember it. I just wanted to never dream about it again.

Bleddyn frowned but reached up to caress my face tenderly. "What did you dream, Krish?"

I shook my head again. "I don't remember. I don't *want* to remember. All I know is it felt like dying, and I was glad to go."

"Do not say that," Bleddyn whispered, holding me tighter and leaning in to kiss my forehead, lingering to murmur something in Welsh I couldn't catch.

"It was just a dream, but it hurt *so much*," I mumbled, shuddering again as the pain of my vanished nightmare resounded in my heart. "It felt like I'd lost everything that mattered to me, and I couldn't lift a finger to stop it. Like I was finally, truly *alone* in the world, and always would be."

"It was merely a dream. A bad one, but a dream, nonetheless," Bleddyn murmured, looking at me with solemn concern. "You are not alone."

"Aren't I?" I asked, remembering what had happened earlier in the morning and trying to push him away from me. But he wouldn't budge. "Bleddyn—"

"You *are not* alone," Bleddyn said again, leaning down to kiss me on the mouth as softly and sweetly as I've ever been kissed. I moaned, parting my lips to allow his tongue entrance. It flirted alongside my own, plundering my mouth and mapping it. I laid back in the hay as Bleddyn's body settled on top of me, heavy and damp and *perfect*.

His touch, his very presence, was the antidote to the way that dream had made me feel. Every time he teased me with his tongue or ran his rough, callused hands down my bare arms and chest, he drove the dream farther away. "Make love to me, Bleddyn. Please."

Bleddyn stopped kissing me to look into my eyes, clearly torn. I could feel how hard he was. He may have stopped kissing me, but he hadn't stopped grinding against me. However, that look of grim guilt was on his face, and he looked so much like his father in that moment I felt almost disgusted.

"Surely I am already hellbound and beyond repentance," Bleddyn breathed, closing his eyes. I felt a surge of anger and pushed him off me, something I only managed because I had the element of surprise on my side. I rolled away from him and sat up, tears in my eyes once more. Only *these* tears were nothing to do with my dream and everything to do with my waking reality.

"Leave me alone, Bleddyn," I said when he put his hand on my arm. I jerked it away and clutched it to me as if it'd been burned. "I'm not gonna be your consolation prize for not being good enough to get into Heaven. I'm not gonna be the one you blame every time you lament your lost redemption and purity. If you wanna hate yourself, go right ahead. Just do it without me."

And with that, I got to my feet as nimbly as I was able, and hobbled out of the stall. Out of the barn, where even I wouldn't be able to tell what was tears and what was the rain.

Chapter Eleven

I stood out there, shivering in nothing but my boots and William's breeches and hose, my arms wrapped around my torso, getting wet all over again and trying my best to calm myself. To put away the rage and despair that were driving me mad.

I shivered and shook as the rain stole the warmth of Bleddyn's embrace and kisses, wondering why I kept falling for the wrong guys. Oh, certainly never this fast or hard before Bleddyn, but still, I had a track record of unsuitable guys. I couldn't tell if it was progress or a lateral move that the most recent guy dumped me *because* I was having sex with him.

It was ironic, if nothing else. I laughed miserably, burying my face in my hands then running them back through my hair. I tugged on it till my teeth ached, barely resisting the urge to scream that'd been building in me since the moment I realized I'd been swept backwards in time.

I'd been able to fight it successfully with Bleddyn to distract me, but now, with bald reality staring me in the face, the urge was undeniable. I opened my mouth and let out a yell, as loud and lonely as any wolf howling. I yelled until my face grew hot and my voice cracked and broke, and all I had left was sobs. Drained, I sank to my knees in a puddle, and held myself, uncaring. I rocked myself and sobbed until I was hoarse and empty.

I was perhaps trapped here, for the rest of my life, in close proximity to a man who could've been everything I'd ever wanted, but for the pesky belief that he was going to Hell for wanting me.

And said man was the only person who knew my true origins. He was maybe the only one I could ever talk to about it and my family and friends without lying.

And the only thing he seemed to despise more than me was himself.

To be fair, the time he was raised in had branded into his bones that he was wrong and deserving of nothing less than an eternity of Hellfire. He wasn't a closet-case directly because of his career or his family, but because he was trying to be a *good man* and to avoid being put to death by the law of the land he lived in. Those were no small reasons to be in the closet. Walking the straight and narrow for the sake of Heaven and one's continued existence on this planet was a hard habit to break, and one that shouldn't have been broken lightly.

But I hadn't asked him to break those habits lightly. Or at all. He'd *offered* to break them, at least in private. Which was more than I could've hoped for or expected. He'd given up, from his point of view, a chance at Heaven to be with me, however briefly. And then his father had found us, and his so-called *sin* was no longer a private matter between Bleddyn and his Savior. Once again, it was fodder for anyone Rhys chose to vent to.

In Bleddyn's eyes I was, no doubt, shaping up to be another William. Could I blame him for wanting to avoid that whole mess twice in a lifetime?

No, I decided. *I can't.*

But that didn't mean it didn't hurt me. More than I'd ever been hurt by a lover before. Bleddyn had his reasons for his choices, but my heart didn't understand that. No, it *did* understand, but that understanding didn't mitigate the pain of rejection. Of coming in second place to Heaven and Rhys's good opinion.

Maybe Gwenllian really does know more than she let on in Trefriw. And if she does, maybe she knows a way to get me home. I don't know that I can live the rest of my life in this time. It's too dangerous, too confusing, and too painful. There's worse than nothing here for me. There's just the stagnant promise of something good fallen through.

Suddenly, I felt Bleddyn's large hands on my shoulders, warm and relatively dry. Instantly angry, I shrugged them off, but he tried again, insistent and unyielding, bare arms embracing mine. Bleddyn sank to his knees behind me in the puddle, pulling me back into a tight, unbreakable embrace as he kissed my hair, my temple, and my neck.

"Why are you doing this to me, Bleddyn?" I asked in a voice as dully miserable as I felt. "You keep pushing me away only to pull me closer and then push me away again. That's *not fair*. Every time you feel guilty about wanting me, *I'm* the one who suffers, and it hurts. Don't you understand?" I sighed, shaking my head. "It hurts."

Bleddyn didn't stop kissing me, but he became more intent and tender. "I do not mean to hurt you," he murmured on the skin of my shoulder. I shivered and a small but traitorous moan escaped my lips. "I only know that I desire you, *all* of you. I wish for you to be mine, and none other's. I want to lie with you and speak with you, and comfort you when you're hurting, not be the cause of that hurt."

"But you are, Bleddyn. You are."

"I know, *fy ngoleuni*, I know." Bleddyn rested his chin on my shoulder before leaning his forehead against it. "You bring me nothing but joy, and yet I bring you nothing but pain."

I sighed, turning my head so I could lean it against Bleddyn's. This closeness after so much strife was as lovely as it was unbearable. "No, that's not true. No relationship is wholly pain or wholly joy. I've hurt you, I'm certain, just as you've hurt me."

"Yet the pain I've caused you is worse, is it not? The pain of not knowing when the one who swore an oath to protect and care for you will of a sudden abandon you, leaving you to think the very worst." Bleddyn exhaled heavily. I knew he was referring to this morning, when his father had caught us and Bleddyn had chosen to go after him rather than stay with me. "I know nothing, anymore, it seems. Nothing but that you deserve better treatment than that which I've bestowed upon you."

"And you shouldn't have to choose between your lover and your father, Bleddyn," I whispered, meaning to pull out of his arms and make for him the choice he was having such trouble making. But he held me fast and stood up, pulling me to my feet, then scooping me up in his arms like I weighed nothing. I wrapped my arms around his neck, not wanting to be dropped on my ass in the puddle.

When I met Bleddyn's eyes, they were solemn and pained, but determined.

"And yet, I *have* chosen," he said, carrying me back into the dim, stuffy air of the barn. Bleddyn had laid our still-damp shirts out over the straw in a stall, and he gently placed me down on them. I gazed up at his face and its warring emotions and reached out to touch his cheek. He leaned into my touch and sighed. "I have made my choice, Krishnan."

"I understand," I replied stoically, removing my hand and looking away. Getting the final brush off didn't hurt as much as I'd thought it would. Maybe that was because at least I'd known it was coming this time. Or maybe I was just numb, and the worst of the pain was still yet to come.

"I have made my choice," he said, and he leaned down to kiss me.

All I could think was, *Oh.*

Then I was laying down and pulling him down on top of me. He came willingly, all damp, chilled muscle, still kissing me, his hands on my chest.

"*Me?*" I gasped as he pinched and tugged on my nipples. "Is it *me?*"

"Yes," Bleddyn breathed, leaning his forehead against mine and rolling us over so I was straddling his thighs. "Always you, *fy ngoleuni.*"

I pinned Bleddyn's hands to the hay and searched his eyes. He looked scared but resolute. He meant what he was saying. His heart was in his eyes and his choice was in his heart. It was all right there for me to see, no dissembling or ambiguity.

It was me. He'd made his choice, and it was me.

"Have I hurt you again?" Bleddyn asked, easily freeing a hand from my hold to wipe away tears that gathered in my eyes and kept falling on his face. "Say not that I've hurt you, when my only aim was to prove my love?"

I laughed and kissed him, joy welling up within me so big and bright I was sure I'd explode. "No, Bleddyn, you haven't hurt me. You've just made me the happiest man in the world, that's all. These are *happy* tears," I told him, kissing him again as he freed his other hand and wrapped both arms around my waist.

"*Happy tears?*" He sounded doubtful. I kissed him silent.

"Not all tears are an evil, my love," I whispered on his lips, reaching behind me to push his hands down to my ass. He squeezed and kneaded, then pushed William's breeches as far down my hips as he could get them. When his hands lighted on my bare skin, I hissed and nuzzled his cheek. "I want you inside me, Bleddyn."

He was the one to shiver this time, and he held me tighter, bucking his hips up. He was hard again.

"And I desire nothing more than your heat and tightness around me, consuming me, burning away all that does not matter," he breathed. "But I've brought nothing to ease the way for us—no oil or salve to—" and he fell silent when I took the small pot of salve out of my pocket. His eyes widened, and he gazed at me with such a mixture of wonder and disbelief that I blushed and shrugged.

"One of these days, I'll actually get around to trying it on my ankle." Bleddyn grinned and kissed me, rolling us over again so that he was on top of me. Laughing and gasping, we touched and kissed and hurried each other out of our breeches, hose, and boots until we lay skin to skin, shimmying and grinding and staring into each other's eyes.

"You are the loveliest piece of Creation I have ever seen," he murmured, brushing his index finger across my cheek, then tracing my lips. He smiled when I kissed his fingertip, and then he drew in a shuddering breath when I licked his finger and sucked it into my mouth. "So versed in carnal delights, yet still so innocently and virtuously do you shine."

I pulled off his finger with an indecent swirl of tongue and kissed him. "You're really gonna turn my head with all this flattery, if you're not careful."

"'Flattery' assumes that I am taking liberties with attributes you may or may not possess. But what I speak is only the *truth*." Bleddyn searched my eyes and smiled again. "You are lovely and sweet, virtuous and good. I have seen so with my own eyes, and nothing anyone says will convince me otherwise."

I thought of Rhys and what would happen the next time Bleddyn saw him, but I held my peace. We would have to see, wouldn't we? Of course Bleddyn *meant* well. I was beginning to see he'd never meant otherwise. Perhaps not in his entire life. But men had done worse things than dump the guy they barely knew to get the approval of their fathers.

"And you," I said to Bleddyn. "You are sexy and smart, funny and earnest, honorable and good. I've never met a man like you before, and everything you do, everything you *are* makes me fall more deeply in love with you. I can't even imagine my life without you in it anymore."

Bleddyn kissed me deeply, intensely, till I could barely remember my own name, let alone his. "And you will not ever have to, for I promise you that for as long as I draw breath, I am yours, body, heart, and soul."

I closed my eyes on the tears that threatened to swamp them again, and I waited till I had some semblance of control before opening them again and looking up into Bleddyn's dark eyes. "And for as long as I draw breath, I'm yours, body, heart, and soul."

Bleddyn leaned up and kissed my eyelids, and then the bridge of my nose. "I love you beyond all other definitions of the word," he breathed, and I felt around in the straw for the pot of salve. When I found it, I pressed it into Bleddyn's hand.

"If you love me, then love me," I murmured, gazing into his eyes and smiling.

❖

I awoke some unknowable time later to murky dimness, the sound of heavy rain, and the safety of Bleddyn spooned up behind, his arm around me, one of his knees between my thighs as he breathed slowly in my ear.

A gust of chill air came from somewhere, and both Bleddyn and I shivered. I reached up and pulled the blanket covering us up higher, till it was practically up to our noses. I sleepily patted myself on the back before the implications of *blanket* hit me.

There'd been no blankets anywhere in the barn before Bleddyn and I had fallen asleep, let alone covering us.

Unless Bleddyn had gone to raid Gwenllian's cottage once I'd gone to sleep, there could be no blanket. Which meant that *someone else* had covered us over. Someone had *seen us* like this and not woken us with accusations or recriminations, but had thought only to make certain we were warm.

Who in the hell would—? I thought, coming fully awake for a few moments before my brain supplied the answer. *Who else, idiot? Gwenllian! She's obviously returned.*

And indeed, a tall, dark-grey mare was in the previously empty stall across from the one Bleddyn and I had commandeered.

Yawning, I settled back into the makeshift mattress of shirt-covered hay, and into my lover's arms. I pulled the blanket up just a bit higher and went back to sleep, despite my brain's sluggish reminder that I had come here for answers, not for a literal roll in the hay and a nap after.

Answers could wait a little while longer. Who knew how long this peace Bleddyn and I had found in each other's arms would last?

When I woke up later, the barn was much dimmer, and there was no patter of rain. All I could hear was the breathing and grunts of the horses and cows.

Bleddyn was clearly awake behind me, thrusting his cock against my ass, one hand between my legs, stroking me off. At some point, he'd hogged the blanket, and I was only barely covered. I shivered from more than just the chill, and I moaned happily. Bleddyn nuzzled my ear and bit the lobe.

"Are you chilled, my love?" he murmured, and I pushed back against him.

"A little. Warm me up?"

Not needing to be asked twice, Bleddyn was already lifting my leg, stroking down my inner thigh as he lined himself up and brushed my hole with the tip of his cock. I moaned again and held my leg up higher, wanting him to have all the access he needed. He kissed his way down my neck, to my shoulder as he slowly guided himself into me.

"*Fy ngoleuni,* oh, *fy ngoleuni…* I wish…"

"What is it you wish?" I gasped out as he filled every inch of me and then some. Despite being pretty slick from earlier, it still burned in the best way.

When Bleddyn could go no farther, when I could've sworn I felt cock nudging my right lung, he exhaled and squeezed me to him. "I wish to be with you like this *forever*," he sighed, running his hand up and down my chest. I smiled and clenched every muscle I could around him, till he groaned and began to pull out a little, only to thrust back in as if trying to get as deep as he could, then deeper still.

"You have me whenever you want, however you want, for as long as you want, Bleddyn."

"Say it again, Krishnan, for never have words sounded sweeter."

I gasped as he began to stroke once more, slow and tight, swiping the head occasionally with his thumb, sliding in pre-come and toying with the slit. For a minute, I was beyond words, fighting not to come. Then I said what Bleddyn wanted as he teased me.

"You have me whenever you want me. However you want me. For as long as you want me."

"Always. In every way. Forever," Bleddyn whispered, biting my ear lobe again as he pulled out but for the very tip of his cock, then drove back in like a battering ram, causing me to wail. Then he did it again. And again. And again. His hand on my cock provided a teasing, agonizingly perfect counterpoint to his powerful thrusts.

When he hit my prostate, I hit a high note I've never hit before. It was damn near operatic.

"There?" Bleddyn asked, stilling in me for a few moments and undulating his hips as the head of his cock put pressure on my prostate. I nodded a frantic affirmative.

"*Right* there," I managed to say, clenching around him and pushing back against him. Bleddyn pulled out a little and drove in hard again at that exact angle, once more tearing that high note from my throat. And he kept doing it, till I was voiceless and senseless, a needy pleasure machine working toward an orgasm that felt like it'd obliterate me. But I was beyond caring. All I knew was the sheer perfection of Bleddyn on me and in me and around me, his voice murmuring endearments or filth in Welsh.

Finally, Bleddyn stopped stroking me to take my balls, squeezing and tugging on them before drifting farther back and pinching the thin strip of skin behind them. He pinched and pulled and twisted, and I actually began sobbing as I started to come in burning pulses.

Bleddyn began groaning, his thrusts losing rhythm but not power, until he thrusted once, twice, a third time, *hard*, and stilled inside me before he came, shouting my name. I could feel each heated throb as he filled me with his thick, lava-hot release, and that kicked my own climax into overdrive. Fireworks went off behind my closed eyes until even they were whited out by pleasure so intense, it bordered on pain.

And that was all I knew for a while.

When sense returned to me, Bleddyn was holding me tight, still thrusting his half-hard cock slowly and gently into my spent body, one hand stroking my abdomen, smearing my come all over my torso. I had no doubt that I looked like a hot mess, and I couldn't have been happier. I sighed contentedly, then started giggling.

"And what amuses you so, *fy ngoleuni?*" Bleddyn asked, nuzzling my hair and kissing the back of my head.

"Nothing, I just love that you're like the Energizer Bunny. You just keep going and going and going." I giggled again, looking over my shoulder just in time to get a lazy, but thorough kiss.

"Never have I desired another the way I desire you. You are a fever in my flesh and blood. I cannot have enough of you. I will *never* have enough of you."

"Mmm, I feel the same way." I stretched a little and clenched my sore ass muscles around Bleddyn till he groaned and his lazy thrusts turned a bit more ambitious. He tightened his right arm around me and he pulled me close. I put my hand back on his slowly pistoning hip and hitched myself back onto him, closer to him.

"When I'm with you—at all times, but especially when I lay with you—I feel as if we are *dau hanner o un cyfan*…two halves of the same whole," Bleddyn whispered, his words tremoring slightly. He linked our fingers together and squeezed tight, bringing our hands forward till they rested over my heart. "I cannot now remember what it is not to love you or be able to touch you. I feel as if I have always loved you and was simply waiting to know it. Waiting to find you."

"And you did. You not only *found* me, you *saved* me. In more ways than I can say." I leaned my head back on his shoulder and he kissed me tenderly, so sweetly, I whimpered and tears leaked from my eyes. My over-sensitized body was shivering and shaking from the echoes of my last climax and the precursors of the one Bleddyn was working it toward.

We rocked together, back and forth, until Bleddyn rolled us over so that he was on top of me. The prickliness of the hay through and around the askew shirts we were laying on didn't even bother me. All that mattered was his body on mine, in mine, and surrounding mine. Anchoring me to Earth lest sheer joy send me spiraling up into the sky, never to return.

"*Rwy'n caru i ti, Krish,*" he breathed in my ear, hot and fervid, as he drove his cock deep into me. I let out a desperate yell as he hit my prostate hard and my pleasure-saturated body *really* began to shudder and shimmy. "*I love you. But I have not the words in Cymraeg or English to wield the feeling...to tell you just how much I love you.*"

I closed my eyes and lost myself in his words. In the juggernaut-pleasure bearing down on me. In the feeling that at last, I was safe and loved, body, heart, and soul.

❖

The sky was truly darkening by the time we emerged hand in hand from the barn and made our way to the widow's cottage door.

Before Bleddyn could knock, I stepped in front of him and straightened his rumpled shirt as best I could, picking off a persistent piece of hay.

"What, I wonder, will she say?" he asked, a trifle chagrined. I smiled, leaning in to kiss the tip of his nose.

"I think that'll depend on what we ask." Bleddyn's eyebrows rose, and I laughed. "C'mon, Butch, let's do this before we wind up having sex on her doorstep."

"I would never!" Bleddyn said, sounding affronted and appalled.

I grinned and leaned close again. "You're saying that if I got on my knees right now and worshiped your amazing, beautiful cock with my warm, wet, willing mouth, you wouldn't let me?"

Bleddyn turned even redder and swallowed. "I—I choose to believe you would not so tempt me on another's doorstep."

"Mm, believe what you like, handsome." I winked and faced the door, raising my hand. Before I could knock, the door opened and our hostess stood smiling in a golden-orange glow of hearth- and lamp-light.

For a moment, my idiot heart thought it was *Dierdre*, and I almost threw myself into her arms and cried, I was so happy to see her. I was so desperate to tell her all that'd happened to me in the past two days. But then my brain reminded me that this was Gwenllian Robert, not Dierdre McConnell.

"Good evening, Master Krishnan, Master Bleddyn," she said, as if two rumpled men who'd just spent the day fucking in her barn turned up on her doorstep every evening. Bleddyn and I exchanged a quick glance, and when I looked back at her she was smiling, as if she'd heard what I was thinking. Then she stepped aside and gestured for us to come in. "Will you come in and sup with me, this evening? For there is much we must talk about, though I gather you must know this, too, else you would not have come all this way to see me."

I exchanged another glance with a still-blushing Bleddyn, and he shrugged as if to say: *It's your safari, Bwana. I'm just following your lead.*

So I took a breath and Bleddyn's hand, and we stepped into the widow of Lake Tynymynydd's cottage.

Chapter Twelve

"I must say, I did not expect either of you to come visiting so soon," Gwenllian said brightly as Bleddyn and I sat at her trestle table. The heat of the fire felt good after a day spent in a drafty barn, despite all the frenzied activity Bleddyn and I had got up to, to keep warm.

"We did not mean to show up unannounced, but we have some questions we hope you may be able to answer," Bleddyn said. At the hearth, Gwenllian was stirring a pot of stew that smelled *heavenly*.

"Yes," she said, glancing over her shoulder with a smile as wry as her tone. "I imagine you do."

Looking into her wise, compassionate eyes, ancient compared to the rest of her, I knew she had answers. If not all of them, then some of them. I looked to Bleddyn, who was watching me thoughtfully. He smiled and made a gesture with his other hand that I should speak.

And suddenly, all my relevant questions flew out of my head. Sitting here, in the comfort of her small cottage, supper at the ready, I could've been bringing my boyfriend over to meet Dierdre, and the familiarity of this tableau disoriented me. So I opened my mouth and said the first thing that came tumbling out of my brain.

"Are you a witch?"

Bleddyn actually facepalmed. I didn't even know that'd been invented before the Age of the Internet. I could see it out of the corner of my eye, and Gwenllian laughed her rich, throaty laugh again.

"I'm a practitioner of the Old Ways, if that's what you're asking. If you define a witch as one who hearkens to the ways of the ancestors, then, yes. I am a witch," she said, still chuckling. Bleddyn, meanwhile, was staring at her, gape-mouthed and goggle-eyed.

"So, are you, like, a Wiccan? I mean, Pagan, I guess?" I asked. Gwenllian hefted the small cauldron and faced the table, and Bleddyn and I. She placed the pot on a flat stone in the center of the table, and I could feel the heat baking off of it. The rich smell, like mutton and vegetables in a savory sauce, grew stronger and my stomach rumbled pitifully.

Gwenllian smiled and put her hands on her hips. "I have many beliefs. Some align with that of the Christian church. Some do not. I do many things of which the Christian doctrine would approve. And I do many things of which it would *not* approve. In that, at least, I am in good company, am I not?"

Bleddyn blanched, then blushed. But I found myself grinning. I *liked* her.

Gwenllian made her way to a small standing cabinet next to the hearth and began retrieving bowls and spoons. She laid them out in front of Bleddyn and me, and set a place for herself on the other side of the trestle table right in front of the hearth.

While she was busy serving the stew and fresh bread she magicked up from somewhere, I looked around her cottage. It was tiny but nonetheless spacious and tidy. Beyond the trestle table and benches there wasn't much to see: a chair to the side of the hearth opposite the cabinet and, in the far corners, a bed and a garderobe. I'd expected the floor to be packed earth, but it was wooden and spotless, despite the rain. Bleddyn and I hadn't tracked much in the way of mud, thanks to the paving stones leading up to the cottage.

Lanterns and candles were everywhere. Gwenllian liked her light. This reminded me of Dierdre, for Dierdre was the polar opposite. She never tolerated more light than absolutely necessary. She was like a bat, could practically see in the dark. John was forever complaining about there never being enough light to see by when she was home.

Sighing, I looked back at Gwenllian to find her sitting across from me, watching me. Her gaze was sympathetic. "You miss your kith and kin," she surmised. I swallowed and nodded.

"I do," I admitted, reaching over and squeezing Bleddyn's hand. "But I've found something here worth missing my friends for."

She nodded, her gaze traveling between Bleddyn and I. "The love you share shines like a beacon for the eyes that would see, like a lighthouse across the darkest, most troubled seas. Neither tide nor time could keep you apart longer than it took for the two of you to call out for each other, and in calling out, find each other."

Bleddyn and I looked at each other, wide-eyed. "So Bleddyn *is* the reason I came back in time?"

"Yes."

"I told you I'd tell you, someday," I said to Bleddyn as his eyes widened. "I mean, it was just a guess, but it felt right. That you were the reason I came back."

Shaking his head, Bleddyn's frowned. "If that is so, how did you manage to travel backwards in time to come to me? How did you even know there was a Bleddyn to come back to?"

I shrugged and looked at Gwenllian, who was dipping a piece of bread into her stew. Bleddyn followed my gaze and together we waited for the answer to the most important question either of us would ever ask.

Gwenllian took a bite of her bread and chewed before answering. "He didn't know. At least not on the top of his waking mind. But he knew in his heart. In his soul." She frowned a little. "But it wasn't Master Krishnan's will that pulled him back in time, Bleddyn, nor his need. At least, it was not only his need. It was also yours."

"*My* need?" Bleddyn asked, startled. "But I have no talent for such dire arts and feats of magic, *Gweddw*. How could *I* have pulled Krish to me from his own time?"

Now, Gwenllian sighed and put her spoon down. "Tell me, Master Bleddyn, what remember you about the day you found me near death? For in that tale lies the beginning of the answers you both seek."

Looking surprised and wary, Bleddyn squeezed my hand and sighed. "I recall everything, *Gweddw*."

"On that day, as I lay too weak to even tend my hearth and keep myself warmed, my husband dead in our bed for days while I lay insensate nearby, you appeared as a guardian angel and saved me from a certain death due to starvation and the lees of my illness."

Bleddyn shook his head. "I was no guardian angel, *Gweddw* Robert. Merely a man sent on a mission by his lord. I did what any would have done in my stead," he said, looking down at his untouched stew and my hand held tight in his.

"I would hear that tale, if you're up for telling it," I said, and Bleddyn looked at me in surprise. I smiled and scooted closer to him along the bench till our thighs were touching. I figured Gwenllian wouldn't mind, and Bleddyn seemed like he might need that contact.

"I, too, would hear the tale," Gwenllian added, "for my memory of that time is scattered and imprecise. I, too, have questions about that day that could do with a spot of answering."

His gaze touching first on Gwenllian then on me, Bleddyn finally sighed again. "It began," he started slowly, somewhat gruffly. "With my father coming to find me while I was at practice with swordplay. He sent me on a small mission on behalf of Lord John to find Eirian Robert, who had not been attending his duties for some days.

"So, I set out at mid-morning, shortly after my father told me what was needed. I rode through Gwydir Forest without incident, till at last I came upon Lake Tynymynydd, and the cottage thereon, from which came no chimney smoke and no signs of life. "

❖

Bleddyn ap Rhys dismounted from his horse, Arwel, and made his way up the clean, smooth path to the door of Eirian's cottage. He raised his hand to knock. No sound came from within, and his knock echoed emptily. Bleddyn frowned and knocked again. "Eirian? It is Lord John's man, Bleddyn ap Rhys! I must speak with you!"

No answer but the echoing of Bleddyn's words and knocking.

Bleddyn put his hand on the latch and pushed it down. With a small creak, the door opened, and immediately let out a smell that Bleddyn recognized, even though he was thankfully not as familiar with it as some.

The smell of death.

He blinked as his eyes adjusted to the dim, near lightless cottage. The first thing he could see and recognize was a body lying limply near the hearth. From its attire of calico dress and apron, it was, beyond all doubt, Gwenllian Robert.

Upon entering the miasma of death and decay, Bleddyn left the door open, and used the collar of his surcoat to cover his nose. Once he began moving toward the back of the small, one-room cottage, the smell grew so strong even the surcoat was no help. But by then, Bleddyn had spotted the bed, and the body which lay on it.

Eirian ap Robert. Dead. Long dead.

And it didn't take more than a moment of wondering to figure out what had happened at this bloodless scene with nothing apparent having been taken. Gwenllian Robert, being on the front lines of the horrible malady which had befallen the town this winter, had finally succumbed to the illness herself. Eirian had done the same.

Bleddyn bowd his head for the soul of this good man and his wife and began to pray. Eirian had been a fine man, and his wife had been a caring, kind, and selfless woman even though she had a strange, off-putting way. But before he was even a third of the way through his heartfelt prayer, he heard a feeble moaning coming from near the hearth, and Gwenllian Robert's poor body.

"Eirian..." she moaned in a faint, cracking voice. Bleddyn gasped, despite the smell, tuning to face the hearth and freezing.

Gwenllian Robert was moving. Barely, but moving. After the initial moment of shock, Bleddyn hurried to Gwenllian's side, kneeling next to her and brushing, lank dark hair from her face. Her skin was snow-white but for hectic red spots at each cheek, her lips were dry and cracked, and the tongue that came out to swipe them more grey than pink. Her eyes, normally a vibrant and canny green, were unfocused and bloodshot.

"Eirian," she sighed, her broken heart in her broken voice. "Don't leave me."

"Hush, now," Bleddyn said, squeezing her hand. It was small and clammy in his own, and she did not squeeze back. "It is Lord John's man, Bleddyn ap Rhys."

Gwenllian Robert blinked several times as if trying to focus her eyes, then squinted. "Bleddyn?"

"Yes."

"Where," she began, then coughed weakly, closing her eyes. "Where is Eirian?"

Bleddyn swallowed and looked away. "He is dead, Goody Robert. Of the sickness. My sincerest condolences for your loss."

She opened her tired green eyes, shimmering with tears of confusion and incomprehension. "But I just now saw him," she croaked, the tears leaking out and down her pale face. "He was hale and—and beautiful. Surrounded by light. And my mother was there, also, and my grandmother. They were all so happy and so young."

She moaned, closing her eyes again, and Bleddyn said nothing. According to Gwenllian Robert, herself, when first she'd arrived at Gwydir castle, her family was all years-dead.

Shaking his head, he let go of the weeping woman's limp hand and stood. The first thing that needed to happen, he knew, was that she needed to be put to bed. A warm bed. And she needed it immediately.

"I will return," Bleddyn told the grieving widow, and he stepped over her toward the small stack of wood and tinder near the hearth. The pile was small, but it would ward off the pervasive chill of the cottage. As he stacked the wood in the dead fireplace, he tried not to think about his next task.

Moving Eirian Robert's body outside.

A silence fell when Bleddyn stopped speaking. With tears in her vivid green eyes, Gwenllian reached out and covered Bleddyn's free hand.

"Thank you," she said softly. Bleddyn looked up from his contemplation of our hands. His surprise was easy to read, and Gwenllian smiled. "For saving my life. For I surely would have followed my Eirian to the next life were it not for you."

Bleddyn frowned. "I only did what any would do in my stead. Verily, it was nothing more than I owed you for caring for me during *my* illness. You and Gwynedd saved my life. In truth, only half the debt I owe has been repaid," he said, and I squeezed his hand. When he looked at me, I raised our hands and kissed them.

"I am only sorry that I did not arrive days earlier, that I might have saved him, too," Bleddyn said.

Gwenllian sighed. "That is a guilt and regret we both share, for I fell ill while caring for Eirian, and had I not succumbed to illness, he might still be alive," she whispered, wiping her eyes.

I looked from her to Bleddyn and back, incredulous. "It's not your fault. *Either* of you," I said, and they both turned miserable gazes to me. I blushed but went on. "Listen, sometimes bad things happen to good people. Sometimes, the, er, Lord works in mysterious ways. It was Eirian's time to go. Nothing either of you could have done would have changed that. I don't know much about your god, Bleddyn, or about yours, Gwenllian, but I do know that they supposedly have a plan, isn't that right?" They both glanced at each other warily and nodded. "Then Eirian's death was a part of that plan. A terrible part—a *sad* part—but a part, nonetheless. No amount of healing or rescuing would have changed that."

I held out my hand to Gwenllian, and the three of us sat holding hands and sneaking glances at each other. Finally, Gwenllian squeezed both my hand and Bleddyn's before letting go and standing up. She took her empty bowl to a large wash basin set on a stool. "I thank you, as well, Master Krishnan."

"Please, it's just *Krish*. And whatever for?" I asked, confused.

"For reminding me that I do not always have control over life and death. That sometimes, those things fall outside my purview." Gwenllian looked over at me with an intense, tear-filled gaze. "Sometimes I forget that such things are, in the end, out of my hands and given over to a will greater than my own."

"Aye," Bleddyn agreed pensively. Gwenllian shifted her gaze to him, and she smiled wryly. "And you, Master Bleddyn, like me, must remember that matters of love also often fall outside of our sphere of control. Do you take my meaning?"

Bleddyn looked at me and nodded. "I do, *Gweddw*."

"Good. Now." Gwenllian came back to the table and sat. "Allow *me* tell you *both* a story. Once upon a time," she began, "there was a brave and true young squire who lived and worked in the service of a just and kind lord. One day, this squire came upon a deathly ill woman and her husband, who'd been laying for many days in their cottage. The squire could do nothing for the woman's husband, for he had been dead for several days. His wife was to shortly join him but for the tender care of the squire, who nursed her until she was well enough for him to venture out.

"He found another goodwife with healing hands to come to care for her. And when he was certain the ill woman was responding to the goodwife's gentle care, he returned to his lord's service and his duties without accepting a word of thanks, saying only that he had done his duty, and that if the situation had been reversed, the woman and her husband would have done the same for him and his kin."

Gwenllian paused and frowned down at the pot, which still steamed gently on the table.

"It was many weeks before the woman was strong enough to properly grieve for her husband. She had never been sick once in her life, but this illness seemed bound and determined to make up for lost time. But once her enervation had passed enough for her to pay a visit to the castle where the good lord lived, she rode her late husband's horse there early one morning, bearing a small token of thanks to present to the young squire.

"He agreed to see her, though he was apprehensive. And the woman could see on the squire's face that he also bore the guilt of not having done enough or come soon enough to save an innocent life.

"It so touched her heart that she forgot the small token of her thanks and asked him, 'If you could be granted one boon, and one boon only—if you could be granted the thing you desire most, what would you have?'

"The young squire frowned, puzzlement showing plainly on his austere face. 'A boon?' he asked quietly. 'Such as money or fine things?'

"Smiling, the woman tilted her head and regarded him before speaking. 'If,' she answered, 'that is what you desire most, from the bottom of your heart.'

"And as she spoke, the squire's face lost the guilt it had worn and reflected. Instead, he took on a heavier and deeper burden. Mixed with a yearning so great and terrible, it hurt the woman's heart. She had known this feeling for many weeks. The feeling of having lost what one has loved most, to circumstances one could not control.

"The squire looked away from her for a brief time, perhaps composing himself before replying. When he spoke, his voice was hard, but underneath that hardness was desperation and grief as plain as daylight.

"'What boon would I have, if I could have what I desire most?' he asked himself aloud. Then he smiled before looking at the woman again and saying that, if he could have any boon, it would be to 'be rid of my abiding affliction.'

"'I see,' the woman murmured, staring not only at the squire, but *into* him. And much she saw there. Much, indeed. 'And what affliction would that be?'

"And the squire opened his mouth to answer, but he didn't. He looked around at the busy front hall and back at the woman.

"He informed her that now was neither the time nor the place to speak of such things. Nor was she his father-confessor, to lift from him the burden of his own 'sinful doings and yearnings.' And his face turned as hard as his voice, so that the woman could no longer divine what he was feeling.

"'I thank you for your visit, *Gweddw*,' he said, 'but I must return to my duties.'

"And he would have turned and walked away, then, but for the woman's hand on his arm, light, yet entreating.

"'I will do my best to aide you in getting whatsoever or *who*soever it is you *truly* desire, Bleddyn ap Rhys. This I swear on my honor and on my late, beloved husband.'

"The squire shook his head once. 'You cannot. You *should* not, *Gweddw*.'

"'And why should I not if, indeed, I can?'

"The squire shook his head. The boon he would have had would be sinful and wrong. It would lead to nothing good.

"'And how do you know this?' The woman demanded.

"The squire shook his head again. "'Because it has *already has* led to nothing good!'

"The woman took her hand away from the squire's arm. 'Love, if that is what you desire, ultimately leads us to good things. It may take time, but love always leads us a-right, if felt truly and unconditionally.' She stepped closer to the squire and spoke so quietly, none could have heard them. 'And did you? Love truly and unconditionally?'

"The squire blinked, and he had tears in his eyes. But he blinked again and they were gone. He squared his shoulders and looked the woman in the eyes. 'I did,' he said. And the woman nodded.

"'You have my word then, Bleddyn ap Rhys, that you will have the deepest desire of your heart. I cannot promise when, but I can promise that you will. Even if it takes my life to accomplish, I will devote nothing less to repayment of my debt.'

"The squire shook his head. 'Art thou a witch?' he asked, clearly torn between intrigue and horror. "'For I will have no part in any devilment,' he went on to say in a low, fearful voice. At this, the woman smiled and inclined her head respectfully.

"'No devilment, you have my word. And I must have your word that you will continue to hold in your heart that love you feel, even though it pains you to do so. Hold on to that love and hope. For someday, that which you desire so strongly and passionately—'"

"—will come back to you," Bleddyn finished with Gwenllian, both their gazes drifting to me. I merely sat there as they stared, Gwenllian with no small amount of pride and Bleddyn with no small amount of confusion.

"So, your heart's desire was for a bitchy, time-traveling, Indian guy from four hundred years in the future and five thousand miles away to come keep you company?" I quipped. Bleddyn raised his eyebrows.

"Not quite." He blushed and looked down, frowning. "I had thought my heart's desire so clear, so certain. And yet—"

"And yet?" I asked, frowning myself. "What was your heart's desire?"

Bleddyn looked up at me but didn't answer. But then, he didn't need to. Of course, he didn't. Who else would be his heart's desire, but William? And since William had been Bleddyn's first, I didn't even have the right to be jealous. Nor should I have been. Not of a ghost.

But *should* and *would* were two different beasts, entirely.

"I'm sorry you didn't get him back," I said, and I meant it. I couldn't imagine losing Bleddyn, then, being presented with a placeholder years later. My heart would rail against such a thing. Even if I found myself growing fond of the substitute, I would always wonder about the love I'd lost.

Bleddyn lifted my hand and laced our fingers together, searching my eyes. "I, for the first time in so many years, am *not*," Bleddyn said, and when my jaw dropped, he smiled. "I loved William dearly. And I always will. But that time in my life is over. The time for William and I to be together is over. And that was, as you said, a part of God's plan that I had no control over. It is true that in my heart, I've always wished for William back. But the good Lord, in his infinite wisdom, has sent me the second treasure of my life. Many people do not see even once in their lives, a love like that which I have felt twice, now. I could have spent the rest of my life mourning William and what I lost. But instead, thanks to the grace of God—and His divine inspiration of Gwenllian Robert, and her part in this—I will choose to spend the rest of my life thanking Him for and taking care of what I now have."

I shook my head, looking down to hide the tears that had sprung up in my eyes. "You don't have to say that. Not if you don't mean it. Not if who you've really been wanting is William."

Bleddyn caught my chin and tilted it up till I was looking him in the eyes. They were shining and slightly red.

"All that I want," he whispered, "is *you*."

"But William—"

"Will always have a place in my heart. But he's my past, now. And you, *you, ngoleuni fy nghalon,* are my present and my future. I love you, Krish. I beg of you to never doubt this, above all else."

I turned my face away and blushed as I saw Gwenllian watching us out of the corner of my eye. I wondered what she must have thought of us, hashing this out in front of her like she wasn't even there. But even that only danced briefly across the surface of my mind. The matters at hand, such as the tenancy of Bleddyn's heart, took precedence. "I don't know if I can," I admitted, sighing heavily.

Bleddyn turned my head back firmly but gently, till we were looking into each other's eyes again. He was smiling a little, once more. "Then it is fortuitous, is it not, my love, that I have the rest of our lives to prove to you that I'm sincere in my plight?"

My jaw dropped again, and I didn't know what to say. I certainly hadn't expected what, in my time, would have been a proposal of marriage. Or at least the pledging of a lifetime to be spent together. "Bleddyn, I…"

"Yes, you *are*. You're everything I have wished for in my heart. Everything I desire. Everything I need. *Rwy'n caru thi*. I love you." Bleddyn's smile was full now, and he leaned in to kiss me, never minding that we weren't alone. When his mouth touched mine, I whimpered, parting my lips to give him access. And as he kissed me and pressed his body against my own, I found that my fears didn't vanish as much as they quieted down. I could accept that Bleddyn loved me, and that having his heart's desire loosely translated into me wasn't going to be keeping him up nights. At least not in a bad way.

But then my other questions came rushing back as Bleddyn kissed me. Questions about the mechanics of time travel, and the mysterious fog I'd stumbled through. Questions of why *then*. Why had the magic spell or whatever chosen *that moment* to suck me back to 1626? Was it simply because I'd been in Wales at that time? What would've happened if I hadn't been? Would it have sucked back any old shmoe to be with Bleddyn? Or was it destined to be *me*? If so, why? What was it that drew Bleddyn's soul and mine together?

Was there any chance that I'd be sucked back to my own time, the next time it got foggy out? Indeed, was there *any* chance I *could* go back? Any way I could summon the fog that had brought me here, just in case things went south with Bleddyn in a way that couldn't be fixed?

All these questions and more weighed heavily on my mind until Bleddyn wrapped his arms around me and pulled me close, breaking the kiss just enough to murmur, "I love you, *ngoleuni fy nghalon*."

This time, the kiss did the trick. The questions receded to the back of my mind where they were shelved but not forgotten. Eventually Bleddyn and I would have to come up for air, and when we did, I now had an entire arsenal of questions for the Widow Robert.

And I meant to have my answers, no matter what they were.

Chapter Thirteen

I don't know for how long we'd kissed for, but the pot was gone when we were done. Gwenllian stood at her open front door, looking out into the fast-approaching night.

"I love you," Bleddyn whispered. "I've been remiss up to this point in showing you proof of that love, but no more."

"You haven't been remiss," I said, reaching up to hold his face in my hand. I leaned back to look into his somber eyes and smiled. "You've just had a lot on your plate to deal with. And no matter what Fate has planned for us, we only just met seventy-two hours ago. I'm a lot to get used to in three days. Even if you love me, I can be difficult."

Bleddyn returned my smile. "You are a marvel of sweetness and kindness. Of *goodness*. And your heart is the bravest, most open heart I've ever known. And I want you to know that from this moment on, I shall try to be more worthy of it."

"Oh, Bleddyn," I laughed a little, embarrassed he seemed to think so well of me, when he didn't know the half of what was *wrong* with me. "There's a reason I was still single back in my time. *I'm* the one who has to be more worthy. And more patient, more understanding, more trusting, *less* precipitous, less sarcastic and spiteful—"

"You are none of the latter to me, *ngoleuni* fy *nghalon*, and all of the former." Bleddyn bussed my lips tenderly. "You are my sweet and lovely Krishnan of Nayar. And nothing will ever change that."

I sniffled and wiped a tear from my face. "And you're my honorable, strong, brave, good-hearted squire," I said around a throat full of tears, stroking his cheek with my thumb and letting myself fall into his dark, dark eyes. "I don't ever want to take you or what we have for granted. I *won't*," I promised him and myself. And with that promise came all my shelved questions, my *fears* about what might happen should Fate decide it had made a mistake after all. Could I truly be whisked back to my own time the next time it got foggy?

Forsaking the comfort and wonder that was Bleddyn's gaze, I looked over his shoulder, to Gwenllian. "Gwenllian?" When she looked in at me, I smiled sheepishly. "Sorry about making out in front of you. Sometimes, it's easy for me to get lost in Bleddyn."

"And I, you, Krish," Bleddyn agreed, leaning into my touch and kissing the pad of my thumb.

Gwenllian's smile was gentle and understanding. "No apologies are necessary. I, too, have lost myself in love at strange moments. And not so strange ones. Eirian and I were an absolute scandal at our wedding."

"So I recall," Bleddyn murmured with a chuckle, and I smiled. I was glad that Gwenllian had had someone to love, even for a short time, who'd loved her back enough to make them both scandalous at their own wedding.

Then I shivered as a chill breeze swept 'round the cottage. Gwenllian noticed and stepped back inside, closing the door. A moment later, she was sitting at the table across from Bleddyn and me.

"I take it you're ready to ask those questions to which I might have answers?" She asked almost playfully, and I swallowed, nodding.

"I'm as ready as I'll ever be." I glanced at Bleddyn once more, and he smiled encouragingly, kissing my palm again and taking my hand in his.

"Is there any chance I could be swept back to my own time?" I ventured. "I know that when I came here, there was a strange fog springing up all around me. Could that happen again any time it gets foggy? I know, it's a stupid question, but—"

"*Any* question is a good question when one doesn't know the answer, Krish," Gwenllian said. "And to answer yours, the only way you might—and I say *might*—be sent back to your own time is...well, let us simply say that it is love and desire and need that keeps you here, and only its absence will send you back."

Bleddyn and I looked at each other, wide-eyed.

"So, you're saying Fate won't just up and send me back to the future alone? It *can't*?"

Gwenllian grimaced. "Far be it from me to tell Fate what it can and cannot do. I have learned a difficult lesson regarding that very subject. But I *will* say that Fate seems to have left that decision in yours and Bleddyn's hands. What holds you here, Krish, is each other. Nothing more, nothing less. Should either or both of your feelings change…"

I sighed. "Then I might get catapulted back to my own time."

"Indeed."

Shaking my head, I let Bleddyn pull me into his strong, comforting arms. "Why me, specifically? Are Bleddyn and I soulmates?"

"*Soulmates*?" Gwenllian blinked and her brows drew together in consideration.

"You know, two souls mated throughout their different lives because they're meant to be together." I made myself small in Bleddyn's arms for a few moments just because it felt good, and because I could. "Is that why we're falling in love so hard, so fast? I mean, we've been pretty much glued together since twelve hours after we met."

And remembering how that twelfth hour had been spent, I blushed. Gwenllian nodded. "*Soulmates*," she said softly, then laughed. "I *like* that term! And it's quite apt at describing what I see when I see the two of you together. As you *should* be. Your souls have always been two sides of the same coin. They always will be. Nothing can truly tear you asunder, unless you let it. *Nothing*, do you understand?"

I looked up at Bleddyn, and he looked down at me. I thought of Rhys and what he would have to say about Bleddyn's new outlook on me. And Bleddyn probably thought of the same thing.

"We understand, *Gweddw*," Bleddyn answered for us both, kissing my forehead. His beard and mustache tickled and I giggled.

"We do," I concurred, smiling at Gwenllian. "I have a few more questions, though. Questions about where my soul is now. I mean, surely my soul must've existed in this time. I don't know if you know what reincarnation is, but in my religion, we believe souls don't just live once. They live different lives over and over again until they reach a state of perfection. But throughout the lives they live, they become stronger, better, more of what they were meant to be. Sometimes, they become weaker and farther from what they were meant to be. But Hindus don't believe that there's one Heaven everyone goes to after merely one lifetime on Earth. We believe many lifetimes must be lived before perfection is reached. So that makes me wonder where and who is my soul, right now?"

Gwenllian looked a bit confused but spread her hands as if to present me with an answer. "It is right here, and right now. It is *you*."

"No, I get that, but what I mean is—" I shook my head, trying to think of a better way to explain reincarnation to a seventeenth century Welsh witch. "If time is a like a straight line," I began, and Gwenllian's face changed from confused to amused.

"And who says that it is?"

Now I was the one to blink. "Uh…"

"Time is a difficult concept to master, even, so I see, for one from four hundred years in the future," she said. "Let it suffice to say that time is *not* a straight line. Time is a curve with no beginning and no end. And we, as souls, do not merely live lives at different points on the curve. We *are* the curve. We exist at every point along it simultaneously. Your soul, Krish, is everywhere at once, but *your* consciousness, what makes you *Krish*, is focused heavily on *this* point. On this *now*. *You are* the you of this time because you are *here*. And when you're in your own time, you are the you of that time, as well." Gwenllian paused, catching the looks of pure confusion on our faces. Then she smiled and sighed.

"There aren't two of your soul wandering around in this now, Krish. You are one soul that stretches along the curve of time, and *many* consciousnesses living at different points on that curve, whose focus is always the here and now you are currently experiencing." She looked between Bleddyn and me, and then she threw up her hands a little, laughing. "I've lost you."

"But not by much," I lied, taking a bite of my heretofore untouched stew.

It really *was* delicious.

"Think of time as a stew!" Gwenllian said suddenly, as a light bulb went on above her head. Bleddyn and I exchanged another glance, shrugged, and settled in to be lost once more.

❖

"And you're both quite welcome to come visit me after church, tomorrow," Gwenllian said as the three of us stood at her door. "Whether it's to ask more questions or simply to pay a lonely widow a visit," she added with a quirky smile.

I glanced at Bleddyn who nodded and smiled, squeezing my hand. Grinning, I turned back to Gwenllian and stuck out my free hand. She looked at it, then made a shooing motion and pulled me into a hug. A big one.

Startled, I nonetheless hugged her, holding back tears. It was like hugging Dierdre, who I supposed I'd never see again.

When we let go, Gwenllian turned to Bleddyn, as if trying to gauge whether or not a hug would be welcome. After a few awkward seconds, I realized neither of them would be making the first move. I elbowed Bleddyn in the side, garnering a stern glance and a muffled jingle for my efforts.

"Er, thank you, *Gweddw* Robert," Bleddyn said almost dourly, opening his arms and stepping toward her. Gwenllian's smile returned and she hugged him—more a brief squeeze than a hug. But it was good enough in my non-exacting book.

"Thank *you* for keeping an open mind, Master Bleddyn."

"It is simply *Bleddyn, Gweddw.*"

Gwenllian grinned. "And I am simply *Gwenllian.*"

Bleddyn almost smiled. "I will remember that in future."

I got the warm-fuzzies, something I almost never got, at least not *this* side of twenty.

After a few more pleasantries and promises to come visit on the morrow, Bleddyn and I went across the yard to the barn, where our horses waited.

"Tell me what you are thinking," Bleddyn murmured as we stepped inside. I smiled over at him and leaned on his arm for a moment.

"Just thinking about time, and how it's all happening *now*," I said, laughing a little. "Wondering what my friends are doing. If they're looking for me. If they've told my mother I've turned up missing." I sighed as we stopped in front of Arwel, who whickered a greeting to his master. Bleddyn patted the horse's nose and smiled.

Men and their horses, I thought with a grin. Then I held the lamp up so Bleddyn could saddle him.

"They may, indeed, be quite worried for you," Bleddyn mused as his fingers flew quickly and automatically over straps and buckles. "I am sorry that your journey here will have caused them consternation and grief, but I am also selfishly glad that you're here with me."

I kissed Bleddyn gently, till he slipped his large, work-roughened hands under my shirt to sweep up and down my chilly back.

"I'm glad I'm here with you, too," I said. "If I had to do it over, I would make the same choices that led me here. I'm certain I always have and I always will," I whispered as Bleddyn kissed his way south to my throat and neck. I set the lamp on the top right wall of Arwel's stall and wrapped my arms around Bleddyn's neck as he kissed and nibbled and licked the hollow junction between my neck and my shoulder.

"The scent and feel of your skin undoes me every time," he murmured, one hand making its way past the small of my back, down my borrowed breeches, gripping my right cheek possessively. I lifted my left leg, wrapping it around his right, and chuckled as his hard cock made contact with mine through our clothes. "I'm probably in dire need of a bath." I said dryly, and then moaned as Bleddyn rubbed the tip of his callused finger insistently at my sore and still pretty sensitized asshole, without pushing in.

"You smell so *good*." Bleddyn exhaled on my shoulder, then inhaled deeply after turning his face back to the crook of my neck. "Like spring and autumn combined, of new grass and wood smoke and nutmeg."

I blushed. "It *must* be love," I joked, but I held him tighter. Bleddyn took that as his cue to run his hands down the backs of my thighs and lift me up, all with an ease that left me gasping and laughing and horny as hell.

He carried me back to the empty stall where we'd had our last assignation and laid me down gently on the blanket Gwenllian had covered us with. Then he gazed down at me hungrily as he undid his mail shirt and removed it along with his undershirt. Next came his breeches and hose which he simply pushed down. In the feeble light coming from the distant lamp, I could see he was as stiff as a flagpole in winter. But he also looked solemn and slightly dangerous, what with all the shadows. I shivered, nearly swept out to sea with wanting him. In me, on me, around me, just so long as I could hold him and be with him.

"Are you chilled, *ngoleuni fy nghalon?*" he asked quietly, and I held my arms open.

"Yes," I said. "Come warm me up."

By the time we arrived back at the road, it was full dark, and the stars and moon were out.

The lamp Gwenllian had lent us helped with navigating our way back, however. Bleddyn and I both rode Arwel, leading my erstwhile horse behind him. It was quite chilly out—springtime in Wales, I suppose—but I barely noticed for Bleddyn's arms around me and his body pressed against my back.

Once we arrived at the castle, Bleddyn stabled our horses while I watched him, and maybe grabbed his ass a few times, causing him to chuckle and blush. Then, when he was done, he caught me in his arms and kissed me passionately till my knees were weak. Not that it took much.

"What *is* it with you and stables?" I asked when he let me up for a quick breather. He was hard again and had been for most of the ride back. "I'm beginning to think this is a fetish, it gets you going so fast."

"Fetish?"

"Never mind. Just take me to bed—preferably *not* here—and fuck me unconscious."

Bleddyn groaned, clenching his hands tight on my waist. "I would ravish you till the sun makes its first foray across the sky, *llawenydd o fy mywyd* but first, I must report to my father and you, I think, may want to speak with Lord Owen about his father's most generous offer."

Now, I was the one to groan, though I really wanted to preen after being called the joy of his life. "Baby," I whined, "can't those wait till after you've ravished me all night?"

Bleddyn leaned his forehead against mine. "I promise I'll not be long."

"Promise? Already broken," I murmured, insinuating a hand between us so I could stroke his cock through his clothes. Bleddyn hissed, and one of his big hands went from my waist, around to my ass, to knead and squeeze and hold me tighter against him.

"My lovely, wanton Krish," he breathed, kissing me teasingly, briefly. "Sooner begun is sooner done."

I sighed and wrapped my arms around Bleddyn's neck, looking into his solemn but heated eyes. "And will you still feel like ravishing me after reporting to Rhys?" I asked hesitantly.

Bleddyn frowned, pursing his lips slightly. "I will never *not* want to ravish you, Krish. Simply to see you is to desire you with a fierce and burning lust that makes even the merest thought all but impossible. My father has long known how to upset me quickest. He is as well-versed in such matters as he is in matters of battle. But I've made my choice. I will no longer let his poisonous words stand between me and the one I love. Nor will I let such slights as he and Dafydd make against you go unchallenged any longer."

"Slights?" I snorted. "There've been slights? Against *me*? I can only imagine."

Making an apologetic face, Bleddyn kissed the tip of my nose. "Never again will I let such insults pass unaddressed. Such disrespectful slander should not stand."

And I wanted to ask what his father had said about me, even though I already had some idea. Likely the medieval version of fag and probably something a good deal more insulting than catamite. I wanted to know exactly what Rhys thought of me, a perfect stranger, and of his only son.

But I sensed rehashing what had been said would do a great deal more than satisfy my curiosity. It'd hurt *Bleddyn* and make it even tougher for me to get along with Rhys, which was something I'd have to be doing for the foreseeable future.

"You won't start any fights or family feuds over me, will you?" I asked Bleddyn, worried because of the stubborn, determined look on his face. I leaned our foreheads together again. "Promise me you won't say or do anything rash, or that you can't take back. He's your father and your superior. Please be careful with him or things could go really bad for us both."

"You cannot expect me to stand by and let you be slandered with vile accusations and falsehoods!"

"What's that saying you Christians love? The one about turning the other cheek?" I raised my eyebrows, and Bleddyn blushed.

"The things he says of you are not fit for gentle ears, Krish. If you but *knew...*" he shook his head. "It hurts my heart to hear the one whom I love spoken of so."

"I know, baby, I know. It would hurt me to hear someone I loved speak that way of you, too. But for now, this is the way it has to be. And maybe it won't be forever." I tried to smile, but failed when Bleddyn sniffed. "Oh, baby, maybe he'll come around someday. He may never like *me* or that you're sharing your life with another man, but he may come to terms with it. Learn to accept it with better grace than he's shown so far."

Bleddyn shook his head again and swiped at his slightly red eyes quickly. But I could see the shine of tears he held back. "He will never believe anything but the worst of me. And of you, *because* I love you. Nothing I do—nothing I have *ever* done is good enough for him," Bleddyn said, his voice raw and cracking with misery. "Nothing I will *ever* do will be good enough. He will never think well of me or feel proud of me."

And before he even finished speaking, I was hugging Bleddyn close, stroking his hair and hushing him. "For what it's worth, *I'm* proud of you, Bleddyn. You're brave and smart and kind and honorable. You're the best person I've ever known. My *favorite* person. Oh, Bleddyn, I wish I could make you see just how amazing you are!"

With a sob as sudden as it was unexpected, Bleddyn crushed me to him, his face a damp oval pressed into the crook of my neck.

I kissed his shoulder and squeezed him tight, stroking his hair once more. "My Bleddyn, my love, you *are* mine, now. And other people's opinions of you don't matter anymore. The only opinion that matters is your own. And mine, of course, but you already know that in *my* unbiased opinion, you're the most perfect and wonderful man who ever walked the Earth."

If I wasn't mistaken, I heard a tiny laugh mixed in with Bleddyn's near-silent sobbing.

"It'll be all right, love, you'll see," I crooned as he shook in my arms. "Do you believe me?"

After a few minutes in which the quiet sobs slowed to hitches and a few shakes, Bleddyn nodded, his breath shuddering out of him in warm gusts. "Forgive me," he whispered. I leaned back in his arms and took his face in my hands. He looked wrecked, red-eyed and wet-faced. He even had tears in his mustache. I brushed them away with my thumbs.

"There's nothing to forgive, nothing to be sorry for. You've done nothing wrong, Bleddyn. Do you hear me?" I gazed into his heartbroken eyes. "You've done *nothing* wrong."

Bleddyn sniffed and looked away. "I've sinned—I *continue* to sin—"

"It's not a sin if your god made you that way. If it doesn't hurt anyone. If it makes you *happy*." I kissed the corner of Bleddyn's mouth. "Look into your heart, Bleddyn, your strong, courageous, noble heart, and ask yourself if you've done anything that warrants the treatment you've received from Rhys or anyone else or would see you damned for eternity. Have you done such a wrong or series of wrongs?"

Bleddyn met my eyes again, then looked away. "I—"

"You don't have to answer me now. Or ever. All I ask is that for now, you let me put you to bed, and leave the reporting till morning, like I said before. Its late now, probably approaching midnight. Neither your father nor Lord Owen will appreciate being dug out of the comfort of a warm bed just to hear a whole lot of nothing. Am I wrong?"

Sighing, Bleddyn shook his head no. I smiled. "I didn't think so. Now." I stepped back out of Bleddyn's arms and took his hands, pulling him out of the dimly-lit stable. Sniffling, Bleddyn followed me.

And so I led him through the castle back to the guestroom. I sat him on the turned-down bed and undressed him wordlessly. For each bit of clothing I removed, I kissed him: shoulders, chest, stomach, the tip of his cock, his knees, even the tops of his feet.

All the while, he watched me with sad, but wondering eyes.

When we were both naked, Bleddyn slipped under the covers, making plenty of room for me. But I had something else in mind and crowded as close to him as I could get, turning on my side, facing the door. Sooner rather than later, he took the hint and spooned up behind me, folding me in his arms with his face buried in my hair.

"I am sorry for my unmanly display," he said. I laced the fingers of our right hands together. "I let myself be overcome by emotions that I've kept back for many years."

"Baby, tears aren't a sign of weakness. They're a sign of strength. A way of showing vulnerability to someone else. That's not an easy thing to do. Some would say it's the *hardest* thing to do."

"But—"

"Only cowards never cry, Bleddyn. And you're anything but a coward."

He sighed in my hair. "Your time must be a very strange one if men go about weeping freely where others might see them."

I laughed. "Well, they don't make a habit of it. But it's not necessarily frowned upon, as long as one doesn't cry for everything."

Bleddyn chuckled, bringing our linked hands up to rest over my heart, the backs of his fingers grazing my nipple. "Ah, so there *are* limits on the respectability of one's every behavior in the far future."

"Well." I shivered as Bleddyn brushed the tip of his forefinger across my nipple over and over. "I suppose there *are* some. It's not a total free-for-all."

"Mm." Bleddyn pressed his body close, all along the back of mine. He was hard again, and I smiled, angling my head so he could kiss my neck. And he did, so lightly that it tickled, and I giggled. "Your *skin*, Master Krishnan, the scent of you drives me to utter distraction."

"Does it?" I asked innocently as he freed his hand from mine and ran it down the length of my torso to my cock, which he took in hand and began to stroke slow and tight. "Too distracted to ravish me till the sun makes its first foray across the sky?"

"Never too distracted for *that, fy nghariad*," Bleddyn rumbled, low and rough, as he pushed his knee between my legs. He let go of my cock and pulled my right leg back over his, tracing the shell of my ear with his tongue and thrusting lazily against my ass. "Never."

"Oh, yeah? Gonna prove it, sweet talker?"

Bleddyn chuckled, rather evilly. Then he was spreading me open, teasing and stretching me with first two fingers, then three. I hissed and rocked myself back onto them, desperate for more, harder, and faster. And Bleddyn chuckled again. "I can promise you will likely *not* be ambulatory in time for church, tomorrow. How's *that* for ravishment?" he murmured, removing his fingers from me carefully and lining up his cock with a few tantalizing brushes and inward feints.

"Fuck—sounds like a win-win, to—oh, *Bleddyn*!"

PART II

Chapter Fourteen

I sat in the accountant's cramped office, quill pen in my left hand, while I used the right to scan down the long list of tiny numbers in the household leger. Despite sitting in front of the window and the lamp burning on Islwyn's desk, it was still tough to make out his writing. No wonder the old man was going slowly, but steadily blind.

But, I reminded myself, *paper is at a premium in this time. Of course he had to write small. And carefully. And that's exactly what* I'm *going to do. Only a bit more legibly, I hope.*

So I scratched out my figures and sums, keeping an eye on Islwyn's figures and sums as I did so. It was easy enough work. Mind-numbing, tempting to zone out on, but I knew if I made a mistake that cost the lord some ungodly sum, I'd be in the shit.

As sweat formed on my forehead, I absently wiped it away so it wouldn't drip on the page. Though it'd been cool enough in the spring and early summer, at the height of summer, Lord John's castle was almost unbearably hot during the day. Especially now, when the sun was on the wester, shining in through the lead glass window that only partially illuminated what I was working on.

I kept at it, moving from accounts to payroll fluidly, managing to both focus on my work and tune out everything else till the clock in the great hall gonged six sonorous times. Both surprised and relieved by the passage of time, I decided I'd finish up what I was doing before calling it quits. And I was a few lines away from being done I heard a knock on the door.

"*Nodwch ar eich menter eich hun!*" I called. *Enter at your own risk!* It was a phrase I'd had Bleddyn teach me almost three months ago, when I'd first become Islwyn's 'prentice. It'd made him laugh when I'd asked, then practiced saying it in my no doubt awful Cymraeg accent. Even after all this time, it still made Bleddyn giggle and snort to hear me say it in my best approximation of a cranky, old Welshman. I'd, of course, picked up such an impersonation from observing my then new boss, Islwyn.

"*Don't I always, Master Krishnan?*" a low voice called, and my heart immediately began to beat faster. I put my pen in its holder and blew on the ink a little to hasten its drying.

"Come in!" I called back. "Or on! Or near!"

Chuckling but looking stern, Bleddyn entered Islwyn's office, closing the door behind him after a glance down the hall in both directions. Then those dark, semi-playful eyes were on me, both heated and slightly reproving. "My love, you know we must be careful, even in Lord John's castle," he tsked. I grinned and stood up, skirting Islwyn's big, space-devouring desk.

"I know, I know. But at this point, everyone *knows*, Bleddyn. Even Lord John, probably. They're just turning a blind eye. They don't care," I dismissed with a wave of my hand. After all, I knew this for a fact. For Gwynedd's girls were the ones who cleaned my room. Technically, it was Islwyn's room, but the old man preferred the small, drafty cottage he'd once shared with his late wife on the lord's land. The girls had more than once come in to clean early and found Bleddyn and I in rather compromising positions. I had no doubt that thanks to their wagging tongues, it was probably all over the damned county by now. It was certainly no secret that Bleddyn didn't sleep in the barracks with the unmarried soldiers and widowers any more. At church, we sat together like any other couple. Even the priest, an Englishman by the name of Father Francis, seemed to take no offense to Bleddyn and I keeping company, seeming instead to view us both with wry bemusement. "No one cares."

"That's as may be, love, but you, in turn, must be more circumspect in repayment of that willful blindness," Bleddyn said and not for the first time. "There is still, after all, the law, and it is stated plain for anyone who might wish to cause us trouble."

Fighting a scowl, I refrained from saying that the only person who seemed to have a genuine problem with Bleddyn and me being together seemed to be Bleddyn's father. After all, it was unlikely even Rhys ap Thomas would use that law to condemn his own son to death just to get at me.

I hoped.

Sighing, I went into Bleddyn's open arms and made myself small and cuddly. "You're right. Of course, you're right. I just forget, sometimes. Where and when I am, if you can believe that. Everyone's been so accepting of us, so far."

"That is because we do not flaunt our affections in front of them."

"Hmm." He was right. This was, after all, *his* time, not mine. His people, not mine. "How was Gareth, today? I got so wrapped up in work, I didn't remember to visit him during lunch," I said, feeling guilty. Though the truth was, I hadn't even taken a lunch break. But I didn't say that aloud. Bleddyn was forever after me not to skip meals, and I was forever on myself to forge an emotional bond with Gareth.

And I had...of a sort. Even though I could understand slowly-spoken Cymraeg startlingly well, for someone with no prior fluency in it, my conversational Cymraeg was still pretty awful, and Gareth's conversational English was nonexistent, but we always wound up laughing when I visited him with or without Bleddyn, mostly at my halting attempts to speak Cymraeg.

Of course it helped that when I visited, I usually brought him and the other boys sweets from the kitchen or toys from Trefriw, if Gwynedd and her girls had been to market. They could always be persuaded with a few coins and my most puppy-dog face to pick up some extras for me.

I was, in short, buying the affections of a bunch of small children. But it was working. Eirwen told me I was the boys' favorite visitor, and that Gareth talked of nothing so much as he talked about "Krish-sir."

It warmed my heart to know I was having a positive impact on Gareth's life in some way.

"Gareth is fine. I just came from putting him down to bed," Bleddyn said, his voice warm and proud, as it always was when speaking of his son. "He missed his *Krish-sir*, today, but he looks forward to seeing him on the morrow."

I smiled. "Well, I missed him, too. Terribly. But I'll definitely see him tomorrow evening. And maybe have a few extra sweets for him," I added, for I knew Gwynedd would be making a special run to the market tomorrow. And Gareth *loved* the little honey candies Gweddw Harmon sold.

"You, my love, are spoiling the boy rotten. Not that you need to, for he already loves you, as do I," Bleddyn murmured, holding me closer, and I blushed.

"I love you, too, Butch. And I love Gareth," I said for the first time, without knowing I was going to say it. And on saying it, I realized it was true. I, who had professed to feel nothing but disdain for children a few months ago, was in love not only with Bleddyn, but with his son.

It was a strange and frightening thought, and yet it warmed me more than anything. I felt like the Grinch, when his heart expanded.

Grinning, I relaxed in Bleddyn's arms and pressed my body against his. He was more than half-hard. "So, what brings you to this humble accounting office?" I asked with fake innocence thick enough to go sledding on, leaning back to look coyly into his eyes. "And at such a late hour? It's almost suppertime, you know?"

Bleddyn smiled, and that heated look was back in his dark eyes. "Aye. And I *am* hungry. But not for food." He kissed me hard before swinging me up into his arms and carrying me to the narrow door just to the left of the one leading out to the main corridor. It led to my room.

As Bleddyn bore me down into the almost-softness of my bed—*our* bed, as I had started thinking of it—I batted my eyes up at him. "But what will the men say if we're not there to dine with them as we usully do?"

Bleddyn snorted. "Naught, if they know what is best for them."

"Hmm. Especially Dafydd, I'm thinking." I chuckled breathlessly as Bleddyn growled into my throat, his thrusts against me becoming harder and stronger.

"*Dafydd* is lucky I let him keep his teeth, after all he's said."

I chuckled again. Dafydd ap Dafydd, was also one of Lord John's squires, the tall, handsome, disdainful blond I'd had the dubious pleasure of meeting when Bleddyn and I had arrived at the castle three months ago. He wasn't exactly under Bleddyn, but I'd noticed that in

Rhys's absence, Lord John's men had a habit of following Bleddyn. Bleddyn had a natural ability to lead and an innate, earnest charisma that even his father must have noticed. There was precious little the men wouldn't do in Lord John's name, if so ordered by Bleddyn.

Of course, that didn't mean those same men wouldn't and didn't "take the piss" with their beloved "lieutenant." Dafydd ap Dafydd was one of those who took the piss with everyone—even Rhys, with whom he got on like a house on fire—and had taken to inquiring of Bleddyn how his husband was, and other versions of that theme.

The first time he did it, he'd casually hailed Bleddyn as *Bleddyn, gwraig Krishnan, ap Karthik,* Or: *Bleddyn, wife of Krishnan, son of Karthik,* which hadn't sat well with Bleddyn. I'd never seen him turn so red. Or so angry. But I guess being referred to as my wife was a bit vexing to him. I didn't like it either, but mostly because of the heteronormative stereotypes and mores it placed on our relationship. Which I tried to explain to Bleddyn with limited success.

If not for my quick thinking the first time Dafydd referred to him that way—leaning in to whisper in Bleddyn's ear that I was hard and could he *please* find us a linen closet in which to fuck *immediately?*—it might have escalated into a fight. And since that evening, Dafydd had been taking the piss with Bleddyn almost daily. He seemed to enjoy getting Bleddyn's goat, which was a rather easy thing to do when I was the topic. In the months since he'd chosen me, Bleddyn had been as good as his word and refused to hear anything pejorative about me.

"He only keeps doing it because he knows it upsets you. If you stop paying him any mind, he'll get bored and move on to someone else," I said as Bleddyn got to his knees and shoved his breeches down. He was hard and fully erect, my favorite sight in the entire universe.

"You speak only the truth, my beloved," he agreed, removing his undershirt. He still smelled of metal from his mail-shirt, however. Metal, sweat, and horse—three things I never would have said would smell like home to me, but Bleddyn was making a liar of me more and more each day. "But I am not adept at hiding myself from the study of others. I fear that no matter what front I present, Dafydd will always know when he has scored a hit upon me. We have known each other for far too long to be able to successfully dissemble around each other."

I thought of the way I sometimes caught Dafydd gazing at Bleddyn but held my peace regarding how well or not Dafydd was able to dissemble.

"How long have you two known each other, anyway?" I asked instead, curious yet hesitant. Bleddyn's frown was absent as he stopped stroking himself.

"I have known Dafydd since I was fifteen. He was fostered to us from *Sir Feirionnydd*, in an exchange of sorts. Him for William. Though, after William's death, their lord was kind enough to allow Dafydd to continue on at Gwydir Castle, a thing for which I was glad. Dafydd had become my steadfast friend in those lonely months."

Bleddyn sighed heavily and I winced.

Having learned from all the previous times I'd stepped on the William-landmine, I sat up a little and licked Bleddyn's cock slowly, with as much obscene slurping as I could manage. He groaned and closed his eyes, murmuring my name.

"So, what you're saying is, in fourteen-plus years, as far as you know of, he's never had *this*?" I licked his cock again, lingering at the head and tonguing the slit till Bleddyn hissed and swore.

"Krish...yes. I all that time, I have never known of him to take a lover, never mind a wife."

"Hmm." Sitting back, I shimmied my breeches down and kicked them and my hose off. "Then maybe we need to find him a wife, so he'll only have time to mind his own affairs." I moaned as Bleddyn ran his hands up my calves, to my thighs. He tugged on the hem of my shirt and pushed it up. I quickly sat up to shuck it, and when it was sailing across my small room, Bleddyn pushed me down to the bed and pinned me, kissing me teasingly and slowly.

"I am no match-maker, to find a woman for Dafydd," he informed me, and I raised an eyebrow.

"I meant wife purely as a euphemism, Butch." I rolled my eyes and bracketed Bleddyn's legs with mine. He ground himself against me till I could barely remember what I'd been saying. "He needs to get laid, and I don't mean by some pretty maiden."

Bleddyn looked confused for a moment and stopped. When the penny finally dropped behind his eyes, I nodded.

"But *Dafydd*?"

"As a purple shilling," I said. "He's frustrated and jealous. He wants what we've got. He won't be happy until he gets it."

Bleddyn frowned. "But I've never known of Dafydd to dally with men, even those few who take on so in the absence of women."

"Ah, but did you know Dafydd to dally with women when there were plenty to go around?"

Bleddyn gave it some thought before answering. "Not even when in his cups. The two of us used to be the odd men out at the pub and various celebrations, before I married and after. I kept to myself because I did not want the women. But I thought 'twas Dafydd's piety that kept him chaste. But now you say he desires other men?"

I don't know about other men, but I know he desires you.

"Yes," I said. "My gaydar—uh, that is, my sense of these things— is very strong. Dafydd is like us. Only he doesn't have anyone to be with. Swell guy like that, it's tough to imagine," I snorted. But then, I was the one frowning as I suddenly realized something.

Dafydd and Bleddyn used to drown their sorrows together for years until…until I showed up and split their bromance in two. Now, Dafydd, who is probably attracted to my lover, if not in full-blown love with him, spends his free time mocking said lover to the point of anger. Basically pulling his pigtails hard.

And remembering the look in Dafydd's eyes after that first time he'd called Bleddyn my wife, I'd gotten a frisson of something. Foreboding. Foreshadowing. For the look in his eyes hadn't been one of just hot jealousy, but of cold calculation, too.

He was testing us, I thought incredulously. He was taking our measure to see just how much ribbing we could take before one of us either left the other or did something precipitous. He'd been doing that for months, and it'd only get worse, no matter how Bleddyn reacted because Dafydd is trying to drive a wedge between us. Either to get Bleddyn for himself or to make sure I don't keep him.

"Enough talk of Dafydd, that gormless clod." Bleddyn swooped in to kiss my neck, right on the sweet spot that turned me into a puddle of Krish-goo. It did so now, driving Dafydd out of my head. "I've been stiff as a rod all day, Krishnan, because I thought of naught but you."

I giggled as Bleddyn skated his fingers lightly over my ribs. He knew how ticklish I was and used that knowledge shamelessly. "Is my brave and dutiful squire telling me that he has neglected his duties for the day?"

"Most egregiously," Bleddyn agreed in a low rumble that made me shiver, as did his hands, which'd turned from tickling to teasing. He sat up just enough to look into my eyes. His were dancing and solemn at once. "Today, I have not earned the sheer delight of your sweet, sheltering arms and tender kisses, but I humbly ask for them, anyway."

I wrapped my arms around his neck and pulled him back down on top of me. "Ask and you shall receive, my love."

Bleddyn's smile was as solemn as his eyes, but his kiss was as wanton as any I'd ever gotten.

We did not make it to supper that night, either.

❖

I was writing. Always writing.

Because of my underwhelming size and lack of prowess at fighting or anything physical, all I'd been allowed to do since my arrival at Sir Feirionnydd, the nearest southward county, was write. I was 'prenticed to the local scribe when it became apparent the only thing I was remotely good at was bookish studies and writing.

It wasn't so bad, really. I had my own room and bed. Back at Gwydir Castle, in Sir Gaernarfon, I had shared both a room and bed with my cousin, which I had done since I was wee. So at the ripe old age of sixteen, I told myself I didn't feel lonely, didn't miss the companionship, or the way we'd used to stay awake and talk into the small hours, or the way my heart beat faster at his every touch and look.

I told myself that I was a filthy sinner and Hellbound, if I didn't stop yearning for that which was an abomination. My uncle had been right to beat me, to see me driven from the only home I'd ever known. If only to protect his own son from my perversion.

If, that was, it wasn't already too late.

Pausing my writing and closing my eyes on my cramped little station, I remembered the way smooth skin covering solid muscle had felt underneath my worshipful hands. The sounds he had made as I kissed him and caressed him and eventually had *him. I remembered the heat of him, like the fires I'd surely spend eternity burning in for my sin, so greatly compounded by my lack of remorse and total enjoyment of this perfect act of love.*

I thought of all this and felt such a pain as I'd never before felt. As if my heart was being squeezed within my breast. As if, despite the suddening stiffening of my manhood and the hot flush of my body, I was quite cold, alone, and about to weep as a bereft babe would.

Would he forget about me? Would he be glad of my absence? Did he blame me for how his father had beaten us? For the fact that now, everyone knew that we were both dirty sodomites?

Or did he miss me as I missed him?

And I missed him terribly.

It had been naught but two months since I'd been fostered to Sir Feirionnydd, and I felt a little more dead inside every day, as if pieces of my soul were rotting away, dying a quiet and unlamented death. For what use was a soul, anyway, when its other half was so far away, and no doubt had either forgotten its lost half or had given it up?

Opening my damp eyes, I got myself under some sort of control. But I couldn't help but remember how he and I used to speak of running away to Caerdyf when we were younger. We'd talk for hours of what it would be like when we were grown men, able to sign onto a ship sailing south, maybe not even debarking at Caerdyf, but traveling all the way to England, where our mothers had come from.

I sighed. If only we still *could* run away, *I thought, morosely imagining the long years I'd be spending at Sir Feirionnydd. Alone, without him.* If only we could still—

Suddenly, my tears stopped and I was taken by a stark, illuminated thought:

Wait. Why *can't* we still run away?

"*Na! Peidiwch â gwneud hyn...os gwelwch yn dda!*"

I bolted up in the bed I shared with Bleddyn, my hands held up in a defensive gesture as I begged shadows to: *please, don't do this.* I was panting and drenched in sweat.

It wasn't the first time over the past three months I'd woken up terrified, moaning and begging in incomprehensible Welsh. In fact, such nights had become more frequent, though I could only dimly remember the dreams responsible. I just knew that I woke, often with a scream locked behind my teeth, clutching my stomach. I was almost always in tears upon such a waking.

Bleddyn slept on next to me, his face solemn in repose, his pale body burnished faint gold by the flicker of the dying lamp. One of his arms was draped over my lap, the other pillowing his head as he slept on his stomach.

I wiped my wet face, carefully disengaged from him, and got up. A minute later, I was dressed and stepping out into the office. The faint light of dawn barely made a dent in the darkness, and I stepped back into our bedroom to grab the lamp.

I meant to start up the work I'd left unfinished yesterday evening, but for some reason, the idea of sitting bent over the page at the desk made me feel unsafe—even in the safest place in *Sir Gaernarfon*, with Bleddyn mere feet away.

Tears began to well up in my eyes as I tried to attend to my work, but I couldn't concentrate for sneaking glances up at the door. I expected to see someone standing there silently, watching me, smiling a merry, empty, merciless smile.

I expected to be *hurt*, and I could do nothing about it.

I was a sitting duck.

Finally, I put down my quill pen and buried my face in my hands, weeping for no reason I could understand.

By the time the clock in the great hall chimed six, I was gritty-eyed and exhausted. I quickly made my way through the largely empty halls to the bathing chambers to make myself look at least somewhat more presentable for Bleddyn. I didn't want him to know about the nightmares, and one look at me without the intervention of a good face-scrubbing would certainly tell him that at least *this* night had not passed well for me.

I was just finishing my ablutions when the door to the chamber creaked open slightly.

"I'll be done in a moment!" I called, not looking away from the piece of highly-polished metal that served as a mirror. From what I could tell, I looked less wrecked than I had before, but my eyes were still suspiciously reddened.

Oh, well. Nothing to be done about it. Perhaps by the time I've gotten us breakfast, they'll have cleared up, some, I thought with tired resignation. I turned away from the "mirror" and started, one hand going up to my chest, over my rabbiting heart.

"Good morning, Krishnan ap Karthik," Dafydd said, smiling his friendly-but-not-really smile as he leaned against the door to the room. "I hope this dawn finds you well."

I shuddered and crossed my arms over my chest, trying not to feel the unease spreading from the pit of my stomach to fill the rest of me with icewater and anxiety.

It's just leftover nerves from whatever it is I dreamed about, I told myself as I mustered up the boldness to approach Dafydd, and thus my only means of escape. *Not to mention the fact that Bleddyn and I were speaking of this very devil last night. Coincidences are just that: coincidence. And there's nothing creepy or spooky about that.*

"It does, Dafydd. And I hope it finds you the same," I replied, taking a few small steps toward him. Dafydd's meaningless smile widened, and he watched me with his hooded, amused gaze.

"And Bleddyn? How fares our lieutenant? I noted neither of you joined us for supper yesterday evening. I hope all is well."

I fought not to roll my eyes. I wanted to say, *As if you don't know why we missed supper, you fucking jerk.* But I pasted on my own smile. "Oh, all's well," I said blithely. "He and I were otherwise engaged, but all is most definitely well. Couldn't be better." And if I was smirking as I said it, what of that? Never mind the prissy, disapproving, downright constipated look Dafydd got on his handsome face.

"That's well, then," he said, caught between his customary easy smile and a scowl. It was almost objectively fascinating to watch the muscles writhe and morph as they tried to settle on an expression.

Almost.

"If you'll excuse me, Dafydd, I have to get Bleddyn's breakfast." I stepped up to him, just inside his personal bubble. He smelled of horse and metal and sweat, like Bleddyn, but slightly wrong. So I held my breath and tried to look nonchalant, even though my nerves were really working overtime with me being so close to him. "After missing supper last night, he'll be ravenous."

Dafydd's face settled on the scowl, at last, and *he* crossed *his* arms like I had a minute ago. "It is no secret, you know," he said, his low voice tight with controlled anger and his pale grey eyes boring into mine. "No secret that you've ensnared Bleddyn in your perversions. No secret he now spends his evenings in your bed, instead of in the barracks where he belongs. No secret that from the day you arrived here, you have sought nothing so much as to lure and subvert a good man into the way of sin."

Dafydd looked me over with a knowing sneer so bald and flat-out disdainful, I wanted to wrap myself in blankets. Then punch him in the face. "The others may not see you for what you are, but *I* do, Krishnan ap Karthik. I do. You are sent by the devil himself to tempt the heart of a good man. To draw him down the path to Hell."

This time, I did roll my eyes, though I was inwardly shocked and appalled at Dafydd's sudden bluntness. Why now? Why here? And why was he, of all the people at Gwydir Castle, the first to confront me? Even Rhys had taken to ignoring me, as he did Bleddyn unless it was something regarding official business.

"Yeah, okay, bored, now," I said, reaching past him for the knob. I was hoping he'd take the hint and get out of the way, but he didn't. He grabbed my wrist and yanked it up hard, squeezing it like he was trying to throttle my arm.

"'Ware me, Krishnan ap Karthik," Dafydd murmured as I tugged on my arm futilely. "'Ware me very well."

"Let me go!"

"If you think I will stand by and let you make off with Bleddyn's honor and his soul, you are very much mistaken, catamite." He clamped down harder on my wrist, till the small bones began to creak and protest. Then Dafydd leaned in close closer and smiled the nastiest smile I'd ever seen on a human being. "You are not the first to try and corrupt him. I don't imagine you will be the last. Great honor and strength of character draws such as you like flies to a dung heap."

Flushed with anger, I finally yanked my aching hand free and cradled it to my chest. "You know, if I actually cared what you thought, that'd be pretty fucking devastating. But since I *don't*, I'm going to ask you again, politely, to get the hell out of my way."

Dafydd sneered, but he moved aside with exaggerated care, even bowing slightly. I opened the door and stepped past him, head held high.

"What are you, that you care not that you impugn his honor and lessen him in the eyes of his kith and kin? Not to mention the eyes of God?" Dafydd asked disgustedly. I paused in the doorway and spoke without looking back.

"Bleddyn's honor isn't impugned because of who he loves. Nor is he lessened in anyone's eyes but those who never held him in any esteem in the first place. As you said, Bleddyn's character *is* strong. Loving and wanting another man isn't going to change that. At least not for the worst." I paused and turned my head just enough that I could see Dafydd out of the corner of my eye, see first his stricken expression, then what could only be a snarl. "Which is more than I can say for some people."

And I strode off toward the kitchen. I didn't realize it until I was halfway there, but I was shaking all over as if I'd just seen the boogeyman. I felt as if I'd faced down a dragon.

But, all in all, it was strangely unsatisfying as telling off assholes went.

Chapter Fifteen

D awn was coming in through the window in the office, so I left the door leading to our bedroom open for the natural light, and made my quiet way to our bed. I sat on my side with the laden tray of food and watched my love sleep soundly, one arm bent under his curly head. Even lax with sleep, every taut inch of him was well-defined muscle and sinew wrapped around strong bones. He was beautiful, and I loved him more than anything or anyone I'd ever known. I loved Bleddyn ap Rhys.

No matter what the Dafydds of the world thought or had to say about my love, it would always shine brightly out of me. I could no more hide my greatest truth than I could hide my dark skin. Both had always marked me as different from those who surrounded me, yet I would not have traded either for all the adulation and approval in the world.

Glancing at my wrist, which was starting to bruise, I pursed my lips with concern. Despite me not caring what they thought, the Dafydds of the world *would* have their say, whatever it was and however they chose to voice it.

Why couldn't he just be like Rhys and ignore both Bleddyn and me unless it was about Lord John's business? I wondered with weary rue. *Or was I right about Dafydd after all, and he's jealous that I got what he couldn't or wouldn't let himself have? And just how far is he willing to go to split us up? Obviously putting his hands on me isn't beyond the pale in his mind.*

I warned myself once more to be very careful of Dafydd ap Dafydd.

Bleddyn had begun to stir when I sat down, rolling toward me with a sigh. He was tenting out the blanket with formidable morning wood, and I grinned, thinking how lucky I was to have a lover who seemed to be able to bookend our days with fantastic sex and never get tired of it. He really was the Energizer Bunny.

Placing the tray down with care, I reached out to brush his curly dark hair away from his pale brow. He made a whiny little sound—his *don't wanna wake up*-noise—and rolled away from me. I smiled. For a man who was used to waking up at dawn or even earlier, he was *not* a morning person. At least, he wasn't before we'd had sex and then a large breakfast.

Well, I'd already taken care of the breakfast.

"Wake up, sexy. It's time to get up," I murmured.

"Say not that it is yet morning, my love," he groaned, squinching his eyes shut tighter. "For I have only just closed my eyes and could not prise them open again for love or money."

"I know, baby, I know," I said, nuzzling his cheek. After all, I knew exactly how he felt. It'd been weeks, maybe *months* since I'd gotten an adequate amount of nightmare-free sleep. "But tomorrow is Saturday, which means it's officially one week and one day until the Jubilee."

Bleddyn groaned again but opened his eyes a crack. They glittered at me, dark and sleepy. "For the Sabbath I am ever grateful, but the Jubilee…"

I stole a quick kiss and sat up. If Bleddyn was talking, he was awake enough to need no further prodding from me. "I know. Rhys has been running you all ragged in preparation for the tourneys."

"That he has," Bleddyn agreed, sitting up with a grunt and scrubbing his face with his fingers. Then he was blinking and staring morosely at the white-washed wall across from our bed. "All must be perfect for the twentieth anniversary of Lord John's knighting and becoming a baronet." Snorting once more, Bleddyn turned to me, quite dour-looking in the meager light before his morning nookie. "And that includes the reenactments of the great deeds of his royal ancestor, Prince Owain of Gwynedd."

"My poor baby," I said, but I giggled just a little. It felt good to laugh, despite mostly holding it in for Bleddyn's sake. "You got the lead in the Christmas play, and you don't want it."

"Christmas play?" Bleddyn looked puzzled.

This time, I *did* laugh. "You're the best warrior for any ten counties around, Bleddyn. You're a natural to play the part of the hero. Even Rhys could see that. And of course, so could Lord John. If not you, whom would they find who would be as convincing as the Prince of Gwynedd?"

Bleddyn thought it over. "Perhaps Gruffudd…"

"Who'll no doubt be drunk before the Jubilee even *starts*." I raised my eyebrows and Bleddyn laid back down, closing his eyes and folding his arms underneath his head. I reached out and scratched my fingers through his chest hair. He closed his eyes and hmmed, almost smiling.

"Perhaps Dafydd…"

"Ugh. He's nobody's hero."

Bleddyn opened his eyes and smiled. "Perhaps not, but he can be a fine actor when the need is near. He is charming and handsome."

Just like any psychopath, I thought, remembering the bruising-tight grip of his hand and somehow refraining from looking at or touching the spot where he'd grabbed me. "That may be the case, but he's not as good a swordsman as you."

"That's debatable, my love. For many's the time he's beaten me during match-ups."

"Recently?"

"Well…"

"I rest my case. You're the best swordsman for ten counties in any direction," I said in a tone that brooked no naysaying, turning to the tray with our breakfast and placing it on the bed's only night table. I could be reasonably certain our flailing around wouldn't knock it over. Again.

I turned back to my lover, smiling my most sultry smile. "Now, let's forget about the Jubilee, the reenactment, and Dafydd, and start another conversation, entirely."

Bleddyn, already sporting morning wood, arched up with a moan when I took hold of him, murmuring something in Cymraeg I couldn't quite make out. But I was flattered, nonetheless, and kissed onto the skin of Bleddyn's sternum one of the first phrases I'd learned in that language. "*Rwyf wrth fy modd i ti am byth bythoedd, Bleddyn...nes y mynyddoedd crymbl, y moroedd yn rhedeg yn sych, ac yr haul a'r lleuad yn methu...Rwyf wrth fy modd i ti..*"

I love thee for ever and ever, Bleddyn...until the mountains crumble, the seas run dry, and the sun and moon fail...I love thee.

Bleddyn's heavy, rough hand landed gently on my head, carding through my grown-out-of-any-style hair. I intended to grow it till I looked more like a man of this time, though I still insisted on shaving my face religiously. Facial hair was a level of butchness I wasn't ready to commit to.

"And my love has no end or beginning," he stuttered out fervently, as he gasped and shivered under my ministrations. "It has always been and it always will be. *"*

Tears began to form at the backs of my eyes. I looked up along the length of Bleddyn's hard, wiry body till our eyes met, and I smiled. He did the same, reaching down until my face rested in his hand.

"Promise you won't ever let me go," I whispered. Bleddyn's frowned, and he stroked my cheek tenderly with his thumb.

"Never will I let you go, Krishnan, though I fear that having said so, I have invited some great evil to come separate us." I shivered and wished I was Catholic so I could cross myself and take comfort in that.

"Remember what Gwenllian said. Nothing will ever separate us for longer than it takes us to call out for the other." I kissed Bleddyn's sternum again and crawled up his body, leaving a trail of kisses until I reached his mouth. But instead of kissing him, I looked down into his eyes. "I love you too much to go without you. Wherever I am, no matter how far—even if it's in another *time* and on another continent—if you call to me, I *will* come to you. Remember that," I pleaded, placing my hand over his strong, steady heartbeat. "Always remember that I love you, and that if you want me, however you want me, I'm yours."

Bleddyn searched my eyes, his gaze somber and vulnerable. "And ever am I—*ever* am I *yours*, Krishnan," he whispered with fierce intensity, closing the slight distance between our mouths for a long kiss. I laughed as we rolled over, and he pulled my legs up to bracket his thighs then wrapped them around his hips as he rocked against me.

Bleddyn's eyes, as he looked into mine, were brimming with happiness and contentment, as they often were these days. "Your beauty outshines the sun and causes the moon to hide her face in shame."

I smiled, smitten and totally okay with that.

Then I reached up to trace his mouth with my finger and he leaned into my touch with a soft sigh, his eyes fluttering shut. I turned my face up to kiss his lips. "Open your eyes, so that my universe can exist again."

"How I love you!" Bleddyn sighed. He caught my hand at the wrist and pulled it to his lips to kiss the palm. I winced and hissed. Bleddyn was holding my wrist in the exact same spot Dafydd had.

Frowning, Bleddyn brushed the fingers of his other hand across my cheek, while he examined my wrist. His eyes turned grim and angry. "Who has done this to you?" he asked in a still, flat voice.

I looked away and pulled my hand from his with another hiss before wrapping both arms around his neck. "It's nothing, baby, nothing. I just banged my hand on the doorpost this morning, being a doof. But it looks a lot worse than it fee—"

"Look at me, Krishnan, and please do not lie to me," Bleddyn said quietly, pulling my left arm from around his neck and examining the wrist again. He traced the bruises with careful, callused fingers. "Only one thing leaves finger-shaped bruises on skin, my light, and it is not a doorpost." Those dark, grim eyes met mine. "Who has manhandled you so roughly?"

I blushed and looked away again. "I promise, it's nothing. Just a misunderstanding."

"Indeed, there *is* some misunderstanding if this person thinks he can so harm my love. You will give me his name that I may address the matter swiftly," Bleddyn said calmly, despite the fire in his eyes. That fire made me afraid not for myself, but for Bleddyn, who I knew would avenge me if I gave him a name. And who knew *what* trouble would follow such vengeance?

"I see fear in your eyes, my love. Be not afraid for, on my honor, this will never happen again." Bleddyn kissed my wrist with such tenderness, tears sprang to my eyes. "I'll not let anyone hurt you so."

"And what, exactly, would you do to stop it, Bleddyn?" I asked, wiping my eyes. Bleddyn sighed.

"I would demand an immediate apology to you or satisfaction in single-combat."

I gaped. "You mean like a *duel*?"

"For your honor," Bleddyn agreed, and I groaned.

"My honor's not worth you possibly getting maimed or even killed."

"Did you not say I am the best swordsman for ten counties around?" he said with a smile. "And as you so flatteringly pointed out, even Dafydd has not won against me in some time, indeed…" he trailed off, his eyes narrowing as he once again searched mine. "You fear that I may lose in combat against your attacker, do you not?"

I nodded reluctantly. "I don't want to see anything happen to you. That's all."

"And to whom would I have any chance of losing, if not the one who has bested me in the past?" Bleddyn asked, sitting up and back on his heels. I was gaping once more as he studied me. "'Twas Dafydd who bruised you so, was it not?"

"Bleddyn…" I closed my eyes for a few moments to gather myself to tell the worst lie I ever had, and all to protect a man I almost hated. No. All to protect the man I *loved* more than life itself. When I opened my eyes, a tear rolled down my right cheek and Bleddyn sighed.

"Do not bother to dissemble or obfuscate further, Krishnan, for I see the truth of the matter in your lovely eyes." Bleddyn jumped up and began to gather his clothes from the floor. Stunned, I watched Bleddyn get dressed, wondering how we'd gone from about to make love to crusading for Dafydd's head.

By the time I could get over my surprise, Bleddyn was dressed and holding out his hand to me. I took it reluctantly, and he pulled me close.

"Come, my love," he said, and I shivered, thinking, *In a perfect universe, yeah, I would be coming, wouldn't I?*

"Where are we going?" I asked as he led me out into the office then out into the corridor. We were at the main staircase before Bleddyn answered me, his voice as grim as his eyes, and tight with restrained anger.

"We're going to see my father."

❖

By the time we got to the barracks where Rhys's office was, I was more than near tears.

"Please, Bleddyn, don't do this," I blubbered as he let us into the barracks and marched past the few men still in residence and not at breakfast. They stared at us as we went by and, for once, neither Bleddyn nor I cared about the fact that Bleddyn was holding my hand. "Rhys won't do anything about Dafydd, and it'll just cause more strife between all of us."

"So, your solution to this matter is to let Dafydd get away with hurting a defenseless person he's supposed to be protecting?" Bleddyn demanded, glancing at me before once more training his eyes on the door set at the back of the barracks, which led to Rhys's office. "If he'd hurt Gwynedd or Mary, would you be so willing to see this matter drop?"

Blushing, I attempted to halt our march, and did for all of three seconds. Then Bleddyn was letting us into the back door and dragging us up the winding staircase. "I'm not a matron or maiden. I can defend myse—"

Somehow, so fast that I couldn't even do anything but huff out a breath and taste stone, Bleddyn had me face first against the wall, pressing his solid body pressed into my back, and yanking my right arm so high behind my back, I could have scratched my own nape.

"Pray, speak to me further about how well you can defend yourself, Master Krishnan," Bleddyn breathed in my ear as I fought to draw even a single breath, trapped as I was between a rock and a hard place. I struggled to be free of my lover and the wall, but it was no use.

"Bleddyn—" he sighed in my ear and let me go slowly. I drew in great whooping breaths while my arm throbbed and complained. When I could breathe normally and my arm let up some, I faced Bleddyn with a glare, only to find him staring at me with some concern and not a little anxiety.

"He could have done anything to you, my love. Absolutely anything. Not only wouldn't *you* have been able to stop him, but *I* wouldn't have been there to stop him, either." He looked down guiltily and shook his head. "I am turning out to be a fine teacher and protector, am I not?"

Anger forgotten, I reached out to Bleddyn, and he came into my arms with a relieved exhalation, his own arms sliding around my waist. He buried his face in the hollow between my neck and shoulder and simply breathed for long moments, while I stroked the curls at his nape.

"I'll be more careful," I promised. "I'll avoid being alone with him in secluded places. I'll do whatever I can not to engage him in so much as small talk. I'll—"

"'Twill not, I fear, be enough, beloved," Bleddyn breathed on my skin, humid and warm. When he straightened and looked me in my eyes, his expression determined and grim once more. "I promised I would teach you how to live like a man of this century, and I have been lax in that duty, for one of the things even the accountants of this century know how to do is defend themselves in a fight."

My eyebrows shot up. "Are you gonna teach me how to fight?"

"No, I am going to teach you how to defend yourself in a fight that is unavoidable. If those lessons go well, then, yes, I will teach you how to fight." Bleddyn frowned his dour frown, the one that made me want to smile. I repressed the smile this time. "But you must do as I say and try your best to do well at it, for I fear nothing less than your safety, and perhaps even your life, is at stake."

I shivered but laughed it off. "Aren't you being a touch melodramatic?"

Bleddyn shook his head no. Eventually, he leaned in and kissed my forehead, then spoke. "I love you. I wish only for you to be safe and happy. I will do anything to make certain that you are both, if you will let me."

I nodded once.

"And we will tell my father what happened, so he knows misdeeds are occurring right under his nose, and wrongs that he should put a-right."

I nodded once more, though it was with trepidation.

"And I will begin training you to defend yourself tomorrow, after church and our visit to see Gwenllian."

Staring into Bleddyn's dark eyes, I nodded yet again and hugged him tight. Then we were finishing the climb up to his father's office, hand in hand.

❖

Rhys was in his office, though I had hoped he wouldn't be.

I'd never been in there before, though I'd known where it was. In my three months here, I'd done my best to avoid my lover's father, and he'd done me the courtesy of attempting the same. I had, of course, seen him around the castle and environs, but I hadn't spoken to him since the Sunday morning he'd knocked on the door to the Islwyn's office, looking for Bleddyn. I'd answered the door still half-asleep, surprised to see who it was, considering that the last time he'd come looking for Bleddyn and suspected him of being with me, he'd just entered without so much as a knock.

"Yes?" I'd asked without inflection. Rhys's eyes were fixed somewhere over my right shoulder, and his hands were behind his back. *Likely so he wouldn't try to throttle me*, I'd thought at the time.

"I'm here for Bleddyn, on Lord John's business," Rhys had said gruffly, still not looking at me. I'd rolled my eyes.

"Wait here, please, I'll get him," I'd said, closing the door to the office and leaning on it for a moment, before going to wake my sleeping, snoring lover, who would no doubt be overjoyed to have been woken just after dawn on the one day he usually got to sleep in.

Now, as Rhys' still-gruff voice bid us to come in, I took a deep breath, glanced at Bleddyn, who was grim once more, and I composed myself as best I could.

Rhys was sitting behind his desk, which was, for this century, anyway, covered in what looked like maps and writs and lists. He was reading one such piece of paper, moving his lips slowly. He did not look up immediately, giving me time to take in my Spartan surroundings: grey stone walls bare of everything except for weapons racks, and one small window set high in the north-facing wall. There was one lamp on a stool near the door, and another lamp on Rhys's desk, well away from the papers.

Bleddyn stopped a few feet from the desk and stood at attention, apparently ready to wait all day to be noticed. I rolled my eyes and stood straighter, but not at attention. I wasn't thrilled about telling Rhys that one of his men was bothering me, when I knew that he'd probably do nothing. Hell, he'd probably give Dafydd a medal. I was pretty disheartened about this whole thing, but I was surprised and warmed by the fact that Bleddyn had not let go of my hand.

At any rate, Rhys didn't leave us waiting long. He looked up, putting whatever he'd been reading down carefully and smoothing it. When he saw us, his grim but attentive expression turned to one of disdain and disappointment that Bleddyn probably couldn't help but notice.

"What is it, Bleddyn?" Rhys asked, sounding put-upon, as if Bleddyn came to bother him on an hourly basis, when I knew for a fact that Bleddyn avoided seeing his father more than necessary. Neither of them enjoyed their interactions, and hadn't since well before William's death.

So, it shouldn't have surprised me that Bleddyn didn't dance about the subject, but cut to the chase, taking my elbow and urging me forward with him. When we were within touching distance of Rhys, practically leaning on his desk, Bleddyn held out my left arm and pulled up the sleeve of my shirt, revealing the blue-black and purple bracelet of a bruise. The shape of the fingers, slightly longer and thinner than Bleddyn's, was really becoming visible and recognizable.

Thinking of my lame doorpost excuse, I blushed.

Rhys saw the bruise and frowned even more, leaning forward as if to examine it. Then he sat back, looking up at Bleddyn. "What is it to do with me how ye choose to handle yer catamite?"

Bleddyn's face turned red, and he took a deep breath before speaking. "'Twas not *I* who grabbed Master Krishnan so harshly, father." Bleddyn paused, as if waiting for his father to ask who, had grabbed me, but I knew not to hold my breath. Bleddyn must've realized that pretty quickly, too, for he went on after a few silent seconds of Rhys' stubborn stare. "'Twas Dafydd."

I saw a flicker in Rhys's eyes I couldn't read. For a moment, he looked concerned, if not about me, then about one of his men wounding another of Lord John's people. But then his expression hardened, and he leaned back in his chair, looking up at the distant ceiling. "And?"

"*And*? Father, Dafydd cornered Master Krishnan in the bathing room and inflicted this damage! He spoke pejoratively of things about which he knows nothing! Master Krishnan neither threatened him nor laid a hand on him, in order to receive such treatment." Bleddyn let go of my arm. and I took that as a signal to put it down. In less than a second, Bleddyn and I were holding hands again, something Rhys did not miss.

"Whatever offense *Master* Krishnan offered Dafydd is none of my concern. Dafydd has obviously handled the matter and brought it to a close. That is, unless Master Krishnan chooses to escalate it further?" Rhys looked at me, and I flushed angrily.

"*Escalate it further?*" I snorted. "There was nothing to escalate until Dafydd accosted me while I was minding my own business this morning. For months he's been doing nothing but provoking Bleddyn and I, and for months, Bleddyn and I have ignored his provocations, thinking they were nothing more than unfunny jokes. If there was any escalation, it was done by Dafydd!"

"Yes," Bleddyn agreed, rather more calmly than I had, his voice several octaves lower. "When he merely jested and mocked us, there was no issue. But now that he's injured Master Krishnan—"

Rhys barked a harsh laugh. "Ye call *that* an injury, Bleddyn?"

"I call it Dafydd intentionally hurting someone under his protection. Someone who is defenseless and who has offered him no offense prior." Bleddyn squeezed my hand and took another deep breath. "As his superior, you are the one I have come to for aid. For satisfaction or punitive measures."

Rhys looked gobsmacked for a moment before his face screwed into a scowl that Bleddyn had inherited but didn't use too often. "Perhaps Dafydd is offended by Master Krishnan's mere existence here. He would not be the first."

My eyes narrowed, but I said nothing.

"And Dafydd's existence offends me," Bleddyn went on, still as calm as if there was ice-water in his veins. "Shall I start harassing and injuring him until he returns to *Sir Feirionnydd*, from whence he came so many years ago? Shall I challenge him to a tourney, so I may at last have the satisfaction which I see you are unwilling to grant me?"

Rhys's eyes widened and after a few seconds he sat forward again, staring at Bleddyn in horror. "Ye would challenge Dafydd, who had the training of ye, when here he first came? Who, until ye took up with this shameless catamite, was like a brother to ye? Truly, Bleddyn?"

I glanced at Bleddyn, just in time to see a slight tic near his eye. But when he spoke, his voice was as calm as ever. "Yes, I would. I know that both you and he do not approve of Master Krishnan, nor of our affection for each other. But that affection is strong, and I will not suffer him to be mistreated because he is an easier target than I am." Bleddyn squeezed my hand again. "I ask that you put an end to this, or my next step will be to take the matter to Lord John and seek redress through combat."

Rhys looked doubly horrified, now. "And what would ye tell Lord John about why ye were championing his accountant's 'prentice? What reason would ye give for defending his honor against Dafydd?"

"I would tell Lord John that I am simply doing my duty, to defend the helpless against the predations of the wicked, because my father would not," Bleddyn said, and this time, Rhys sat back as if stung.

"Ye—ye—" Slowly, Rhys's face began to turn red with anger. "Are ye giving *me* an ultimatum? Do ye *dare*?" he demanded. Bleddyn sighed.

"I will do much and dare greatly to protect that which I love," Bleddyn said.

"And what of yer love of all that is right and good? What of yer love of God? What of yer love for me?" Rhys stood up, his voice growing louder. His next words were almost a yell: "Where is yer honor, boy?!"

"Where is yours*?!*" Bleddyn yelled back suddenly, startling both Rhys and me. In the silence that followed, punctuated by Bleddyn's heavy breathing and Rhys's glaring, I looked from son to father and back again. They could have been twins in that moment.

"Keep the cur on a line, father," Bleddyn finally said, in a voice that shook just a bit. "Keep him on a line or see him put down."

Rhys squinted. "Is that a threat, then? Has yer unseemly desire for this catamite driven ye to make threats against yer own father?"

"I don't threaten. I merely promise." Bleddyn pulled me closer to his side and, overtaken with that sense of foreboding again, I went happily, glad of the arm he put around my shoulders. "I will not stand idly by while Dafydd harms my love. I would sooner put him in the ground than see him lay another finger on Krishnan."

Rhys shook his head and sat down with a near-silent grunt, his eyes never leaving Bleddyn, gauging and measuring, weighing and calculating. "Ye would flout the law of this land to defend this creature ye've barely know for a season, against a man who has shown ye nothing but loyalty and camaraderie for fourteen years?"

Bleddyn's jaw firmed. "Yes. For at the first sign of a challenge, his loyalty and camaraderie have fled like a thief in the night."

"Ye cannot expect such virtues to remain in the face of yer continued sinning!" Rhys gestured at me, but didn't look at me.

"It is no sin to love, father. If ever *you* had loved, you would know that," Bleddyn said in a soft, almost pitying tone. Once more, Rhys looked stung. "I will say only this. Do not make me go to Lord John for satisfaction or resolution. For if I am forced to do so, I will no longer look upon you as my father. Never again will I address you in a familiar fashion, and I will hail you only on his Lordship's business. You have until after the Jubilee to make your choice. Captain."

And before that stung look on Rhys's face could deepen, Bleddyn turned on his heel and left, dragging me with him.

When I glanced back before the turn of the stairwell blocked him from my sight, Rhys was staring after us, looking stricken and betrayed.

Once we arrived back at Islwyn's office, I shut the door behind us and locked it. Bleddyn didn't say anything, merely made straight for our bedroom. I followed him and saw him sitting on my side of the bed, hands dangling between his knees, head hanging almost to his breast bone. He looked miserable.

And it was all my fault.

"I'm sorry, Bleddyn," I said, fidgeting and shifting in the doorway. Bleddyn looked up at me, his dark eyes shining with tears.

"But it is not your fault, beloved," he said so earnestly, I believed him for a few moments, anyway. "It is Dafydd's fault for daring to touch you. And father's for being petty."

"Maybe. But if I wasn't here—"

"If you weren't here," Bleddyn cut in to say, smiling a little and standing up. He took my hands and pulled me closer, until he could wrap his arms around my waist, pinning my hands behind my back. "If you weren't here, my love, then I would have continued on in the same benighted state of loneliness and guilt that has dogged me for fourteen years. I would not know the sweetness of your lips or the tenderness of your arms." Bleddyn leaned his forehead against mine and met my gaze. His eyes were merely a dark glitter, so close. "I would not know the fragrance or softness of your skin, or the heat of you around me, or the simple perfection of falling asleep next to you and waking up next to you.

"I would know none of these things, Krishnan," Bleddyn said, bussing my lips and freeing my hands. I wrapped my arms around his neck. "And for that lack of knowledge, my life would be poorer, indeed."

"Oh, Bleddyn," I murmured, closing my eyes as he kissed me hard, scrabbling under my shirt and down the back of my breeches. When he touched my warm flesh with his cool hands, I moaned. "Yes, please. Make love to me."

Bleddyn palmed the cheeks of my ass, and I hooked my right leg around his left. He carried me to our bed and stared down at me with eyes that seemed to burn, while he began removing his clothes.

Watching him watch me, I toed off my boots, shimmied out of my breeches and hose, and shucked my shirt. When we were both undressed, Bleddyn kneeled on the bed next to me and ran his hand down my chest and stomach, over my abdomen and to my cock. Then he was swooping down like a hawk, his mouth closing around me, so warm and wet I gasped.

As Bleddyn licked, sucked, and teased me, my guilt, fear, and worry slowly retreated to a more manageable distance. I spread my legs wide when he left off the blowjob to get the salve out of our night table. As he slathered salve up and down his hard, reddened cock I hiked my right leg up to my torso. Bleddyn locked his eyes on me, and he let go of his cock to finger and scissor me open. I closed my eyes, and I clenched around his fingers.

But soon enough, Bleddyn lowered his body to mine, guiding his cock forward with one hand and bracing himself with the other. I bit my lip and gazed up into his eyes as he breached the first ring of muscle.

By the time he'd gone as far as our bodies would allow, my eyes were closed again, my lip bitten nearly bloody from fighting not to cry out in pleasure. Bleddyn was kissing, licking, and biting my left nipple, stroking my cock slow and rough. He matched his thrusts to his stroking, driving himself into me slow and powerful before withdrawing, teasing me until only the tip of his cock was in me and I was whimpering to be filled again. And fill me Bleddyn did. Over and over.

And over.

And so that morning passed, Bleddyn blowing off his usual Saturday morning duties, and both of us ignoring the occasional knock on the door. Some of those knocks were, I'm certain, Islwyn, who insisted on coming in for at least a few hours a day to make sure I wasn't messing up his ledgers. Then we ate our very cold breakfast in bed, smiling at each other, but not speaking. After breakfast was done, with silent but tacit agreement, we cleaned up, got dressed, and prepared for our respective duties.

Just as I was about to unlock the door to the corridor, Bleddyn pulled me close and turned me to face him, kissing me intently. He reached down the back of my breeches again, his fingers sliding between my cheeks to brush and tease my sore and swollen asshole.

"I will return 'ere the clock chimes six," he murmured, his index finger penetrating me shallowly.

I grinned. "Six o'clock," I agreed, and Bleddyn kissed me with a hungry moan. A few seconds into our kiss, the knocking started again, and we broke apart with wry smiles. Straightening out each other's clothes, we whispered our *I love you*s, and I unlocked the door and opened it.

There stood Islwyn, looking rather small and disgruntled, red about the cheeks. His canny, but rheumy eyes went from me to Bleddyn, then back to me, and he *hmph*ed, shouldering his way between us into the office, making for his precious, tomelike ledger.

I rolled my eyes. Islwyn didn't care *who* I fucked, so long as I got my figuring right. Though he was probably pretty put out at being locked out of his office for several hours while Bleddyn and I made love repeatedly.

When I came back from the place thinking about making love with Bleddyn sent me, Bleddyn's lips were twitching like he wanted to smile. He was probably already thinking of six o'clock, and I'd be lying if I said I wasn't, too.

Bleddyn glanced behind me at Islwyn, then stole a quick, teasing kiss before striding off down the hall. I watched him go till he turned a corner, then I shut the door to the office, leaning against it with a happy sigh.

At least until Islwyn began complaining about my handwriting.

Chapter Sixteen

The next morning, Bleddyn and I were up extra early. Rather, *I* was up from nightmares, and had been for hours, before finally waking Bleddyn up so we could have the bathing room to ourselves.

Working in tandem, we filled the large metal tub, locked the door to the room, and took our bath together though there was more horseplay than actual bathing.

But by the time the first knock on the door sounded, Bleddyn and I were already dressed and emptying the tub into the drain in the floor."Just a moment!" I called as we righted the tub. Bleddyn smiled at me, and I smiled back.

"You look so handsome," I said besottedly, reaching out to smooth down wet cowlicks that refused to be tamed. Bleddyn laughed and pulled me into his arms.

"And *you* are simply ravishing," he replied, one hand squeezing my ass, the other brushing my hair back from my face as he kissed me. "I wish church and our visit to Gwenllian were already over, and Gareth already a-bed, because then, oh, *then*, Krishnan…"

"Then, you'd be teaching me self-defense, remember?" Normally, after church and Gwenllian, Bleddyn and I would spend the rest of the afternoon and the beginning of the evening with Gareth, then the end of the evening and a goodly portion of the night making love in our tiny room off the accounting office.

Not so, today.

We both sighed, and Bleddyn's smile made a limp comeback. "Well, we needn't stay at it for more than an hour. 'Twould defeat the purpose to inundate you with more than that."

"Are you sure you're not just saying that so we'll have more time to fuck?" I teased, and Bleddyn shivered. He loved it when I talked what passed for dirty then.

"I'm certain, beloved. The important thing is to learn the very fundamentals of defense thoroughly, and practice them daily before moving on to more specific counters and defenses." Bleddyn's smile firmed up. "But you are graceful and light on your feet. I have no doubt such learning will come easily to you if you approach it with an open mind and heart."

"Okay, okay, I get it," I said, chuckling a little and stealing a kiss. "I'll stay open and try my best."

"That is well, then." We leaned in to kiss each other, when we heard a discreet knock on the door. It was quiet, but a bit rushed. "C'mon," I said, taking his hand and tugging him toward the door. "Let's go see about breakfast."

"An inspired idea, my love."

When Bleddyn opened the door, two of Gwynedd's girls—Bryn and Anwen, identical twins of about fourteen—were standing there, chatting. Their eyes widened as they saw us, and they giggled behind their hands.

"Top of the morning, ladies," I said jauntily, and Bleddyn wished them a good morning in Cymraeg.

The girls shared a look, giggled again, and curtsied. "Good morning, Master Krishnan, Master Bleddyn," they said at the same time. Then they giggled again and inched their way past us to the bathroom, whispering among themselves in a language that wasn't Cymraeg.

Bleddyn and I made our way down to the dining hall, at which point we stopped holding hands. There were very few people in the hall, so Bleddyn and I got our food and sat in a secluded corner, eating and talking in private about inconsequentials. That lasted for all of ten blissful minutes, till Rhys walked in with none other than Dafydd, the two of them speaking quite companionably.

I glanced at Bleddyn in time to see him notice them. The blood slowly drained from his face as he processed the fact that his father was talking so chummily with his enemy, for lack of a better word. They walked past the area where Bleddyn and I were seated—perhaps they noticed us, perhaps they didn't—got their food, and sat in the center of the hall, still chatting. Bleddyn, meanwhile, had gone from blanched white to mottled red.

I put my hand on his and leaned closer to whisper, "Hey, wanna take breakfast back to our room? We can have a little fun after we eat and before it's time to get Gareth and go to church."

Bleddyn barely seemed to hear me, staring so hard at his father and Dafydd that I thought they would burst into flame.

"How little he respects me," Bleddyn mumbled in disbelief, closing his hand tightly around mine. I didn't know which of the two he meant, or if he meant both. I'm not sure even Bleddyn knew which he meant.

"We don't know what they're talking about. It could be about Dafydd's little attitude problem," I said, hoping that would calm Bleddyn. But that hope was in vain.

"They're as thick as thieves! There is no disciplining or remorse whatsoever in their postures or their faces!" Bleddyn spat, then he stood up.

"Fuck!" I hissed, jumping up and following him as he approached Rhys and Dafydd's table. I took his hand and tried to tug him back the way we'd come, but Bleddyn wasn't having any of it. So, sooner rather than later, we were standing over Rhys and Dafydd, who looked up from a conversation that seemed to be pleasant, identical looks of polite disdain on their faces, though Dafydd's grey eyes shone with malice, whereas Rhys's dark eyes were just grim.

"Good morning, Bleddyn!" Dafydd said mockingly, popping a bit of sausage into his mouth. "Good morning, Master Krishnan! How fare you both on this, our Lord's day?"

Bleddyn didn't even dignify that with an answer, didn't even look at Dafydd. He only had eyes for Rhys.

"So," he said, his normally even voice cracking with hurt and accusation. "I see now where your true loyalties lie."

Rhys glanced down at our clasped hands, then back up at Bleddyn with the same look of accusation on his face that Bleddyn wore. "And I see where *yers* lie, boy."

Bleddyn paled and squeezed my hand. "My loyalty lies with those of good heart, who don't wish or visit ill on the innocent. I wonder now if that can be said to include my own father."

Rhys's eyes widened for a moment, then narrowed venomously. "It seems to me I could say the same of ye, Bleddyn. Where is the son I raised? Where is the young man who lived as virtuously as a saint and strove to be as near to Christ as possible? Did this *catamite bugger* it all out of ye?" Rhys demanded in a low voice. Both Bleddyn and I paled this time. Bleddyn even more so when Dafydd snickered, and added under his breath, in Cymraeg, something that sounded low and mean even in another language. And my name, as well as the word for gonorrhea was stuck dab in the middle of whatever was said.

Oh, dear, I thought, glancing at Bleddyn. *This will end badly..*

And, as if in slow motion, I saw Bleddyn turn toward Dafydd, who was taking another bite of sausage. Bleddyn didn't even blink, simply swung on the other man. Clocked him in the face hard enough that I heard the *crunch* as his nose broke. Dafydd squawked and tumbled backwards out of his chair, to the floor in a small spray of blood.

"Bleddyn, no!" I cried, interposing myself between the two of them as Bleddyn started to advance on Dafydd, who was scrambling back away from the table, one hand coming up to his bloody, gushing face as he began to make awful, aborted coughing sounds.

"Stand aside, Krishnan," Bleddyn was saying angrily but calmly. "He needs to be taught a lesson in manners. Since no one else appears willing to teach him, I will!"

"No, Bleddyn—damnit, Rhys, help me out, here!" I called, trying to block Bleddyn from a still-coughing Dafydd. But Rhys wasn't paying me or his son any mind. Instead he was staring at Dafydd in horror, just starting to stand up.

"Dear God, he's choking" fell from Rhys's lips. Bleddyn, who'd gotten past me by moving me to one side as if I was a chair or a box, stopped his advance on Dafydd and blinked. We both looked at Dafydd, who was struggling to get up and, from the sound, clear his windpipe. He was having no luck with either.

"Fuck!" I said again, turning away from Bleddyn. I approached Dafydd reluctantly, Bleddyn and Rhys on my heels. "Fuck. Twenty-first century? Don't fail me, now," I muttered, then I glanced back at Bleddyn and Rhys.

"Get him on his feet. *Now!*" I added when they both merely stood there. Bleddyn was the first to move, darting in to tug Dafydd's left arm. Rhys was a second behind him, taking Dafydd's right, and together they got the taller man to his feet. He was still coughing and wheezing, his face turning purplish at the cheeks, white at the forehead, and blue around the mouth. His grey eyes were rolling wildly, fear writ large in them. They rolled from Rhys and Bleddyn to me. Then I was walking past all three of them till I was behind Dafydd.

"Now, hold him still and upright," I said, as grim as Bleddyn or Rhys ever was.

I stepped up behind Dafydd, wrapped my arms tight around his waist, locked my fists together under his ribcage, and said a prayer.

Then I invented the Heimlich maneuver.

It took nearly a minute, during which I broke out in a flop-sweat like nobody's business. Dafydd struggled against the three of us, and Bleddyn and Rhys stared at me with equal parts horror and interest, as if I was going insane right before their very eyes.

I performed the maneuver over and over, ignorant of the crowd forming around us, though I did hear Bleddyn saying: *"Arhoswch yn ôl!"* Stay back!

It was weird, since I'd never performed the Heimlich on someone who was actually choking. I didn't know how long I should keep trying. Till he was dead? Till he yakked up the bit of sausage? How would I know when he had?

And just as I was thinking that, I heard and felt him puke it up. And I *do* mean puke. For it wasn't just that bit of sausage that came out, but the rest of his breakfast and, I'll wager, some of last night's dinner, in what I was later told was a projectile spew of enormous proportions.

Shaking from adrenaline and stunned that it'd worked, I let go of Dafydd, backing a few steps away. For nearly a minute, he intermittently barfed and coughed and sobbed. Bleddyn and Rhys held him up when he drooped like week-old laundry, but both of them were staring back at me like I'd just done a truly astounding magic trick.

Bleddyn let go of Dafydd's arm and faced me. After a moment of staring at each other with wide, shocked eyes, we hugged and kissed, then hugged again, regardless of the onlookers. Dafydd was still hitching and dry-heaving, half-held up by Rhys.

"You—you saved him from certain death!" Bleddyn exclaimed looking at me with such wonder and tenderness, I felt about ten thousand feet tall. "Never before have I seen anyone save a man's life in that manner. 'Twas a most wondrous thing to behold!"

I laughed, adrenaline still rushing through me, making me shake and twitch. "I don't know about that, but it's definitely something I'm glad I learned how to do! Though I never thought I'd get the chance to use it!"

Bleddyn leaned close. "More learning from the twenty-first century?"

"Indeed." I grinned and let Bleddyn kiss me again, but briefly. I was suddenly aware of all the people standing around and asking questions.

"Uh," I said when Sawyl ap Rhodri stammered an enthusiastic question at me in Cymraeg, made even more incomprehensible by his lack of teeth. Bleddyn put his arm around my waist and steered me away from the crowd, saying something fast and firm in Cymraeg as he did. And though it took a few reluctant moments, the crowd before us parted to let us through. But as I passed, no few of them reached out to touch me reverently, murmuring: *"Bendithia di. . . mae'r Arglwydd gyda thi."*

Bleddyn led me away from them to the exit, and when I glanced back, everyone including Rhys and a bloody, puke-faced Dafydd was staring after us, varying expressions of awe and surprise on their face. Even Rhys looked gobsmacked. And Dafydd—Dafydd was glaring at me with hot, *hot*, unhidden hatred as he coughed up and spat bile and blood.

❖

When we got back to the accountant's office and our bedroom, I flopped on the bed, feeling drained and as if I might float away without something to weigh me down. And I knew just the thing, too.

Bleddyn stood over me, smiling down, still alight with wonder. I grinned and held open my arms. As ever, he went into them, kneeling before me and pulling me close.

"I love you," he murmured. I sighed.

"And I love you."

"You are a miracle," Bleddyn said, brushing his fingertips across my cheek. "Everything about you is miraculous. If ever more proof were needed of your goodness and honor, then you have just given it in front of everyone."

I laughed again. "Oh, Bleddyn, I don't care what any of them think of me. Just what you think of me."

"I think you are, simply put, the most amazing man I ever have and ever will meet, and I love you more than word can adequately wield the matter." Bleddyn kissed me so sweetly that I moaned.

We were both disrobing again without saying a word, kissing and touching each other with reverence and something that was almost shyness.

And despite the pleasure of Bleddyn's solid weight on me, pinning me to the Earth, I spent the morning floating amongst the clouds nonetheless. We didn't make it to church that Sunday. Neither of us, however, had any complaints about that.

Early afternoon found the three of us, Bleddyn, Gareth, and me at Gwenllian's cottage.

Bleddyn had, from his arrival, started on his continuing mission to fix every little thing that was wrong with her cottage and barn since there'd been no one else to do such work in the years since Eirian Robert's death.

For a while, the three of us watched Bleddyn work. Gareth had to be physically restrained to keep from trying to climb up into the hayloft onto the roof to "help" his father. But he finally stopped his antics when Bleddyn called from the roof: "*Gareth, rhoi'r gorau i gamymddwyn a gwneud fel eich Krish-syr a gofynnodd i'r Gweddw Robert. A oes gan fy mod yn gofyn, ac yn setlo i lawr." Gareth, stop misbehaving and do as your Krish-sir and the Widow Robert asked. Do as I ask, and settle down.*

"*Le, tad!*" Gareth called back obediently as he stopped leading Gwenllian and I a merry chase around the back of the barn. He just stopped in his tracks and ran back toward us, jumping as soon as he was within catching distance. I *oofed* as I caught him and hoisted him above my head for "birdie," which was really the seventeenth century version of "airplane,"and Gwenllian laughed.

When we'd both had enough of birdie, I hugged Gareth and kissed his cheek, and he giggled and wiped his face. Just for that, I gave him a wetter kiss right on the forehead, and he made the universal sound of the grossed-out, "Yuck!"

I chuckled and put him down, taking his tiny hand. Together, he, Gwenllian, and I strolled back to the cottage.

Once inside, Gareth was talking a mile a minute to Gwenllian and me. I got the feeling that even Gwenllian could only understand a little of what he was saying, despite her fluent Cymraeg. Though she did ask him questions and listened closely to his responses.

The three of us got lunch together, and I went to call Bleddyn in from roofing. When he came down, he smelled of sweat and the outdoors. It was all I could do to keep my hands off him.

Okay, since we were alone in the barn, maybe I didn't keep my hands *strictly* to myself. Bleddyn was partly at fault for encouraging me by already being half-hard and submitting gratefully to my patented, three-minutes-to-Heaven-or-your-money-back stroke-off.

Afterwards, we meandered back to Gwenllian's cottage hand in hand, while Bleddyn used his shirt to wipe himself down. Just before we reached the open doorway, he pulled the shirt on and pulled me close for a kiss, then we went inside.

Gareth led the conversation over lunch, his gabbling bright and uncomplicated. He asked Gwenllian about ten thousand questions, all of which she answered with patience and gentle indulgence. While she did, Bleddyn and I made calf-eyes at each other and played footsie under the table.

An hour after lunch was over, Bleddyn was back on the roof, Gareth was asleep in Gwenllian's bed, and Gwenllian and I were catching up on all that'd happened to each other over the past seven days while we cleaned up. It was, in some ways, like spending time with Dierdre, thus it was, as the Sundays before it, a good one.

❖

By late afternoon, Bleddyn had finished with the roof of the barn and was some distance away, chopping wood for Gwenllian's cottage, as he also did every Sunday.

For once, I wasn't out there with him, cheering Bleddyn on and ogling him as he made short work of the logs. Gwenllian and I were sitting at her table in comfortable silence, sipping mugs of spearmint-raspberry tea.

My mind began to drift, till I was starting to nod off. It'd been so long since I'd had a full night's sleep, it was amazing that I didn't face-plant during these visits. Or church, which was not the most exciting place on Earth.

In all honesty, I'd barely been able to stay awake for either, so tired was I from a night spent in part getting banged like a Salvation Army drum, but in part spent waking up from nightmares which I could not remember but filled me with fear.

Snapping myself mostly awake, I finally found the courage to broach the subject of my sleepless and nightmare-ridden nights with the one person who might be able to help me.

"Gwenllian?"

"Yes, Krish?" She smiled over at me, and I returned it lamely.

"Is it possible...that is, would you know of any sleeping tonics that would allow me to sleep without dreaming?"

Gwenllian's canny green eyes were measuring and penetrating. "I know of quite a few. Why, pray tell, do you ask, Krish?"

I looked away from her to the steaming mugs on the table. "Well," I muttered, uncertain how much to tell Gwenllian, but knowing I had to tell her *something*.

But what? What could I say?

Gwenllian, I haven't been sleeping for so long that I'm either a zombie during my days, or an emotional wreck from spending what little sleep I do get fending off nightmares. Is there any *way you could help me drug myself insensate every night so I can finally,* finally *get some rest before I have a psychotic break?*

Something like that?

Finally, as the silence drew out, I decided to be forthright. After all, what did I have to hide from *her*?

So, I told her everything. Not specifically about the dreams, for I could never remember them in any coherent way upon waking. But I told her they'd become more frequent, and I was barely getting any sleep because of them. I also told her that Bleddyn did *not* know about them. That as far as he was concerned, I was sleeping like a baby every night.

Gwenllian frowned and sat back in her chair. I avoided her eyes. "Secrets such as that can do worse than make one feel alone and in pain. They can cause divisions between two hearts that are otherwise one," she said with gentle concern, and I snorted.

"I know that, Gwenllian, I do, it's just...I don't want him to worry. Not when there's nothing his worrying would accomplish. After all, it's not like *he* can control whether or not I have nightmares."

Gwenllian made a noncommittal noise and stared at me some more, until I braved her gaze. Her face was worried and knowing. "I can, of course, supply you with such a tonic. Though, in the long term, such tonics are deleterious to one's health," she said, giving voice to a soft, ponderous sigh. "I can offer you a tonic, or I can offer you a chance at knowledge."

I frowned. "*Knowledge*? Of what?"

"Of what you *dream*, Krishnan. Of what vexes you every time you close your eyes."

I barked a desperate laugh. "I don't want to remember these nightmares! I wanna *forget* them till I stop having them!"

Gwenllian shook her head. "These are not mere dreams, do you understand? These are *memories*, struggling to assert themselves and be acknowledged by your waking mind."

Thinking of the feelings I'd been waking up with for weeks, the weeping and silent sobbing till dawn, the feeling that I wasn't safe, even with Bleddyn's arms around me, I closed my eyes and shuddered.

For I didn't have any memories that were *that* bad, did I? Not that I could remember, anyway. Nothing worse than that awful night I got date-raped when I was too drunk to say no with my fists or otherwise fight off the guy who would be my first. And if there were worse memories lurking within me, I just didn't want to know. Didn't want to remember. I wanted them to stay buried *deep*. The bad memories I *could* remember were bad enough.

"The longer you resist them, the longer you let them stagnate under your waking mind, the worse they will become, until…" Gwenllian went on, as if reading my very thoughts. And when she trailed off, I opened my eyes and looked at her solemn face.

"Until?" I ventured.

Gwenllian drew her fine dark brows together. "Until, ultimately, you are driven mad, Krishnan."

Horrified, I covered my mouth with my hand. Then I forced myself to put my hand back down, and wrap it around my mug. "C'mon," I said with admirable calm. "You're being a little dramatic, aren't you?"

"Do *you* think I'm being dramatic? Does it *feel* as if I'm being dramatic?"

I looked away from her, unable to lie but unwilling to tell the truth. "All I know is that I need to get some sleep," I said, briefly meeting her eyes again. "I can, of course, pay you for the tonic."

"I neither want nor need money to help you, Krish, if this would actually be helping you," Gwenllian said, and I swallowed, feeling tears well up in my eyes. She went on. "I can and will make you a tonic right now, but only as a temporary measure. In return, you must let me also help you to recover the memories that plague your sleeping mind."

I blinked. "Wouldn't that kind of defeat the purpose of the tonic?"

"The tonic will be to allow you to rest for a while, to give you the time and space necessary to gather yourself and face that which you find so impossible to face. And once you retrieve these memories, you will be more able to control when and how often you *do* remember." Gwenllian paused and put her hand on mine. Hers was cool and dry. "But remember you must. Or it *will* send you mad."

I closed my eyes on more tears. "What if it's something really awful, Gwenllian? What if someone did something terrible to me that I don't want to remember, or maybe I did something terrible to someone else, and I've pushed it out of my mind for that very reason?"

"Either way, Krish, do you really think forgetting will solve the problem?"

After a few moments, I shook my head but didn't open my eyes.

"The only way out is through, Krishnan."

I snorted again, then laughed, wiping my eyes and opening them. "You sound like my mother."

"An undoubtedly wise and compassionate woman."

I laughed again. "Yes, she is. Was. Is. Fuck!" I wiped my eyes, and Gwenllian squeezed my hand again.

"You'll see her again."

I shook my head. "If I do, that'll mean I've lost Bleddyn. I can't have them both, can I?"

Gwenllian's smile was gentle and fond. "Krishnan, you can have whatever you want. And you will. If this adventure through time has proved to you nothing else, it's that love is the most powerful force in the universe, and through it, all of our dreams can come true! Yes, it may take us some time, but in the end, we'll have everything we ever desired. Now." Gwenllian stood and moved to her herbal closet. One of them. "I'll get started on the tonic, and you must speak with Bleddyn, I'm thinking."

I gaped at her. "Tell him? About the not sleeping? And the tonic? And having to remember the awful things I dream about?"

Gwenllian nodded. "He loves you and will want to aid you through this. And I fear that without his aid and love, you'll have a much tougher time of it than necessary."

I groaned and buried my head in my arms, on the table. Gwenllian's put her hand on my head and stroked my hair for a few moments.

"The tonic for dreamless sleep will be ready in an hour. The tonic to help you remember what it is you dream will take somewhat longer. It will be ready by Friday evening."

I sighed. "Okay."

"Take heart, Krish, for you are stronger than you think."

I snorted. I was the weakest person I knew. And come Friday, Bleddyn would know it, too. Would he still want me if he knew the horrible secrets I kept even from myself?

Suddenly I jumped up. I needed air. I needed to get outside, where I wouldn't feel so closed in and trapped, a feeling I'd never associated with Gwenllian's cottage until that moment. I got that feeling everywhere these days. I always felt trapped wherever I was, as if I was being hunted, and my pursuer was always just out of sight taunting me. And when he grew tired of playing games, when he finally decided to catch me...

"Excuse me—" I managed to say as I made for the door and flung it open. I ran outside, down the path and out of the clearing into the woods, which were a green, fuzzy wall, as seen through my tears.

"Krishnan!" Gwenllian called after me but did not follow. Something for which I was obscurely grateful. I hated for people to see me cry.

I didn't realize I'd been following the sounds of chopping until I was almost upon Bleddyn.

He didn't immediately notice me, and so I wiped my teary face and watched him hew wood, while I thought of nothing at all. I ogled him, all sweat-shiny skin and oiled muscle, as he swung the ax over and over, until I started to get hard. Wide-eyed, I watched him to the end of his labors, when he put down the ax, took up his shirt, and began to wipe himself down.

He'd barely run the shirt over his hair before he noticed me and started. Then he smiled and approached me. "Hello, my love," he said, seeming so happy to see me that I doubt he even noticed that I took a step back and averted my no doubt reddened eyes. But then I forced a step forward and tried to act as if nothing was wrong.

"Hey, baby," I said, smiling a sultry smile that felt about as real as cubic zirconium. "I missed you."

Bleddyn's smile, open and welcoming, widened, and as he drew near to me, he pulled me into his arms. I went into them with a relieved sigh, wrapping my arms around his neck and burying my face in the sweat-damp hollow between his neck and shoulder.

"I missed you, too, my gentle dove." Bleddyn kissed my temple. I shivered and clung to him so close that he chuckled, and the hand that rested at the small of my back moved down to my ass, and he pulled me flush against him. He was just as hard as I was. But then exertion always did that to Bleddyn. He was never hornier than when he'd been through drills or doing some onerous labor.

Like wood-chopping and roof-mending, I supposed, leaning back to look into his eyes. They were dark and contented.

"Take this not as a sign of displeasure, but you are unusually aroused at such a strange moment," Bleddyn noted, squeezing my ass and pushing his hard-on against mine.

"Watching you exert yourself always gets me hard," I said, kissing him intently, before whispering: "I *need* you to fuck me, Bleddyn."

He tightened his hand on my ass, and then he plucked at the back of my breeches. "And I wish nothing more than a sojourn in the tight confines of your lovely form, but I brought nothing with me to ease the way," he said, his fingers nonetheless teasing between my cheeks, brushing feather-light at my entrance. Breathless, I laughed.

"That's why God—*somebody's* God—gave us spit."

Bleddyn pressed his questing finger against me lightly enough that he didn't enter me, just teased and tortured me. "Beloved, I would take you here now, but for the fear of harming you."

"I swear, if we take it slow, you won't harm me." I tipped my head back so Bleddyn could kiss and nibble and lick that erogenous zone. And he did, bending me back slightly.

"Or," he said, pinching a small section of skin between playful teeth, "I could pleasure you with my hands and my mouth."

I shivered. "Okay. That could work."

Bleddyn chuckled and walked me backward until I hit a tree. Then he sank to his knees and took my breeches with him, all without breaking eye contact.

Nothing more was said until the sun neared the horizon, and we were walking back to Gwenllian's cottage to pick up Gareth and go home.

"Gwenllian will be giving me a tonic," I said with annoying uncertainty as we neared the clearing. Bleddyn's step didn't falter, but I felt his keen gaze on me.

"Are you ill?"

"Not ill, just…I'm having trouble sleeping," I paused to let that sink in, then went on. "I have nightmares that I can't remember, and I wake up several times per night until I eventually just stay awake for the day."

He was silent. For several minutes. By the time Bleddyn took my hand and spoke, we were on the path to Gwenllian's cottage. I could already hear Gareth's laughter coming from within.

"For how long?" Bleddyn asked.

I sighed. "From almost since the day I got here," I admitted, and Bleddyn stopped walking. I stopped with him and waited for whatever blame and recriminations he would make. I felt his gaze on me, heavy and considering, for nearly a minute before I found the strength to meet it. When I did, I saw solemn concern on Bleddyn's face.

"We will speak of this more after Gareth is to bed and we're alone," he said softly, and it was *not* a question.

Resigned, I nodded. "All right."

He sighed. "But why did you not tell me, Krishnan?"

"I didn't want to worry you."

Bleddyn shook his head irritably. "Is that not what a husband is supposed to do? To care for, protect, and, yes, worry over his spouse?"

I blinked, surprised at the word *husband* from Bleddyn's lips. But Bleddyn was still speaking.

"Is this not exactly like what happened yesterday with Dafydd? You did not see fit to tell me you were in a bad way with him. Had I not spotted the bruises, I would never have known he'd accosted you! You must learn to tell me when you are troubled or when others trouble you, so that I may help you, for I love you, and would take away all your pain, if I could. If you would but let—*mmph*!"

Bleddyn didn't get to finish his sentence because I'd thrown my arms around him and kissed the words from his lips. I could still taste myself on his lips and that, along with him using the H-word, sent little zings of arousal throughout my body.

When I felt the need to breathe again, I broke the kiss and leaned my forehead against his. "You just called yourself my husband."

Bleddyn, also panting, chuckled nervously. "So I did."

"I love you, Bleddyn," I said, injecting every drop of feeling for Bleddyn I had into my voice. "I love you, husband."

Bleddyn shivered and held me tight. When we could bear to let go of each other, we didn't go far. We gazed into each other's eyes, until we both laughed. Then, arms around each other's waists, we made our way to up the path to Gwenllian's front door.

We arrived back at Gwydir Castle by sunset. Bleddyn led the way into the courtyard, on Arwel. I was close behind him on the gelding I often rode, Ifan, with Gareth asleep in front of me. We dismounted at the stable, and the boy came to take our horses. His eyes widened when they landed on me, and he smiled for the first time in my experience, and kept staring.

I smiled back uncertainly, holding a still sleeping Gareth in my arms and glancing at Bleddyn, who shrugged.

"Er, thank you, Gronw," I said, nodding. Gronw nodded back, then gabbled something out in Cymraeg. Bleddyn's brows drew together in concern, and he replied in Cymraeg. There was a brief back-and-forth, then he and Gronw both looked at me. I stroked Gareth's fine blond hair, kissed his forehead, and said: "What?"

"Welcome, Master Krishnan and Bleddyn!"

Lord John's welcome was warm and sincere, and he shook my hand. I shook his back, a little limply, I was so nervous.

As Lord John shook Bleddyn's hand, I took a moment to meet the eyes of the other dinner guests in the lord's private dining room. There was Richard and Owen, of course, and two advisors whose names I didn't remember, but they'd been present at the dinners I'd had with his lordship three months ago. Finally, Rhys and...Dafydd.

The former was staring at me in seeming disgruntlement and plain confusion. Dadydd wasn't looking at me at all, but instead examining a tapestry as if it held the secrets of the universe. Though his face was in profile, I could tell it was still bruised from Bleddyn breaking his nose. Dafydd appeared to have a raccoon mask.

"Come, let us sit and eat, for it has been a long day!" Lord John said. The other guests, lingered and talked with each other, all except Rhys and Dafydd, who was now staring at Bleddyn with a look of abject misery and thinly-veiled betrayal.

Then everyone moved to the large, round dining table, talk flowing among them like wine. One of the nameless advisors even managed to engage Rhys in chat. No one, however, bothered to speak to Dafydd who, once seated, stared at his plate and would not lift his gaze.

Bleddyn and I sat next to each other. I was to the left of Lord John, at the lord's request, and Bleddyn next to me. To his right sat his eldest son, Richard, then Owen, followed by the advisors, Dafydd, then Rhys, who was next to Bleddyn.

Rhys cast a few glances Bleddyn's way, but Bleddyn steadfastly ignored him and focused on my conversation with Lord John.

"I must say, I'm surprised to be invited to supper with you, my lord, but I'm honored, as always," I said when there was a break in our exchange of pleasantries. Lord John smiled, glancing at Bleddyn before patting my hand.

"But surely, you mustn't be, Master Krishnan," he replied with a laugh. I couldn't help the questioning look I'm certain was on my face. Lord John sat back in his chair. "After you miraculously saved the life of one of my men, the very least I could do was to invite you to supper!"

My eyes widened, and I refrained from glancing at either Bleddyn or Dafydd. So *this* was why I'd been invited to supper with his lordship.

I could feel eyes on me, and I glanced around the table. I stopped on Owen, who raised his wine goblet in a toast and winked at me. I blushed and looked at Lord John. "Oh, that," I said, pasting on a smile. "I just did what anyone would have done."

"Would have? Perhaps. *Could* have...?" Lord John shook his head. "I'm not so certain of that. You are a young man of rare and impressive talents, Master Krishnan."

I blushed and looked at my own wine goblet. Then I snatched it up to take a rather large sip. I needed the fortification. "Really, it was just something I picked up in my, er, misspent youth."

"If only more people misspent their youths learning such things," Lord John said, taking a sip of his own wine. Then he fixed me with his canny, blue gaze and said, "What boon would you ask of me, Master Krishnan?"

I blinked. "Uh, boon, my lord?"

"Yes, for your quick thinking and skill. For saving a young man's life. I would grant you a boon. Ask of me anything, and if it is in my power to grant it, I will."

Gobsmacked and caught completely off guard, I stammered for a few seconds, then looked to Bleddyn, who seemed wide-eyed and surprised as well. Indeed, the rest of the table had fallen silent and was watching me, even Dafydd, whose expression was now blankly unreadable, and only partly because of his swollen face.

I realized Lord John was waiting patiently for my reply. "I—I—" I glanced at Bleddyn again, and he shrugged almost imperceptibly. "There's nothing Bleddyn or I want for. You have provided for us admirably, my lord." And I inclined my head to him. "There's nothing I want for. I have everything I need."

"Is that so, Krishnan ap Karthik?" Lord John asked, sounding so amused that I immediately looked up at him. His eyes *were* amused, but still kind. And knowing. "Have you no thought for the future? Perhaps a cottage of your own, or a horse, or a plot of land—anything such as that?"

Frowning, I thought about what his lordship had offered. A cottage? But what good was a home if I couldn't risk Bleddyn and Gareth living in it with me?

A horse? Hah, I could barely ride well enough to keep my seat. Ifan or Queen were good enough to ride to church or to Gwenllian's or to Trefriw and Llanrwst.

A plot of land? To what end? I was no farmer and certainly had no interest in building a home I couldn't share with my husband and his child on whatever land I was given.

Bleddyn and I lacked nothing, at least nothing Lord John could fix. But what about *Gareth*? What about *his* future? The kid was smart. Clever and intelligent. With his quick, sharp, curious mind, he could be anything he wanted, but his station in life would limit him in this time, as surely as being none too bright in *my* time might have.

In that moment, I knew exactly what I wanted.

"My lord, the boon I would ask of you would be that you, Lord John, be Gareth ap Bleddyn's benefactor. That upon reaching the age for university, should he show an aptitude for his studies, he be sent to the university of his choosing to continue his education, and build a life upon that learning, if he is able." I paused when Rhys gasped, and smiled as Bleddyn covered my hand with his and squeezed. "And if he is not, or chooses not to, then I would ask that he always have a place here at Gwydir Castle."

Lord John saw Bleddyn's hand where it covered mine, then back up to me."Is this how you would spend your boon? On Gareth ap Bleddyn?"

"On his future, yes," I replied firmly.

Lord John searched my eyes, then looked at Bleddyn. "And is this in accordance with *your* wishes, as well, Bleddyn ap Rhys?"

I could hear Bleddyn swallow. "'Tis, indeed, my lord."

"Well, then." Lord John looked from Bleddyn, to me, his eyes grave, but approving. "It shall be as you ask. The boy, Gareth ap Bleddyn, will be tutored like one of my own sons and, if he shows the aptitude for learning, he shall attend any university he wishes." Lord inclined his head to me slightly. "On my honor, Master Krishnan, I swear this."

I smiled.

The rest of dinner was a pleasant affair.

After granting my boon, Lord John turned the talk to other matters, for which I was grateful. I drank rather too much wine and laughed rather too loud at Lord John's humorous stories. But he didn't seem to mind.

Next to me, Bleddyn was a mostly-silent, but rock-steady presence that occasionally held my hand, or nudged my knee.

Whenever I glanced at him, he would smile at me in such a way that the whole table, had to have known we were in love, if they hadn't known it before.

But I didn't care. I chatted with their lordships and the advisors and ignored Rhys and Dafydd. When dinner was over, after good nights had been wished, and Bleddyn and I were halfway out the door, Rhys called Bleddyn's name, I would have ignored that, too. So would Bleddyn, if Rhys hadn't caught his arm.

As it was, Bleddyn stiffened and froze before shaking off Rhys's hand, slipping an arm around my waist and escorting me from the room. Rhys neither called after Bleddyn nor followed. But when I looked back, he was staring after us with that same miserable, confused expression on his face.

As soon as the door of the office shut behind us, Bleddyn pulled me back into his arms and began nuzzling behind my ear.

"I love you," he murmured, squeezing me tight around the waist. I relaxed back into his arms, practically purring. Then hiccupping. I was *so* drunk.

"I love you, too, husband."

Bleddyn groaned. "When you call me that, I wish nothing more than to fulfill my marital duties until I am utterly spent."

"I wouldn't complain if you did."

Bleddyn turned me to face him and gazed into my eyes. His brimmed with so many emotions, I couldn't read them. "You are the most generous person I have ever known," he said. I grinned and hiccupped again, and he chuckled. "You have given me a love that I have never known before, happiness that I scarce deserve, and you've given my son a better future than I ever could have. Is there anything you *cannot* do, my angel?"

I thought it over, then shook my head. "Nope."

"I thought as much," Bleddyn agreed with indulgent amusement. Then he kissed me lightly. Then less lightly. And then I was trying to climb him like a tree, horny and needing to do something about it.

In short order and as usual, we found ourselves in bed, kissing and touching, moaning and groaning, humping, and screwing. It was *amazing*. Even for us.

And I had somehow managed not to drink *so* much that I got whiskey-dick, so I was good to go all night. Or at least for *part* of the night. After all, I had Gwenllian's tonic to take.

When I finally wore Bleddyn out for the evening, we lay in each other's arms, catching our breath and cooling off. Bleddyn was sprawled on top of me, his face tucked against my neck, as he played absently with my Parvati necklace. I blamed it on all the wine I'd had, but I had an idea.

Bleddyn grumbled as I sat up a little. Shushing him, I reached behind my neck for the clasp of the necklace. When I got it undone, I took the necklace off. Bleddyn, meanwhile, had rolled off to my left and was watching me curiously.

"What is the meaning of this?" he asked. I grinned and leaned over to kiss him silent.

"With this necklace," I said quietly, reaching around the back of Bleddyn's neck and brushing his hair out of the way. I fastened the clasp, Bleddyn gazing at me with wide, uncomprehending eyes. "With this necklace, Bleddyn ap Rhys, I, thee wed."

CHAPTER SEVENTEEN

G wenllian's tonic *worked*.
For five nights after dinner and after Bleddyn screwed my brains out, I got some of the best sleep of my life. No dreams, no nightmares. And by the third day after taking it, everyone had taken to telling me how chipper I was and how well I looked. Bleddyn told me that I was somehow even more radiant and lovely than usual. It was like some sweet idyll, and then I woke up Friday morning.

It was two days until Lord John's Anniversary Jubilee, and I awoke feeling rested and at peace. Bleddyn was already up and gone, probably on Jubilee business, and I was sorry he was, because I woke up with a real rager. But, being ever resourceful, I took care of it with focus and diligence, if not as much satisfaction as Bleddyn would have. Then I was up for the day.

On my way to breakfast, I stopped to lock the door and dropped the key with a small tinkling clatter. I bent to pick it up, but as I was straightening, turning the key over between my fingers, I got the sudden and strong feeling I was being watched.

The feeling wasn't an unfamiliar one. Not over the past few days. From time to time, I would feel as if someone observing me. And yet when I looked around, I saw no one. At least, no one who wasn't busy doing their own thing working or talking or whatever.

So I just chalked the sensation up to being a side effect of Gwenllian's tonic. I figured that, like getting stoned, being on the sleep tonic made me paranoid, as well as well-rested, chipper, and radiant.

It seemed a small price to pay to feel sane again, so I was willing to put up with it. I'd be taking a different tonic tonight, remembering whatever horrible memories had been plaguing my sleep since I arrived.

Sighing, I locked the door and started down the hall, determined to ignore the creeping, crawling sensation that worked its way down my spine.

Then I literally ran into Owen. Or rather, *he* ran into *me* rounding the first corner from the office and nearly knocked me down, but he caught me by the biceps and righted me, both of us laughing.

"Well, this was quite the fortuitous act of clumsiness. I was just coming by Islwyn's office to ask you and Bleddyn to join me for breakfast," he said, making a sardonic, but graceful bow. I blushed and bowed back.

"Bleddyn was gone when I woke up, but *I'd* be delighted to have breakfast with you," I said, batting my eyes. Owen smiled, his blue eyes dancing as he took my hand and brought it to his lips, bowing again.

"And I'd be delighted about your delight," he said, kissing my hand and lingering over it before straightening up with a sigh. "And, in truth, I'd be glad of any company that is not father or Richard. They speak of nothing but that damned Jubilee."

I laughed. "Poor Bleddyn feels the same way about it."

"I can imagine, the poor fellow! Having to play father for the reenactment!" Owen snorted. "'Tis an honor, to be sure, but one I am thankful to do without."

"You and me, both," I agreed, still chuckling. Owen grinned and folded my hand on his forearm, covering it with his own. Then he started us down the corridor, toward his chambers.

"So, how fare you on this lovely morning, dearest Krish?"

"I fare very well," I answered. "And you?"

"Far better, for having stumbled across you in so timely a fashion."

"Charmer."

"I speak only the truth." Owen chuckled. "And how fares Bleddyn, other than harried by the reenactment-brouhaha?"

"He's well. A bit tired, but I expect that once the Jubilee has passed, that situation will remedy itself."

"I imagine there is very little wrong in Bleddyn's life that cannot be cured by a few, er, *restful* nights in your arms."

"Got *that* right," I said smugly, and then we both laughed and continued to his chambers, my feeling of being watched temporarily forgotten.

❖

I spent the morning hard at work, as usual, on the castle's books when I heard a hard, yet hesitant knock on the door.

The tenor of the knock was demanding and urgent, so very different from Bleddyn's discreet, gentle three-rap knock. I should have known it wasn't my sexy squire. But I was still half distracted and automatically called: *"Dewch i mewn. Neu ar. Neu gyda."*

And I called it in my most innuendo-laden purr.

I looked up as the door opened, a promising smile on my lips at the prospect of the crippling nooner that was no doubt about to happen. But that smile turned into a goggle-eyed gasp and deep blush as I scratched the pen across the formerly clean page. "Dafydd!"

The tall, blond bruiser had let himself halfway into the office, as if he disdained coming in all the way. "Aye," he said, then sniffed— actually *sniffed*, as if he smelled something bad—before squinting at a spot just above my right shoulder. "My captain wishes you to join him in his office for the midday meal. If, that is," Dafydd added, his dropping to Islwyn's desk for a moment before he frowned and looked over my right shoulder again. "If, that is, you are not too busy at his lordship's accounting."

Still blushing, I blinked as the import of what Dafydd had said, hit me. "Um. Wait—*what*?"

Dafydd's grim face acquired hints of annoyance and impatience. "Captain Rhys wishes you to join him for lunch, if you please."

Shaking my head, I put the pen in the inkwell, wincing at what I imagined Islwyn saying when he saw the mess I'd made of his precious ledger, a big black streak of ink that lightning-bolted across both pages like Lord Voldemort had been doing the books. "Uh, I can't. I'm pretty tied up with the ledger."

"Aye. He said you'd say no."

I snorted. "Smart man, your captain."

Dafydd shrugged again, moving out from between the door and the doorpost. "T'was *Bleddyn* who said you'd not join them." Then he was gone, nothing but his stomping footsteps and the faint jingle of his armor to signal his passing.

After another few wasted seconds of blinking, I skirted the desk, blew through the open door, locked it, and dashed after Dafydd, calling his name.

❖

At the top of the stairs that lead to Rhys's office, I paused, taking a minute to regain my breath and my composure after a flat-out sprint to the barracks that left a sauntering Dafydd far behind.

Smoothing my hair and brushing imaginary wrinkles out of my clothes, I took the last few steps calmly and knocked on Rhys' door.

"*Mewnbynnu, os gwelwch yn dda,*" came Rhys' stern, heavy voice. It was so like Bleddyn's, only imperceptibly grimmer. But still, somehow equally vivid.

At least, it *usually* was. Today, he sounded, unusually muffled. If he were anyone but this person who had ice-water in his veins, I'd have sworn he was *unsettled*.

Whatever *his reason for wanting to see me* and *the son who hasn't spoken to him on anything but Lord John's business for almost* three months, *it must be something big. Oh,* God, *has Lord John decided to banish Bleddyn and I? Is this our eviction notice? Leave the county on pain of death? It can't be, can it? Lord John is a live-and-let-live sort of guy, very cool. He's known about Bleddyn and me almost since the beginning, I'm sure. So why would he banish us* now?

Then, another chilling thought took me. *At least he'd be giving us a chance to escape with our necks unstretched. By the law of this land, he can put us to death.*

Shuddering, I took another deep, unsatisfying breath, let it out, and turned the knob.

❖

"Bore da, Meistr Krishnan. Sut wyt ti?"

I closed the door behind me discreetly, taking in the sparse, neat office and its lone occupant behind his desk, sitting ramrod-straight, his resigned gaze resting on me, missing nothing. I tried on a smile that felt more like a seasick grimace. *"Er, yn dda. Ac chwi, Capten?"*

Nodding once, Rhys replied in Cymraeg. If he was surprised my Cymraeg had improved enough to have a basic polite bit of chat, he didn't show it. *"Wel, yn canmol yr Arglwydd."* He cleared his throat and glanced out the room's lone window, as if he was considering jumping out of it.

Ha, not if I beat you to it, pal, I thought with nervous gallows humor, taking this moment of distraction to wipe flop-sweat off my forehead.

When Rhys looked at me again, I clasped my hands in front of me like a schoolboy reciting a lesson.

"Well," he said gruffly. "I must say I am somewhat surprised ye did not decline my invitation."

Only because I was lead to believe Bleddyn would be here, and I thought he could use the moral support, I wanted to say, but wisely did not. "I must say that I'm more than a little curious as to why you'd invite *me* to lunch. That alone was enough to send me running," I lied, and Rhys cracked a small, craggy smile, as if his bullshit detector had been set off.

He might be a dick, but he wasn't an idiot. And I'd be smart to remember that.

"I'm assuming there *is* a reason for the invitation," I went on before Rhys could think *too* long and hard about my lie. "That you weren't just overtaken by a strong desire to dine with me."

Rhys' snorted, his craggy smile widening a bit, as if he was surprised. I must say, I found myself surprised by a lot of things that morning. Not the least of which was the ease with which I was speaking to Rhys without someone else around to act as a buffer between us.

"Yer assumption is correct," Rhys said with a sigh, his smile fading as he studied me. I resisted the urge to fidget or lean against the door just behind me. "I wish to speak with ye and with Bleddyn about…"

I raised an eyebrow when Rhys trailed off, looking fantastically uncomfortable and at a loss for words. But despite my outer *sang froi*, inside I was shaking like a leaf. "About?"

Another sigh, this one followed by Rhys standing and walking to the window. He leaned against the sill and looked out. "About the obvious affection ye have for my son. And the reciprocated affection he has for *ye*."

Wiping my brow again and ignoring the gibbering capuchin that was my nerves, shrilling at me that Bleddyn and I were about to be banished. "Is that so?"

"'Tis."

Sighing myself, I finally gave in and leaned against the door. "Then shouldn't Bleddyn be here, too?"

"Aye, he will be." Rhys glanced at me briefly, then back out the window. "He went to tell the kitchen that there'll be three dining here instead of one."

"Oh." No wonder Rhys was looking out the window, then. I was certain he was counting the seconds until he saw his son's familiar figure striding toward the barracks. It all made sense now. Well, except for the bit about why Rhys wanted to talk about my relationship with his son *now*? And why had Bleddyn relented enough to allow that conversation to be initiated?

The silence between Rhys and I stretched out for uncomfortable minutes. Finally, I broke it with no prior authorization from my brain by saying, "I love your son."

"Aye. I know," was the terse, unhappy reply.

"And I could not love Gareth more if he was my own son."

Rhys glanced at me—almost glared at me, his mouth opening as if he was about to say something snappish or condemning. But before the expected jibe or condemnation could be spat out, Rhys looked away at his rack of shields and sighed yet again. "There is no repaying the boon with which ye've gifted my grandson," he began with a humility that must've tasted bitter, indeed.

Not wanting to force anything of the sort from such a proud and hide-bound man, I interrupted him. "I didn't do it for repayment, Rhys." I shrugged when he looked at me again, his face conflicted and suspicious. "I did it because Gareth is an intelligent, inquisitive, wonderful child who deserves the best from life. I found myself in a position to give him that. How could I *not* give it to him when I was able?"

Rhys studied me hard for a minute before making a frustrated sound and aiming his glare back out the window. "Why? *Why* do *ye*, a near-stranger to this place and its ways, care so for my son and grandson? Why do ye claim to love Bleddyn, when the unnatural form of that love will surely drag ye both to Hell, someday?" He turned away from the window and skirted his desk, approaching me, but stopping well before we were arms' length away from each other, his expression ragged and despairing. "Why, if ye claim to love my son and grandson, would ye jeopardize Bleddyn's immortal soul, his place by the Savior's side for eternity, by continuing to lay with him?"

And there it was. Out on the proverbial table like a bad hand of poker.

Well, I told myself with dubious optimism, *at least Bleddyn and I aren't about to be banished. I think.*

"Rhys," I began, not knowing what I was going to say. What I could possibly say to convince him everything he'd ever been taught or told or learned about homosexuality was flat-out wrong. What could I tell this man that he would believe, if not what the sense of his heart and gut told him? That his son was one of the best men, and not in spite of his attraction to other men?

Looking into his dark, angry, and hurt eyes, I knew I could say nothing. Nothing at all. And despite having known it before that moment, having it confirmed, irrefutably hurt me. Hurt like the Hellfires Rhys so feared for his son's sake.

"I love Bleddyn, Rhys," I repeated around a throatful of tears. "I *love* him. More than anyone or anything in the world. Do you really think that if I believed that Bleddyn would suffer for eternity, I would be within a thousand miles of him, let alone share a bed with him? Do you think that I would condemn the man I love to Hell?"

Rhys drew his brows together and shook his head. "I think ye are so addlepated by yer so-called love that ye cannot see the forest for the trees!"

"You're wrong." I looked down, not wanting Rhys to see the tears in my eyes, which threatened to spill over at even one more harsh word. "You don't know what you're talking about."

"Truly, say ye?" Rhys shook his head again. "What proof have ye that ye're not Hellbound and dragging my poor son with ye?"

"No proof that you would believe, unfortunately for you. Fortunately for *me*, Bleddyn isn't as close-minded as his father," I said finally, sniffing and risking a look up. It was just in time to see Rhys draw back as if gobsmacked. I wiped my eyes and went on. "If there is such a being as God, then it is surely love and will not condemn a man for loving another man. Not when those two men were made in God's own image, to love and be loved."

Rhys was shaking his head again. "Heresy," he said without inflection, but he looked more despairing than he had just a few minutes ago. "Heresy of which ye've no doubt convinced my son."

"Truth, Rhys. Hope. And faith. I have faith that if there is a God, then it is a God of love and acceptance. Why can't you believe that?"

"Because the world isn't the way ye wish it to be, simply because ye wish it to be that way!" Rhys almost yelled. I pressed myself back against the door, momentarily cowed. Then I squared my shoulders and took a step toward him. Rhys took a matching step back from me.

"Perhaps. But that doesn't mean the world is the way you think it is, either." I spread my hands and shrugged once more in the face of the walls I saw going up behind his eyes. I knew I was fighting a losing battle, but I had to try. I had to. "Look, neither of us can claim to know the mind of God. But we can have faith we're following the path God wants us to be on. And I understand your faith comes from the words in a book that's sixteen centuries old. My faith comes from my heart. From the still, small voice inside of it that tells me which way to go, even when I'm lost. I cannot do anything other than follow that voice, for to me it *is* the voice of God. And it tells me that as long as I love without doing harm, I am not wrong."

"Ye *are* doing harm, Krishnan. Can ye not see it?" Rhys demanded desperately. "Ye're doing harm to Bleddyn's reputation! To...to..." he faltered, and I took another step toward him.

"What harm have I done, that you had not already started by outing him and William all those years ago, as if their love was shameful and sinful and awful? By chasing them into the courtyard to face public scrutiny for a private act? By beating them both so badly that Bleddyn still has nightmares about it?"

Rhys flushed angrily and turned away from me. "I need not make an accounting of myself to the likes of ye. I did what I did because, unlike ye, I care for my son's eternal reward."

"So, I see. Even more than you care for your actual son."

He aimed his glare at me again. "Do not *dare* doubt my love for my son," Rhys hissed. "He and that innocent child are all I have in this world. And I am bound to protect them and look after them until the Lord calls me home. If *ye* had a son, ye would understand. Understand that I did what I did and do what I do to keep them safe from any manner of harm or evil that would interfere with them."

I let that sink in for a few moments before responding. "So. You think I'm evil."

At this, Rhys frowned. "Evil? No. At least not a-purpose. I think ye are misguided, foolish, and undisciplined. A heathen and a heretic, to boot. Arrogant and thoughtless of the harm ye might bring others simply by going about yer way. Ye chase blindly after whatever yer heart desires with no thought to consequence. In yer own fashion, ye are worse than evil. Ye're a *lure*, that which convinces men to act unwisely and dishonorably because ye believe so deeply that ye are in the right when it is obvious that ye are not."

Stung because he was close enough about some of what he said, I crossed my arms defensively. "The same could be said of you, Rhys ap Thomas. I think you are misguided and foolish. Worse, in your own way, than outright evil. It's people like you that convince others to act unwisely and dishonorably. Because you fear Hell so much, fear judgment from a God who cannot possibly be as petty and narrow-minded as you'd have it be, that you would beat and shame two children for loving each other, even going so far as to banish one of them. Is that how love is shown, here?"

Rhys turned away from me again, his own arms crossed tightly. Neither of us said anything for a while. This time, however, Rhys broke the silence.

"Perhaps further discourse of a more civil nature should await Bleddyn's arrival."

"Perhaps it should," I agreed just as flatly.

I moved away from the door, going to the weapons rack to admire the specimens on display, while Rhys gazed out the window, his shoulders a tense, stiff line.

From the way they ached, I imagined mine were much the same.

Thankfully, before long I heard Bleddyn's familiar footsteps coming up the stairs. Both Rhys and I turned toward the door in anticipation, but I was the one who went to greet Bleddyn as he came in.

His eyes lit up upon seeing me, as usual, not that I'd *ever* get blasé about such a warm welcome, and he brushed his knuckles against my cheek.

"I have seen Dafydd, and he told me you were already here, my light," he said quietly, his gaze darting to his father, then back to me. "Are you all to rights?"

"As all right as can be expected," I said, smiling at him and basking in the warmth of his concern for a few precious moments. Bleddyn even leaned in as if he would kiss me, but another glance at his father and he was straightening, clearing his throat, and nodding.

"Captain."

"Bleddyn."

Rolling my eyes, I took Bleddyn's hand and faced Rhys. His gaze lay arrested at the place where Bleddyn's hand linked with my own.

"The midday meal should be here, shortly," Bleddyn announced stiffly. "Now that we are assembled, sir, will you reveal your purpose for bringing us here?"

Rhys left off staring at our hands and looked up to search his son's face. Whatever he saw there didn't please him, for he turned away and went to sit behind his desk.

"If ye will be seated," he said, just as stiffly as Bleddyn had spoken.

Bleddyn lead me to the two chairs facing Rhys's desk and we sat, still holding hands. Rhys sat, too, and looked from Bleddyn to me and back to Bleddyn. "I brought ye both here to tell ye that Lord John is most impressed with yers and Master Krishnan's care for Gareth's future. Especially with Master Krishnan's foresight and selflessness. He is also most impressed with the way ye saved Dafydd's life."

Bleddyn and I shared a glance. Lord John had already made as much plain to us both the day it happened. And while he was generous with his praise, Lord John was not what I'd call *effusive* with it. And of that I was glad. My safety and comfort in this time involved me keeping a low profile. Even acts of arguable altruism were dangerous for me. What if someone took it into their head to call me a witch for knowing the fucking Heimlich Manuever? The people that witnessed it had seen it was no magic, but time had a way of erasing and embellishing facts that might not work out in my favor.

At any rate, both Bleddyn and his father were waiting for me to say something.

"Um, that's…it's just a technique I learned back where I come from. Everyone can do it," I exaggerated, hoping that Rhys, at least, bought *this* lie. "Even children get taught as soon as they're old and strong enough."

"Indeed?" Rhys looked thoughtful, and that half-constipated look of disapproval and disappointment had mostly left his face. Mostly. "And would ye be able to teach another to implement this technique of yers?"

Surprised, I blinked then nodded. "Yeah. I mean, I guess I could. It's not difficult to learn. It's just a matter of placing your hands correctly and using the right amount of force."

That craggy smile made its second appearance in the same hour. "This is fortuitous, and it brings me to the other reason I invited ye to break your fast with me, Master Krishnan." Rhys leaned forward, his gaze intent and intense. "I wish ye to teach my men this technique so that they may teach others. 'Twould be a valuable bit of knowledge to have, I doubt it not."

Bleddyn and I glanced at each other again, then back at Rhys. I was about to tentatively say yes, when Bleddyn spoke first. "*This* is why you have brought us here? To take advantage of Krishnan's skill at life-saving? Not to make peace with him?"

I blushed. "Bleddyn—"

"I was not aware that he and I were at war," Rhys huffed, sitting back in his chair and looking mulish. A quick peek at Bleddyn showed an identical look on his face.

Oh, Jesus, I thought wearily, pinching the bridge of my nose to stave off a headache that had been building since before I entered Rhys's office.

"You know what I mean, fath—*sir*. Since the day of his arrival, you have been nothing but contemptuous of Krishnan ap Karthik, disdaining his skills, his company, and his value to this castle. You have belittled him and sided against him, accused him and called him despicable names. And now, you seek to plunder his precious knowledge when it suits you?"

Rhys blanched. Then blushed, getting to his feet to lean forward on his desk and glare. "I am yer father and yer captain, boy! Do not speak to me so!"

Bleddyn scowled. "Or what, pray tell? You'll chase me out into the courtyard and beat me in front of the whole of the castle?" Standing up also, fists clenched, Bleddyn's gaze was hard and hostile. "Try me, old man. I *beg* of you. You'll be surprised yet."

Again, Rhys drew back, gazing up and down Bleddyn as if taking in a stranger, and a dangerous one, at that.

"Ye would turn on yer own father for *him*?" Rhys demanded, sounding more lost and resigned than angry. Bleddyn's glare and stance didn't change one iota.

"I could and I would. I would have done for William, had I the chance of it. But you were bigger and stronger, and I thought that I needed your approval, your love." Bleddyn spat the word as if it was so much phlegm. "And I let you send away the one person who'd ever loved me without condition, who always thought well of me, no matter what. The one person who filled the empty, gaping hole in my heart. I let you ruin the best thing that had ever happened to me..." Bleddyn's voice faltered with remembered horror for a moment, then hardened, like his gaze. "Once. I let you nearly destroy me. But I won't let you do it again. You doubt that not."

Bleddyn turned to me and took my hand, pulling me to my feet as I stared at him with wide eyes. He smiled his fondest smile and kissed first my left hand, then my right. "Come, my love. Let us seek our meal somewhere more conducive to retaining it."

"O-okay," I said, glacing at Rhys, who was staring, shocked, at us, his mouth open and working, as if he would say something but couldn't quite decide what.

Without a look back at his father, Bleddyn lead me to the door, I opened it and preceded him down the narrow staircase. We made it to the bottom of the stairs without Rhys calling Bleddyn back, either in anger or regret.

And despite the hard set to my lover's face, I could see every moment he didn't hear his father's voice calling after him put a nail in the coffin of their relationship.

I awoke in our bed in what I guessed was late afternoon. I smiled a little at the myriad aches I always relished after a nooner with Bleddyn.

I was alone in bed, the lamp burning low, but bright enough to see by even in our windowless little room. I lay in bed for a few minutes, reliving the afternoon and wishing Bleddyn were there to relive them with me.

But, eventually, the great clock chimed four. Just enough time for me to get a little work done before it was time for dinner.

And then I remembered Bleddyn and I were having dinner at Gwenllian's. Which meant knocking off work early and going to see Gareth before we left. I'd soon find out whatever had been causing me nightmares I couldn't remember, and maybe my sleep patterns would get back to normal. Getting up with a groan, I spot-cleaned myself as best I could with my washcloth and the ewer of water at my bedside, then dressed quickly. I could get at least an hour and a half of work done. And it'd take my mind off of…well, everything.

I'd cross the nightmare-causing bridge when I came to it.

Chapter Eighteen

The ride to Gwenllian's cottage was silent and thoughtful, for two different reasons, I was sure.

While I couldn't stop fretting over what Gwenllian's tonic would bring to the front of my mind, I was certain Bleddyn, who'd been in a pensive, terse mood since we'd departed his father's office that afternoon, was thinking about the things he'd said to Rhys and the things Rhys hadn't said back.

We each rode our own horses, and I found myself missing the early days of my tenure in 1626, when Bleddyn and I would ride Arwel together, him slowly but surely getting hard against my ass, and me squirming shamelessly to get him harder.

"A penny for your thoughts, my light."

Bleddyn's voice startled me out of my reverie and back to our scenic ride through the forest, with the westering sun's golden light turned greenish by the filter of the leaves. Tiny patches of blue sky could be glimpsed through the heavy canopy and the very air was thick with heat and humidity. But not unpleasantly so. Though it *did* incline one to sleepiness, even if one was on the back of a horse.

I smiled over at Bleddyn, and he smiled back, tense and strained. "Just thinking about getting you hard," I said offhandedly, without elaborating on all the other things I'd been thinking about before that.

Bleddyn's eyes widened and that tense smile became less so. "Think you of only that?"

"I won't lie and say it's not my favorite and most persistent thought."

Chuckling, Bleddyn nudged Arwel closer to me and my horse, Aderyn, till he was close enough to reach out and brush his fingertips down my cheek. "You are my bright light," he said. Had we not both been horsed, I would've shown him what that kind of sweet talk did to me.

I settled for catching his hand and kissing it. And we held hands, sometimes awkwardly because of Arwel and Aderyn's gaits, but we didn't let go until we arrived at the clearing in which sat Gwenllian's cottage.

Exchanging glances, we finally let go of each other's hands and got off our respective horses. Bleddyn stepped around Arwel as I petted Aderyn's nose, and he put his hands on my shoulders, slowly kneading them. He gave the best massages, and soon I was moaning and getting into said massage, Aderyn forgotten.

"You are worried about the memories Gwenllian's tonic will reveal?"

"A little, yeah," I admitted, though with a casual tone that implied I wasn't nearly as worried as I actually was.

Bleddyn wasn't buying it. He kissed my ear lobe. "My love, you do not have to hide your fears from me. Tell me what you dread, that I may reassure you."

I laughed a bit breathlessly. "Oh, Bleddyn, if only it was that simple. If only I could be reassured about a complete unknown! I mean, I have some bad memories of things I've done and things that happened to me—my father's heart attack, his death, my mother's grief, the stupid things and bad people I got mixed up with afterwards trying to displace that grief. Partying, skipping school, drinking, drugging, stealing, vandalism, stupid, petty crimes with stupid petty people. I was messed up. Did messed up things and had messed up things done to me, and if there's something in my past that's worse than the worst thing I remember…"

I fell silent, forcing down the memories, confused as they were. Most of it was a haze of drunken semi-awareness; the blur of whirling, spinning colors going dark as my face was suddenly pushed into tacky leather that muffled my *nos* and *don'ts*; the somewhat sobering fear of asphyxiation; the feeling of hands scrabbling at my jeans, then the rough rasp as they were yanked down my hips; the weight of a larger, heavier body on my own, sweating, callused hands on my ass for just long enough for spit-sticky fingers to stab into me, and my own startled and muffled shout, which wavered and hitched in my throat until those fingers were replaced with something a lot larger, something that hurt a lot more and turned my yells into screams.

I'm certain I was screaming for him to stop and that he was hurting me. Fairly certain, anyway. Not that it mattered, because he'd pushed my face into that muffling tackiness, until I couldn't breathe at all, until I'd stopped struggling and mostly lost consciousness. Mostly, for I was aware enough that when the pain eased up, when he was done, I rolled onto my side immediately, coughing and hacking, my face covered in tears and snot.

I remember hearing laughter—*familiar* laughter, and from more than one person—before I really did pass out. And after that, I have no memory until I woke up fully dressed in the park the next morning, with a hangover, a nasty taste in my mouth, and a whole new world of aches I'd never felt before.

I remember it was dawn: beautiful, blameless, and blank, and that the walk home took forever, sore and achy as I was. If I thought anything on that endless, agonizing walk, I don't remember it. I only remember needing to get home before my mother woke up, so I could shower away the evidence of the night before.

"A penny for your thoughts," Bleddyn murmured again, but his voice was worried and solemn this time, his perfectly punishing massage turned to a soothing stroke. I sighed and stepped away from him to lean on Aderyn.

"I think if I told you, you'd demand your money back," I joked, but it sounded false and too anxious even to my own ears. When I dared look at Bleddyn, he was watching me with that too-perceptive, too-serious expression.

"Will you not tell me what memory casts into shade the light that shines from you, my love?"

I looked away, blinking back sudden tears. "*Damnit*, Bleddyn, why do you have to be so...so..."

"What?"

"So *sincere*?" I complained, laughing even as a sob came out of me like a bark in between the giggles. "You care about me more than just about anyone ever has, and you're so interested in me, and I'm really not that interesting or worthy of your concern."

Bleddyn frowned. "You are worthy of every ounce of concern of which I am capable. And to me, you are interesting in no small measure, and to no end."

"Oh, Bleddyn," I laugh-sobbed again and buried my face in my hands. After a few moments of that, Bleddyn wound his arms around me tentatively, then more certainly as the laugh-sobs turned into just sobs, which soon turned into silent weeping.

And that, too, eventually turned to hitching and shuddering, until I was just resting in Bleddyn's arms, letting him hold me as he imparted silent comfort. One of his hands rested against the small of my back and the other cradled my head and held it against his neck, where I breathed in the scents of sweat, horse, and metal that had come to mean home to me.

"If you wish it of me," Bleddyn whispered. "I will take you back to the castle and never will I bring you here again. If the memories you carry burden you so greatly, to add yet another set to that burden may be disastrous, despite what the *Gweddw* Robert thinks."

Sniffing, I straightened up and looked into Bleddyn's eyes. Mine were still wet and probably red.

"Let's just get this over with, all right? So that I can sleep without the aid of a sleeping potion."

"But—"

I tried to smile. "It'll be all right, Bleddyn," I said, with more hope than certainty. But at least I didn't promise. I couldn't lie so hugely to Bleddyn, of all people. I kissed him, wrapping my arms around his neck. "It may not be easy, but eventually, it'll be all right."

After searching my eyes for the better part of a minute, Bleddyn nodded. "If you say so, my light."

"I do."

At last, returning the small smile I conjured up, Bleddyn held me close and kissed me thoroughly, intently.

"*Rwyf wrth fy modd i ti, fy olau llachar a disgleirio.*" *I love thee, my bright and shining light.*

"*Rwyf wrth fy modd i ti, yn ogystal, mae fy sgweier golygus.*" *I love thee, as well, my handsome squire.*

Bleddyn hugged me close and tight before stepping back. "Go and let the *Gweddw* know we have arrived, and I will care for Arwel and Aderyn," he murmured, taking their reins and walking them to Gwenllian's barn.

I watched him go, letting my heart fill with love for him, like a strong wind fills the sails of a ship. Then I turned toward Gwenllian's cottage and marching to what I told myself was not my doom.

❖

"You've arrived in quite a timely fashion," Gwenllian said as soon as she opened the door, her green eyes seeming to spark and glow in the last of the day's golden light. She was wearing a white, brown, and black calico dress, and her hair was piled into a messy upsweep on her head. Her sleeves were rolled up, and she looked ready for business.

I tried not to believe the snarky voice in the back of my brain that suggested this did *not* bode well for me. She waved me in, and turned to go back to her table, which was covered in vials and pots, small and large.

"Gee, is all this for little ol' me?" I asked as I stepped in, closing the door. Bleddyn would, even if I left it open, knock as if he'd never been here before. The thought made me smile.

Gwenllian glanced up from where she was mincing or mashing a small pile of herbs, caught my smile and returned it fondly.

"Of course it is. And I have just finished your tonic." She paused her mincing or whatever and picked up a tiny clay vial about a quarter the size of my palm.

I approached Gwenllian, gaping, and took the vial. "This is it?" I demanded, letting out a relieved laugh. Though I knew even as I laughed, my relief was premature. After all, sometimes powerful things came in tiny packages. Like tabs of LSD, for instance.

At any rate, I eyed the vial and sniffed it. "Smells minty. Like mouthwash."

"The mint is to improve the flavor somewhat, for I fear the tonic is…not pleasant to taste. And you know, as well as I, Krishnan ap Karthik, that sometimes, powerful things come in small packages."

I nearly dropped the vial and I was gaping again, this time at Gwenllian. It wasn't the first time. "Can...can you hear what I'm thinking?" I asked in a quiet, stricken voice.

"Of course not!" she said, snorting a little as she giggled. Relieved yet again, I felt tension flow out of my shoulders like water out of a sieve.

"Well. Okay, then," I said, laughing a little, too. But I noticed that Gwenllian didn't seem unfamiliar with the concept of hearing the thoughts of others. Discretion being the better part of me not flipping the fuck out on one of my few friends in 1626, I filed that detail away under: Not Even Gonna Go There. "Okay," I said, composing myself, "so, the tonic is done. Are there any special instructions for it. Any use-by date?"

Gwenllian went back to mincing with a chuckle. "It is, of course, most efficacious if taken sooner rather than later. And it's best for you if not taken on a full stomach."

"And why is that?"

Gwenllian glanced at me, then away. "I think the memory that torments you might manifest itself as physical illness. There'll be less for me to clean up if you don't eat before you take it."

I grimaced and nodded. "Makes sense. Wait a minute. Less for *you* to clean up?"

"Of course. You were not considering taking the tonic at the castle, were you?"

"Well..."

"My dear Krishnan, should you start to call or scream for aid while in the grips of memory, can you imagine how the castle will react to that, especially in the middle of the night?"

To that, I had nothing to say. I wasn't going to lie to Gwenllian and say that my memories weren't so bad that they'd cause me to scream in my sleep? Stupor? Whatever the tonic did.

But still, to do it here where not just Bleddyn, but Gwenllian would see me at my less than best?

"She is right, Krishnan."

I started and turned around to see Bleddyn standing in the open doorway, looking as grim as Rhys ever had. But he still looked good enough to eat.

I really hope you can't hear what I'm thinking now, Gwenllian, I thought absently as I met Bleddyn halfway across the room and he pulled me into his arms. We gazed into each other's eyes for a while before he spoke. "Gwenllian is right. Best to do it here, where she can care for you if the tonic affects you in ways which I cannot treat."

"But…"

"Yes?"

I sighed and looked down. "I just want as few people as possible to witness me in whatever state I'll be in."

"Then here is where you will take the tonic," Bleddyn insisted. "For if you do begin to yell or shout in the castle, it will not go unmarked. Many would come to your aid, there."

"Oh, God, you're right," I said as the realization hit me that as much as I didn't want anyone to see me compromised, at least one person had to see me that way. And it might as well be the person who could treat me if something went pear-shaped. I glanced over my shoulder at Gwenllian. "You're *both* right. Okay. Here, it is. When would be least inconvenient for you?"

"Why, you were planning to take it tonight, were you not? And it will be most potent tonight, the fifth night of its brewing." Gwenllian spread her hands as if to say *there you go.*

"Of course." I turned back to Bleddyn, who was watching me with the most melancholy expression on his face, his mouth pursed unhappily. Smiling, I darted in and kissed his mouth till he, too, began to smile. "Here and now, it is," I said. "On one condition."

"And what is that, my love?"

I searched his fond, tender gaze. I'd catch him totally off-guard, and maybe even get what I wanted. After all, I had the element of surprise on my side. I hoped. For I was about to say something Bleddyn was not only not going to like, but would probably hate. And he'd be mad at me for demanding it. Well, that was just too damn bad.

"My condition is," I said, nudging Bleddyn's boots with my own, backing Bleddyn toward the open door. He looked confused but wasn't resisting me. When his boots crossed the threshold, I stepped back out of his arms. "My condition is that you wait outside till Gwenllian lets you back in."

And I shut and latched the door in Bleddyn's suddenly understanding, suddenly *furious* face.

❖

"Are you certain you wish it to be this way?" Gwenllian asked as I laid myself down in her bed. She stood at the bedside, holding the small vial containing my tonic.

In the recent silence—Bleddyn had finally stopped pounding on the door and demanding to be let in about two minutes ago, after nearly fifteen minutes. I hoped he'd gone to curry the horses or something and wasn't just sitting out there waiting to be let back in. Because if I pictured him like that, I knew that I'd cave and go let him in. And then he'd see me. Whatever lurks below the masks I wear. And who's to say he wouldn't be disgusted? Pitying? Revolted?

I steeled myself and looked Gwenllian in the eyes. "I'm sure."

Sighing, she unstoppered the vial and handed it to me as I leaned back on my elbows. I took it after a brief hesitation, then brought it to my nose to sniff it.

"Ugh! Vile! It smells like someone pissed out a garbage fire!"

"It is not a sipping sherry, Krishnan. It is a powerful calmative among other things."

"And what other things would those be? You never *did* tell me exactly how this stuff is supposed to work."

Gwenllian sat on the edge of the bed next to me. "Aside from its sedative qualities, the tonic also has hallucinatory properties. It will allow you to have waking dreams. Dreams that you will remember even after the tonic has worked its way out of your system."

"And how long will *that* be?" I asked, thinking of LSD again. "How long till this shit wears off? I don't wanna be trippin' balls during Lord John's Jubilee!"

"It won't last that long, Krishnan. The effects will wear off within an hour." Gwenllian said sternly, and I felt bad for having doubted her. "Now, soon begun is soon done. Drink."

Which was her way of saying, *Quit stalling and take your medicine, already!*

Holding up the vial to the light as if I could see through the dark clay it was made of, I thought one last time of Bleddyn—*my Bleddyn*—and of Gareth. Of Owen and Islwyn. Of the friends I'd made since arriving here.

I had reasons to remember this nightmarish memory. People to be well for. And I *would* be well once I remembered and accepted whatever it was, and began to move on.

"Bottoms up," I said, tilting the bottle up to my mouth and closing my eyes. It tasted green-brown and was vaguely minty. I nearly gagged, but I swallowed until the vial was empty, perhaps a mouthful and a half.

Shuddering, I handed off the bottle to Gwenllian without opening my eyes and laid back into her relatively soft bed. I kept swallowing spit in an attempt to hasten that taste out of my mouth.

"I'll get you some water for the taste," Gwenllian said.

"Thank you."

When I opened my eyes, I meant to turn my head to watch her go, but instead, my glance fell on the window next to the front door. The shutters were pulled most of the way closed, but they were just open enough for Bleddyn to peer in. And peer in, he did.

Glancing away from Bleddyn's dark, worried, angry eyes, I took the cup of water from Gwenllian. "Thanks."

"Of course."

I sipped at the water, swishing it around in my mouth. Thankfully, the tonic wasn't oil-based, so it didn't linger too long in my mouth or throat. After a couple minutes, there was just the taste of cool water and mint. I handed Gwenllian the cup and I laid down when I was done.

"Bring it on," I muttered to my subconscious, even as I felt Gwenllian and Bleddyn watching me. I closed my eyes and noticed with faint amusement that there were already pretty colors swirling and writhing on the backs of my eyelids like groovy, psychedelic snakes. "Just bring it the fuck *on*."

And, as if in answer to my challenge, the colors and lights on the backs of my eyelids winked out, leaving me floating and helpless, immobilized in total darkness.

Chapter Nineteen

*D*arkness.

I was running through darkness, running like I was being chased. By what or whom, I couldn't imagine. Couldn't imagine who I was that I would be chased at all.

So, since running seemed to make no sense, I stopped. Stopped running.

And then as if someone flipped a switch, light flooded the world, and I was in a room that looked very familiar. It seemed large, but some part of me found it to be rather small. A big bed was in one corner of the room, windows with real glass in them—three!—and shelves brimming with books. A closet filled with clothes that seemed as unfamiliar and familiar as the grand-small room I was in. On the walls were pictures—no, posters of singers and bands and...

"Demotivational posters," I breathed, the words feeling both oddly unfamiliar and perfectly right. I drifted over to one that pictured a kitten at a gallows. A hand was fitting a noose around its neck and the kitten seemed to be smiling. "I remember these. HANG IN THERE!" I intoned, reading the caption below the cuddly little furball and laughing.

Then I was drifting to a door next to the demotivational poster. I opened it, already knowing what I'd find.

"Well, looka here, Maw. An indoor outhouse," I said, looking around the bathroom with both disinterest and awe. Everything seemed to be in place: toilet, shower, sink, mirrored medicine cabinet, and towel-rack with three towels on it.

"Mom, you're such a neat-Nazi," I murmured, and while part of me thought that was funny, another part of me wondered what in blazes a Nazi was.

Clearly, I needed to sit down and regroup. Figure out what was going on. But first, it was time to splash my face. Maybe that would help. Maybe a cold, bracing faceful of water would—

"Oh, fuck me!" I screeched when I moved to stand in front of the mirror, and saw my face.

Only it wasn't my face.

Except that it was.

But clearly it was not.

(Though, obviously, it was. Most certainly my face)

(Nope. Not at all my face. Nor my body.)

I—we?—I stared at the reflection in the mirror. Its mouth was agape, just as mine was agape, and raising its hand to touch the mirror, just as I was. And it, too, stopped at the last second, just as I did, to look at that hand.

The hand in the reflection was almost fishbelly-white. My hand was a rather lovely sienna color, so I knew that couldn't be my reflection.

Only I knew that it was. From the fine, mouse-brown hair to the long, straight nose, and the thin-lipped mouth. Those wide, wide-set eyes in that narrow face, terminating in a strong chin and jaw were mine, as well.

And yet, I knew my face was oval-shaped, with dark-brown eyes, a shorter, wider nose, a much lusher, more kissable mouth. My chin and jaw were nothing to write home about, however.

But they were mine.

And so, it seemed, was the face in the mirror. It was even wearing the same black jeans and a grey t-shirt, though the clothes seemed a bit too large and too short on it.

Otherwise, it was me.

That was impossible, of course, and yet...

And yet.

I stuck my tongue out at the reflection, and it reciprocated. I blinked, and I presume it, too, blinked. I made a few more funny faces, crossed my eyes, stuck out my teeth, even turned my eyelids inside out.

The latter brought on an irritated huff that seemed to come from everywhere and nowhere all at once. Even with my compromised vision, I could see that the reflection had rolled its eyes and put its hands on its hips.

"If you think I'm doing that, you're daft," it said, and I blinked so hard and fast, my eyelids slipped back into place.

Glaring at me, my erstwhile reflection gave me a once over, then opened its mouth to speak again. But before it could, I covered my ears and eyes and began to hum as loud as I could. "Hmm-hmm-hmm...I can't hear anything...hmm-hmm-hmm..."

"Fat lot of good that'll do you, since I'm in your head!" That same voice, low, musical and lilting, not entirely different from my own except for its funky UK accent.

"My accent is neither here nor there. Not that I have one. You're the one with the accent."

So, *I thought cavalierly,* this is what it feels like to go insane. Should I call 9-1-1, or just start making tinfoil hats now?

"Oh, you're not going insane, Krishnan. You're going sane. As sane as you'll ever be."

Gee. That's comforting.

"I'm not here to comfort, I'm here to enlighten. So stop behaving like a horse's arse and take your hands down! Look at me!"

No! *I told the voice. Then I realized I had already lost the battle if I was arguing with it. So I sighed and put my hands down. My reflection crossed its arms over its chest and smiled at me like the cat that got the cream.*

"There. That's better," it said with great satisfaction. I sighed.

For whom? *I wondered silently, since it seemed to really be inside my head.*

The reflection tutted. "Oh, don't take on so. You know you're not insane, and that I'm more than just your skewed reflection."

Oh, I know that, do I? *I sighed again.* Then who *are* you?

The reflection's smile widened into a much nicer version of the smug one. Its teeth weren't the whitest or the straightest, but it was still a charming smile. "The name's William ap Warren, Gwil, to a few friends and the man we both love. I'm also Krishnan Nayar." The reflection winked. "I'm you. And we need to have us a wee talk before that witch's tonic wears off."

❖

I shook my head, backing away from the mirror. When my butt hit the towel rack, I closed my eyes tight, counted to ten, and then opened them again.

Gwil was still there, staring at me as if I was the one who was insane. He rolled his eyes. "I told you, I am not merely a reflection and you *are not insane. Leastaways, not in this instance.*"

Thanks.

Gwil laughed. "Oh, you're bloody delightful when you're flustered. Just like me."

I'm not you!

"Of course not. I'm you." Gwil snorted. "There's some as say it makes no difference, but since I was walking around incarnate before you...you get where I'm going with this?"

No, I don't! You don't make any sense! None of this makes any sense! I screamed into my own head, closing my eyes tight and sliding down the wall to the floor. I tucked my knees up under my chin and felt like crying. This is all crazy! I'm crazy!

"No, mate. I promise, you're not," Gwil said with an awkward sort of gentleness as I began to sob. He let me blubber and feel sorry for myself for at least five minutes before knocking on the glass of the mirror. From his side, of course.

Startled, I looked up. His left hand was splayed flat on the glass, and he was watching me with the most intent and intense gaze anyone had ever focused on me. "Listen, Krishnan. Krish, yeah? I need you to listen to me for just a little longer, right? And then, when I'm done, you can go back to wallowing or..."

"Or?" I asked.

"Or you could go back to where you belong. To your home. Our home."

"But I am home," I said, sounding less than certain about that. I looked around the bathroom and into the bedroom to make sure they hadn't changed on me. And they hadn't.

Gwil was shaking his head. "No, I don't mean the home you had with your Mum and Tad, when you were a child. I mean the home you've carved out for yourself. Out of space and time, with determination and love."

I frowned and slowly got to my feet. "What do you mean?"

He smiled. "One word for you, mate: Bleddyn.*"*

And with that one word came an entire universe of love and affection so great and so all-encompassing I couldn't even tell where it ended and the rest of me began.

As the feeling swept over me, I gasped, and Gwil's smile widened. He nodded at his hand, which was still splayed on his side of the mirror. "Yes. You've got two options now. Once you've made your choice, there's no turning back.

"Yon door leading out of your precious indoor-outhouse, will take you back to the life you left behind when Bleddyn called you. You walk out that door, boyo, and it's POOF!" Gwil made a starburst motion with his free hand. "All a dream or a head injury or temporary insanity—whatever you choose to believe. But it's over. For keeps.

"But if you want to know what's behind that name and the feeling you got when I said it, you'll touch the mirror."

I looked out the bathroom door. If I listened hard, I could hear the television in the living room downstairs. My mom was down there, watching her shows, I knew. And I could go down there and watch with her. Have a normal life with my friends and family, and pretend that none of this had ever happened.

But the thing was, I didn't remember clearly what any of this was, just that some bits had been horrible, and some bits divine.

Just like my life outside the bathroom door.

I closed my eyes for a few moments before speaking. "Say that name again. Please."

*I could sense Gwil's smile as he said, "*Bleddyn.*"*

And without opening my eyes, I reached out and placed my hand on the glass of the mirror, expecting it to be cold and hard. Instead, it was warm, soft, and almost yielding, like living skin.

Opening my eyes one micron at a time, I peered out at Gwil, who stood there smiling, his hand pressed to mine. I opened my eyes wider and looked around the bathroom. Yet again, nothing had changed.

"Wow, that was—" I began with snooty snarkiness, when Gwil winked and suddenly, my life—no, Gwil's—flashed before my eyes. From first memories to last.

❖

The sound of laughter shook me awake in my cramped resting place, where I'd finally felt safe enough to fall asleep after days and days of traveling. Not that it'd been restful sleep, jammed as I was in the space below the deadfall that'd once barely fit two young boys between games of tag and hide-and-seek, and was now accommodating a half-grown man.

The laughter wasn't threatening, though I'd thought it was for a moment. But no, it was the laughter of boys my own age or thereabout, and one of the laughs was achingly familiar.

Parting a couple of leafy tangles of the vines that hid me, I looked out as the laughter drew closer and waited. Shortly, I could see them coming down the foot-worn path that led past the once-more hiding spot.

There were two boys, one of whom was a year younger than me, with dark hair and eyes, broad shoulders, and the assured gait of someone who knows his place in the world. His hair, unevenly, indifferently cut straggled down to those broad shoulders, which shook with laughter. Laughter no doubt caused by the blond boy at his side.

Though I suppose I should've thought man, *since the boy was as tall as one, and handsome like someone who'd walked out of a ballad. Like a prince. He walked with a certain swagger that showed off his brawny, solid frame. He was clearly strong and probably a fighter, which I never had been.*

If he was an eagle, golden and regal and made to soar, I was a wren, plain and scrawny, and meant to stick close to the ground.

But my eyes slid immediately back to the other boy, who was a bit small for his age, much like me, but who, unlike me, had a wiry musculature and an air of speed and agility. As ever it had been, whenever the other boy was in viewing distance, I couldn't keep my eyes off him. He was beautiful. Golden in a way the eagle at his side would never and could never be.

My heart rising to my throat, I allowed myself to think the name I hadn't let cross even the threshold of memory in months:

Bleddyn.

It was Bleddyn's laughter that I had heard, that and the laughter of the other boy, of course. Which was odd, because everyone knew that only I could get Bleddyn to laugh like that, right?

But a lot can change over the course of a summer, can it not?

I told that voice to stuff it. I couldn't bear to think about what it meant that Bleddyn had already found someone who made him laugh the way I used to, had found a companion to take my place. Couldn't bear to think of what would happen if I were to reveal myself now. Spring out of our old hiding spot and present myself to him. Ask him to run away with me, only to be told that he had no intentions of doing so, and that I was a fool to have thought he would.

I couldn't bear to think of my Bleddyn not only laughing with someone else, but in this other's arms. Being kissed and held and touched and taken by this boy. Jealousy as hot as branding irons welled up within me, only to be cooled by a chill rush of despair.

What if Bleddyn worse than no longer cared for me? What if he'd forgot me altogether?

Oh, I knew that wasn't possible. Not after the beating his father had given us after he'd caught us.

Well. If nothing else, he'd remember the beating and what it had been for. Especially having survived it, against all odds, *I told myself, and then a frequent thought assaulted me again, one I hadn't had since running away from my fosterage, a fortnight ago.* What if he *hates* me because of what his father did to us? What if he *blames* me for it? For surely he should. What if—

And there, the voice fell into blessed silence, for Bleddyn and his companion were on me, standing right in front of the deadfall. Bleddyn swore, his booted feet turning abruptly back the way they'd come.

"What's this?" the other boy asked, his voice cracking and creaking in a way that made me snort silently. He might have been bigger and taller than the average boy, but he still had the voice of a half-grown child. Mine had deepened and stayed that way rather early in my adolescence. "Where're you going, Bleddyn?"

"Forgot my bloody slingshot. Can't go hunting without it."

"You'd forget your head if it wasn't sewed to your neck!"

"Stuff it—I'll be back in two shakes. Wait here."

"I won't wait long. I can hunt rabbit perfectly fine on my own."

Bleddyn laughed, already running back down the path. "But where's the fun in that?" he called back, disappearing around a turn.

The legs of the boy still near the deadfall turned in a full circle before the boy finally approached the deadfall and—not too surprisingly, sat on it. Right above my head.

Holding my breath, I hoped Bleddyn hurried.

After a few minutes that felt like brief eternities, of listening to the boy sitting above me sing in his creaky, awful voice, belch, fart, and sing some more, I was sweating and aching from holding my body so perfectly still. I wished he'd get up, maybe follow Bleddyn back to the castle or something. Anything. Just so long as I could ease myself out from under the deadfall, which was really quite cramped. My legs were burning, and I was certain at least a few dozen ants and spiders were crawling on them. My arms were stiff from being held in the same position as well, and I feared even to blink, lest I be heard.

Suddenly, the boy stopped his singing and muttered something that sounded like: "Here, now…"

He stood up and walked almost silently around the deadfall, as if looking for a better place to sit. I held perfectly still, knowing that even a twitch might betray me. Finally the boy came to a stop right back where he'd started, and he squatted low enough that I could see the tip of his chin as he examined the dirt right in front of where my face was.

Now, I'd taken care, or so I'd thought, to brush away my tracks after I'd climbed in, but I had no doubts that if given a chance, Bleddyn would have noticed something off. Who was to say this boy wasn't as good at tracking as Bleddyn? The boy stood up and backed away from the deadfal, until all I could see were his feet.

"I'm armed," he said in his cracking but unafraid voice. "Come out where I can see you, or I'll come in there."

And while I knew that last part was rather unlikely given the size of the space I was in, I believed the first part for the threat it was.

"All right! I'm coming out!" I called, my voice muffled by the dead air in the deadfall.

I had to struggle with my numb limbs, and in the end, I tumbled through the vines like a disoriented hedgehog, rolling tail over tea kettle. I stopped at the other boy's feet and groaned, finally laying flat.

Suddenly, after a silence in which I could feel his bestartlement, he started laughing, like a rusty gate swinging in a stiff breeze.

I opened my eyes and looked up at him. He was standing over me, clutching his stomach as he laughed, though in one hand he held a dangerous looking dagger. He squinted at me, his teeth practically hanging out of his mouth. He looked like a braying donkey, and much less handsome than he had before. I felt myself grin as I realized Bleddyn could never and would never love such a guffawing jackass of a boy. He might not love me anymore, but he'd also never love a boy such as this.

Laughing, I got to my feet slowly, so as not to startle my new, dagger-wielding acquaintance, and dusted myself off. When he saw that I was laughing too, he stopped and scowled at me, brandishing the dagger. "Here, now! What're you *laughing at?"*

I'm laughing at you*, you dullard, I thought. "Just laughing at the sight I'm sure I posed. Tumbling out of the verge like that."*

The other boy's narrow gaze narrowed even more. "What were you doing in there anyway, hiding on Lord John's land? Poacher? Thief? Beggar? Vagrant?"

All equally bad things, his tone said, so I hastened to reassure him I was none of those. "I'm a humble scribe on his way to Caerdyf, passing through here, hoping to see my kin before I go."

Which was true.

The other boy snorted and didn't sheath his dagger. "A likely story. You're probably a poacher, just like them two was caught a fortnight ago. C'mon," he ordered, gesturing with his dagger for me to precede him on the path back toward the castle. "I'm taking you to Captain Rhys. He'll get an honest answer out of you."

"No!" I said, terrified beyond the capacity to move, even with the threat of the dagger to prod me along. The other boy smirked cruelly and paced in a tight circle around me. He smelt of old sweat and old food, with hints of stable.

I did not make a face, however. I merely stood there, contriving to look as helpless as I actually was.

"You've heard of Captain Rhys, then?" he asked, and his tone made it a taunt. He knew I was frightened, and it amused him.

"Y-yes." No sense in hiding it or lying, just yet.

"Then you must have heard that an honest man has naught to fear from him."

I met the other boy's murky grey eyes and between the stupid, anticipatory expression on his face, his stench, and his obvious enjoyment of my discomfort and fear, I wondered: How could I have mistaken him for an eagle? *Bleddyn's* the eagle, not this bottom-dwelling, belly-crawling snake.

And then I was wondering: How has Bleddyn not seen through you? Is it that he's been so *lonely,* he'd settle on *anyone* for companionship? Is this what Rhys has driven him to? Driven *us* to? Me, a runaway fugitive and Bleddyn forced to associate with this bully just for the sound of someone else's voice?

Oh, Bleddyn…oh, my love.

"Oi!" The other boy snapped his fingers in front of my face to regain my attention. "Answer me, boy. Or should I just march you straight to Captain Rhys right now?"

"Don't. Please," I said, though it stung to humble myself to someone I'd have once ignored. Someone Bleddyn and I would've once taken great joy in cutting down a peg or two. *"I'm telling you the truth. I'm here to see my cousin before I leave for Caerdyf."*

The boy snorted again. "And who would this cousin of yours be? Perhaps he can vouch for you without having to see Captain Rhys, after all," he said, though he sounded far from happy at the idea of losing his afternoon's sport.

I took a deep breath, let it out, and said, "He's just gone to get his slingshot. His name is Bleddyn ap Rhys, and I'm—"

"William ap Warren," the other boy said, his face caught in a rictus of unpleasant surprise. "You're William ap Warren, fostered this past summer to Sir Feirionnydd.*"*

I nodded warily as the words fell from the boy's lips like stones. "Yes, but how do you know me? Have we met before?"

A muscle near the boy's right eye twitched so quickly I was scarce certain I'd seen it, but then he was smiling, a charming smile, meant to put one at ease. Which was why I didn't trust it for a moment.

"No, we haven't, William ap Warren of Sir Gaernarfon,*" he said, and then stuck out his free hand. When I reached out to take it, the other boy grabbed my hand and pulled me close, his murky grey eyes*

colder and deader than any I'd ever seen. "And we never will." Agony suddenly bloomed in my gut like a dark blossom. I grunted and looked down to see the other boy's dagger sticking out of my abdomen like a quill from a porcupine. At least until he drew it back out and drove it in again. I grunted again, looking up to meet his dead gaze questioningly, even as my life's blood began to pour out of me. "We never will."

And he dragged the dagger up.

❖

I crumpled to the ground, sliding off the dagger and to my knees, unable to look away from the other boy's lifeless eyes. I fell over on my side, jarring the wounds given me. I moaned and clutched at my abdomen with both hands, curling into a ball as I tried to hold my insides—which I could feel against my palms, waiting to slither out of me should I move my hands. Above me, the other boy stood, breathing hard and loud. He was speaking, and even though I was rapidly descending into shock and unconsciousness, I struggled to understand his words.

". . . after what you did to Bleddyn, how could I not know who you are? Tongues will wag, after all, even about Rhys ap Thomas' son." A wild, unpleasant laugh punctuated that claim. "Even now, months later, the men still talk about Rhys' fancy son. About how he loved buggery just fine till Rhys caught him and beat that love out of him. They think I don't hear them talk, but I do. I know what they say in the barracks when they think Bleddyn and I are asleep. But what they should *be talking about is you. How William ap Warren, so smart and so charming, turned those smarts and that charm to the task of seducing his younger cousin. For Bleddyn would* never *have strayed so far from the righteous path if* you *hadn't taught him to crave the pleasures of the flesh. You. His own* cousin!*"*

I felt a sharp pain in my side. I could only imagine the other boy had stabbed me there, too. But I couldn't tell because my eyes were closed, and I was more focused on the slippery pulse of my intestines against my palms than I was on any new and ancillary wounds.

"—won't let you take him to Hell with you, you Hellbound, Godless sinner! I'll send you there myself *before I let you further*

corrupt Bleddyn's pure, sweet soul." I felt another sharp pain in my side, and I moaned. It sounded like:

"Bleddyn..."

When next I drew a breath, it was redolent of that old sweat/ old food/manure scent and made me open my eyes. The other boy's face was mere inches from my own. His eyes were all I could see as darkness nibbled away at the edges of my vision.

"Rot in Hell, knowing that you'll never see him again and that he will hate you forever for besmirching him so."

"B-Bleddyn," I spat out in a coppery-tasting froth that made the murderous boy's face scrunch up as he moved out of further spitting distance. "Bleddyn...loves me...mine...always."

The boy snarled and grabbed a handful of my hair, yanking my head back and putting his bloody dagger to my throat. I was barely conscious and about to die, when I heard...hoofbeats!

Bearing down on us from deeper in the forest, they were coming at a good clip. The dagger that had been held to my throat disappeared.

As did the murderous boy.

Meanwhile, the sound of the hoofbeats was getting louder. I struggled to open my eyes wider and clutched at my gushing gut. It barely seemed to hurt, though I was very cold. "Help!" I called in a voice barely louder than a chuffing whisper. "Please! Help!"

Reflex made me try to sit up, and agony came back to me with the effort, hot and immediate. When darkness took me this time, it was for real. My last thought before it caught me up in its clutches was, I may go to Hell, but Bleddyn was *worth it*. He was worth it. Do you hear me, God or Satan, or whomever is listening? *Bleddyn. Was. Worth—*

Gwil really did expect to wake up in Hell for all his troubles. Instead, he—*we*—woke up someplace a lot less balmy.

"Bleddyn!" Gwil was screaming from *my* mouth as I bolted upright in Gwenllian's bed, clutching my abdomen, still feeling the agony of what we'd experienced in that dream? Memory? At the moment, we were too frightened and in shock, too traumatized to even begin such a line of inquiry. All Gwil knew was he was dying, and that he'd never see Bleddyn again. All I knew was that I had woken up with a whole different person inside my head. One who could, with just the power of his cyclonic emotions, control my body as if it was his.

Gwil kept screaming Bleddyn's name and screaming it, despite Gwenllian—Dierdre?—no, *Gwenllian*, at my bedside trying to calm him. A loud rhythmic thudding came from everywhere, making it hard for me to hear even my own screams, let alone her soft, soothing voice. She rested her gentle hands on my shoulders, but Gwil shuddered, and she withdrew. He was inconsolable. He felt cold and numb, surely the precursors of death, and once he was dead, that was it. He'd never see Bleddyn again. Never get a chance to tell him that he loved him, no matter what Rhys had said or done, no matter what had happened in the time since Gwil had seen him.

He loved Bleddyn. Always had and always would.

A thud, louder and harder than the others, seemed to rock Gwenllian's cottage, and both Gwil and I were so shocked, we turned toward the sound. The sturdy, oaken door hung from the top hinge, off to the side. Gwil's screams stilled for the moment, and we saw him standing in the doorway of the cottage, backlit by the final light of the orange sunset, his eyes darting everywhere, as if for danger. Brother, lover, best friend, *savior*.

"*Bleddyn!*" Gwil and I called, bursting into tears. Bleddyn looked at, grim and anxious, then he strode across the room toward the bed.

We held open our arms, and Gwenllian jumped up so Bleddyn didn't sit on her in his haste to reach Gwil and I. Once in each other's arms, we held on tight. Neither Gwil nor I could stop weeping and laughing and sobbing and hitching.

"Never again," Bleddyn said, and then he sat back to catch our chin between his index finger and thumb, his dark eyes boring into ours with a mix of anger, pain, and relief. "You will *never* put a locked door between us again. Not when your well-being is of concern."

"Never again," I agreed for myself and for a gobstruck Gwil, tucking my head under Bleddyn's chin and making myself small in his arms. "I never want to be more than an arm's length away from you ever again."

"Hush," Bleddyn said, resting his head upon mine and rocking us.

I don't know how long we sat like that, but I felt the bed dip on the other side when Gwenllian sat down. For my part, I was curled up in Bleddyn's strong, protective, *possessive* arms, and had no plans to be elsewhere any time soon. I wasn't even planning on opening my eyes. Gwil had quieted, almost to the point of me being certain he'd gone.

"I have no wish to disturb you, but I must ask. It is imperative that I know, did the tonic work?" Gwenllian asked from a few feet away. "Did it help you to remember what you've forgotten?"

I nodded once against Bleddyn's chest. "Yes."

Silence, as Gwenllian thought that over, then: "And what *do* you remember?"

I shuddered and started sobbing again. Or, I should say, Gwil and I started sobbing. He was still there, hovering near the edge of hysteria. I supposed experiencing one's own attempted murder for the second time around would do that to just about anyone.

As would having lost and regained Bleddyn.

"*Everything*," I said as a phantom pain, like a sharp cramp, rocketed through my abdomen. I discreetly touched the area to reassure Gwil it was whole. And he quieted again, moving somewhere farther back in my consciousness. It was a strange feeling. Like having a passenger in one's head, only this passenger had a steering wheel, gas pedal, and brake, as well. "I remember everything, Gwenllian."

It was then that I realized that all four of us had been speaking Cymraeg since Gwil and I had woken up.

"Krishnan? My light? Speak, and tell me what disturbs you that I may address it. You've gone as stiff as a plank in my arms and as chill as winter." Bleddyn kissed the crown of my head. "Tell me what is the matter."

"Bleddyn, I—" pausing at the strange, yet utterly familiar sound of Cymraeg—coming from my mouth, I sighed and forced myself to sit up and look at my cousin? My lover?

Neither appellation seemed to fit.

My one and only reason for being?

Yes. *That one* seemed to fit.

"I love you," I said, and Bleddyn smiled. I smiled back and reached up to take his face in my hand. "I love you more than life, itself. And apparently not even death will keep me from being with you." I laughed, jagged and slightly hysterical. "Enough belaboring the obvious, love, there's so much I have to tell you, so much I'm remembering even as I sit here, talking to you like I'm just one person when there's more than just *me* to me, now."

Bleddyn was looking confused. Adorably so. "I do not understand, my love."

"I know." I smiled and kissed him briefly. Then I looked at Gwenllian, who was watching me with her warmest, most knowing gaze. I smiled at her, too. "I have a lot to tell you, but I get the feeling that you already know most of it."

Gwenllian winked. "I know enough. Though if you ever feel like telling this particular tale from the beginning, I am, as always, all ears. But for now," she said, standing and clapping her hands together. "For now, I think a little supper might be in order, yes?"

I nearly gagged. "Uh, I think I'll pass on that tonight. You were right about not eating before I took the tonic, too." I offered Bleddyn a reassuring grin. "But I'm more than happy to sit and watch *you* eat."

Bleddyn took a breath and looked up at Gwenllian. "If you don't mind, Gwenllian, I think it would be best if I took Krish home to get some rest. How does that sound?" he asked me. I let myself be folded into his arms again, Gwil all but purring in the back of my mind.

"That sounds like Heaven to me."

Gwenllian and I stood on her porch while Bleddyn readied the horses, and I avoided her gaze for a few minutes before finally meeting it. I saw the same friendliness and curiosity I'd always seen. Some tense muscle within me slowly began to relax.

"How do I tell him, Gwenllian?!" I burst out suddenly, but it didn't feel exactly like *I* was speaking. Well, at least not *just* me. "'By the way, Bleddyn, I'm not just your lover, I'm the reincarnation of your dead first love?' I mean, do I let those words actually come out of my mouth? Or do I just not tell him?"

Gwenllian took my face in her hands and leaned in to kiss me right between the eyes, the way my mother always had. "I think that you *must* tell him and tell him soon, William, if ever you *will*, for I fear..."

Shuddering, I caught her gaze, ignoring the surprise that emanated from within, but wasn't entirely mine. Gwil was *in there*, all right, and he had a say in what we said and did. And Gwenllian could tell us apart. I didn't know how I felt about that, so I decided to focus on what she had said. "*What* do you fear?"

But Gwenllian merely shook her head and tried to smile. It didn't look very convincing. "Nothing. It's ridiculous."

"Well, good. I could use a laugh to take my mind off everything for a bit. So tell me."

Gwenllian sighed, ran a hand across her forehead, and laughed. "It's really nothing, Krish. Don't worry about it, just go home, both of you, and be with him."

She turned and went back into her cabin, moving the heavy door with some effort so that she could latch it. That left me standing on the porch, wondering and worrying. For Gwenllian, that parting was abrupt and odd.

But Arwel wickered from across the clearing, and I turned to see Bleddyn leading our horses out of the barn. He smiled and waved, and I managed to put Gwenllian's fears, at least, out of my mind, in stark favor of my own.

Chapter Twenty

We rode back through Gwydir Forest in the deepening twilight gloom on Arwel, Bleddyn behind me with his left arm tight around my waist, his breath stirring my hair.

We didn't speak until we neared the edge of the forest, when I put my hand on Bleddyn's rein-hand.

"What is it, my love?" he asked, still in Cymraeg. I doubt he'd noticed my sudden fluency with all the foofaraw that'd gone down before. And now, since speaking his native tongue was natural to him, I guessed he wouldn't notice someone else in his Cymraeg-speaking country was speaking the same language.

"There was a place near here," I began hesitantly, only it didn't feel like *I* was saying it. Not quite. "A place where you and I—I mean, you and *Gwil* used to play tag and hide-and-seek. There was a large, old deadfall covered in vines, and—"

"How did you know about that place?" Bleddyn asked, sounding surprised and amused, even laughing a little. "How did you know Gwil and I used to play there?"

"It's a long story. But can you take us there, now? Even though it's getting dark?"

"I could take you there in my sleep, my love." Turning the horses slightly west, he lead us off the main path.

We arrived in mere minutes. Bleddyn stopped Arwel just outside the glade containing the deadfall and dismounted, helping me down, then leading me to it. I ruthlessly tamped down the memories of nearly dying in front of it and focused on all the memories William wanted to show me of fun times spent near the deadfall camping, playing, and just *being* with Bleddyn.

"There—see that spot right there?" Bleddyn pointed at a spot a few feet away from the deadfall. The grass there was sparse and rather stunted in comparison to the rest of the ground. I nodded and Bleddyn went on with a chuckle. "When I was ten and Gwil was eleven, we stole a bottle of Cadwgan ap Talfryn's, er, spirits used chiefly for horse-doctoring. That didn't stop Gwil and I from drinking ourselves sick on it. That patch of grass, right there, is where Gwil vomited, and I not a minute behind him, in almost the exact same spot."

"Um, how charming," I said, wracking Gwil's memory for a recollection of the incident. I couldn't find anything close to what Bleddyn was describing and got the mental equivalent of a shrug from Gwil. Was Bleddyn making it up, or embellishing?

"Gwil passed out immediately after, of course. Nearly landed face-first in the puddle of puke he'd made, but I caught him and laid him down. Then it was *my* turn to be sick," Bleddyn said with a wistful laugh. "When Gwil woke up well into the next day, he had no memory of anything after noon of the *previous* day."

Ah. That would explain it. Even in my past life, I was a blackout drunk.

"The grass there never *did* grow quite right, afterward. When it grew at all." Bleddyn sounded almost proud of this fact. I rolled my eyes and turned to face him, wrapping my arms around his waist and kissing him teasingly. He moaned and pulled me close.

We stood there for long minutes, making out in the summer twilight. Bleddyn dropped his hand from my waist to my ass, squeezing and urging me even closer, till I was flush against him. He was, of course, hard. But then, so was I.

It would have been so easy to just get lost in wanting him, as I had so many times before. To just let him bend me over the deadfall and fuck me, even just a few feet from where I—where *Gwil*—had been stabbed over and over.

But I could hear Gwenllian telling me that if I would tell Bleddyn, I must do it soon. Indeed, I felt some of her urgency sweep through me, as if it was contagious and had lain in wait like a common virus, only to show its hand now.

"Bleddyn, *my Bleddyn*..." I broke the kiss to say, gazing into his dark eyes. He smiled at me, his heart shining out of those eyes like beacons to guide and give hope.

"Krishnan, my light."

Embracing him, I sighed. "Don't you wish to know what it was that I remembered? Aren't you curious as to what Gwenllian's tonic unearthed in my soul's deepest reaches?"

Bleddyn cradled the back of my head with his hand, his other hand on my waist. "I am, of course, curious. But I have little wish to push you or demand of you what you will not or perhaps *could not* share," he murmured, kissing my neck. Then he, too, sighed. "I had hoped that in your own good time, you would feel confident in sharing with me what you learned tonight."

"Oh, Bleddyn, it isn't a matter of feeling confident. I'm not certain *how* you'll take what I must tell you. And I *must* tell you, for honesty's sake—for *my* sake and for yours as well."

Bleddyn leaned back and searched my eyes grimly. "Then I promise I will listen with an open mind and a willing heart to whatever you tell me."

I nodded and pulled free of his arms, feeling instantly chilled for their absence, despite the warmth of the summer evening. I walked over to the deadfall, brushed aside a few of the bigger vines revealing the hiding space behind, and smiled.

"It's as if it was designed with children playing hide-and-seek in mind," I noted, letting go of the vines and facing Bleddyn, who was watching me solemnly. "Come," I invited, "sit by me."

I sat in front of the deadfall in full lotus. Not even a few hours ago, I'd have been wary of doing so for getting ants in my pants and spiders in my hair. But whether it was Gwil's influence, or I was just far too nervous and overwhelmed with what I had to tell Bleddyn, that thought only crossed my mind briefly.

Bleddyn closed the distance between us in a few strides and stood over me for a few moments, his face hidden by darkness, so that for a few moments, I felt as if a stranger was observing me.

But then he sat next to me, dropping gracefully into tailor-fashion, taking my hand and squeezing it. And this time when I looked at his face, it was no stranger gazing at me, but the man whom I loved more than anyone, whose love had come to define not just *my* life, but at least one *past* life.

Well, nothing to it, but to do it, I told myself, clutching at Bleddyn's arm and leaning against him, my head on his shoulder.

"In my religion, Hinduism, there is a central religious and/or philosophical concept that after the death of the body, the soul or spirit can begin a new life in a new body. Start over from birth until death, birth until death, and so on. This cycle, called *samsara*, is repeated until the universe itself dies and is reborn. Or until the soul, through its lifetimes of experience, has reached a state of purity and desirelessness called *moksha*, which is when one achieves *nirvana*. The word means *blown out* in Sanskrit, the ancient language of my people. It is literally an extinguishing of the self, the ego, of all desire and want, of suffering and pain, as one blows out a candle. It is *liberation* from the cycle of death and rebirth, suffering and pain. It is *enlightenment*."

I paused here, in case Bleddyn had any questions or comments. There was a long silence before he said. "And when this *moksha* is reached, and *nirvana* is achieved, *then* what happens?"

I smiled. "There is a Zen koan, which is like a riddle or epigram or parable that goes: '*Before enlightenment: chop wood, carry water. After enlightenment: chop wood, carry water.*' Do you understand?"

I could practically sense Bleddyn's contemplative frown as he thought it over. "I feel as if I do one moment, then I do not the next," he finally said, sounding quite put-out.

I laughed. "Well, Zen koans are usually meant to provoke such confusion and thought. It is believed that they are one path of many, to enlightenment. Some other paths are mediation or prayer, for example." I hugged Bleddyn's arm. "There's even chanting."

"One can sing one's way to this *nirvana*, this enlightenment?" Bleddyn sounded equally scandalized and amused. I laughed again, leaning up to kiss his cheek.

"Yep."

"Astounding," he said, chuckling, too. Then, before the silence between us could grow *too* comfortable, I went on.

"Anyway, this is, in part and simplified, what many millions of Hindus and Buddhists believe."

"Do you believe?"

Not really. Not till today. "Yes," I said. Then amended. "No, I don't *believe*, I *know*. For I've seen with my own heart, that it's true. We have all lived many lives before this one. Maybe even, as Gwenllian insists, at the same time as this one. And when I drank that tonic, I witnessed one of my previous lives." *I met my freaking previous life, and he did some sort of Vulcan mind-meld thing to me so that now he's floating around in my head and occasionally taking control of my body and emotions.*

Bleddyn's breath caught. "And, I take it, this is not a common experience, even among Hindus and Buddhists?"

"No, it's not, though some claim to not only remember their past lives, but to be able to help others remember *their* past lives, either for vanity or curiosity's sake, or even as a supposed fast-track to enlightenment." I snorted. "I was never all that interested in fast-tracking the inevitable. I'll reach enlightenment in my own time. However I will *not* be chopping wood and carrying water, one hopes."

Bleddyn laughed and I smiled in the darkness. "Right. So. This past life I witnessed, I remember it in its entirety."

"*Truly*, say you?"

I nodded. "Yes."

"And *who*, pray tell, were you in this other life?"

Here was the moment. I didn't know what to say. "He was a young man. A young *Welshman*."

Bledding was the one to nod now. "Would that be why your fluency in Cymraeg has increased so dramatically?"

Had I thought Bleddyn so inobservant as not to notice that I now spoke Cymraeg like a native? More fool me, then.

"Yes, it is."

Bleddyn pulled me into his arms and kissed me. "I have known almost since the beginning that despite our many differences, you have a Welshman's heart, noble and great."

"Well, I don't know about that," I murmured, and he kissed me again—would've kept kissing me had I not sighed my way out of it. "Well, actually, he was born in England, but his family relocated to Wales shortly after his birth, and he grew up Welsh in his heart, if not his lineage."

"Truly?"

"Truly. And he, too, loved a man. That love came to define him, and it was with him till death and beyond."

Bleddyn looked into my eyes, his own a mere glitter in the dark. "Beyond? Does that mean that he—that *you* still love this man?"

"Oh, yes."

Bleddyn stiffened in my arms. "And this man he loved you back?"

"More than anyone ever has. He loves me truly and well."

"*Loves*?" I nodded. "So, this man yet lives?"

"He does."

"And do you wish to be with him, still?"

"More than I have ever wished anything, Bleddyn."

Bleddyn looked down, putting a bit of space between us. "I am sorry, then, that he is beyond your reach, lost to another time."

I reached up and caressed Bleddyn's cheek tenderly. "But that's the thing. He is *not* in another time. He is in *this* time. Here and now."

Bleddyn wouldn't look up at me, when all I wanted was for him to do that. If he looked at me, I could blurt out the truth in one fell swoop rather than continue letting him question his way to it. But he would not look at me.

"He is a good man, brave and true. One of Lord John's men. And by far, his *best*, in my opinion," I said, and Bleddyn nodded yet again, still not looking at me.

"And does he wish to be with you, too?"

"I sure hope so."

A moment later, my right thumb was wet. A tear drop had rolled down Bleddyn's cheek. "Then be with him with my blessing, Krishnan, and my sincerest hope that you are happy always."

My jaw dropped. Whatever capricious whim of mine let Bleddyn think the worst while I played Twenty Questions shattered, and I shook my head, tears gathering in my eyes, too. "Bleddyn, there's something else I must tell you—"

"But know that if ever you need me for anything, I am still yours, heart and soul." At last, Bleddyn looked up at me, his eyes shining more than the meager light could account for. "Ever will I be your protector and guide, should you have need of me."

"Bleddyn, I will *always* have need of you!" I took his face in both my hands now. "I *love* you!"

Bleddyn's mouth dropped open, then closed, and he shook his head. "Krish—Master Krishnan—"

I tried on a grin that felt both familiar and strange to me. "I'm master of nothing, Bledd. And you once knew me by another name."

"Another name?" Bleddyn looked completely confused now. I leaned close and brushed our noses in an Eskimo kiss.

"Yes, my April Fool, *another* name. One not nearly so exotic as Krishnan ap Karthik."

Frowning again, Bleddyn looked into my eyes desperately. "Krish, I…I don't take your meaning."

I silenced him by kissing him softly, putting all my love, all my yearning and desire into it. Bleddyn, kissed me back with all the desperation and urgency I would expect of a man who thought this kiss would be the last. But this time, *he* was the one to break it. To stare into my eyes with feverish intensity, clenching my biceps with his hands.

"This man whom you love so, in what year was he born? What was his name?"

I smiled. "He was born April 1st of the year 1597, and his name is Bleddyn ap Rhys."

And at the speaking of his name, Bleddyn blinked once, another tear rolling down his face as he shuddered violently in my arms. "*W-William*?" he asked, realization and disbelief, hope and fear warring in his eyes. Then he stared into my eyes with intensity and intent. "Is it…my own *Gwil*?"

I couldn't speak for the tears that threatened, so I simply nodded and smiled. Bleddyn studied my face for a few seconds before he reached up and brushed the tips of his fingers down my cheek and over my lips. He let them trail down my throat and chest, and he placed his hand on my heart.

"It has always beat for you," I managed to say.

"But how can this be?" he whispered. "How is this possible?"

"Because you love me. And I love you."

Bleddyn licked his lips and the tears fell. "But Gwil is dead. My William is *dead*."

"No, your William, your Gwil, is *here*. He died, and then he lived again. And it was the love we feel that reached out across time and brought us together once more. To finish what we started. Although," I wondered, "how can we finish something that doesn't have an end? For *never* is the day I will stop loving you, and you me."

Bleddyn searched my eyes some more, this time for a *long* time, before shaking his head in negation. Then his face crumpled, and he broke down into hitching sobs, pulling me against him and holding on to me so tight I could barely draw breath.

"I love you, Bledd," I murmured into his hair, stroking it as I held him, laughing and weeping. "Oh, how I love you, my April Fool."

Bleddyn shook in my arms like a large leaf, or a small earthquake, and laughed in between sobs. "Gwil, my love, my *life*. I love you, and I never stopped."

And there we sat, both of us sobbing and laughing till twilight was become night and the horses had begun to stamp and whicker. I laughed one last time and leaned back in Bleddyn's arms, but only far enough to kiss him. He tasted like tears and happiness.

"Oh, Gwil—*Krish*—" he chuckled a bit raggedly. "I do not even know what I am to call you!"

"Call me *yours*, and I'll be happy," I said, and I meant it. For in that moment, I finally accepted not only that I could love someone as much as I loved Bleddyn, but that I was indeed William "Gwil" ap Warren.

Actually, noted a soft, amused voice that was fading into the morass of my mind, *I am Krishnan ap Karthik. Seeing as I was here first. There's some as would see no difference, however.* Then, the voice was gone, leaving behind only memory and emotion.

Leaving behind *love*.

I looked into Bleddyn's eyes and saw the same. He brought my hand up to his lips and kissed my palm repeatedly, without breaking gazes. In that moment, I only needed and wanted one other thing. One element to make my happiness complete. To give me the wings I'd always wanted.

"Let's go back to the castle, husband. Let's go *home*."

Bleddyn smiled, and just like that, I could fly.

❖

Back at the castle, we peeked in to check on Gareth, who was sleeping soundly, and then we walked hand in hand to our bedroom just off Islwyn's office.

Once there, I came over shy. Not suddenly, for it'd been building all the way back from the deadfall. Bleddyn seemed unable to stop staring at me, the heat and passion and yearning he felt for me so blatant, anyone who'd seen us had surely seen it. And I, for that matter, was unused to such a sustained look of worship and wanting, even from Bleddyn. Even the part of me that was still and would always be *Gwil* found it disconcerting.

As Bleddyn shut the door that opened onto Islwyn's office and latched us in our bedroom, I put the lamp down on the night table and held my breath. When he turned to me, his eyes burning and intense, I blushed and looked down.

"You are *beautiful*," he said softly. "I desire you no matter what form you wear, though I must say I find this form *at least* as pleasing as the last."

My blush deepened, and I swallowed nervously, linking my hands together in front of me. "And you are, and have always been my brave and handsome squire. Merely to see you is to find my reason overwhelmed."

Bleddyn chuckled and approached me slowly. When he was within touching distance, he put his hands on my waist and pulled me close. When we were flush against each other, Bleddyn tilted my face down so we were eye to eye. He made no attempt to hide how hard he was. "Never doubt that I love you, Krishnan."

And as if my name was a shibboleth, my nerves vanished, and I smiled at Bleddyn. He pulled me closer and kissed me. I wrapped my arms around his neck and soon, he was backing me toward our bed.

In a matter of minutes, we were undressed and writhing against each other, Bleddyn clearly torn between stroking me off and retrieving the salve from the night table. Neither of us could stop giggling and hushing each other. Finally, I smacked Bleddyn's hand away from my cock and looked into his eyes. "I want you inside me, Bledd."

Bleddyn made one of those hoarse groans, as if he was about to come, even though I'd barely touched him so far. He scrabbled in the night table for the salve, nearly tumbling us off the bed in his haste. I laughed and brought my knees up to my chest.

Downstairs in the hallway, the great clock struck nine. And by that ninth resound, Bleddyn prepared me with efficient, reverent fingers, brushing my prostate and putting pressure on it till I was a moaning wreck, my head tossing on the pillow, tears leaking from my clinched-shut eyes, and biting my lip almost bloody. In the silence that followed, all I could hear besides my own moans and the blood pounding in my ears, was Bleddyn's murmured praise and encouragement.

Then, just when I thought I couldn't bear being teased anymore, Bleddyn withdrew his fingers and shifted closer to me, pushing my legs wider apart. As he braced himself above me, I opened my eyes to see him looking down at me, tears in his eyes again.

"I love you, my light. Even more than I once did, if that is possible."

I let go of my left leg for long enough to brush my fingertips down Bleddyn's cheek. "And yet still only a fraction as much as I love you."

Bleddyn kissed me once more. Then he pressed me down into the bed and, with one quick, sharp thrust, he was past the guarding ring of muscle, driving himself to my very core.

Never once did our locked gazes stray until we stilled, on the cusp of our climaxes. I threw my head back into the pillow, eyes shut once more, and Bleddyn buried his face in the hollow space between my shoulder and my neck, and gasped. And then the universe died and was reborn in the same explosion of light and color.

When reality had resolved itself once more into our dim, shadow-splashed bedroom, I sighed happily. Bleddyn kissed me anywhere and everywhere, rolled us over and arranged us into our usual sleeping positions, pulling the blanket over us.

Smiling to myself as he kissed my damp hair and squeezed me to him tight, I sighed again as my body shivered and tingled with orgasmic aftershocks, and we lay in silence for a while. But then curiosity got the better of me, and I dared to shatter the afterglow by speaking.

"Bledd?"

"Hmm?"

I turned my head from where it rested on his shoulder, and looked into his sleepy, sated eyes, made lambent by the dreamy, dim lamplight. He smiled at me, reaching up to caress my cheek ever so gently. I leaned into his touch. "May I ask you something? I mean, you don't have to tell me if talking about it pains you, but I was just wondering…"

"Yes, my light? You may ask me anything, and I will answer as truthfully as my knowledge allows," Bleddyn said, and I bit my lip for a moment.

"All right. But first I want you to know I'm not jealous or envious, angry, or resentful. If anything, I'm glad about her, because it meant you had someone, for a little while, anyway. And then, there's Gareth, whom I couldn't love more if he was my own son. And—"

"Krish," Bleddyn interrupted me, smiling wryly. "Krishnan, would you like me to tell you of Rhiannon?"

"Yes, please," I answered, nodding, blushing, and looking away. "I just—she was there for you when I…I couldn't be. And she gave you a beautiful son, something I *can't* do. I'm glad she did. But no one ever talks about her, even when I try to be sneaky and worm information from them. I think they don't want to hurt my feelings or make me feel insecure about my place in your life. But the thing is," I said, looking up at Bleddyn again. "The thing is, I *don't* feel insecure, and it *won't* hurt my feelings to know that you had someone who *loved* you, and whom you maybe loved when I couldn't be there with you. So, I suppose what I'm curious about is, did Rhiannon love you? And did you love her?" I asked, anxious for and fearing the answer at the same time.

Bleddyn's smile turned wistful and sad. "Yes. She loved me and I would have had a heart of stone not to love her in my own way. She was comely and fair, innocent and gay. She was kind and beloved by all who knew her, and I believe you would have loved her, too."

If Bleddyn believed, then so did I. Which only made me sorrier for the loss of this woman I had never known.

"She was impossible not to love. I was still in despair over losing you, but Rhiannon was able to shine a small light into my heart. To bring a little joy into my despair." Bleddyn sighed, and I snuggled closer to him.

"Were you in love with her?"

Another sigh. "I loved her. Very much. As you said, she was my companion when I had none. I would have died for her, if my dying would have prevented hers. But I did not desire her. I lay with her as part of my marital duty and as a duty to my father and our line. I did not yearn for her the way I yearned for you, Gwil. Though it shames me to admit it, I'd have given her up a thousand times over to have had even one more hour with you."

"Oh, Bleddyn..."

Bleddyn's smile firmed a bit. "But that is neither here, nor there, I suppose," he said. "I loved her as best as I was able to, with my heart in tatters. Then, when Gareth was born, it was as if my heart began to mend."

I grinned. "Gareth has that affect on people. He's a marvelous child."

"A *miracle* child," Bleddyn amended, frowning just a little. "He was born frail and sickly, almost too weak to nurse. Even Gwynedd didn't think he'd last a fortnight. But Rhiannon never gave up on him. She barely slept, caring for him. And she only ate so that she might more ably nurse him. She fought harder for the life of our child than any man on any battlefield I have ever seen. And she *won*," he said, sounding rather proud and more than a little awed, "though it was many months before he was well enough that she dared sleep through the night, rather than hover over his cradle, watching him in his poor, fitful slumbers."

"She sounds formidable and very caring."

"She was both. She reminded me more than a little of you. And I think that's part of why I loved her so. When I lost *her*, too, the only thing that kept me from taking my own life in utter despair was Gareth. He deserved a better father than I've ever been, but I'm the only father he's got. I intended to do the best I could to see his life was a good and happy one."

"And you've done admirably, Bleddyn. I've never seen a happier child," I promised. "How...how did she die?"

Bleddyn blinked and swallowed, his Adam's apple bobbing almost comically, but it did nothing to dispel the shine in his eyes. "'Twas poison."

I gaped. "But…but who? *Why?*"

"'Twas none other than ill-fortune that killed my good wife." Bleddyn closed his eyes for a few moments. "She loved blueberries, you see. Especially in her morning porridge. One morning…" Bleddyn shook his head, his Adam's apple bobbing again. "One morning, I sent one of the kitchen girls to pick fresh blueberries for my Rhiannon. The girl was young, barely old enough for the responsibilities she had. She could not tell the difference between the blueberry and nightshade plants. The berries of the former are, of course, harmless. The berries of the latter—"

"Oh, my God." I covered my mouth and closed my eyes, sorry I'd even asked. That I'd dredged up this nightmare for the man I loved. "Bleddyn, I'm so sorry. You don't have to—"

"She was ill within minutes of eating her porridge. She did not even finish it before the delirium had begun. By the time Gwynedd came to our chambers, Rhiannon was fully delirious and fainting. By evening, she was dead. Most horribly dead. As was the poor child who'd picked the berries, for she'd ingested some herself."

Tears leaked from my eyes, and I wiped them away, hoping Bleddyn wouldn't notice. "I'm sorry, Bleddyn, my Bleddyn…sorry you lost her so terribly."

Bleddyn hugged me closer and kissed my temple. "It is not me for whom sorrow should be felt, but for my poor motherless Gareth. If only he'd known her longer. If only *she'd* lived to see him grow into such a strong, fearless child."

He fell suddenly silent and lay back, looking at the ceiling. I placed my hand over his heart. "She sees. She watches over him and over you, I think. She's your guardian angel. And she's proud of you both."

Bleddyn covered my hand, then pulled it to his lips to kiss it. His face was wet with tears, and when I sat up and pulled him into my arms, he didn't protest. He simply held on to me like I was his only lifeline.

"I lose everyone I love," he whispered. "Everything I love is taken from me. Am I *cursed?*"

"Baby, no. Of course not!" I kissed his hair and rocked him the way he'd rocked me earlier at Gwenllian's cottage. "The ones we love don't *really* leave us. They live forever in our memories and our hearts. And in time, we meet them again and again. So, no one is ever really lost. Not really. Sometimes, our paths diverge for a little while. But in the end, they always come back together."

Bleddyn shuddered. "But the times of separation are unbearable."

"Only because it seems like it's permanent. But the trick is knowing that no separation, not even death, is permanent. Even if we both died right now, some day in a future neither of us can imagine, we would meet on a crowded street and be floored by the perfect stranger whom, it seems, we know better than ourselves."

Bleddyn sighed and looked up, his face a wet, red, miserable wreck. I wiped away tears that were instantly replaced by fresh ones. "If I knew that tomorrow, we were to be separated for a long time, perhaps even by death, you know what I would say?"

He shook his head no, and I smiled. "I would say, 'I love you, husband. I'll see you next time.'"

Bleddyn drew his brows and he blinked, but this time, no more tears fell.

"Is it truly as simple as that?" he asked, hope and fear warring in his eyes.

I nodded. "More or less." I held his gaze and smiled. "I know now, there's an eternal love, like I've never known, waiting for me throughout the rest of time. I just have to find it, and until then, keep hoping. I think I can do that. Can you?"

Bleddyn's pensive face grew more so as he thought it over. Finally, he nodded.

"Yes. I can. I would do anything to be with you. Even go on for centuries before I see you again."

"And I'd do the same."

Bleddyn took my face in his hands and kissed me. Softly at first, then with increasing passion and intensity, till he was pushing me to the bed and rolling on top of me. I spread my legs, my thighs were bracketing his hips so we could grind against each other frantically, without coordination, till Bleddyn urged me onto my stomach.

It wasn't a marathon screw, far from it. It was quick and desperate and incredibly *hot*. I was moaning and groaning so loud, I'm certain the whole castle heard it, and Bleddyn called me his light and his love, his Gwil and his Krish. His hands were bruising-tight on my hips—I really did have hand-shaped bruises in the morning—his pace pleasantly punishing and practically perfect. I was hoarse from yelling by the time he gave me a reach-around. All he did was stroke me once, and I went off like a firecracker. Then he came moments after me, hissing and hollering.

The dead silence that followed was unbroken by any noise, save the sound of flesh impacting flesh when Bleddyn collapsed on top of me, and the harsh pant of our breathing. By the time Bleddyn pulled out of me, our sweat had cooled and dried, and the stillness of the castle no longer seemed so preternatural.

Without speaking, we curled up on our sides, spooning, and lay there in the semi-darkness, listening to the quiet and each other's breathing. I fell asleep to Bleddyn nuzzling the nape of my neck and stroking my flank.

If I had dreams, they were good ones.

CHAPTER TWENTY-ONE

The next morning, I woke up late for me. Bleddyn was, of course, already off practicing and preparing for the Jubilee. But he'd been to breakfast and back, leaving my breakfast on a tray on the night table. It was porridge and bread with butter. The porridge was, unsurprisingly, berry-free.

I decided to be a layabout, for once. Islwyn wasn't in yet, and might not come in today if he was saving his strength for the Jubilee tomorrow. And I knew a lot of the castle would be so busy with preparations that my slacking off wouldn't be noticed. Especially since the office was in an out-of-the-way spot.

I quickly got bored and lonely, however, and was up eating breakfast in a matter of minutes. I took advantage of having the washing room to myself, and then I got dressed. By the time the clock chimed ten, I was already at Islwyn's desk, glaring at the long, black streak I'd left across the pages yesterday. I sat there glaring at it for about ten minutes before I finally gave up, at least for this particular Saturday, and almost skipped out of the office.

I even had a destination in mind.

"…and then—and then, Ceiriog caught the froggy, and he named it Mr. Tudur!"

"Did he, really?" I asked as I carried Gareth down the front hall. He nodded fervently, staring at me with large, dark eyes the same color as Bleddyn's, though their wide, round shape and fringe of pale lashes must have been all Rhiannon. He kept pushing his fine blond hair out of those eyes impatiently with sticky, tiny hands. "How did he know the froggy wasn't a girl-froggy?"

Gareth laughed, bright and tickled. "Krish-sir! All froggies are boys!"

"Ah," I said, deferring to his superior knowledge for a moment as we stepped outside. The sun was shining and the air in the courtyard was not as revolting as usual. "But *some* froggies are girls, you know. Otherwise, who would the boy-froggies marry?"

"Each other," Gareth said simply, and I stopped walking and looked at him, surprised. He watched me back with his mother's eyes.

"Um…" I said. We were treading on dangerous ground, here. I wanted Gareth to be open-minded, but he still had to live in the seventeenth century. Bleddyn knew that and I knew that. We'd tried our best to keep the true nature of our "special" friendship a secret from Gareth. At least until he was older. "Boys don't usually marry other boys, sweetpea."

"Uh-huh," Gareth said, nodding. "You and daddy are married. That's why you kiss each other so much."

My jaw dropped. "Uh, when, uh, do your daddy and I ever kiss, Gareth? I mean, you know. Boys kissing other boys is kinda yucky, don't you think?"

Gareth shrugged. "But kissing girls is yucky, too."

Well, he's got me, there, I thought. "When did you see your daddy and me kissing?"

"At Aunt Gwenllian's house. When you think I'm asleep." He giggled. "Mummies and daddies kiss when they're married. Are you going to be my new mummy?"

"Whuh?"

"I *already* have a daddy, so you *have* to be the mummy."

"Boys, uh, boys can't be mummies, sweetpea."

"Why not?" Gareth asked, his little face set in Bleddyn's frown. "Froggies can be girls."

They say you always remember the big firsts in your life. I will never forget the morning I was outwitted by an almost-four-year-old for the first time.

I started walking again, still trying to think of some rational rebuttal as we passed through the gate. Gareth, seeming bored of the subjects of kissing, and mummies and daddies, continued regailing me about Mr. Tudur and other things as I carried him toward the field where Bleddyn and the rest of Lord John's men were practicing for the Jubilee.

We reached the top of a grassy, gentle slope and could see the pavilions and tents being set up. Amidst the seeming chaos, the squires were easy to spot even from a distance, all dressed in full plate armor, instead of just their usual mail, parrying, blocking, and lunging in the midst of their staged fights. At the sight of them, even my little chatterbox fell silent and I forgot about trying to rebut his unwitting argument for gay marriage and same-sex parenthood.

The squires truly looked magnificent.

We stood there for a few minutes, watching them mock-fight. Then Rhys called out, "*Hold!*" All the men paused at almost exactly the same moment. It was strange. Eerie and beautiful.

"*Wow,*" Gareth breathed. "Is my daddy down there?"

"Yes, he is," I said with undimmed pride. "See the one in the green surcoat with the three golden eagles across the front of it? That's him."

"Can we go see him?" Gareth asked with such hope and yearning, still staring at Bleddyn, who appeared to be taking a break along with the other squires. Even if I hadn't been planning on taking him down to see his father, I would've done so anyway.

"Of *course* we can, sweetpea. That's where we were going all along." I kissed his cheek and the crown of his head, and he giggled, wrapping his small arms around my neck as I started down the slope. "You know your daddy is always happy to see you. You know you're his brave little squire."

"Yay! We're going to see my daddy!" Gareth exclaimed in my ear, and I winced, but laughed. Then I made a mental note to speak with Bleddyn about how often he visited Gareth. Perhaps their quality time together could be increased. I was careful to not take up too much of Bleddyn's time during the day, when Gareth was awake and could benefit with a visit from his father. Well, I was careful except for the occasional nooner. But I never kept Bleddyn for his entire lunch, often shooing him off so he could spend some time with Gareth, too.

But was that time enough? Was I keeping Bleddyn, who was not really *all* mine, away from his son?

As Gareth and I encountered the first of the tents and construction, I was suddenly very pensive, in spite of the friendly hails sent our way by sweaty workers and sweatier squires, some still at their jobs, some heading back to the castle for well-earned breaks.

Even Rhys passed us with a grim nod, given only when sweet, guileless Gareth waved cheerily and shouted, "Good morning, Granddad!"

Rhys did not once glance at me.

❖

"Daddy!"

Gareth squirmed and almost spilled himself out of my arms as we drew closer to his father. Bleddyn, who was drinking water from a ladle he'd dipped from the barrel, looked up in surprise, then grinned, stepping out from under the shade of the large, green awning.

"Well! If it isn't my two most favorite persons in the whole of the world!" he said, catching a running, jumping Gareth. He swung his son up into his plated arms and spun him over his head in a game of "birdie" before hugging him close and kissing his cheek. "How is my little man doing? What are you doing here?"

"We came to see you, daddy!" Gareth bounced in his father's arms. "Krish-sir came and got me!"

"Did he, now?" Bleddyn glanced at me, and the look in his eyes was as heated as it was affectionate. I smiled and closed the distance between us. Bleddyn put his free arm around my waist, pulling me against him, without a care for the eyes that might see us. And indeed, everyone seemed busy doing whatever job they'd been given. Even the few squires on break had taken to helping those erecting tents. The others were scattered about the grounds of the Jubilee. No one was paying us any attention, it appeared.

So I leaned in and gave Bleddyn a quick peck on the lips. As I was pulling away, he squeezed me tighter and kissed me again, holding it before letting it and me go. But not far.

"I've missed you *both*," he said, looking from me to Gareth, then back again. "I cannot wait for this cursed Jubilee to be over," he muttered in English. I grinned and replied in the same.

"Aw, you'll miss wearing that fancy armor and swinging Lord John's sword."

He snorted. "I shall be glad of resuming my regular duties."

"And our regular schedule," I added, thinking of all the missed sex we had to make up for. Perhaps Bleddyn was thinking of the same, for he chuckled and put Gareth down. The boy ran into and began exploring the tent next to us. Bleddyn faced me, putting his hands on my shoulders.

"Is it safe for him to be running around in there?" I asked in English, nodding at the tent. Bleddyn chuckled.

"Yes, that's a refreshment tent. Naught in there but tables, chairs, water, ale, bread, and dried meat for the squires who are in the reenactment. No one and nothing else is in there."

"Ah," I breathed as Bleddyn pulled me closer, staring into my eyes. "Perhaps we should find a similarly empty tent to run around in, hmm?"

"I would like nothing more than to find some quiet, empty space in which to ravish you…" he trailed off, his hands traveling down and around my waist, then to my ass.

"Thinkest thou of *nothing else*, my randy squire?" I asked playfully, taking a quick glance around us before pressing myself against Bleddyn who, in his plate armor, was indeed hard. All over.

"When you are in my arms, my light, I am unable to think of *anything* else," Bleddyn murmured, leaning in to steal a kiss. I wound my arms around his neck, threading my fingers through his hair, and let him tickle and tease, then plunder my mouth.

I don't know how long we were standing there like that, but suddenly I felt a tug on the hem of my shirt. Startled, we looked over and down with wide eyes. Gareth was standing there, looking up at us curiously.

"See? You're kissing! You're married!" he said, and Bleddyn and I looked at each other, eyes still wide.

"Um," I said.

"Er," Bleddyn said.

Gareth looked from me to Bleddyn, still curious. "Is Krish-sir going to be my new mummy, now, daddy?"

Bleddyn looked at me and I shrugged. "I don't know what to tell him."

Letting go of me to scoop up Gareth, Bleddyn said. "Gareth, men can't be mummies—"

"I already tried saying that, Butch," I cut in to whisper in English.

"—but I suppose they can be second daddies."

"Second daddy?" I asked in a small, breathless voice, shocked and uncertain as to what to say or how to feel.

"Yes, Krishnan. If aught were to ever happen to me, I would want you to have the raising of my...of *our* son. I would want him to call you father, just as he calls me, for you love him, just as I do, and would give your all for him just as I would." Bleddyn smiled a small but sincere smile. "That is, if you would shoulder such a responsibility. You are, of course, not obligated."

I put my arms around Bleddyn and Gareth, kissing each of them on the cheek ringingly. Gareth said, "yuck!" Meanwhile, Bleddyn merely smiled a little wider, looking rather surprised.

"Are you kidding?" I demanded, laughing. "This is no obligation, this is only everything I've ever wanted, Bleddyn. Once more, you're the one who's giving it to me. Thank you! Thank you!"

I kissed Bleddyn again, this time on the lips, this time for a lot longer. Long enough that Gareth began singing a song about having two daddies, and how kissing was yucky. Then I think there was something about froggies, but to be honest, I was too busy kissing Bleddyn to keep track.

"I love you," I whispered when I had to come up for air or pass out.

"And I love you," Bleddyn panted back, pecking my lips briefly.

"I have *two* daddies now," Gareth sang happily. "And froggies are girls!"

Bleddyn blinked and looked at me, about to ask a question, but I just shook my head, meaning to tell him I'd explain later, when a familiar voice, fairly dripping with horror, exclaimed from beyond the green tent:

"Bleddyn ap Rhys, have you lost your mind?! Have you any idea the damage you're doing to that child, Bleddyn?"

Bleddyn glared coldly as Dafydd ap Dafydd approached. He even let go of us, pressing Gareth into my arms before facing Dafydd full-on, fists clenched.

Dafydd wore armor like Bleddyn's and a green surcoat, only with the three-eagle device in silver-grey instead of golden-yellow. He looked every inch the noble, honorable squire, which only seemed to highlight just how wrong the words *noble* and *honorable* were when keeping company with him.

"I'd advise you to mind your own affairs, Dafydd," Bleddyn warned in the meanest, angriest tone I'd ever heard from him. "And to do so as far from me and mine as possible." But Dafydd paid no heed, still approaching us, stopping only when he was within an arm's distance from us. Which was far too close for me. I clutched Gareth close and began to slowly back away.

Bleddyn's hand was settling on the hilt of *Lord John's* sword. But Dafydd, again, didn't seem to notice as he was too busy glaring at me.

"And *you*," Dafydd said in English, with towering disdain. "'Twas not enough to seduce and subvert the father, but now you must drag the child into your evil? Do you know no shame?"

I kept backing away, unable to even blink for fear of what would happen if I were to take my eyes off him for even a second.

"Have you no sly answer? No quick response to the discovery of the depths of your perfidy?" he taunted, taking a step closer to me. Bleddyn blocked him, half-drawing Lord John's sword. "Where is that blasphemous, heathen tongue now that you have been caught out?"

"I warn you, Dafydd, stay back, or—" Bleddyn began, drawing the sword three quarters of the way out of its sheath. In my arms, Gareth was shaking and starting to cry.

"You're scaring him, you sadistic piece of shit!" I hissed in English.

Dafydd sneered. "He should be scared! You've corrupted his father's immortal soul and now you're trying to corrupt his, you filthy catami—"

Bleddyn shoved Dafydd with a low growl, and he went stumbling backwards a few feet, only barely keeping his balance. He caught himself before he fell and, with a look of pure hatred rushed Bleddyn, slamming into him and tackling him to the ground not five feet from where I stood holding Gareth.

I jumped and kept backing away as Gareth screamed and cried, burying his face in my neck, clutching at me tight, sobbing.

I stood there, dumbfounded, watching them punch and bash at each other, neither going for their sword yet, but it was inevitable, right? I turned away from the fighting men and ran around the awning set up for Lord John and his family, and I would've kept going till I reached the castle until I heard Dafydd's triumphant roar. My heart went still, and my body went cold. My plan had been to get Owen or his brother—or even Rhys, but the sounds of metal impacting metal had stopped, and there was nothing but silence back the way I'd come. Gareth must have noticed, too, for he leaned back and looked at me, his wide eyes red and frightened as he turned to his second daddy for an answer that would reassure him.

I had none. I could only look back at him.

Finally, I turned toward the castle and started running. I was halfway up the slope that led back to the castle when I saw Rhodri and Meurig, two woodworkers from Trefriw who were always working at Lord John's castle, holding steins of the strong ale the men around here favored and laughing. They were obviously taking a no doubt deserved break. I instantly course-corrected and hailed them by name. When they saw me, they paused and watched me approaching with my crying son, and exchanged a glance.

"You have to take him!" I said when I was close enough to hand off Gareth, who wouldn't let go of me without a fight. When I *did* manage to pry his strong little hands free, he began to sob louder, reaching for me and calling, "Daaaaaaaa! Wanna stay with *you*!"

The two squires exchanged another glance, then Rhodri took a flailing Gareth from me. Meurig merely stood there with his eyes wide.

"Please, get Lord Owen or Lord Richard or—or Rhys! Dafydd's attacked Bleddyn and—and—" I didn't know what to say after that, only that my eyes were blurring and the sense of urgency I felt had grown stronger, as had the icy chill. Rhodri and Meurig just watched me, looking like gobstruck cows. I felt the first stirrings of anger and I shoved Meurig, since Rhodri was holding my son. "Just—*go*! Get help!"

I turned and ran back toward the Jubilee and the green tent.

When I got back to Lord John's awning, I paused, took a deep, steadying breath, and peered around the back edge. I saw a still body with dark hair on the ground. Bleddyn.

Dafydd was nowhere in sight.

My heart in my throat, I ran to Bleddyn with a bitten-back sob. When I reached him, I fell to my knees at his side and looked him over. He was pale and unconscious. His face was bloody at the lip and nose, and he had a huge bruise already coloring his left jaw. I checked at his throat for a pulse, and there it was. Even and steady.

I let out a sigh of relief and started to cry, leaning down to kiss Bleddyn's bloody lips. Then I sat up, licking away salty copper, and brushed his damp hair away from his clammy forehead. "It'll be all right, Butch, I promise. I won't let anything happen to you. I'll protect you."

Bleddyn didn't even so much as stir. I carefully removed his breastplate and rerebrace, then his chausses, tossing them aside. His heavy, grey undershirt and breeches were sweat-stained but not *blood*-stained, for which I gave thanks.

"Please, wake up, my love," I whispered, leaning down to kiss his forehead. As I did so, a glint of sunlight off of something shiny caught my eye, near Bleddyn's right hand. Lord John's sword. Unsheathed, but unbloodied. That meant that Dafydd was not only alive, but likely still around.

Leaning across Bleddyn's supine body, I reached for the sword and clasped the hilt. I dragged it carefully over Bleddyn's body, then got to my feet with it, hefting it experimentally. It wasn't as heavy as

I had feared it might be, but it was solid. Smaller than a claymore, but still long and difficult for me to wield.

But I'd have to, until Owen, Richard, or Rhys arrived.

I had no doubt that Dafydd would be back.

Standing over Bleddyn's unconscious form, sword raised, I turned in a circle, seeing nothing but tents, awnings, and people working to set up more in the distance. Even more distant was the castle.

I kept an ear out for the clink of plate armor and continued looking around for what felt like eternity under the hot sun. Sweat beaded on my brow and gathered in my hair. I thought I heard the rustling of fabric from the direction of the refreshments tent.

I brandished the sword expertly, which for me meant not dropping it and severing part of my foot. Unfortunately, the Gwil-memories didn't involve memories of learning swordplay. I stepped over Bleddyn and committed the cardinal sin of going to investigate the strange noise. When I got closer to the refreshments tent, I heard it again, and I froze, holding the sword out and swinging it once in a clumsy arc. Then I stepped around the side of the tent quickly, expecting to see Dafydd there, sneering at me, sword at the ready.

I saw nothing.

Confused, I lowered the sword slightly. It was getting heavy and even more unwieldy. I didn't know how Bleddyn could brandish it, let alone *fight* with it for hours on end. I walked to the tent's flap. It'd been open before, and now it was closed.

Dafydd.

I clutched the sword tight and tried to wedge my boot under the edge of the flap so I could kick it open. But that didn't work. I stood on one side of the flap, so I'd be behind it when I whipped it open. Bending over to grab the leading edge, I nearly had it in my grasp when a sharp blow to the wrist of my sword hand caused me to cry out and drop it.

As I turned to face Dafydd, a punch to the face sent me falling backwards against the tent, which was the only thing that kept me upright. I groaned and turned my ringing head toward the sound of familiar laughter. It was laughter I remembered from yesterday evening. From fourteen years ago. From four hundred years ago. It was the same creaking laughter of the boy who'd gutted Gwil, then tried to cut his throat. He'd run away like the coward he was at the sound of hoofbeats coming swiftly down the path. In the end, though he hadn't the guts to kill me outright, Dafydd ap Dafydd had gotten his way and had gotten away with it for fourteen years.

No more.

I straightened up and willed my ringing, spinning head to stop doing at least one of those things. Dafydd stood in front of me sans armor, which was how he'd sneaked up on me, holding Lord John's sword expertly. He was still laughing. His golden hair shone in the sunlight, but his dead-grey eyes were like chips of dirty ice in his handsome face.

"What kind of man are you?" he taunted in a voice made rich with contempt. "None, at all, I think."

Hot-cold anger seemed to fill my veins, electrifying me, as Dafydd started laughing again. The world stopped spinning and, instead of ringing, the only sound in my ears was my own heartbeat. I clutched my aching, stunned wrist. "That's a fine thing for a filthy sneak and a spineless, honorless coward to say."

Dafydd's laughter stopped like his throat had been cut. If only. "Be careful how you address me, catamite, or I'll cut out your lying tongue," he said flatly.

"I'm not afraid of you, Dafydd." In saying it, I realized I *wasn't* afraid of him. No matter how many times he hurt or killed me or Bleddyn, our souls would always find each other in time. And that was what mattered. "You're the one who's afraid of me, and you're right to be."

Dafydd snorted. "And why should I be afraid of a man who is less than a man?"

I smiled, even though it made my jaw hurt. "Because *I win*, asshole. I always win, and I always will. You can't stand against me because I have something you've never had and never will have. Bleddyn's love."

Now, all traces of laughter or even a smile were gone. *My* smile only got wider. "You want Bleddyn so much, it drove you to gut an innocent boy and to poison an innocent woman," I added, knowing without question, I was right. Never mind the girl who had given Rhiannon the poisonous berries, Dafydd had been behind it. Likely smirking as he sent a child to kill a woman whose only crime had been to love and be loved by Bleddyn.

Dafydd's mouth dropped open, then quickly shut. "You know not of what you speak."

"Don't I?" I laughed and straightened up, letting go of my wrist. I was wobbly without the tent holding me up, but I managed to at least *look* like I was fine. I wasn't swaying or listing, anyway. "'*I'm a humble scribe on his way to Caerdyf, passing through here, hoping to see my kin before I go.*'"

Dafydd immediately tensed, looking almost guilty for a moment before his face screwed itself into a smug, ugly smirk. "Witch," he said with a merry sort of loathing. "Only a witch would know that."

I rolled my eyes. "Prove me a witch, and you prove yourself a murderer," I said, in case he was thinking of going to Lord John with what he thought he knew. But I was wrong. I was dead wrong.

"I don't have to prove anything," Dafydd said with menacing gentleness, raising Lord John's sword and taking a step forward. He was still wearing that awful smirk. "Thou art a witch, and the Good Book says to suffer not a witch to live."

I didn't even stop to think or fear. I simply dove out of the way before he lunged forward with a growl, Lord John's sword skewering nothing but tent with a loud ripping sound. I rolled to my side, my feet in the still-damp grass. Dafydd yanked the sword free and turned toward me. He didn't look too pleased, but neither did he look terrifically put out. I posed no threat to him, physically. I knew it, and so did he.

He advanced on me cautiously but steadily, as I backed away, hands held up as if in defense. I doubted he'd let me stall him long enough for Owen or Rhys to get there, but I had to try.

"Admit it, Dafydd. You killed William and Rhiannon because Bleddyn loved them, and not you. That's why you're trying to kill me. You're so jealous, you can't stand the fact that someone else is making Bleddyn happy. That we've had the chance to feel his love and his affection, and that we've lain with him, something you could never have the courage to do."

Dafydd's face was murderous by now, but he'd paused his approach. So I took a leap and went on. "William was his first love.

He had Bleddyn first, and nothing anyone could ever do, no amount of fostering could change that. No amount of murder. And Rhiannon was his spouse in the eyes of God and man. She bore him a son. No amount of wishing or hatred or poisons could change that. And I—"

"What *of* you?" Dafydd demanded angrily, his face red and almost hideous in its rage. "You, who have swooped in here like a carrion-bird to take Bleddyn from me when he was mine at last! Mine and no one else's! What of you?"

I closed my eyes—unwisely, but there you have it—and asked myself the same question. What of me? "I—" I began, but I had nothing to say, nothing in my brain to answer Dafydd's question. I knew without opening my eyes Dafydd was moving in for the kill.

I was about to die.

CHAPTER TWENTY-TWO

*B*ut at least I've had this time with Bleddyn and Gareth. I've had a chance to have a family of my own, no matter how brief the time. I know, now, what it is that I want—what I've always wanted. And I will always know it deep down, no matter how many lifetimes pass. And I will search for Bleddyn, and I will find him. This life is not the only one, and this death is not the end.

There is no end to Bleddyn and I. We are eternal. Our love is forever.

And with that, my fear of death and regrets about my life vanished like dew in the midmorning sun. I'd said it before, but now I truly understood its meaning: *The ones we love never truly leave us.*

No, nor we, them.

I smiled, and that's when the words came.

"What *of* me, Dafydd? I loved well, and was loved well, and I will be loved well again. Even if I die here, now, Bleddyn's soul and mine are bound together. You can't sever that tie with a thousand swords, nor can you kill it with a thousand blows. But you'll try, anyway. I know that. You'll kill me like you killed William and Rhiannon and think that's the end of it, but it won't be. It *never* ends. I think you know that, and that knowledge is eating away at you like acid. Because you've never loved or *been* loved that way, and you begin to fear that you may *never* be so loved. And you're right to fear."

Dafydd made a sound of inarticulate rage, and from much closer than I'd expected. I opened my eyes and saw him not an arm's length away from me, Lord John's sword poised at the top of an arc meant to behead me. I gasped when I saw the motion out of the corner of my eye. I glanced over Dafydd's shoulder and he started to turn, changing the direction of his swing even as he brought the sword in its downward arc, but it was too late. Bleddyn had tackled him, knocking him into me, and all three of us went tumbling to the grassy ground. I hit spine and head first.

I groaned as Bleddyn and Dafydd rolled off me and I curled onto my side, trying to breathe. I could hear the two of them fighting and screaming at each other in Welsh.

"You killed them! You killed my William! And Rhiannon!"

"I did it to protect you, Bleddyn. To save you from their perfidy. Just as I would save you from *his*."

"You murder innocents with impugnity and dare to speak to me of the perfidy of those you've murdered?"

"William corrupted you, can't you see? That corruption left you vulnerable to the machinations of this vile catamite!"

"How dare you speak of my husband in such a fashion!"

"Husband?" A twisted, mean laugh. "You're mad if you've let him convince you that the two of you are married! Bad enough he's got the child believing it, but you, Bleddyn? *You*?"

"You're the one who's mad, Dafydd, and I was a fool not to see it before now!"

By this time, I'd managed to push myself upright. The world was spinning worse than ever, and my head hurt so bad I thought I was going to throw up. But I quickly forced the nausea away, and began crawling toward the forgotten sword.

Out of the corner of my eye I could see the two of them rolling around, throwing punches, landing them, all while still screaming at each other, Bleddyn angrily, Dafydd more despairingly with each blow Bleddyn landed.

"I don't want to hurt you, Bledd—agh!" When I glanced over at them, Bleddyn was throttling Dafydd, sitting on his chest, his right knee pinning Dafydd's left arm. Dafydd's right arm flailed about. And Bleddyn was really *squeezing*, banging Dafydd's head against the ground.

I let out a breath and dragged Lord John's sword to me, using it to lever myself first to my knees, then to my feet. *It's over*, I thought tiredly, around the buzzing, dull ache in my skull. *Soon, Owen will come and Dafydd will be arrested, and Bleddyn, Gareth, and I will finally be sa—*

Bleddyn grunted and cried out suddenly. And when I looked over at him, I saw a spreading red spot on the left side of his undershirt at about kidney level. And that's when I saw Dafydd's dagger. A *familiar* dagger.

All the strength flowed out of me as Bleddyn let go of Dafydd's throat, his hands coming up to his side, surprise and agony writ large on his face. Dafydd coughed and drew the dagger back. Before Bleddyn could defend himself, Dafydd brought it down into Bleddyn's chest, high on the left side. Bleddyn grunted again and fell partially off Dafydd, onto his wounded side. Dafydd coughed again and sat up slowly, pushing Bleddyn off him completely.

Without any input from my brain, almost stumbling, I made my way over to Dafydd, raising the suddenly feather-light sword over my head. When my shadow fell over him, Dafydd, still coughing and swaying as if he was fighting not to lose consciousness, looked up at me, his dazed eyes wide.

For a moment, those dazed, empty eyes met mine. There was no hope in them and, I'm certain, no mercy in mine. I let the sword arc downward over and over. It craved blood. *Dafydd's* blood. Who was I to deny it?

I don't remember well the minutes immediately after I let the sword do its business. I only remember letting it swing upward and downward repeatedly, then turning away from a churned, bloody mess I couldn't entirely focus on.

My lover had rolled onto his back, the dagger sticking out of his chest like the mast out of a ship. I thought I would be sick, even after what I'd done to Dafydd, and I turned away, my stomach roiling.

All I could think was: *What have I done? What have I done?* And on the heels of that: *I've done what needed doing for fourteen years. For four hundred years.*

And yet, I couldn't even *focus* on what I'd done. On the horrible action I'd taken with no more malice than an automaton. I had been acting on autopilot. As agents of retribution went, I was hardly a fount of towering rage. I was just another instrument, just another tool of the cycle of *samsara*, which was almost inescapable because of human nature and an inability to take the long view of things.

For did it matter in the end that Dafydd had been erased from this life, when in his next life, he'd likely be worse? And what did it matter, when in my next life I'd pay for taking the life of another?

But then, hadn't I *already* received a punishment worse than any other that could be exacted? Wasn't my punishment Bleddyn's maimed body on the ground, churning out trickles and sprays of blood with every labored and slowing breath?

Yes. I was a murderer. And I would surely pay for that, but not with Bleddyn, right? Not with the only person I would ever have killed for, save Gareth?

Right?

Oh, gods, oh, *please. Right?*

Bleddyn's eyelids fluttered. He coughed up more dark blood, and I realized I had more important things to worry about than my own bad karma. Lord John's bloody sword fell out of my numb hands, and I staggered over to Bleddyn, an anguished cry trapped behind my teeth, my uncertain stomach forgotten. Because this couldn't be *real*, could it? Bleddyn couldn't be wounded so badly, so *mortally.* Could he?

When I reached Bleddyn, I knew the dagger sticking up out of his chest was real, as was the blood spreading out from the wound every time he took a shuddering, coughing breath. One especially wracking cough brought a froth of blood to his lips, and he moaned weakly, trying to sit up, his eyes wide.

Tears suddenly rolling down my face, I fell to my knees at his side and took his bloody left hand in both of mine. "Don't, Bleddyn. You're hurt badly. Don't try to sit up, baby. Not yet. Help is coming."

"Krish—" he coughed out, his eyes locking on mine, his face sheet white but for their dark glitter. "Krishnan…"

A soft sob escaped me, and my tears dripped on Bleddyn's face. He blinked and frowned.

"Dafydd…?"

"He won't hurt us anymore, Bleddyn," I said, trying to smile and failing miserably. My vision was now so blurred, I could barely see.

"Then you…have done what I should have…a long time ago." Bleddyn coughed and his face scrunched into a pained grimace. "I am…only sorry that I did not prevent this…from happening. Sorry… that I am leaving you and Gareth…"

I shook my head frantically. "No, no, you're not leaving anybody, baby. You're just—you're just a little hurt, that's all. Gwynedd'll fix you right up," I promised, unwilling to consider any other possibility. "She'll have you back chopping Gwnellian's firewood in no time."

Bleddyn almost smiled. More blood frothed out of his mouth.

"There *is* no fixing this, my light." He coughed again, this time for nearly a minute before he could go on. "No fixing *me*."

"Bleddyn—"

"I'm dying, Krishnan," he said calmly, blinking up at me.

"Don't say that!"

"It's true. I'm not long for this world. I—" Bleddyn's face grew annoyed, as if dying was getting in the way of saying what he wanted to say. "I have…two boons I would ask of you."

"No," I said firmly, even though I was trembling inside, on the verge of shattering. "If I say yes to your boons, you'll think it's all right for you to let go."

Bleddyn smiled again, faint but unmistakable; his gaze was fond and loving. "I would ask," he said, as if I had not spoken, "that you look after our son…I would further ask…that you not grieve overlong, for me. That if…if you find love with another to cherish it. Hold on to it. Take care of it. And know that…whether it be in the next lifetime… or the next after that…I will be searching for you. I will love you. Even if I don't…remember you."

"No, Bleddyn," I moaned, curling up next to him in the grass and tucking my head under his chin. "There'll be nobody else. No one, if not you. Please, baby, just hold on till help comes. Please. Gareth needs you, and and I need you. please…"

"Hush, my love," Bleddyn said, his voice gone as ragged as ancient cloth. I maneuvered and tugged till I got Bleddyn's left arm around my shoulders. And with the last of his strength, he pulled me even closer, squeezing my shoulders and kissing the crown of my head.

"I love you Krishnan, my darling Krish. I'll see you next time." His voice was a mere shuttling of air, no more than a sound.

"I love you, too, husband. And I'll s-see you next time."

And after that, nothing more was said. Nothing more *needed* to be said. So we lay for minutes that felt like eternities, but which were still not nearly long enough to suit me. I felt safe and loved with his arm around me, but then a cloud passed across the face of the sun, and I shuddered, noticing how *cold* I was. How inhumanly cold the world suddenly seemed.

I closed my eyes tight. I didn't want to see, let alone be a part of any world where Bleddyn wasn't, and I drew in a shaking breath that came out as the anguished cry trapped behind my teeth. I screamed loud and long, till it felt as if my throat would rupture.

And just as unexpectedly as it started, it stopped.

I pushed Bleddyn's arm off me and sat up. I didn't need to look at the body to know he was dead, so I didn't. I got to my uncertain feet, and stumbled away from Bleddyn. Away from Dafydd. Away from the Jubilee.

Away from Gwydir Castle.

❖

Somehow, I made it to the Great Road unnoticed and unap-prehended. I stumbled along the roadside, parallel to Gwydir Forest until the sun proclaimed it midday. Then, for no reason I could decipher, I crossed the road and went into the woods. I felt nothing, thought nothing, *did nothing* but walk and walk.

In fact, I was walking in the woods for about twenty minutes before I heard hoofbeats coming swiftly down the road from in the direction of Gwydir Castle. I paid them no mind until they seemed to be getting closer to where I'd for some reason stopped.

It was Owen and Lord John's squires, coming after me. I was, at the very least, witness to two murders, and at worst, the perpetrator of both. I looked up through the trees at the overcast sky. It was getting cloudy and dark, the leaden light fading quickly. It was likely to rain, not that I cared one way or another.

I buried my face in my bloody hands and leaned against a tree.

I tried to think beyond the fact that Bleddyn was dead and I couldn't. Couldn't think *or* feel, so I stood up and started walking again. I was utterly lost and couldn't have cared less. Didn't know where I thought I was going and couldn't have cared less about that, either.

As I traveled on, the hoofbeats got closer, though they were slowing down, likely hampered by the fog that had sprung up out of nowhere. It crept and crawled and clung to the ground like pearl-grey leeches, spreading and growing higher and denser, until I couldn't see my own hand in front of my face.

But I kept walking anyway. Pushed on until the hoofbeats faded into silence.

Pushed on until the world was nothing but pearl-and-white fog.

Pushed on until I tripped over a root or branch and fell forward. I was so numb, I didn't even put out my hands to catch myself as a reflex. I just fell forward into blankness. My temple glanced off a stone or something hard, and I knew no more.

When I woke, it was to darkness broken by cloudy moonlight.

My head ached so much, even that meager light caused sharp, shooting pains through my skull. So I closed my eyes and lay there, my face in the dirt, till a spider walked across my cheek. Screeching, I practically levitated to my feet, brushing and slapping at my face.

Where am I? I wondered, staggering back till I hit a tree. The jarring impact made my skull ache even more. *What happened? Where's Bleddyn?*

And at the thought of his name, it all came rushing back.

"Oh, oh, God," I sobbed, burying my face in my sticky, tacky hands. The blood on them had dried brown. "Oh, *no!*"

I leaned against that tree, weeping and sobbing for I didn't know how long. I couldn't face the world just yet. Couldn't face Owen, or Rhys, or Gareth, whose father was dead because of his love for me.

No, a voice in my head said firmly, sternly. It sounded like Bleddyn at his most reasonable. *Gareth's father is dead because of Dafydd and no other reason. Dafydd killed him, not you or your love for each other. Place the blame where it belongs and don't take Dafydd's bad karma on your shoulders.*

I didn't know if I believed that voice, but I had to get back to Gwydir Castle and tell everyone how Bleddyn had died. I had to be there for Gareth, and even Rhys if he'd let me, in his grief.

I had to clear Bleddyn's name of murder and my own, for Dafydd had been murdered with Lord John's sword, which had last been in Bleddyn's possession. And I had done the killing, but only in self-defense. Only so Dafydd couldn't hurt us anymore.

Wiping my face on my dirty sleeve, I sniffed and blinked away tears. Now that I was thinking, and it wasn't misty and foggy anymore, I knew exactly where I was, thanks to Gwil's memories. So I started walking again.

This time, as I passed familiar landmarks—a boulder, broken and splattered with bird shit; a fallen tree blocking the path that I remember John and Dierdre clambering over on the way to the campsite, while I'd simply gone around; a small pond that we'd *all* walked around, I felt a chill work its way up my spine.

It…it *couldn't* be. Could it?

The moon was setting quickly now, but even by its dim, cloudy light, I could make out the green markers on some of the trees I passed. By the time I passed the third such marker, false dawn was lighting the sky. I broke into a shambling run, despite what I was coming to believe was a decent concussion. I ran and ran till I burst out of the trees and onto hard, grey macadam, which stretched as far as my blurry eyes could see.

I was home.

Stumbling down the center of the road for a few yards in utter disbelief, I finally collapsed to my knees in despair, sobs once more wrung out of me. I sobbed and wept till a sound I hadn't heard in months startled me into looking up.

A car was coming down the road from the direction of Llanrwst and coming *fast*. It was bearing down on me, its not-so-bright brights not yet illuminating me. By the time they did, it'd be too late. I'd be street pizza.

Maybe, I thought wearily. *Maybe that's for the best. Maybe I'll get to see Bleddyn again sooner, this way.* So I knelt, there, waiting for my fate, and thinking of Bleddyn.

Chapter Twenty-three

Huw Davies was fantastically early for once in his life.
The call had come in at almost four a.m. precisely, that Colin had fallen ill—something about bad clams the night before—and wouldn't be able to play his part in the first of the upcoming reenactments of the season at the old castle.

As soon as he'd got the call, Huw had rolled out of bed and gotten dressed. He'd made a cup of instant coffee that tasted like shite, guzzled it while it was still scalding, then grabbed his wallet, keys, mobile, and costume, and was out the door.

He was early and, for once in his life, he felt *ready*.

Perhaps it was the nasty coffee, but he was completely pumped and prepared for his first turn as Lord John Wynn. And certainly he couldn't do any worse than Colin had done for the past two seasons running.

"For once in my life," Huw murmured to himself, clutching at his lucky necklace and giving it a squeeze as he sped down the dark streets of his hometown. "For once, things are really starting to go my way, though I *am* sorry about Colin's bad clams."

He was speeding along the road from Llanrwst to Gwydir Castle, rehearsing his lines as he went, when he saw what appeared to be a person, kneeling in the road about a hundred yards ahead of him. Before he could be entirely sure, instinct kicked in, and he pumped the brake as his older brother had told him to do *ad nauseam* whilst teaching him to drive.

The Audi slowed down, but not enough to stop before Huw ran whatever it was over.

"Fuck me!" He swerved and jammed on the brake, going into something of a spin.

When his car had come to a complete stop, leaving him facing the direction he'd come from—Huw sat there, panting, trying to catch his breath. He had asthma, and sometimes, the attacks could be brought on by stress—like, say, the stress of nearly running down some knob who'd been kneeling in the road.

When he'd achieved some semblance of composure, he shut the engine off and glanced out the windshield. By the lights of Huw's Audi, the figure was still kneeling in the same spot, head bowed like a penitent, shoulders slumped as if in defeat.

Huw felt the first stirrings of anger begin to displace his relief.

Unbuckling his seatbelt, he opened the driver's side door of his outmoded Audi and levered his tall, brawny frame out into the pre-dawn morning.

"Beg pardon, but what the bloody *hell* was that, mate?!"

I looked up at the low, strained voice coming from my left. And up. And up.

An angry young guy who must've been six-foot-everything stood over me, arms akimbo like he thought he was Yul Brynner. He was glaring down at me from his prodigious height, waiting for an answer. His AC/DC t-shirt, jeans, and battered-looking sneakers looked strange to me after so many months spent in 1626. I couldn't stop staring and gawping at him.

"Well?" he demanded irritably, brushing his shoulder-length strawberry-blond hair out of his face. "I could've killed you kneeling in the road, like that!"

"You were *supposed* to kill me," I said, because it was the first thing I thought and my brain-to-mouth filter seemed to have been left in 1626.

The guy glared at me again. Then his eyes narrowed as if he was really looking at me and seeing me. I can only imagine what he saw, with all the dirt and blood I was covered in. His glare became an uncertain scowl. Then a worried gape.

"Jesus on a postcard, mate, is that blood?" he asked, kneeling in front of me and looking at my bloody shirt. Then my bloody face. "B-loody hell!"

"What year is it?" I asked, and the guy shook his head, as if shaking himself out of a nightmare. He looked up at my face, his eyes lingering at my right temple, the one I'd bashed on the rock when I tripped. I reached up and tentatively touched it. My fingers came away sticky and a bolt of pain lanced through my head. "Ow!"

"Don't—don't touch it. You'll only make it worse, or get it infected," the guy said, his voice cracking with concern. "You need to go to hospital—"

"What day is it?" I asked him desperately. "What date?"

He told me, blinking, and looking generally wary. He even added the time, too, glancing at his watch. I couldn't believe it. It was only about ten hours after Dierdre and John and I arrived at our campsite three-plus months. or four hundred years ago. I felt very faint and started to sway.

"Oh, bloody hell—are you all right? I mean, of *course* you're not. But *are* you all right?" the guy asked quietly, and I nodded, looking away and wiping at my wet face.

"Yeah, I'm fine," I said, shuddering away when he put his large hand on my shoulder. "I just...it's...I'm sorry I tried to kill myself with your car. I wasn't thinking straight."

The guy snorted. "That's the understatement of the year. Listen, you really *do* need to go to hospital. Let me take you to town and we can get you looked over, yeah?"

I laughed a brief, brittle bark, hysterical around the edges. "Hospital can't fix what I've got."

"I think you're wrong, there, mate." The guy stood up and up and up, and then reached out his hand for me to take. He must've underestimated his own strength, because he accidentally pulled me to my feet a little too hard, and I collided with him.

"Oh, I—"

"Sorry, I didn't mean to—"

"No, *I* didn't mean to—" I chuckled wryly, but not without that edge of hysteria I so feared. "I didn't mean to go all pro-wrestler on you. Sorry."

"No, it's *my* fault for yanking you up so forcefully. I'm sorry," the guy said, sounding like he meant it. His eyes were very dark and round but slanted just a bit at the corners. I frowned and stared into his lightly freckled face as he stared into mine, looking rather confused himself.

"I..." he began, but he didn't finish his thought. He seemed to be searching my eyes as if he was trying to figure something out. "That is, you..."

My eyebrows shot up. "Yes?"

"Are far too gorgeous to be kneeling in the road, waiting for someone to turn you into roadkill," he said solemnly, and I felt my eyebrows climb up under my bloody, messy fringe. I waited for him to walk back what he'd said, but he didn't. He merely stared into my eyes.

"Looks aren't everything, you know," I replied bitterly, thinking of the compliments Bleddyn had always lavished on me with his words and his gazes. Just that morning, in fact, he'd told me...nothing. Bleddyn hadn't told me anything in four hundred years. He and my little Gareth were so long dead, no one remembered them but me. "Pretty don't solve every problem, believe me."

The guy stared into my eyes for a few seconds longer before looking down at his battered sneakers. "No, I don't suppose it does."

We stood there, sneaking glances at each other for a minute, before the guy turned beet-red and opened his mouth. "I'm Huw. What's, er, what's your name?"

"Krishnan Nayar."

"Well, I'm, er, pleased to meet you, Krishnan. Despite the circumstances."

"Likewise," I said automatically. Then I realized we were still holding hands like a couple of morons. I pulled mine free and the guy—Huw—shoved both of his in the pockets of his jeans for a few seconds.

Then blinking and shaking his head, he smiled nervously, removing his hands from his pockets, and he took my elbow, leading me to his car.

❖

When Huw and Krishnan got to the Audi, Huw opened the passenger side door and helped the injured man into the car, feeling a touch awkward.

It's as if I'm taking my girlfriend to prom or some such, he thought bemusedly as he leaned on the door and watched Krishnan take in his messy car. The back seat was a disgrace of clothing, take-away cartons, and CDs.

"Homey," Krishnan said dryly.

"Sorry for the mess," Huw replied, shutting the door and jogging around the front of the car to get in the driver's side. "I sort of live in my car, sometimes."

Krishnan met his gaze wryly. His eyes were deep and dark, the kind of eyes a man could fall into and get lost. Happily.

"I have a friend like that. Her boyfriend's always trying to clean out her car, but as soon as he's done, it looks like a sty again," Krishnan said with an absent smile, glancing out the passenger side window.

Feeling suddenly awkward and stupid, a feeling he was quite familiar with, Huw sighed and started the car. "Let's get you to hospital," he said with probably inappropriate cheer.

Krishnan merely leaned his head against the passenger side window and closed his eyes. Huw couldn't help staring at him. The guy was ridiculously gorgeous despite the blood on his face and hands and his weird, also-bloody Amish clothes, and he seemed somehow *tragic*. It was the only word that seemed to fit besides gorgeous. At least so far.

Huw started up the Audi and pulled into the correct lane before heading for Llanrwst again. The reenactment, though not forgotten, had been utterly eclipsed.

A few minutes into the ride, Huw glanced over at his passenger, thinking the other man had fallen asleep, he was so quiet. But in the faint light of dawn, Huw could just make out tear tracks on Krishnan's sienna cheeks.

"Are you...are you all right?" Huw asked again, knowing it was still a stupid question. Krishnan, bloodied and bruised, dirty and crying, was anything but all right, but Huw had to ask.

"I'm fine," Krishnan claimed in a shaking, water-logged voice. "Just tired."

Which Huw believed not at all. "Maybe talking about whatever it is will help?" he said, and Krishnan laughed. It was an alarmingly wild and desperate sound.

"No, I don't think it will," Krishnan said flatly, still laughing, though it sounded more like rapid-fire sobs.

Huw hated to push, but he felt obliged to. After all, he had nearly run Krishnan over with his car. And while that had been at least partly Krishnan's fault, Huw still felt some culpability, some responsibility for the life he'd saved. "Obviously something is wrong, or you wouldn't have been trying to kill yourself with my car, right? You can tell me. I'm a good listener, and—"

"My husband and child are dead." Krishnan said, meeting Huw's startled gaze again. His eyes were more despairing than any Huw had ever seen. "My husband died and I wandered off in a fit of grief and left my son. And now, he's dead, too. He and everyone else probably spent the rest of their lives thinking I'd run off like a coward because it was all my fault. They probably cursed my name. Maybe they were right to. If not for me, my husband would've lived a full life, and our son would've grown up knowing his father, living in the light of his love instead of orphaned and alone. My family is long dead, and it's my fault."

Stunned by what was said and by the level of grief Krishnan must be feeling, Huw looked back at the road, illuminated for a hundred feet ahead of him. He tried to imagine losing a spouse *and* a child and couldn't.

"I'm sure that's not true," he said, after an uncomfortable minute had passed. Then he felt Krishnan's gaze on him again, like a spotlight. "You don't seem like the sort of man who'd hurt someone he loved, intentionally or not."

"The appendices of what you don't know about me could fill the Grand Canyon to overflowing, Huw," Krishnan said, and then that spotlight feeling was gone. Out of the corner of his eye, Huw could see Krishnan splay his right hand on the passenger side window. "My husband and our son, our sweet little Gareth, are gone. And I'll never see them again. At least not in *this* lifetime."

Krishnan slowly lowered his hand and sighed, more tears leaking out of his lovely but swollen, reddened eyes.

"I'm so sorry," Huw said quietly, unable to imagine what that kind of loss could do to a person. In his admittedly short life, he'd never lost anyone except an elderly, senile great-aunt, whom Huw had barely known.

Even in his lowest moments, Huw knew his life was a charmed one. A *good* one. The only shame was that the same couldn't be said for everyone.

Krishnan sighed again. "What're *you* sorry for? It's not *your* fault, Huw."

"I'm sorry for your loss. Sorry that you're hurting, Krishnan."

Krishnan looked over at Huw and smiled the most miserable smile Huw had ever witnessed. "Thanks, I guess."

Silence fell again, and Huw cast about for a way to break it. They needed a distraction to change the mood in the car and take Krishnan's mind, however temporarily, off of the family he'd lost.

Then Huw remembered he'd been somewhat startled and bemused not a minute before, when Krishnan had said the name of his son. As a man frequently beset and distracted by the vagaries of coincidence, Huw could think of no better change of subject. Of course, bringing up something tangential to the man's dead son wasn't exactly a *distraction,* but it certainly was an *odd* coincidence. And one that Huw, who believed whole-heartedly that there was no such thing as coincidences, felt he had to share.

"You know," he began lightly, casually, "my maternal great-grandfather was named Gareth. That name's very popular in my mother's family."

"Oh, really?" Krishnan said, without any genuine interest. But Huw went on, anyway.

"Truly. My mum named my older brother Gareth to honor great-granddad. And we've got Gareths in the family going back for at least three hundred years. It's a cool old name. Better than Blethyn, anyway."

He glanced over at Krishnan, smiling and hoping for agreement or even amusement, only to see the most stricken look on his face. In fact, Krishnan looked almost grey in the unforgiving first light of morning.

"What's wrong with Blethyn?" Krishnan asked in a hoarse and husking voice. "I think that's a fine name."

Huw's smile turned lopsided as he realized he might have somehow put his foot in it. "It *is* a fine old name, I suppose. But I don't know that it suits me as well as Huw does. It's a bit *too* old-fashioned.

But Mum wanted to name me after this local-legend ancestor of ours—the only one, I suppose, besides the first Gareth." Huw shrugged as he followed a turn in the road. Up ahead, he could see the lights of Llanrwst like a beacon. "I guess I'm just lucky mum decided that if she was gonna stick me with Blethyn, she'd better give me a couple of middle names that were a little more modern."

"You...your name is Blethyn?" Krishnan asked in a faint, breathless voice.

Huw nodded. "Blethyn Huw Daniel Davies, at your service," he said brightly, only to hear Krishnan gasp. When he glanced over at the other man, Krishnan was staring at him as if he had three heads. "But everyone just calls me Huw. Even mum, except when she's upset with me. Then it's all four names and a few others, besides."

Krishnan continued to stare at him, his dark eyes wide. Till Huw started to get a bit uncomfortable.

"Have I said something?" Blushing, Huw decided to keep his eyes on the road from then on. "If I've offended you, or upset you—"

"No, no, you've done neither, it's just..." Krishnan said in that same faint voice. "Do you believe in coincidences, Huw?"

"Nope. Why?"

Silence until Llanrwst loomed large ahead of them, at least as large as it could loom. "No reason, just...no reason." Krishnan sounded disappointed.

But Huw could feel that curious, confused gaze on him the rest of the way into town. And though neither of them spoke another word until they arrived in Llanrwst proper, the other man always seemed on the verge of speaking. One thing was certain, though, more tears were leaking out of his dark eyes, and that hurt Huw. Made him want to pull Krishnan into his arms and...and...Huw decided it was time to change the subject again. Hopefully this one would be more fortuitous. "Say, do you like historical reenactments?" When he felt Krishnan's gaze change from curious and confused to outright disbelieving, Huw blushed.

"I can't say I've ever been to one," Krishnan said stiffly, leaving Huw feeling as if he'd put his foot in it again, but he'd already brought it up. He supposed he had to carry on the conversation until he could find a way to make a graceful exit from it.

"Well, the local historical society holds weekly reenactments starting in spring and going through summer, of Lord John Wynn's elevation to knighthood, his creation of the almshouses and other high points in his life. Every Saturday morning, in fact. That's where I was speeding off to when we crossed paths."

"They hold the reenactments at dawn?" Krishnan asked doubtfully.

Huw laughed. "No, they're held at nine a.m., but the actors are supposed to show up two hours in advance to do a last run through and get into costume." Huw waited at a stoplight, drumming his fingers on the steering wheel. "But I like to be at the old castle early when no one else is there. It's become like a second home to me." Shrugging, Huw drove on when the light changed. "I'm a big history nerd, if you haven't guessed. And today was going to be my first turn as Lord John Wynn."

"*Was?*"

Huw glanced at Krishnan. The other man was staring out the window again. "Well, I can't very well be in two places at once, you know."

"What other place do you have to be?"

"Erm, at hospital, of course."

Krishnan looked at Huw, his face wary and defensive. "You don't have to stay at the hospital with me."

"Well, I can't very well leave you alone there, can I?"

"Why not?" Krishnan looked back out the window. "You don't owe me anything."

"I know I don't," Huw said, getting a bit defensive, himself. "It's not about what I owe you."

"Then what *is* it about? Christian duty?"

Huw snorted. "Pagan-born and raised, so, no. And it's not some misplaced sense of duty that's making me worry about you, Krishnan."

Shaking his head, Krishnan sighed. "You don't want anything to do with me, Blethyn. I'm bad news."

"Who says?" Huw demanded. But Krishnan refused to be drawn out on the matter. When they pulled up outside of the hospital's emergency entrance, Huw put the Audi in park, and let it idle for a few moments before speaking. "Here we are."

"Thanks." Krishnan said, opening the passenger side door and swinging his legs out. He took a deep breath, got out, then slammed the door shut. He made his way slowly around the front of the car toward the automatic doors, looking small and defenseless in his bloody, Amish clothes.

Huw leaned out the window. "I think I should wait with you."

"Go do your reenactment, Huw."

"You're hurt!"

"And I'm at a hospital. Where hurt people go."

"You're being ridiculous, Krish!"

Krishnan paused. For so long that the automatic doors swept shut in his face. His entire body shuddered and shook as he stood there.

"Are you okay?"

"Go to Hell," Krishnan said shakily but without inflection, and he stalked forward into the hospital. Stung, Huw sat there idling, for some reason feeling more rejected than all the times Colin had refused him put together. And it hurt. Incredibly.

"All right," he said, scowling to himself. Krishnan was right. It wasn't like Huw owed him anything. "All-bloody-*right*."

He threw the Audi into drive and laid rubber out of hospital property.

Hospitals are, it turns out, the same wherever one goes.

Except for the accents, I could've been in any hospital back in the States. As soon as I presented myself at the front desk, the attendant took one look at me, gasped, and the next thing I knew, hospital folk were rushing a gurney out just for little ol' me.

I was flattered.

They did all sorts of tests on me that told them one thing: along with a bunch of scrapes, scratches, and bruises, I had a concussion. Not as bad a concussion as I'd suspected, but still a concussion.

I was given a bed, stitches, and told I'd probably be kept till the next day for observation.

Great, I'd thought, rolling my eyes. Though with the way my head was still pounding, I wasn't too upset about that. And when they got me settled in, I could call Dierdre's satellite phone and tell her and John where I was. I might not have been gone for almost four months, but they must've still been worried sick.

When the orderly wheeled me to my unit and my bed, he whipped the curtain back, and I saw a familiar face parked in the chair next to my bed, flipping through television channels.

"*You*," I said disbelievingly. He looked over at me and smiled his daffy, adorable smile. It made his scruffy face boyishly handsome, and something in my chest turned over like a rusty engine.

"Close," he said in his lyrical lilt. "You've left off a letter."

The orderly tried to help me out of my wheelchair and into bed, but I smacked his hands away and got out of the chair and into bed without his help, holding the back of the gown together. Huffing, the orderly drew the curtains shut behind him as he turned and left.

I looked back to Huw, who was still flipping through six channels at light-speed. "How'd you find out where I was?" I asked. "How'd you even get onto the unit?"

Huw blushed and cleared his throat, finally putting the remote down on the night table. He wouldn't meet my eyes. "I, er, told them I was your fiancé."

I gaped, uncertain whether I was pissed off at his presumption or admiring of his quick thinking. I think it was C, all of the above. But pissed off soon raced to the fore, leaving admiration behind.

"I was worried about you, Krishnan," Huw said earnestly, just before I'd have verbally ripped him a new one. That, of course, took all the wind out of my sails. I sat there, mouth open, staring at Huw, who was watching me with a solemn gaze that put me in mind of Gareth, my sweet Gareth. And also, by extension, Bleddyn.

And just like that, I was weeping. Burying my face in my hands and shaking and quaking and weeping.

Huw put a hand on my shoulder, then again when I shrugged it away. The second time, I let it stay. I told myself I didn't have the strength or energy to keep fighting him on it.

The next thing I knew, Huw was standing up and sitting on the bed next to me, pulling me into his arms. I went with ill grace, but I went.

I don't know how long we sat like that, but eventually, my weeping turned to hitches and shudders, until I was still and numb, just resting in Huw's long, strong arms, my face pressed against his throat.

Finally, I sat up a little, and Huw loosened his grasp, but he didn't disappear. He watched me with his solemn, searching eyes. I looked down, unable to bear the questions I saw in them, and that's when something metallic just below his collar bone caught my eyes.

I reached out and touched the small figurine on the silver chain with reverent, awed fingers, remembering.

"What is the meaning of this?" Bleddyn had asked curiously. I'd grinned and leaned over to kiss him silent.

"With this necklace," I'd said quietly, reaching around the back of Bleddyn's neck and brushing his hair out of the way. After a few moments, the necklace had been clasped and Bleddyn gazed at me with wide, uncomprehending eyes. "With this necklace, Bleddyn ap Rhys, I, thee wed."

Bleddyn's wide eyes had grown even wider as I swallowed around the words stuck not only in my nervous throat, but in my forgetful mind. Luckily my heart, steadfast and true, had supplied something pretty close to official-sounding for me. "I will have and hold you from this day forward, for better or for worse, for richer, for poorer, in sickness and in health, and I will love and cherish you—how I will love and cherish you!—and I promise to be faithful to you forever after. With this necklace I thee wed, Bleddyn. Wear it as a symbol of our love and commitment. Will you have me as your lovingly-wedded husband?"

Bleddyn had been the one to swallow this time, his eyes filled with more emotions than I could count, let alone name. "I will, Krishnan. I will have and hold you from this day forward, for better or for worse, for richer, for poorer, in sickness and in health, and I will love and cherish you. I promise to be faithful to you forever after, and I will wear this necklace as a symbol of our love and commitment," he'd said roughly, a single tear falling from the corner of his eye, to roll down his cheek. But Bleddyn'd kissed me yearningly before I could track its progress.

I shook my head slowly as the memory faded. *No. It can't be—*

"Oh, that?" Huw chuckled, tilting his head up so I could get a better look at the necklace, not that I needed one despite my denials. "It's a family heirloom. Lucky Parvati. Been in the Davies family for—"

"Four hundred years," I mumbled through numb lips, looking up at Huw, who nodded, his eyes wide.

"Thereabouts, yes. How'd you know?" he asked wonderingly. I let the necklace fall back against his skin. I remembered I hadn't ever seen Bleddyn take it off, not once. Even up to the day before the Jubilee.

Someone must've taken it off of Bleddyn before he was buried and—and gave the necklace to Gareth, who then gave it to one of his children, and so on, until...no, that's not possible. That can't be true. Can it? It can't be the same *necklace—and Huw can't be Bleddyn's descendent, right? Even if it* is *the same necklace and Huw* is *a descendent of Bleddyn's...that's just a coincidence, right? Right? It doesn't have to mean anything!*

But as I looked into Huw's—*Bleddyn* Huw Daniel Davies's— eyes, dark and compassionate as a dove's, I knew that my belief in coincidence didn't extend quite *this* far.

"Lucky guess," I said glibly, before my eyes rolled up into my head and the world went gently dark.

They lay in their tiny bed just off the accountant's office, spooning and snuggling in the sumptuous semi-darkness.

"A penny for your thoughts, my light?" Bleddyn asked nibbling Krishnan's ear and slipping his hand up under Krishnan's shirt. He was only half-hard so far, and both he and Krishnan were still dressed, but those two problems were easily solved.

"I was just thinking it should always be like this," Krishnan replied with a wistful sigh.

"It always will *be like this. I promise."*

Shivering as Bleddyn's fingers grazed his right nipple, Krishnan sighed. "Don't make promises you can't keep, Bleddyn."

Bleddyn turned Krishnan to him and, seeing the worry and fear in the dark eyes that he adored, leaned down and kissed the tip of his lover's nose.

"It will always *be like this, if I have to move Heaven and Earth to make it so for you, my love."*

Krishnan's eyes welled with tears. He blinked, but he hid his face in Bleddyn's chest before Bleddyn could see the tears fall.

"But what if—"

"Always."

"But, Bleddyn..."

"Always," Bleddyn averred, tilting Krishnan's beloved face back so he could see into the depths of those dark eyes. Every time he did, he got lost in them. Happily.

After searching Bleddyn's eyes intently for most of a minute, Krishnan finally smiled like the sun rising, and Bleddyn's heart skipped a beat. Or several. "Always," Krishnan agreed, leaning in to kiss Bleddyn, who tenderly, passionately kissed him back.

Epilogue

He woke from a sound sleep—the best he'd had in ages—and squinted open his eyes. Glanced over at the clock on the night table. Twelve thirty-seven p.m.

He was laying not in his own bed, alone, in his own flat, but in a hospital bed, spooned up behind a slim, dark young man with stitches in his bruised temple and the most gorgeous profile that'd ever graced this world…

*Krishnan…he's Krishnan. And I'm Huw…*Blethyn *Huw Daniel Davies.*

For some reason, it seemed important to keep that straight. Not that it was terribly hard to do so. After all, who else *would* he be?

Huw watched Krishnan sleep for a few minutes, entranced by the sight of him, drawn, as helpless as a moth to a flame, to the other man. Indeed, after Krishnan had fainted, Huw had tucked the other man in, meaning to sit a quiet vigil in the uncomfortable bedside chair… but as he'd stood there, watching the tragically gorgeous (gorgeously tragic?) young man sleep deeply, getting in bed *with* him had seemed to be not just the *right* option, but the *only* one.

He wanted nothing more, in that moment, than to stay like this for…well…

"*Always* is what I pledged thee, and *always* is what I meant," he whispered in Cymraeg, as soft and final as a promise, smiling at the sleeping man. "Ever am I a man of my word."

Then he was frowning again, wondering what in the *bloody* hell he was talking about. And in his rather poor Cymraeg—honestly, his French was *loads* better—no less.

Shaking his head, he lay back down, burying his face in Krishnan's dark hair. The other man would no doubt have something scathing and...accurate to say when he woke up in Huw's arms, but Huw would stumble across that bridge when he came to it. In the meantime, he continued to do what felt *right*: he draped one arm protectively, possessively over Krishnan's waist, and was soon asleep once more.

THE END

About the Author

E. L. Phillips was born in the Bronx, raised in Brooklyn, and has an attitude to match. After four years in a fancy-pants arts college, E. L. obtained a bachelor's degree that hasn't been used to pay a single bill, including the astronomical student loan debt attending such a fancy-pants arts college incurred. It should be known that E. L. sometimes hates writing, but *always* loves having written, and has spent many an hour daydreaming about novels published, accolades won, and royalty checks cashed. Ca-ching! That private island in the Mediterranean won't buy itself, after all.

In the meantime, E. L. can be reached at Author_ELPhillips@Yahoo.com.

Books Available from Bold Strokes Books

Crimson Souls by William Holden. A scorned shadow demon brings a centuries-old vendetta to a bloody end as he assembles the last of the descendants of Harvard's Secret Court. (978-1-62639-628-9)

The Long Season by Michael Vance Gurley. When Brett Bennett enters the professional hockey world of 1926 Chicago, will he meet his match in either handsome goalie Jean-Paul or in the man who may destroy everything? (978-1-62639-655-5)

In Shining Armor by E. L. Phillips. Krish Nayar has traveled back to Medieval Wales, where homosexuality is punishable by death. Will he find a way home, or risk everything for Bleddyn, the squire he loves? (978-1-62639-827-6)

Triad Blood by 'Nathan Burgoine. Cheating tradition, Luc, Anders, and Curtis—vampire, demon, and wizard—form a bond to gain their freedom, but will surviving those they cheated be beyond their combined power? (978-1-62639-587-9)

Death Comes Darkly by David S. Pederson. Can dashing detective Heath Barrington solve the murder of an eccentric millionaire and find love with policeman Alan Keyes, who, despite his lust, harbors feelings of guilt and shame? (978-1-62639-625-8)

Men in Love: M/M Romance, edited by Jerry L. Wheeler. Love stories between men, from first blush to wedding bells and beyond. (978-1-62639-736-1)

Slaves of Greenworld by David Holly. On the planet Greenworld, the amnesiac Dove must cope with intrigues, alien monsters, and a growing slave revolt, while reveling in homoerotic sexual intimacy with his own slave Raret. (978-1-62639-623-4)

Final Departure by Steve Pickens. What do you do when an unexpected body interrupts the worst day of your life? (978-1-62639-536-7)

Love on the Jersey Shore by Richard Natale. Two working-class cousins help one another navigate the choppy waters of sexual chemistry and true love. (978-1-62639-550-3)

Night Sweats by Tom Cardamone. These stories are as gripping as the hand on your throat. (978-1-62639-572-5)

Soul's Blood by Stephen Graham King. After receiving a summons from a love long past, Keene and his associates, Lexa-Blue and the sentient ship Maverick Heart, are plunged into turmoil on a planet poised for war. (978-1-62639-508-4)

Corpus Calvin by David Swatling. Cloverkist Inn may be haunted, but a ghost materializes from Jason Dekker's past, and Calvin's canine instinct kicks in to protect a young boy from mortal danger. (978-1-62639-428-5)

Brothers by Ralph Josiah Bardsley. Blood is thicker than water, but you can drown in either. Jamus Cork and Sean Malloy struggle against tradition to find love in the Irish enclave of South Boston. (978-1-62639-538-1)

Every Unworthy Thing by Jon Wilson. Gang wars, racial tensions, a kidnapped girl, and a lone PI! What could go wrong? (978-1-62639-514-5)

Puppet Boy by Christian Baines. Budding filmmaker Eric can't stop thinking about the handsome young actor that's transferred to his class. Could Julien be his muse? Even his first boyfriend? Or something far more sinister? (978-1-62639-510-7)

The Prophecy by Jerry Rabushka. Religion and revolution threaten to bring an ancient civilization to its knees…unless love does it first. (978-1-62639-440-7)

Heart of the Liliko'i by Dena Hankins. Secrets, sabotage, and grisly human remains stall construction on an ancient Hawaiian burial ground, but the sexual connection between Kerala and Ravi keeps building toward a volcanic explosion. (978-1-62639-556-5)

Lethal Elements by Joel Gomez-Dossi. When geologist Tom Burrell is hired to perform mineral studies in the Adirondack Mountains, he finds himself lost in the wilderness and being chased by a hired gun. (978-1-62639-368-4)

The Heart's Eternal Desire by David Holly. Sinister conspiracies threaten Seaton French and his lover, Dusty Marley, and only by tracking the source of the conspiracy can Seaton and Dusty hold true to the heart's eternal desire. (978-1-62639-412-4)

The Orion Mask by Greg Herren. After his father's death, Heath comes to Louisiana to meet his mother's family and learn the truth about her death—but some secrets can prove deadly. (978-1-62639-355-4)